In war, Clausewitz says, everything is very
simple, but the simplest things are very
difficult. Indeed, the simple truths of war are
difficult to understand. The study of war
is a study in contradictions. Men of war must,
to be successful, be willing to risk death.
An army not willing to die is an army
that wins few victories.
Until it does

THERE WILL BE WAR

THERE WILL BE WAR

created by
J.E. POURNELLE

Associate Editor
John F. Carr

TOR

A TOM DOHERTY ASSOCIATES BOOK

THERE WILL BE WAR

Copyright ©1983 by Jerry Pournelle

A TOR Book

Published by Tom Doherty Associates, Inc., 8-10 West 36th Street, New York, New York 1001&

First TOR printing: January 1983

ISBN: 48-555-7

Printed in the United States of America

Distributed by:
Pinnacle Books
1430 Broadway
New York, New York 10018

Acknowledgments: The stories contained herein were first published and are copyrighted as follows:

REFLEX by Larry Niven and Jerry Pournelle has never been previously published. Printed by arrangement with the authors and the authors' agent, Blassingame, McCauley, and Wood. Copyright©1982 by Niven and Pournelle.

SPANISH MAN'S GRAVE by James Warner Bellah was first published in *The Saturday Evening Post* in 1947. It is reprinted by special permission of the James Warner Bellah Estate. Copyright©1947 by The Curtis Publishing Company.

MARIUS by Poul Anderson is Copyright©1957 by Street & Smith Publications, Inc.. Originally published in the March 1957 issue of *Astounding Science Fiction.* Reprinted by special permission of the author.

THE THREAT by the Committee on Space War of the Citizens' Advisory Council on National Space Policy. Copyright©1981 by the L-5 Society. Published by special arrangement with the officers of the L-5 Society.

ENDER'S GAME by Orson Scott Card was first published in the August 1977 issue of *Analog Science Fiction/Fact Magazine.* Copyright©1977 by Conde Nast Publications, Inc..

A DEATH IN REALTIME by Richard Sean McEnroe appeared in *DESTINIES.* Published by permission of the author. Copyright©1981 by Richard Sean McEnroe.

OVERDOSE by Spider Robinson was previously published in *Galaxy,* September 1975 issue. Copyright©1975 by UPD Publishing Corporation. Included by special arrangement with the author.

For the Men and Women of the
Armed Forces of the United States;
in appreciation.

CONTENTS

PREFACE
by
Jerry Pournelle

Everyone desires peace; but there have been few generations free of war. Paradoxically, the few eras of peace were times when men of war had high influence. The *Pax Romana* was enforced by Ceasar's Legions. The *Pax Britannica* was enforced by the Royal Navy and His Majesty's Forces. The era of (comparative) peace since 1945 has been marked by deployment of the most powerful weapons in history.

The Swiss Republic has long enjoyed peace; but ruthlessly enforces universal manhood conscription and military training.

Historically, peace has only been bought by men of war. We may, in future, be able to change that. It may be, as some say, that we have no choice. It may be that peace can and must be bought with some coin other than the blood of good soldiers; but there is no evidence to show that the day of jubilee has yet come.

In war, Clausewitz says, everything is very simple, but the simplest things are very difficult. Indeed, the simple truths of war are difficult to understand. The study of war is a study in contradictions. Men of war must, to be successful, be willing to risk death. An army not willing to die is an army that wins few victories. But why will they risk their lives?

It is fashionable to say there are as many reasons as there are soldiers, but in fact that is not so. There are not so very many reasons why soldiers will stand and

11

face the enemy. Sometimes the reasons are very simple, and easily understood.

When you enter West Point, you find that the Army doesn't care a hang about the first verses of the Star Spangled Banner. It's the third verse that you must learn. It goes:

Oh thus be it ever when free men shall stand,
Between their loved homes and the war's desolation!
Blest with victory and peace, may the heaven rescued
    land,
Praise the Power that hath made and preserved us a
    nation.
Then conquer we must,
When our cause it is just,
And this be our motto: 'In God is our trust!'
And the star spangled banner in triumph shall wave
O'er the land of the free and the home of the brave!

To stand between one's home and war's desolation is an ancient and glorious military tradition, and certainly one reason why men fight.

There are others. When the Black Company marched during the German Peasant Wars of 1525, they sang:

When Adam delved and Eve span,
    Kyrie Eleison
Who then was the gentleman?
    Kyrie Eleison
Lower pikes, onward go!
Set the red rooster on the cloister roof!

To set the red rooster on a thatch roof is to set fire to it; the Black Company and other peasant military units were so thoroughly successful at destroying religious establishments that Martin Luther turned to the princes of Germany, bidding them to burn and slay and kill. Yet the Black Company was certain that it did the Lord's work in liberating the lower classes from domination by the nobility.

Not all warriors have the excuses of the Black

Company. There was once recorded a remarkable conversation between Genghis Khan and one of his soldiers. The Kha Khan asked a guard officer what, in all this world, could bring the greatest happiness.

"The open steppe, a clear day, and a swift horse," said the officer. "And a falcon at your wrist to start up the hares."

"Not so," replied the Khan. "To crush your enemy, to possess his wife as he watches, to see enemies fall at your feet. To take their horses and goods and hear the lamentations of their women. That is best."

Mephistopheles tempts Faust: "Is it not pleasant, to be a king, and ride in blood to Samarkand?"

Some soldiers fight for money. Scottish troops have often fought for pay; in the words of the song, "Not for country, not for king, but for my Mary Jane," which is to say, for enough to buy a crofter's hut and support a wife and family. Yet surely no one dies for a standard of living? Why, then, have some paid soldiers been feared and admired, while others, equally well trained, have merely been despised?

There are also the legions of the damned, who have often been responsible for deeds thought glorious; men who marched into battles for nothing more than the honor of the regiment. The best known of these is the French Foreign Legion, whose marching song, stirring as its music may be, glorifies nothing more glamorous than blood sausages.

It is no easy thing to determine why men fight. For those who live in free lands, it may be enough to rejoice: until now, at least, we have always found enough defenders, even if we have not always appreciated them.

History shows another strong trend: when soldiers have succeeded in eliminating war, or at least in keeping the battles far from home, small in scope, and confined largely to soldiers; when, in other words, they have done what one might have thought they were supposed to do; it is then that their masters generally despise them.

This too is an established tradition, old when Kipling wrote of it:

> Yes, makin' mock o' uniforms that guard you while
> you sleep
> Is cheaper than them uniforms, and they're starva-
> tion cheap;
> An' hustlin' drunken soldiers when they're goin' large
> a bit
> Is five times better business than paradin' in full kit.
>> Then it's Tommy this, and Tommy that, and
>> "Tommy, 'ow's yer soul?"
>> But it's "Thin red line of 'eroes when the drums
>> begin to roll—
>> The drums begin to roll, my boys, the drums
>> begin to roll,
>> O it's "Thin red line of 'eroes" when the drums
>> begin to roll.

It may be that in this Century of Grace the drums will not again roll. It may be that we have seen the last of war.

It may be that we will not; that it will not be long before we in the United States, like the Israelis and the Afghanis, must again turn to warriors for protection; for that is the oldest tradition of all.

> While it's Tommy this, and Tommy that, an' "Tommy
> fall be'ind,"
> But it's "Please to walk in front sir," when there's
> trouble in the wind—

Jerry Pournelle
Hollywood, 1982

EDITOR'S INTRODUCTION TO:

REFLEX

Larry Niven and Jerry Pournelle

My partner Larry Niven and I have written five novels in collaboration. Whenever we go to conventions, we are inevitably asked "How do you two work together?"

We always answer in unison: "Superbly."

The first book Larry Niven and I wrote together was called MOTELIGHT. It opened with a battle between rebels and Imperial troops.

It was quite a good battle; the problem was that the battle wasn't really relevant to the main theme of the novel, and the book was more than long enough already. Eventually we solved the problem: we cut about 60,000 words out of MOTELIGHT. We also changed the name to THE MOTE IN GOD'S EYE, under which title the book has done very well indeed.

Scenes chopped from a novel don't usually make a story; but among the scenes we cut was that introductory battle, which was a complete story all by itself. The novel assumes that the battle happened as originally presented; but the actual story has never been published until now.

The tradition of military honor is very old and very strong, and with good reason. Total war is seldom just war; while a just cause has considerable military value to inspire the army and populace.

Query: can military honor be more important than the cause you fight for?

REFLEX
by
Larry Niven and Jerry Pournelle

Any damn fool can die for his country.
> General George S. Patton.

3017 AD

The Union Republic War Cruiser *Defiant* lay nearly motionless in space a half billion kilometers from Beta Hortensi. She turned slowly about her long axis.

Stars flowed endlessly upward with the spin of the ship, as if *Defiant* were falling through the universe. Captain Herb Colvin saw them as a battle map, infinitely dangerous. *Defiant* hung above him in the viewport, its enormous mass ready to fall on him and crush him, but after years in space he hardly noticed.

Hastily constructed and thrown into space, armed as an interstellar cruiser but without the bulky Alderson Effect engines which could send her between the stars, *Defiant* had been assigned to guard the approaches to New Chicago from raids by the Empire. The Republic's main fleet was on the other side of Beta Hortensi, awaiting an attack they were sure would come from that quarter. The path *Defiant* guarded sprang from a red dwarf star four-tenths of a light year distant. The tramline had never been plotted. Few within New Chicago's government believed the Empire had the capability to find it, and fewer thought they would try.

Colvin strode across his cabin to the polished steel cupboard. A tall man, nearly two meters in height, he was thin and wiry, with an aristocratic nose that many

Imperial lords would have envied. A shock of sandy hair never stayed combed, but he refused to cover it with a uniform cap unless he had to. A fringe of beard was beginning to take shape on his chin. Colvin had been clean-shaven when *Defiant* began its patrol twenty-four weeks ago. He had grown a beard, decided he didn't like it and shaved it off, then started another. Now he was glad he hadn't taken the annual depilation treatments. Growing a beard was one of the few amusements available to men on a long and dreary blockade.

He opened the cupboard, detached a glass and bottle from their clamps, and took them back to his desk. Colvin poured expertly despite the Coriolis effect that could send carelessly poured liquids sloshing to the carpets. He set the glass down and turned toward the viewport.

There was nothing to see out there, of course. Even the heart of it all, New Chicago—Union! In keeping with the patriotic spirit of the Committee of Public Safety, New Chicago was now called Union. Captain Herb Colvin had trouble remembering that, and Political Officer Gerry took enormous pleasure in correcting him every damned time. —Union was the point of it all, the boredom and the endless low-level fear; but Union was invisible from here. The sun blocked it even from telescopes. Even the red dwarf, so close that it had robbed Beta Hortensi of its cometary halo, showed only as a dim red spark. The first sign of attack would be on the bridge screens long before his eyes could find the black-on-black point that might be an Imperial warship.

For six months *Defiant* had waited, and the question had likewise sat waiting in the back of Colvin's head.

Was the Empire coming?

* * *

The Secession War that ended the first Empire of Man had split into a thousand little wars, and those had died into battles. Throughout human space there were planets with no civilization, and many more with too little to support space travel.

Even Sparta had been hurt. She had lost her fleets, but the dying ships had defended the Capital; and when Sparta began to recover, she recovered fast.

Across human space men had discovered the secrets of interstellar travel. The technology of the Langston Field was stored away in a score of Imperial libraries; and this was important because the Field was discovered in the first place through a series of improbable accidents to men in widely separated specialties. It would not have been developed again.

With Langston Field and Alderson Drive, the Second Empire rose from the ashes of the First. Every man in the new government knew that weakness in the First Empire had led to war—and that war must not happen again. This time all humanity must be united. There must be no worlds outside the Imperium, and none within it to challenge the power of Emperor and Senate. Mankind would have peace if worlds must die to bring it about.

The oath was sworn, and when other worlds built merchantmen, Sparta rebuilt the Fleet and sent it to space. Under the fanatical young men and women humanity would be united by force. The Empire spread around Crucis and once again reached behind the Coal Sack, persuading, cajoling, conquering and destroying where needed.

New Chicago had been one of the first worlds reunited with the Empire of Man. The revolt must have come as a stunning surprise. Now Captain Herb Colvin of the United Republic waited on blockade patrol for the Empire's retaliation. He knew it would come, and could only hope that *Defiant* would be ready.

He sat in the enormous leather chair behind his desk, swirling his drink and letting his gaze alternate between his wife's picture and the viewport. The chair was a memento from the liberation of the Governor General's palace on New Chicago. (On Union!) It was made of imported leathers, worth a fortune if he could find the right buyer. The Committee of Public Safety hadn't realized its value.

Colvin looked from Grace's picture to a pinkish star drifting upward past the viewport, and thought of the Empire's warships. Would they come through here, when they came? Surely they were coming.

In principal *Defiant* was a better ship than she'd been when she left New Chicago. The engineers had automated all the routine spacekeeping tasks, and no United Republic spacer needed to do a job that a robot could perform. Like all of New Chicago's ships, and like few of the Imperial Navy's, *Defiant* was as automated as a merchantman.

Colvin wondered. Merchantmen do not fight battles. A merchant captain need not worry about random holes punched through his hull. He can ignore the risk that any given piece of equipment will be smashed at any instant. He will never have only minutes to keep his ship fighting or see her destroyed in an instant of blinding heat.

No robot could cope with the complexity of decisions damage control could generate, and if there were such a robot it might easily be the first item destroyed in battle. Colvin had been a merchant captain and had seen no reason to object to the Republic's naval policies, but now that he had experience in warship command, he understood why the Imperials automated as little as possible and kept the crew in working routine tasks: washing down corridors and changing air filters, scrubbing pots and inspecting the hull. Imperial crews might grumble about the work, but they were never idle. After six months, *Defiant* was a better ship, but . . . she had lifted out from . . . Union with a crew of mission-oriented warriors. What were they now?

Colvin leaned back in his comfortable chair and looked around his cabin. It was too comfortable. Even the captain—especially the captain!—had little to do but putter with his personal surroundings, and Colvin had done all he could think of.

It was worse for the crew. They fought, distilled liquor in hidden places, gambled for stakes they couldn't afford, and were bored. It showed in their discipline. There wasn't any punishment duty either, nothing like cleaning heads or scrubbing pots, the duties an Imperial skipper might assign his crewmen. Aboard *Defiant* it would be make-work, and everyone would know it.

He was thinking about another drink when an alarm trilled.

"Captain here," Colvin said.

The face on the viewscreen was flushed. "A ship, sir,"

the Communications officer said. "Can't tell the size yet, but definitely a ship from the red star."

Colvin's tongue dried up in an instant. He'd been right all along, through all these months of waiting, and the flavor of being right was not pleasant. "Right. Sound battle stations. We'll intercept." He paused a moment as Lieutenant Susack motioned to other crew on the bridge. Alarms sounded through *Defiant*. "Make a signal to the fleet, Lieutenant."

"Aye aye, sir."

Horns were still blaring through the ship as Colvin left his cabin. Crewmen dove along the steel corridors, past grotesque shapes in combat armor. The ship was already losing her spin and orienting herself to give chase to the intruder. Gravity was peculiar and shifting. Colvin crawled along the handholds like a monkey.

The crew were waiting. "Captain's on the bridge," the duty NCO announced. Others helped him into armor and dogged down his helmet. He had only just strapped himself into his command seat when the ship's speakers sounded.

"ALL SECURE FOR ACCELERATION. STAND BY FOR ACCELERATION."

"Intercept," Colvin ordered. The computer recognized his voice and obeyed. The joltmeter swung hard over and acceleration crushed him to his chair. The joltmeter swung back to zero, leaving a steady three gravities.

The bridge was crowded. Colvin's comfortable acceleration couch dominated the spacious compartment. In front of him three helmsmen sat at inactive controls, ready to steer the ship if her main battle computer failed. They were flanked by two watch officers. Behind him were runners and talkers, ready to do the Captain's will when he had orders for them.

There was one other.

Beside him was a man who wasn't precisely under Colvin's command. *Defiant* belonged to Captain Colvin. So did the crew—but he shared that territory with Political Officer Gerry. The Political Officer's presence implied distrust in Colvin's loyalty to the Republic. Gerry had denied this, and so had the Committee of Public Safety; but they hadn't convinced Herb Colvin.

"Are we prepared to engage the enemy, Captain?"

Gerry asked. His thin and usually smiling features were distorted by acceleration.

"Yes. We are doing so now." Colvin said. What the hell else could they be doing? But of course Gerry was asking for the recorders.

"What is the enemy ship?"

"The hyperspace wake's just coming into detection range now, Mister Gerry." Colvin studied the screens. Instead of space with the enemy ship black and invisible against the stars, they showed a series of curves and figures, probability estimates, tables whose entries changed even as he watched. "I believe it's a cruiser, same class as ours," Colvin said.

"Even match?"

"Not exactly," Colvin said. "He'll be carrying interstellar engines. That'll take up room we use for hydrogen. He'll have more mass for his engines to move, and we'll have more fuel. He won't have a lot better armament than we do, either." He studied the probability curves and nodded. "Yeah, that looks about right. What they call a 'Planet Class' cruiser."

"How soon before we fight?" Gerry gasped. The acceleration made each word an effort.

"Few minutes to an hour. He's just getting under way after coming out of hyperdrive. Too damn bad he's so far away, we'd have him right if we were a little closer."

"Why weren't we?" Gerry demanded.

"Because the tramline hasn't been plotted," Colvin said. And I'm speaking for the record. Better get it right, and get the sarcasm out of my voice. "I requested survey equipment, but none was available. We were therefore required to plot the Alderson entry point using optics alone. I would be much surprised if anyone could have made a better estimate using our equipment."

"I see," Gerry said. With an effort he touched the switch that gave him a general intcom circuit. "Spacers of the Republic, your comrades salute you! Freedom!"

"Freedom!" came the response. Colvin didn't think more than half the crew had spoken, but it was difficult to tell.

"You all know the importance of this battle," Gerry said. "We defend the back door of the Republic, and we are alone. Many believed we need not be here, that the

Imperials would never find this path to our homes. That ship shows the wisdom of the government."

Had to get that in, didn't you? Colvin chuckled to himself. Gerry expected to run for office, if he lived through the coming battles.

"The Imperials will never make us slaves! Our cause is just, for we seek only the freedom to be left alone. The Empire will not permit this. They wish to rule the entire universe, forever. Spacers, we fight for liberty!"

Colvin looked across the bridge to the watch officer and lifted an eyebrow. He got a shrug for an answer. Herb nodded. It was hard to tell the effect of a speech. Gerry was said to be good at speaking. He'd talked his way into a junior membership on the Committee of Public Safety that governed the Republic.

A tiny buzz sounded in Colvin's ear. The Executive Officer's station was aft, in an auxiliary control room, where he could take over the ship if something happened to the main bridge.

By Republic orders Gerry was to hear everything said by and to the captain during combat, but Gerry didn't know much about ships. Commander Gregory Halleck, Colvin's exec, had modified the intercom system. Now his voice came through, the flat nasal twang of New Chicago's outback. "Skipper, why don't he shut up and let us fight?"

"Speech was recorded, Greg," Colvin said.

"Ah. He'll play it for the cityworkers," Halleck said. "Tell me, skipper, just what chance have we got?"

"In this battle? Pretty good."

"Yeah. Wish I was so sure about the war."

"Scared, Greg?"

"A little. How can we win?"

"We can't *beat* the Empire," Colvin said. "Not if they bring their whole fleet in here. But if we can win a couple of battles, the Empire'll have to pull back. They can't strip all their ships out of other areas. Too many enemies. Time's on our side, if we can buy some."

"Yeah. Way I see it, too. Guess it's worth it. Back to work."

It had to be worth it, Colvin thought. It just didn't make sense to put the whole human race under one government.

Some day they'd get a really bad Emperor. Or three Emperors all claiming the throne at once. Better to put a stop to this now, rather than leave the problem to their grandchildren.

The phones buzzed again. "Better take a good look, skipper," Halleck said. "I think we got problems."

The screens flashed as new information flowed. Colvin touched other buttons in his chair arm. Lt. Susack's face swam onto one screen. "Make a signal to the fleet," Colvin said. "That thing's bigger than we thought. This could be one hell of a battle."

"Aye aye," Susack said. "But we can handle it."

"Sure," Colvin said. He stared at the updated information and frowned.

"What is out there, Captain?" Gerry asked. "Is there reason for concern?"

"There could be," Colvin said. "Mister Gerry, that is an Imperial battle cruiser. 'General' class, I'd say." As he told the political officer, Colvin felt a cold pit in his guts.

"And what does that mean?"

"It's one of their best," Colvin said. "About as fast as we are. More armor, more weapons, more fuel. We've got a fight on our hands."

"Launch observation boats. Prepare to engage," Colvin ordered. Although he couldn't see it, the Imperial ship was probably doing the same thing. Observation boats didn't carry much for weapons, but their observations could be invaluable when the engagement began.

"You don't sound confident," Gerry said.

Colvin checked his intercom switches. No one could hear him but Gerry. "I'm not," he said. "Look, however you cut it, if there's an advantage that ship's got it. Their crew's had a chance to recover from their hyperspace trip, too." *If we'd had the right equipment*—No use thinking about that.

"What if it gets past us?"

"Enough ships might knock it out, especially if we can damage it, but there's no single ship in our fleet that can fight that thing one-on-one and expect to win."

He paused to let that sink in.

"Including us."

"Including us. I didn't know there was a battle cruiser anywhere in the trans-Coalsack region."

"Interesting implications," Gerry said.

"Yeah. They've brought one of their best ships. Not only that, they took the trouble to find a back way. Two new Alderson tramlines. From the red dwarf to us, and a way into the red dwarf."

"Seems they're determined." Gerry paused a moment. "The Committee was constructing planetary defenses when we lifted out."

"They may need them. Excuse me . . ." Colvin cut the circuit and concentrated on his battle screens.

The master computer flashed a series of maneuver strategies, each with the odds for success if adopted. The probabilities were only a computer's judgment, however. Over there in the Imperial ship was an experienced human captain who'd do his best to thwart those odds while Colvin did the same. Game theory and computers rarely consider all the possibilities a human brain can conceive.

The computer recommended full retreat and sacrifice of the observation boats—and at that gave only an even chance for *Defiant*. Colvin studied the board. "ENGAGE CLOSELY," he said.

The computer wiped the other alternatives and flashed a series of new choices. Colvin chose. Again and again this happened until the ship's brain knew exactly what her human master wanted, but long before the dialogue was completed the ship accelerated to action, spewing torpedoes from her ports to send H-bombs on random evasion courses toward the enemy. Tiny lasers reached out toward enemy torpedoes, filling space with softly glowing threads of bright color.

Defiant leaped toward her enemy, her photon cannons pouring out energy to wash over the Imperial ship. "Keep it up, keep it up," Colvin chanted to himself. If the enemy could be blinded, her antennas destroyed so that her crew couldn't see out through her Langston Field to locate *Defiant*, the battle would be over.

Halleck's outback twang came through the earphones. "Looking good, boss."

"Yeah." The very savagery of unexpected attack by a smaller vessel had taken the enemy by surprise. Just maybe—

A blaze of white struck *Defiant* to send her screens up into the orange, tottering towards yellow for an instant. In that second *Defiant* was as blind as the enemy, every sensor outside the Field vaporized. Her boats were still there, though, still sending data on the enemy's position, still guiding torpedoes.

"Bridge, this is damage control."

"Yeah, Greg."

"Hulled in main memory bank area. I'm getting replacement elements in, but you better go to secondary computer for a while."

"Already done."

"Good. Got a couple other problems, but I can handle them."

"Have at it." Screens were coming back on line. More sensor clusters were being poked through the Langston Field on stalks. Colvin touched buttons in his chair arm. "Communications. Get number three boat in closer."

"Acknowledged."

The Imperial ship took evasive action. She would cut acceleration for a moment, turn slightly, then accelerate again, with constantly changing drive power. Colvin shook his head. "He's got an iron crew," he muttered to Halleck. "They must be getting the guts shook out of them."

Another blast rocked *Defiant*. A torpedo had penetrated her defensive fire to explode somewhere near the hull. The Langston Field, opaque to radiant energy, was able to absorb and redistribute the energy evenly throughout the Field; but at cost. There had been an overload at the place nearest the bomb: energy flaring inward. The Langston Field was a spaceship's true hull. Its skin was only metal, designed only to hold pressure. Breech it and—

"Hulled again aft of number two torpedo room," Halleck reported. "Spare parts, and the messroom brain. We'll eat basic protocarb for a while."

"If we eat at all." Why the hell weren't they getting more hits on the enemy? He could see the Imperial ship on his screens, in the view from number two boat. Her field glowed orange, wavering to yellow, and there were two deep purple spots, probably burnthroughs. No way to tell what lay under those areas. Colvin hoped it was something vital.

His own Field was yellow tinged with green. Pastel lines jumped between the two ships. After this was over, there would be time to remember just how *pretty* a space battle was. The screens flared, and his odds for success dropped again, but he couldn't trust the computer anyway. He'd lost number three boat, and number one had ceased reporting.

The enemy ship flared again as *Defiant* scored a hit, then another. The Imperial's screens turned yellow, then green; as they cooled back toward red another hit sent them through green to blue. "Torps!" Colvin shouted, but the master computer had already done it. A stream of tiny shapes flashed toward the blinded enemy.

"Pour it on!" Colvin screamed. "Everything we've got!" If they could keep the enemy blind, keep him from finding *Defiant* while they poured energy into his Field, they could keep his screens hot enough until torpedoes could get through. Enough torpedoes would finish the job. "Pour it on!"

The Imperial ship was almost beyond the blue, creeping toward the violet. "By God we may have him!" Colvin shouted.

The enemy maneuvered again, but the bright rays of *Defiant's* lasers followed, pinning the glowing ship against the star background. Then the screens went blank.

Colvin frantically pounded buttons. Nothing happened. *Defiant* was blind. "Eyes! How'd he hit us?" he demanded.

"Don't know." Susack's voice was edged with fear. "Skipper, we've got problems with the detectors. I sent a party out but they haven't reported—"

Halleck came on. "Imperial boat got close and hit us with torps."

Blind. Colvin watched his screen color indicators. Bright orange and yellow, with a green tint already visible. Acceleration warnings hooted through the ship as Colvin ordered random evasive action. The enemy would be blind too. Now it was a question of who could see first. "Get me some eyes." he said. He was surprised at how calm his voice was.

"Working on it," Halleck said. "I've got minimal sight back here. Maybe I can locate him."

"Take over gun direction," Colvin said. "What's with the computer?"

"I'm not getting damage reports from that area," Halleck said. "I have men out trying to restore internal communications, and another party's putting out antennas—only nobody really wants to go out to the hull edge and work, you know."

"Wants!" Colvin controlled blind rage. Who cared what the crew wanted? His ship was in danger!

Acceleration and jolt warnings sounded continuously as *Defiant* continued evasive maneuvers. Jolt, acceleration, stop, turn, jolt—

"He's hitting us again." Susack sounded scared.

"Greg?" Colvin demanded.

"I'm losing him. Take over, skipper."

Defiant writhed like a beetle on a pin as the deadly fire followed her through maneuvers. The damage reports came as a deadly litany. "Partial collapse, after auxilliary engine room destroyed. Hulled in three places in number five tankage area, hydrogen leaking to space. Hulled in the after recreation room."

The screens were electric blue when the computer cut the drives. *Defiant* was dead in space. She was moving at more than a hundred kilometers per second, but she couldn't accelerate.

"See anything yet?" Colvin asked.

"In a second," Halleck replied. "There. Wups. Antenna didn't last half a second. He's yellow. Out there on our port quarter and pouring it on. Want me to swing the main drive in that direction? We might hit him with that."

Colvin examined his screens. "No. We can't spare the power." He watched a moment more, then swept his hand across a line of buttons.

All through *Defiant* nonessential systems died. It took power to maintain the Langston Field, and the more energy the Field had to contain the more internal power was needed to keep the Field from radiating inward. Local overloads produced burnthroughs, partial collapses sending busts of energetic photons to punch holes through the hull. The Field moved toward full collapse, and when that happened, the energies it contained would vaporize *Defiant*. Total defeat in space is a clean death.

The screens were indigo and *Defiant* couldn't spare power to fire her guns or use her engines. Every erg was needed simply to survive.

"We'll have to surrender," Colvin said. "Get the message out."

"I forbid it!"

For a moment Colvin had forgotten the political officer.

"I forbid it!" Gerry shouted again. "Captain, you are relieved from command. Commander Halleck, engage the enemy! We cannot allow him to penetrate to our homeland!"

"Can't do that, sir," Halleck said carefully. The recorded conversation made the executive officer a traitor, as Colvin was the instant he'd given the surrender order.

"Engage the enemy, Captain." Gerry spoke quietly. "Look at me, Colvin."

Herb Colvin turned to see a pistol in Gerry's hands. It wasn't a sonic gun, not even a chemical dart weapon as used by prison guards. Combat armor would stop those. This was a slugthrower—no. A small rocket launcher, but it looked like a slugthrower. Just the weapon to take to space.

"Surrender the ship," Colvin repeated. He motioned with one hand. Gerry looked around, too late, as the quartermaster pinned his arms to his sides. A captain's bridge runner launched himself across the cabin to seize the pistol.

"I'll have you shot for this!" Gerry shouted. "You've betrayed everything. Our homes, our families—"

"I'd as soon be shot as surrender," Colvin said. "Besides, the Imperials will probably do for both of us. Treason, you know. Still, I've a right to save the crew."

Gerry said nothing.

"We're dead, Mister. The only reason they haven't finished us off is we're so bloody helpless the Imperial commander's held off firing the last wave of torpedoes to give us a chance to quit. He can finish us off any time."

"You might damage him. Take him with us, or make it easier for the fleet to deal with him—"

"If I could, I'd do that. I already launched all our torpedoes. They either got through or they didn't. Either way, they didn't kill him, since he's still pouring it on us. He has all the time in the world—look, damn it! We can't shoot at him, we don't have power for the engines, and look at the screens! Violet! Don't you understand, you blithering fool, there's no further place for it to go! A little more, a miscalculation by the Imperial, some little failure here, and that field collapses."

Gerry stared in rage. "Maybe you're right."

"I know I'm right. Any progress, Susack?"

"Message went out," the communications officer said. "And they haven't finished us."

"Right." There was nothing else to say.

A ship in *Defiant's* situation, her screens overloaded, bombarded by torpedoes and fired on by an enemy she cannot locate, is utterly helpless; but she has been damaged hardly at all. Given time she can radiate the screen energies to space. She can erect antennas to find her enemy. When the screens cool, she can move and she can shoot. Even when she has been damaged by partial collapses, her enemy cannot know that.

Thus, surrender is difficult and requires a precise ritual. Like all of mankind's surrender signals it is artificial, for man has no surrender reflex, no unambiguous species-wide signal to save him from death after defeat is inevitable. Of the higher animals, man is alone in this.

Stags do not fight to the death. When one is beaten, he submits, and the other allows him to leave the field. The three spine stickleback, a fish of the carp family, fights for its mates but recognizes the surrender of its enemies. Siamese fighting fish will not pursue an enemy after he ceases to spread his gills.

But man has evolved as a weapon using animal. Unlike other animals, man's evolution is intimately bound with weapons and tools; and weapons can kill farther than man can reach. Weapons in the hand of a defeated enemy are still dangerous. Indeed, the Scottish *skean dhu* is said to be carried in the stocking so that it may be reached as its owner kneels in supplication. . . .

Defiant erected a simple antenna suitable only for radio signals. Any other form of sensor would have been a hostile act and would earn instant destruction. The Imperial captain observed and sent instructions.

Meanwhile, torpedoes were being maneuvered alongside *Defiant.* Colvin couldn't see them. He knew they must be in place when the next signal came through. The Imperial ship was sending an officer to take command.

Colvin felt some of the tension go out of him. If no one had volunteered for the job, *Defiant* would have been destroyed.

Something massive thumped against the hull. A port had already been opened for the Imperial. He entered carrying a bulky object: a bomb.

"Midshipman Horst Staley, Imperial Battlecruiser *MacArthur,*" the officer announced as he was conducted to the bridge. Colvin could see blue eyes and blonde hair, a young face frozen into a mask of calm because its owner did not trust himself to show any expression at all. "I am to take command of this ship, sir."

Captain Colvin nodded. "I give her to you. You'll want this," he added, handing the boy the microphone. "Thank you for coming."

"Yes, sir." Staley gulped noticeably, then stood at attention as if his captain could see him. "Midshipman Staley reporting, sir. I am on the bridge and the enemy has surrendered." He listened for a few seconds, then turned to Colvin. "I am to ask you to leave me alone on the bridge except for yourself, sir. And to tell you that if anyone else comes on the bridge before our Marines have secured this ship, I will detonate the bomb I carry. Will you comply?"

Colvin nodded again. "Take Mr. Gerry out, quartermaster. You others can go, too. Clear the bridge."

The quartermaster led Gerry toward the door. Suddenly the political officer broke free and sprang at Staley. He wrapped the midshipman's arms against his body and shouted, "Quick, grab the bomb! Move! Captain, fight your ship, I've got him!"

Staley struggled with the policial officer. His hand groped for the trigger, but he couldn't reach it. The mike had also been ripped from his hands. He shouted at the dead microphone.

Colvin gently took the bomb from Horst's imprisoned hands. "You won't need this, son," he said. "Quartermaster, you can take your prisoner off this bridge." His smile was fixed, frozen in place, in sharp contrast to the midshipman's shocked rage and Gerry's look of triumph.

The spacers reached out and Horst Staley tried to escape, but there was no place to go as he floated in free space. Suddenly he realized that the spacers had seized his attacker, and Gerry was screaming.

"We've surrendered, Mister Staley," Colvin said carefully. "Now we'll leave you in command here. You can have your bomb, but you won't be needing it."

EDITOR'S INTRODUCTION TO:

SPANISH MAN'S GRAVE
by
James Warner Bellah

This story is not science fiction; but it has its place in
this anthology, for this is one of the stories that inspired
Robert Heinlein to write *STARSHIP TROOPERS*.

When I met Colonel James Warner Bellah, he was a
crusty retired military officer. He was quite famous;
Bellah's stories inspired more than half of the best Duke
Wayne movies directed by John Ford. "She Wore A
Yellow Ribbon," "Red River," "Rio Grande," "Thunder
of Drums," all those and more were his, and indeed
shared the characters: Lt. Pennell, Captain Brittles who
couldn't be promoted, Sergeant Tyree (that was Tyree's
department . . .), Trooper Smith who had been a Major
General in the Army of the Confederate States—those
and many more.

His own biography reads:

"I was born three months before the Century of Wars
began to unfold itself. The faded, drink-wrecked blue
shirts of El Caney and San Juan Hill cut our laws
in Westchester County when I was a boy, for my father
had raised a company of infantry in the Spanish-
American War and was soft, ever after, to anyone who
called him Captain.

"During my growing-up, a flamboyant cousin in
cavalry yellow-and-blue was perennially in the house
from chasing Aguinaldo in the Philippines—and, as late
as 1916—from chasing Pancho Villa deep into the Sierra
Tarahumare in Mexico.

"In my mother's closet, there were the epaulettes and
sabres of her infantry captain father, wounded seven
times from Cold Harbor to Appomattox—which he
reached in an ambulance, still doing duty, because he
had had a bellyful of field hospitals.

"On the inertia of all this, a fugitive from school at

seventeen, I was in France with the Army Transport Service. At eighteen I was a De Haviland 9 pilot in the 117th squadron, Royal Air Force, which had, when I joined it, been still the old, original Royal Flying Corps.

"The years between, I wrote for a living, but in 1939, the bugles screamed again, and being too old to fly but still young enough to walk, I was a lieutenant in F Company, 16th Infantry, First Infantry Division, ending up in the Burma War, variously under Stillwell, Wingate, and Phil Cochran.

"None of which is to be construed as vainglory, but merely as an explanation of the fact that a great deal of my writing has had the background of war. With some pardonable reason.

"The experience of war never quite leaves a young man or woman. A great many are utterly destroyed by it. All are indelibly and subtly marked by it, because, for good or evil, the memory never quite leaves any of us."

Col. Bellah wasn't an easy man to get to know, and I was a bit awed by him anyway. We were both members of the Order of St. Lazarus of Jerusalem, as well as St. Nicholas Church. I last saw him at his funeral which was conducted jointly by the Knights of Lazarus, the US Army, and a personal piper. Since then his son and I have become friends.

I have never read a story that tells more about why one might be a soldier.

SPANISH MAN'S GRAVE
by
James Warner Bellah

The fears of man are many. He fears the shadow of
death and the closed doors of the future. He is afraid for
his friends and for his sons and of the specter of
tomorrow. All his life's journey he walks in the lonely
corridors of his controlled fears, if he is a man. For only
fools will strut, and only cowards dare cringe.

The Barrels Patrol wound on down across the far
corner of the West, riding easily for the long haul, the
long swing around. Day after deadly day. Week after
weary week. Never the same route, for fear of forming
military habits hostiles could depend upon.

There was that smudge of smoke ahead, straight up on
the horizon, like coarse and thinning hair swept across
yellow linen. And nothing else. Nothing but the empty
miles that echoed in from the rim of the world, from the
northern wastes of the Dakota country, from south of
the Rio Grande, from Kansas back in the States. And in
the center of this utter loneliness, like a fly caught in
amber, Ross Pennell writhed inwardly in loathing of it.

For there are no soft-handed girls on the lone plains;
only the echo of their laughter in dreams. And a plains
uniform is a poor badge of glory. Worn leather, reeking
of horse sweat and body sweat. Shirts bleached to the
blue of distant rain, the armpits white with salt rime.
Battered gray beaver felt, threadbare on the head, with
the sweatband stinking when you ease up the brim. And
no violins. No flowers. No band music. Only the
dreariness and the loneliness and the final knowledge
that you have flung down your youth into this empty

void and that there your youth will die, far from the
lights of cities, wasted forevermore.

"I don't like that smoke too much, Mr. Pennell,"
Sergeant Tyree spat sideways, and the brown ribbon of
tobacco, flat and gleaming in the sunlight, twisted over
once and struck into the dust with the muffled slap
of dropped playing cards. "Ain't prairie fire; it's focal-
ized."

It is odd how you come to understand things. Tyree
wanted an opinion. He had a faint doubt, but that wasn't
enough for Tyree. From years of habit, he needed
an opinion to ease that doubt and to rationalize it. And
the opinion had to have shoulder straps on it, no matter
how new the straps were.

Lieutenant Pennell glanced down the column. Corporal Bartenett and seven men. Sergeant Tyree, the
captain and himself. Taking it on the downslope at a
walk. Twisting in and out in single file, broadside on to
the trail, head on to it, picking the best footholds, riding
carefully. Thinned down to bone and muscle they were,
after five weeks of this. Griped silent. Their faces were
drawn with monotony, their minds were seared raw
with it. The pack animals creaked along in the rear.

Pennell said, "Homestead chimney smoke, probably."

For a moment, as he said it, Ross Pennell saw the
broad sweep of Claymont Street in his memory. The
sunlight in the green arch of the ancient elms. The smell of
bonfire smoke and the broad white verandas. The cold
throat bite of well water. Ginger cookies in the crockery
jar. Fresh bread in the oven. His mother in lavender silk,
and the snap of his father's hunting-case watch. And a
great and silent scream tore through him, for there was
no going back to that now. No one there, waiting, any
longer. It was almost as if cold hands pressed that silent
scream up from his diaphragm, forced it up his throat,
until it died in silence behind his clenched teeth.

So it is always, if you listen to the music of the band.
Down the street it swings, and the boys and the fools
follow it, and there is a great and powerful uplift
as the crowds cheer, as feet tap in cadence. Then
suddenly your soul is gone with it—gone on ahead
to wait for you in the memories where the old men
live. The town is far behind, and those who waved

you off have gone back home to loneliness and tears. The band is silent and there are no more parades. Only your soul to plod on after—to try to own again, once more before you die.

"Effen it's a homestead," Tyree said, "it's burnin' down."

Captain MacAfee reined in, and the column rattled and jangled slowly to a stop behind him. Ross Pennell rode up to it from the rear. Brown acid smell of horses. Green acid smell of men. MacAfee sat straight-backed—a miniature man, delicate in bone, but long-limbed. His face was drawn so thinly across the frontal bones of his head that it was as if it had been laced up too tightly in back. His fleshless hands at fifty-six were gray talons, and there was not enough blood left in him, after the years of his service, to take the iridescent blue from his lips.

"Mr. Pennell," he spoke haltingly, "this is as far as I go," and he sat there with his eyes closed, like marbles in his skull. Marbles covered with chicken skin. A worn-out man, old before his time, drained by the Colors, sitting his mount a thousand miles down the wastelands, staring at distant smoke with his eyes closed.

"Please, sir, I beg your pardon?"

MacAfee soughed his breath in heavily. "My left arm and leg went dead a ways back—" his voice was thickening and the words were falling clumsily out of his slackened mouth "—and now I've gone blind."

"Hold steady, sir; I'll dismount you."

"Mr. Pennell, there are only three things to remember out here. Always make them think you are in force, or will be soon. Always frighten them until they stop thinking and take refuge in Medicine. Then turn it against them, spoil its power and break it, so they can't trust anything. And always treat your luck with respect, so that it will never turn against you. This time I was going to take the patrol down and try to find Spanish Man's Grave. I wanted to show dirty shirt blue down there and spoil that Medicine for them. The Apaches have been living too long on that old massacre story—believing too much in their immunity. Flout it in their faces, show them that the gods hate them, too, and you've gone a long way toward making them behave. I want you to take the patrol down."

"Yes, sir. I'll take it down just as you say. If you'll let me have your arm now, I'll dismount you. You'll be all right in a minute."

"It's a damn long journey, Mr. Pennell."

"Sergeant Tyree!" But MacAfee's candle guttered before the sergeant could ride in. He died straight-shouldered in the saddle. Only his head snapped. For a moment, the years of habit still held him upright; then he went loose all over and pitched out headfirst. Ross Pennell caught him by the scrawny left arm, and the captain dangled there, toes down, tongue out and head hanging. Both horses shied apart, nostrils wide, blowing, eyes rolling white, heads tossed up in quick panic. Corporal Bartenett threw off and grabbed the captain under the arms.

Tyree threw off. "My God, Mr. Pennell! He's dead!"

For a moment, everyone just stared down at what Royal Forsythe MacAfee had finished with suddenly after fifty-six years of living with it. Then they hauled off their stained hats and dismounted. "MacAfee, R.F., Capt.—from duty to deceased, 2 P.M., 17 Sept.—"

There were the soft beds back on Claymont Street, white-sheeted, and hand-polished mahogany. Brides' beds, childbeds, deathbeds in slow, respectable rotation. People said, "I was born in that bed, and my father before me. My mother died in that bed."

"Captain MacAffe's wife died years ago," Sergeant Tyree said, "and there were two little boys, but they died too. They're buried at Fort Starke. Never knew the captain to get letters from anyone or send 'em, in all the eight years I served with him. I guess he's just like all of us. People kind of forget when you're away." Tyree shrugged and looked off down horizon.

"I won't have it!" Pennell almost shouted. "There must be some kinfolk somewhere. Somebody who cares if a man lives his life like this. Damn it to hell, he was a captain of cavalry, wasn't he? All his life he served something, somebody, didn't he? And is this all there is when it's finished?" Ross Pennell held out the dirty tied handkerchief with its still-ticking watch and the locket and chain and the Louis d'Or pocket piece—for luck ever since Cerro Gordo. "Is this all there is?"

Tyree said, "Mr. Pennell, that's all there is, except that smoke on the horizon. He's left that too. The watch don't matter and the locket don't matter, and neither does the good-luck piece, but the smoke does. You inherit that smoke, I guess, Mr. Pennell. Like it says in law, 'an heir and an assign . . .' "

This far the gods will let a man go—to a cairned grave on a lonesome downslope where he may lie in sleep forever. But here another man takes over, for there is always smoke still ahead and the march goes on. "Prepare to mount—"

Your first man dead in violence is a sick thing in your mind for many suns and many moons, until the others fade its picture. But you never forget the first white woman you see that the Apaches have worked over.

It had been a three-sided cabin of clay-chinked rails. No one but a fool or a very brave man would have put it in as far west as that, unless he had pushed out beyond the other people so far that he was lost and didn't know it.

There was the scrabbled corn patch lying under the bitter pall of smoke. The hot air held it just off the ground. It rose from the embers of the cabin, coiling lazily in white ropes, spreading, rising straight in a thin veil. Almost burned out when they got there. They saw the two halves of the dog first, and the dust and hair and clotted abomination of the ax, flung under the broken wagon. Flies were there, green and translucent, glutted lazy.

The name in a torn book was "Alice Downey, Fairfax, Virginia." The book was Robert Browning's poems. On other papers that fluttered in the corn there was "Charles Graeme and Alice Downey Graeme, his Wife—" and there were blackened brass drawer pulls and broken splinters of mulberry china and a bent spoon of silver.

The man was roped and arched in final protest at the little field's edge. Cold in his agony now, and blue stiff. His outraged face seemed to howl at them for vengeance—to howl in black and tortured silence. He had fought like a panther. The ground was lacerated with his fight. "I, Charles Graeme, farmer, will hold this land or die on it."

Corporal Bartenett found the woman—"Alice Downey Graeme, his Wife." And there it was, and how can you say what it was? For the ground about showed that fight, too, and there was sickness in all of them as they read the ground, and the dark maroon anger that makes for murder, even though its ice takes the strength from fingers for the moment.

Thirty Apaches, by the pony marks, blood-drunk and beast hot. Reeking to defile. Hair-tearing hands, grease slick. Fetid-breathed and shrieking with obscenity.

Sergeant Tyree turned sharp around, as if someone had moved behind him, as if he would draw gun on whoever it was. "Two days," he growled, "by the condition of the carcasses. Washday Monday—that's what these clothes is," and he toed his boot into the strewn and trampled clothing, twisting his leg slowly as he did it, almost as if he were in agony. "A two-day start on us they got, and the girl they got, about ten, eleven years old. See there," and he pointed. "Her go-to-meetin' dress." He shook his head at Pennell's question. "No," he said. "I don't think the girl, yet. Only the mother. But I sure hope the girl ain't big for her age, 'cause we gotta long haul to catch up on 'em, sir. I sure hope she ain't—"

Ross Pennell stood still, looking off toward the western horizon again, as if there would be more smoke down there to guide him on. Smoke to the west, drawing a man on down his destiny, on down his years until there was no more Claymont Street behind him forevermore. Until the Chew girls next door, in their white dresses with the pink sashes, their patent-leather slippers and flop-brimmed leghorns, their prayer books and their crocheted mittens—until the Chew girls . . .

But there were no Chew girls left in Pennell in that moment. And suddenly there was no place in him for them to come back to if they ever tried.

"Tyree," he said, "you and Marcy fix Mrs. Graeme decently for burial. I want her to have something on. Unmarried men clear out of the area . . . Gustafson and Newkirk, get the man ready . . . Bartenett, take the rest of the details and unsaddle. Graze wide. Pack train as well. We move out again at seven o'clock."

The book tells you how to force the march, but a good sergeant is better than the best of books, and deep anger is better than a sergeant. Space out to fifty-five paces and stagger the odd files twenty yards to the right. That keeps the dust down and gives the mounts air to breathe. Unbit to graze on all halts, even the shortest. Halt ten minutes in the hour, and forty minutes every sixth hour for watering. Trot twenty minutes every second hour, and lead for the full hour before watering call. And talk up the horses. Tell them what you want out of them, for you can always bring a horse in on your side with the right kind of talk. A horse is a child on the surface, but he's got a mind underneath that is capable of telling him how to die like a gentleman, if the need comes. And a horse can get regiment-conscious as hell, and don't you ever forget it.

The patrol had had five full weeks of conditioning before Pennell put them to it on a hot stern chase, for there isn't anything but a stern chase on the plains—for there is only the trail to follow. They began to force it unbelievably. They cut the bivouac time to half the dark hours, and they ate up the space between themselves and the thirty Apaches with the Graeme girl. But they ate up their own minds doing it; they wore them down like old knife blades. They were all in it—all ten—all reading the trail when it was written, guessing at it when it wasn't, cramming in food when their bellies screamed, and watching their mounts like young mothers with a first babe. They got crotch stiff and neck stiff, and they stumbled wooden-legged when they led. They gave it all to the horses, and the horses knew it and gave back what they could. Their eyes got red and their beards got foul, but the anger stayed in them, and it stayed cold—frozen in yellow-legged discipline.

On the day the first Apache fire spot was still warm when Ross Pennell put the palm of his hand on it, the night of that day he put in his own fires. Squad fires. Fifty paces apart along the skyline. Enough fires to indicate two companies and their escort train. The simulated hands of vengeance, clawing upward with crimson fingers for the Apaches to read as fate. Pennell did it almost to dictated order. "Always make 'em think you're in force . . . or will be soon."

And in three hours again, when the fires were burned down, "Prepare to mount. Mount!"

"Tyree, tell me about Spanish Man's Grave."

Sergeant Tyree spat left and looked squint-eyed under his hat brim at Ross Pennell. "Can't rightly tell much, sir. Never been there. Only hearsay. He drawed a picture of it once—Captain MacAfee did. Spanish soldiers ridin' an' marchin' up from Sante Fe coupla centuries ago, all shinin' in armor and golden helmets, with plumes and yellow silken flags. Must 'a' been purty." Tyree shook his head. "But it didn't work out. The Apaches caught the whole kit and kaboodle of 'em in the tablelands and killed every mother's son. Got 'em like at the bottom of the well, they say. Ever since then it's been Apache holy ground. It did something to their bad god for all time. Only their good god lives at the Grave. Once the Apaches get in to Spanish Man's, they're safe home. Big and powerful Medicine protects them."

"Anybody from Fort Starke ever been there?"

"No white man was ever there, is what I think. A lot of 'em will lie they was, but I think only them dead *caballeros* know where it is, and they ain't a one of 'em ever talked since the massacre."

"Tyree," Pennell said, "I wonder what those Spaniards did wrong?"

"I ain't a man to blame dead men," Tyree said, "but the captain used to say an army ought to have a lotta brains before it shows a lotta flags. He used to say it ought to be able to shoot 'possible' before it lets the band play too loud. And he used to say that only a well-trained veteran looks right in a bright uniform, and that dirty uniform shirts make the best empires. But maybe we'll find out what the Spaniards did wrong, Mr. Pennell. I've knowed you was goin' to the Grave fer four days."

They didn't talk all at once, Ross Pennell and Tyree. A word here and the long miles between, and then another word, for talk is like a chewing twist when men are alone. Bite fresh and something new comes into the flavor. Chew it out alone until it's flat, then spit and bite again. That way the mind keeps quieter to do its own thinking. Sometimes by moon they spoke. Sometimes in the sun's heat. A word and then another word, until it wove a slow and inexorable pattern of deep understanding, unadorned with the furbelows of chatter.

"We're going to the Grave because the Apaches are going. They're going because they're running to Medicine, for protection, to get away from what they think is two companies. Drive 'em to Medicine, turn it on 'em, show 'em it's no good either! That's the second thing you always do."

Tyree could see Pennell's white teeth, bare and alkalidry in the starlight. He said, "Somethin' crazy about any man who'll stay out here, Lieutenant. Longer he stays, crazier he gets. Crazier he gets, the more he knows, and the less he knows how he knows. Crazy is like fever. On and off. But every time it comes, it stays a little longer, until you die of it or it breaks. We're all talking to ourselves now, sir. We're all worn through the crust now, and we ain't goin' to get better till we catch up with the little girl or die trying. We're worn through, like our pants. Thin and stringy and gristly. Any minute and we can go loco. If we do, I want you to know I can take my lootenints or leave 'em lay. Always could. I take you, sir. But just remember, when we get there, we're only ten men all told, and there won't be any trail left in, so's you can follow it, unless you've got the luck of the damned."

"That's the third ingredient, Tyree—respect for your luck."

And hours later again: "And, Sergeant Tyree, I think I've got that luck, for I am damned now. There is bitter smoke hanging in the elms above Claymont Street and across the brick wall of Christ Churchyard where my father and my mother are buried; there's somehow a mat of green flies. The people of the United States are a frightened little white girl eleven years old. Tyree, I take you too. Pass the word to halt, dismount and lead."

At first you can't believe it when you come to plains' end, for no painting can ever show it as it is. The frost blues and the silken yellows of the tablelands. The reds that are watered out to the color of broiled lobster claws. The purples that have distant church music in them. The greens that you can smell for sweet mown grass. All worked into one breathlessness and swept across the horizon. At dawn, there is a golden rim around it. At sundown, nothing contains its endlessness. Ten miles away to the eye, two hundred miles to the march.

When the night comes down in blue fog so thick that you can hold it at arm's length in your two clutched hands, the mesas move in on the bivouac and cut the mileage down. And the stars hang under the rims of them so close that you can touch their iciness with the tip of your tongue. But in the morning, just before you open your eyes, the mesas race away again.

The afternoon that you give up all hope of ever riding them down they turn suddenly to slate gray, shot with dull chrome, and you are in among them.

"What now, Mr. Pennell?"

The faces jerked as Sergeant Tyree said it. The worn and hollow faces. Skin and stubble, with deep and filthy trenches in the cheeks. And one of them crackled, "So here we are; where are we?" And another tried twice, and had to claw it into sound with grimy fingers at his mouth and throat. "They'll know now we're only ten men! They can see by daylight, from the high ground, that there are no two companies behind us."

"But the Apaches may not *be* on the high ground!" Pennell snarled at them.

A hand stretched out, palm upward, dirty fingers clawing. "Apaches always camp high!" the faces said, "no matter where water is, or wood." And the faces snarled, "Yea-Yea! A fine answer. How high? Tell me—where are they?"

The horses skittered in fear, twitched deeply in the flank with long nerve whips, tossed up their heads, whistled.

Pennell threw back his own head and laughed in the jerking faces. "For two days now, by daylight, they could have watched from the high ground and seen that there were no two companies behind us! If they had done so, they would have circled wide to try to hit us from behind. But they didn't do that, so that means they still believe we are two companies, and they have run to Medicine to get away from us, they've run to Spanish Man's Grave for sanctuary . . . and that's what I've been trying to make 'em do!"

"But where is the Grave?" the faces jerked. "You ever been there? I ever been there? Any of us ever been there, mister?"

Tyree drew his revolving pistol and muzzle up, twirled the cylinder with his thumb. The spinning metal whined loudly in the stillness. "A man here opens his mouth again," Tyree said, "I'll shoot his eyes out. I trained you. Show your training!"

Then Pennell couldn't stop laughing. "The louder the band plays the worse the shooting! The less brain the more flags! Only a trained soldier looks right in a bright uniform! Listen, Tyree. If we get up high ourselves—" and he pointed up toward the mesa tops "—Spanish Man's Grave will stand out to you and me like a cut thumb, for it'll be a bottleneck on a route that no well-trained soldier would ever think of taking through the tablelands."

The faces stopped jerking and stared red-eyed with their dried-out mouths hanging open.

"Those dead Spaniards," Pennell said, "came through the easiest route. The fact that they were all killed means they must have laid themselves wide open to tactical murder. They've done it all through their history; that's why they've got no history left to make." Ross Pennell kneed his horse around and faced the towering gateways of the tablelands. The sun was in his face in long, slanting rays, heavily dust shot, so that it looked as if great rough boards were thrust up through the brilliant beam of light, holding it high for all of them to see by. And all of them looked in through the gateways and saw the wreckage of that ancient erosion, the serried ranks of its vast silence. Then, for a moment, it was as if Ross Pennell had lost something and was searching with his eyes to find it. He pointed. "It will be an approach like this one," he said. "If we were high enough, I believe we would see their passage winding up the draw, winding around the easiest slopes, winding all the miles back to Sante Fe."

There was a trace to the right that wound up the side of the mesa. Pennell dismounted, stiff-legged. He almost fell when he tried to stand alone and sling his glasses case high behind his left shoulder. Tyree threw off beside him and stumbled down on one knee before he could control his legs. They started up, clinging, and drawing themselves by their arms and by their hands, for there was slow blood flow still in their legs.

The patrol sat below, watching their painful progress upward. Watching them cling to handholds and swing on up, scrabbling, clawing. Once they slipped and tumbled back rump-over, kicking and trying to catch hold again, spurring into the sand to brake themselves to a stop. To start on up again.

Then the last of the direct rays of the sun flooded down the draw and flared for a moment like a great fire flame. The shadows slowly rose like purple mist, and the two climbing men were lost in them. But not to themselves were they lost. There was still light above when they stood together on the mesa's rim.

"There's the draw, Tyree!" Ross Pennell reached for his glasses case. "It traces due west and goes in behind the second table. Do you see—?"

Tyree said, "Yellow thread don't make chevrons, but brains in the right head can sure make luck. You don't need them glasses. Look," and he swept his arm to the left. "There's Spanish Man, where that bivouac smoke is! The Medicine is supposed to hide that too. I'd say south a half mile, west to the second table and due west about seven miles from there. Come on, Lieutenant; let's get the hell down while there's still enough light—"

The silver moon wash was almost as light as early dawn.

"I'll go in first, Tyree, twenty yards ahead of you. Follow me, keeping to the opposite side, in case they fire at me. Keep bunched to concentrate your own fire. Fire only on my order."

The Apaches sat about their fires, safe in the ancient power of Medicine. Sat on the robes of their long-dead warriors, robes that were sewn with the symbols of the massacre story. Robes that boasted and lied and gloated in their needle tracery. Robes that had been used so long that they were no longer thick enough to hold smells in them for long. They sat frozen in fear when they saw Pennell, their faces turned toward him, or rose in white, unbelieving panic as he called through cupped hands and his voice rang in the narrow defile like the voice of doom:

"The little Graeme girl! Lie flat where you are!" Then he saw her . . . "She's by the fire on our left, Tyree! Hand these bastards the bill!"

And Tyree snarled, "At fifteen yards, fire by squad! The aim is right oblique! Steady . . . *Fire!*"

Pennell called to the little Graeme girl again to lie flat and wait, and again the patrol fired, and again, until there was no more sound of thrashing agony, no more panther rush to get away, no more Apaches to teach the niceties to.

The little girl stood there in the moonlight, looking large-eyed at Ross Pennell and his ragged patrol.

"And is your name Alice, too?"

"Yes, sir," she curtsied, "Alice Graeme."

"And are you all right, Alice?"

She curtsied again. "Yes, sir; I am now, sir." She walked toward them slowly with the ancient and solemn dignity of all of womanhood. And she said, "But I'm awfully glad you came, for I was very frightened . . ." not to Pennell alone, but turning her head to all of them, looking at their red eyes and their scraggly beards, their haggard faces, but knowing them for her own, with silent gratefulness that seemed to reach out and touch them with warm hands, and soft. And the way of their own hard living was suddenly more worthwhile in that moment than all the emeralds of Hind and all the gold of Cathay.

MARIUS

by

Poul Anderson

Poul Anderson has been one of my closest friends for twenty years. I recall fondly the many nights we have until dawn debated history and philosophy and the future of mankind; alas, such evenings have become all too rare.

In every generation there are those who can lead men to Hell. There are never many, for the secrets of that kind of leadership have not been written in books. No one quite knows where the great captains come from. They appear when needed—or they do not, and homelands die.

The great captains are not immune to the temptations of power; indeed, for those who can lead men to Hell, there is always the suspicion that they might be able to lead them to Heaven. If the generals do not think this way, we can be certain they will have followers to suggest the possibility.

Great soldiers are not often great governors. Sometimes they are: Julius Caesar was certainly preferable to most of his immediate successors and predecessors, Washington was certainly an able president, Mustapha Kemal was the best governor Turkey ever had. England has had able soldier kings. Napoleon reformed French society and developed a code of laws that has spread throughout the world, making one wonder what might have happened had the Allies left him in peace after his return from Elba.

Far too often, though, the habits of military power have been ingrained, so that the great captain becomes tyrant or incompetent—or both—as head of state.

MARIUS
by
Poul Anderson

It was raining again, with a bite in the air as the planet spun toward winter. They hadn't yet restored the street lights, and an early dusk seeped up between ruined walls and hid the tattered people who dwelt in caves grubbed out of rubble. Etienne Fourre, chief of the Maquisard Brotherhood and therefore representative of France in the Supreme Council of United Free Europe, stubbed his toe on a cobblestone. Pain struck through a worn-out boot, and he swore with tired expertise. The fifty guards ringing him in, hairy men in a patchwork of clothes—looted from the uniforms of a dozen armies, their own insignia merely a hand-sewn Tricolor brassard—tensed. That was an automatic reaction, the bristling of a wolf at any unawaited noise, long ago drilled into them.

"*Eh, bien,*" said Fourre. "Perhaps Rouget de l'Isle stumbled on the same rock while composing the 'Marseillaise.' "

One-eyed Astier shrugged, an almost invisible gesture in the murk. "When is the next grain shipment due?" he asked. It was hard to think of anything but food above the noise of a shrunken belly, and the Liberators had shucked military formalities during the desperate years.

"Tomorrow, I think, or the next day, if the barges aren't waylaid by river pirates," said Fourre. "And I don't believe they will be, so close to Strasbourg." He tried to smile. "Be of good cheer, my old. Next year should give an ample harvest. The Americans are shipping us a new blight-preventive."

"Always next year," grumbled Astier. "Why don't they sent us something to eat now?"

"The blights hit them, too. This is the best they can do for us. Had it not been for them, we would still be skulking in the woods sniping at Russians."

"We had a little something to do with winning."

"More than a little, thanks to Professor Valti. I do not think any of our side could have won without all the others."

"If you call this victory." Astier's soured voice faded into silence. They were passing the broken cathedral, where child-packs often hid. The little wild ones had sometimes attacked armed men with their jagged bottles and rusty bayonets. But fifty soldiers were too many, of course. Fourre thought he heard a scuttering among the stones; but that might only have been the rats. Never had he dreamed there could be so many rats.

The thin, sad rain blew into his face and weighted his beard. Night rolled out of the east, like a message from Soviet lands plunged into chaos and murder. *But we are rebuilding,* he told himself defensively. Each week the authority of the Strasbourg Council reached a civilizing hand farther into the smashed countries of Europe. In ten years, five perhaps—automation was so fantastically productive, if only you could get hold of the machines in the first place—the men of the West would again be peaceful farmers and shopkeepers, their culture again a going concern.

If the multinational Councillors made the right decisions. And they had not been making them. Valti had finally convinced Fourre of that. Therefore he walked through the rain, hugging an old bicycle poncho to his sleazy jacket, and men in barracks were quietly estimating how many jumps it would take to reach their racked weapons. For they must overpower those who did not agree.

A wry notion, that the feudal principle of personal loyalty to a chief should have to be invoked to enforce the decrees of a new mathematics that only some thousand minds in the world understood. But you wouldn't expect the Norman peasant Astier or the Parisian apache Renault to bend the scanty spare time of a year to learning the operations of symbolic sociology. You would merely say, "Come," and they would come because they loved you.

The streets resounded hollow under his feet. It was a world without logic, this one. Only the accidents of survival had made the village apothecary Etienne Fourre into the *de facto* commander of Free France. He could have wished those accidents had taken him and spared Jeanette, but at least he had two sons living, and someday, if they hadn't gotten too much radiation, there would be grandchildren. God was not altogether revengeful.

"There we are, up ahead," said Astier.

Fourre did not bother to reply. He had never been under the common human necessity of forever mouthing words.

Strasbourg was the seat of the Council because of location and because it was not too badly hit. Only a conventional battle with chemical explosives had rolled through here eighteen months ago. The University was almost unscathed, and so became the headquarters of Jacques Reinach. His men prowled about on guard; one wondered what Goethe would have thought could he have returned to the scene of his student days. And yet it was men such as this, with dirty hands and clean weapons, who were civilization. It was their kind who had harried the wounded Russian colossus out of the West and who would restore law and liberty and wind-rippled fields to grain. Someday. Perhaps.

A machine-gun nest stood at the first checkpoint. The sergeant in charge recognized Fourre and gave a sloppy salute. (Still, the fact that Reinach had imposed so much discipline on his horde spoke for the man's personality.) "Your escort must wait here, my general," he said, half-apologizing. "A new regulation."

"I know," said Fourre. Not all of his guards did, and he must shush a snarling. "I have an appointment with the Commandant."

"Yes, sir. Please stay to the lighted paths. Otherwise you might be shot by mistake for a looter."

Fourre nodded and walked through, in among the buildings. His body wanted to get in out of the rain, but he went slowly, delaying the moment. Jacques Reinach was not just his countryman but his friend. Fourre was nowhere near as close to, say, Helgesen of the Nordic Alliance, or the Italian Totti, or Rojansky of Poland, and he positively disliked the German Auerbach.

But Valti's matrices were not concerned with a man's heart. They simply told you that given such and such conditions, this and that would probably happen. It was a cold knowledge to bear.

The structure housing the main offices was a loom of darkness, but a few windows glowed at Fourre. Reinach had had an electric generator installed—and rightly, to be sure, when his tired staff and his tired self must often work around the clock.

A sentry admitted Fourre to an outer room. There half a dozen men picked their teeth and diced for cartridges while a tubercular secretary coughed over files written on old laundry bills, flyleaves, any scrap of paper that came to hand. The lot of them stood up, and Fourre told them he had come to see the Commandant, chairman of the Council.

"Yes, sir." The officer was still in his teens, fuzzy face already shriveled into old age, and spoke very bad French. "Check your guns with us and go on in."

Fourre unbuckled his pistols, reflecting that this latest requirement, the disarming of commanders before they could meet Chairman Reinach, was what had driven Alvarez into fury and the conspiracy. Yet the decree was not unreasonable; Reinach must know of gathering opposition, and everyone had grown far too used to settling disputes violently. Ah, well, Alvarez was no philosopher, but he was boss of the Iberian Irregulars, and you had to use what human material was available.

The officer frisked him, and that was a wholly new indignity, which heated Fourre's own skin. He choked his anger, thinking that Valti had predicted as much.

Down a corridor then, which smelled moldy in the autumnal darkness, and to a door where one more sentry was posted. Fourre nodded at him and opened the door.

"Good evening, Etienne. What can I do for you?"

The big blond man looked up from his desk and smiled. It was a curiously shy, almost a young smile, and something wrenched within Fourre.

This had been a professor's office before the war. Dust lay thick on the books that lined the walls. Really, they should take more care of books, even if it meant giving less attention to famine and plague and banditry. At the rear was a closed window, with a dark wash of rain flowing across miraculously intact glass. Reinach sat with a lamp by his side and his back to the night.

Fourre lowered himself. The visitor's chair creaked under a gaunt-fleshed but heavy-boned weight. "Can't you guess, Jacques?" he asked.

The handsome Alsatian face, one of the few clean-shaven faces left in the world, turned to study him for a while. "I wasn't sure you were against me, too," said Reinach. "Helgesen, Totti, Alexios . . . yes, that gang . . . but you? We have been friends for many years, Etienne. I didn't expect you would turn on me."

"Not on you." Fourre sighed and wished for a cigarette, but tobacco was a remote memory. "Never you, Jacques. Only your policies. I am here, speaking for all of us—"

"Not quite all," said Reinach. His tone was quiet and unaccusing. "Now I realize how cleverly you maneuvered my firm supporters out of town. Brevoort flying off to Ukrainia to establish relations with the revolutionary government; Ferenczi down in Genoa to collect those ships for our merchant marine; Janosek talked into leading an expedition against the bandits in Schleswig. Yes, yes, you plotted this carefully, didn't you? But what do you think they will have to say on their return?"

"They will accept a *fait accompli*," answered Fourre. "This generation has had a gutful of war. But I said I was here to speak to you on behalf of my associates. We hoped you would listen to reason from me, at least."

"If it is reason." Reinach leaned back in his chair, cat-comfortable, one palm resting on a revolver butt. "We have threshed out the arguments in council. If you start them again—"

"—it is because I must." Fourre sat looking at the scarred, bony hands in his lap. "We do understand, Jacques, that the chairman of the Council must have supreme power for the duration of the emergency. We agreed to give you the final word. But not the *only* word."

A paleness of anger flicked across the blue eyes. "I have been maligned enough," said Reinach coldly. "They think I want to make myself a dictator. Etienne, after the Second War was over and you went off and became a snug civilian, why do you think I elected to make the Army my career? Not because I had any taste for militarism. But I foresaw our land would again be in danger, within my own lifetime, and I wanted to hold myself ready. Does that sound like . . . like some new kind of Hitler?"

"No, of course not, my friend. You did nothing but follow the example of de Gaulle. And when we chose you to lead our combined forces, we could not have chosen better. Without you—and Valti—there would still be war on the eastern front. We . . . I . . . we think of you as our deliverer, just as if we were the littlest peasant given back his own plot of earth. But you have not been *right*."

"Everyone makes mistakes." Reinach actually smiled. "I admit my own. I bungled badly in cleaning out those Communists at—"

Fourre shook his head stubbornly. "You don't understand, Jacques. It isn't that kind of mistake I mean. Your great error is that you have not realized we are at peace. The war is over."

Reinach lifted a sardonic brow. "Not a barge goes along the Rhine, not a kilometer of railroad track is relaid, but we have to fight bandits, local warlords, half-crazed fanatics of a hundred new breeds. Does that sound like peacetime?"

"It is a difference of . . . of objectives," said Fourre. "And man is such an animal that it is the end, not the means, which makes the difference. War is morally simple: one purpose, to impose your will upon the enemy. Not to surrender to an inferior force. But a policeman? He is protecting an entire society, of which the criminal is also a part. A politician? He has to make compromises, even with small groups and with people he despises. You think like a soldier, Jacques, and we no longer want or need a soldier commanding us."

"Now you're quoting that senile fool Valti," snapped Reinach.

"If we hadn't had Professor Valti and his sociosymbolic logic to plan our strategy for us, we would still be locked with the Russians. There was no way for us to be liberated from the outside this time. The Anglo-Saxon countries had little strength to spare, after the exchange of missiles, and that little had to go to Asia. They could not invade a Europe occupied by a Red Army whose back was against the wall of its own wrecked homeland. We had to liberate ourselves, with ragged men and bicycle cavalry and aircraft patched together out of wrecks. Had it not been for Valti's plans—and, to be sure, your execution of them—we could never have done so." Fourre shook his head again. He would not get angry with Jacques. "I think such a record entitles the professor to respect."

"True . . . then." Reinach's tone lifted and grew rapid. "But he's senile now, I tell you. Babbling of the future, of long-range trends—Can we eat the future? People are dying of plague and starvation and anarchy now!"

"He has convinced me," said Fourre. "I thought much the same as you, myself, a year ago. But he instructed me in the elements of his science, and he showed me the way we are heading. He is an old man, Eino Valti, but a brain still lives under that bald pate."

Reinach relaxed. Warmth and tolerance played across his lips. "Very well, Etienne," he asked, "what way are we heading?"

Fourre looked past him into night. "Toward war," he said quite softly. "Another nuclear war, some fifty years hence. It isn't certain the human race can survive that."

Rain stammered on the windowpanes, falling hard now, and wind hooted in the empty streets. Fourre glanced at his watch. Scant time was left. He fingered the police whistle hung about his neck.

Reinach had started. But gradually he eased back. "If I thought that were so," he replied, "I would resign this minute."

"I know you would," mumbled Fourre. "That is what makes my task so hard for me."

"However, it isn't so." Reinach's hand waved as if to brush away a nightmare. "People have had such a grim lesson that—"

"People, in the mass, don't learn," Fourre told him. "Did Germany learn from the Hundred Years' War, or we from Hiroshima? The only way to prevent future wars is to establish a world peace authority: to reconstitute the United Nations and give it some muscles, as well as a charter which favors civilization above any fiction of 'equality.' And Europe is crucial to that enterprise. North of the Himalayas and east of the Don is nothing anymore—howling cannibals. It will take too long to civilize them again. We, ourselves, must speak for the whole Eurasian continent."

"Very good, very good," said Reinach impatiently. "Granted. But what am I doing that is wrong?"

"A great many things, Jacques. You have heard about them in the Council. Need I repeat the long list?" Fourre's head turned slowly, as if it creaked on its neckbones, and locked eyes with the man behind the desk. "It is one thing to improvise in wartime. But you are improvising the peace. You forced the decision to send only two men to represent our combined nations at the conference planned in Rio. Why? Because we're short on transportation, clerical help, paper, even on decent clothes! The problem should have been studied. It may be all right to treat Europe as a unit—or it may not; perhaps this will actually exacerbate nationalism. You made the decision in one minute when the question was raised, and would not hear debate."

"Of course not," said Reinach harshly. "If you remember, that was the day we learned of the neofascist coup in Corsica."

"Corsica could have waited awhile. The place would have been more difficult to win back, yes, if we hadn't struck at once. But this business of our U.N. representation could decide the entire future of—"

"I know, I know. Valti and his theory about the 'pivotal decision.' Bah!"

"The theory happens to work, my old friend."

"Within proper limits. I'm a hardhead, Etienne, I admit that." Reinach leaned across the desk, chuckling. "Don't you think the times demand a hard head? When hell is romping loose, it's no time to spin fine philosophies . . . or try to elect a parliament, which I understand is another of the postponements Dr. Valti holds against me."

"It is," said Fourre. "Do you like roses?"

"Why, why . . . yes." Reinach blinked. "To look at,

anyway." Wistfulness crossed his eyes. "Now that you mention it, it's been many years since I last saw a rose."

"But you don't like gardening. I remember that from, from old days." The curious tenderness of man for man, which no one has ever quite explained, tugged at Fourre. He cast it aside, not daring to do otherwise, and said impersonally: "And you like democratic government, too, but were never interested in the grubby work of maintaining it. There is a time to plant seeds. If we delay, we will be too late; strong-arm rule will have become too ingrained a habit."

"There is also a time to keep alive. Just to keep alive, nothing else."

"Jacques, I don't accuse you of hardheartedness. You are a sentimentalist: you see a child with belly bloated from hunger, a house marked with a cross to show that the Black Death has walked in—and you feel too much pity to be able to think. It is . . . Valti, myself, the rest of us . . . who are cold-blooded, who are prepared to sacrifice a few thousand more lives now, by neglecting the immediately necessary, for the sake of saving all humankind fifty years hence."

"You may be right," said Reinach. "About your cold souls, I mean." His voice was so low that the rain nearly drowned it.

Fourre stole another look at his watch. This was taking longer than expected. He said in a slurred, hurried tone: "What touched off tonight's affair was the Pappas business."

"I thought so," Reinach agreed evenly. "I don't like it either. I know as well as you do that Pappas is a murderous crypto-Communist scoundrel whose own people hate him. But curse it, man, don't you know rats do worse than steal food and gnaw the faces of sleeping children? Don't you know they spread plague? And Pappas has offered us the services of the only efficient rat-exterminating force in Eurasia. He asks nothing in return except that we recognize his Macedonian Free State and give him a seat on the Council."

"Too high a price," said Fourre. "In two or three years we can bring the rats under control ourselves."

"And meanwhile?"

"Meanwhile, we must hope that nobody we love is

taken sick."

Reinach grinned without mirth. "It won't do," he said. "I can't agree to that. If Pappas' squads help us, we can save a year of reconstruction, a hundred thousand lives—"

"And throw away lives by the hundred millions in the future."

"Oh, come now. One little province like Macedonia?"

"One very big precedent," said Fourre. "We will not merely be conceding a petty warlord the right to his loot. We will be conceding"—he lifted furry hands and counted off on the fingers—"the right of any ideological dictatorship, anywhere, to exist: which right, if yielded, means war and war and war again; the fatally outmoded principle of unlimited national sovereignty; the friendship of an outraged Greece, which is sure to invoke that same principle in retaliation; the inevitable political repercussions throughout the Near East, which is already turbulent enough; therefore war between us and the Arabs, because we must have oil; a seat on the Council to a clever and ruthless man who, frankly, Jacques, can think rings around you—No!"

"You are theorizing about tomorrow," said Reinach. "The rats are already here. What would you have me do instead?"

"Refuse the offer. Let me take a brigade down there. We can knock Pappas to hell . . . unless we let him get too strong first."

Reinach shook his head goodnaturedly. "Who's the warmonger now?" he said with a laugh.

"I never denied we still have a great deal of fighting ahead of us," Fourre said. Sadness tinged his voice; he had seen too many men spilling their guts on the ground and screaming. "I only want to be sure it will serve the final purpose, that there shall never again be a world war. That my children and grandchildren will not have to fight at all."

"And Valti's equations show the way to achieve that?" Reinach asked quietly.

"Well, they show how to make the outcome reasonably probable."

"I'm sorry, Etienne." Reinach shook his head. "I simply cannot believe that. Turning human society into a . . .

what's the word? . . . a potential field, and operating on it
with symbolic logic: it's too remote. I am here, in the
flesh—such of it as is left, on our diet—not in a set of
scribbles made by some band of long-haired theorists."

"A similar band discovered atomic energy," said
Fourre. "Yes, Valti's science is young. But within admitted limitations, it works. If you would just study—"

"I have too much else on hand." Reinach shrugged. A
blankness drew across his face. "We've wasted more
time than I can afford already. What does your group of
generals want me to do?"

Fourre gave it to him as he knew his comrade would
wish it, hard and straight like a bayonet thrust. "We ask for
your resignation. Naturally, you'll keep a seat on the Council, but Professor Valti will assume the chairmanship and
set about making the reforms we want. We will issue a formal promise to hold a constitutional convention in the spring and dissolve the military government within one year."

He bent his head and looked at the time. A minute and
a half remained.

"No," said Reinach.

"But—"

"Be still!" The Alsatian stood up. The single lamp
threw his shadow grotesque and enormous across the
dusty books. "Do you think I didn't see this coming?
Why do you imagine I let only one man at a time in here,
and disarm him? The devil with your generals! The common people know me, they know I stand for them
first—and hell take your misty futures! We'll meet the
future when it gets here."

"That is what man has always done," said Fourre. He
spoke like a beggar. "And that is why the race has
always blundered from one catastrophe to the next. This
may be our last chance to change the pattern."

Reinach began pacing back and forth behind his desk.
"Do you think I like this miserable job?" he retorted. "It
simply happens that no one else can do it."

"So now you are the indispensable man," whispered
Fourre. "I had hoped you would escape that."

"Go on home, Etienne." Reinach halted, and kindness
returned to him. "Go back and tell them I won't hold this
against them personally. You had a right to make your
demand. Well, it has been made and refused." He nod-

ded to himself thoughtfully. "We will have to make some change in our organization, though. I don't want to be a dictator, but—"

Zero hour. Fourre felt very tired.

He had been denied, and so he had not blown the whistle that would stop the rebels, and matters were out of his hands now.

"Sit down," he said. "Sit down, Marius, and let us talk about old times for a while."

Reinach looked surprised. "Marius? What do you mean?"

"Oh . . . an example from history which Professor Valti gave me." Fourre considered the floor. There was a cracked board by his left foot. Cracked and crazy, a tottering wreck of a civilization, how had the same race built Chartres and the hydrogen bomb?

His words dragged out of him: "In the second century before Christ, the Cimbri and their allies, Teutonic barbarians, came down out of the north. For a generation they wandered about, ripping Europe apart. They chopped to pieces the Roman armies sent to stop them. Finally they invaded Italy. It did not look as if they could be halted before they took Rome herself. But one general by the name of Marius rallied his men. He met the barbarians and annihilated them."

"Why, thank you," Reinach sat down, puzzled. "But—"

"Never mind." Fourre's lips twisted into a smile. "Let us take a few minutes free and just talk. Do you remember that night soon after the Second War, we were boys freshly out of the Maquis, and we tumbled around the streets of Paris and toasted the sunrise from Sacre Coeur?"

"Yes. To be sure. That was a wild night!" Reinach laughed. "How long ago it seems. What was your girl's name? I've forgotten."

"Marie. And you had Simone. A beautiful little baggage, Simone. I wonder whatever became of her."

"I don't know. The last I heard—No. Remember how bewildered the waiter was when—"

A shot cracked through the rain, and then the wrathful clatter of machine guns awoke. Reinach was on his feet in one tiger bound, pistol in hand, crouched by the window. Fourre stayed seated.

The noise lifted, louder and closer. Reinach spun

about. His gun muzzle glared emptily at Fourre.

"Yes, Jacques."

"Mutiny!"

"We had to." Fourre discovered that he could again meet Reinach's eyes. "The situation was that crucial. If you had yielded . . . if you had even been willing to discuss the question . . . I would have blown this whistle and nothing would have happened. Now we're too late, unless you want to surrender. If you do, our offer still stands. We still want you to work with us."

A grenade blasted somewhere nearby.

"You—"

"Go on and shoot. It doesn't matter very much."

"No." The pistol wavered. "Not unless you—Stay where you are! Don't move!" The hand Reinach passed across his forehead shuddered. "You know how well this place is guarded. You know the people will rise to my side."

"I think not. They worship you, yes, but they are tired and starved. Just in case, though, we staged this for the nighttime. By tomorrow morning the business will be over." Fourre spoke like a rusty engine. "The barracks have already been seized. Those more distant noises are the artillery being captured. The University is surrounded and cannot stand against an attack."

"This building can."

"So you won't quit, Jacques?"

"If I could do that," said Reinach, "I wouldn't be here tonight."

The window broke open. Reinach whirled. The man who was vaulting through shot first.

The sentry outside the door looked in. His rifle was poised, but he died before he could use it. Men with black clothes and blackened faces swarmed across the sill.

Fourre knelt beside Reinach. A bullet through the head had been quick, at least. But if it had struck farther down, perhaps Reinach's life could have been saved. Fourre wanted to weep, but he had forgotten how.

The big man who had killed Reinach ignored his commandos to stoop over the body with Fourre. "I'm sorry, sir," he whispered. It was hard to tell whom he spoke to.

"Not your fault, Stefan." Fourre's voice jerked.

"We had to run through the shadows, get under the wall. I got a boost through this window. Didn't have time to take aim. I didn't realize who he was till—"

"It's all right, I said. Go on, now, take charge of your party, get this building cleaned out. Once we hold it, the rest of his partisans should yield pretty soon."

The big man nodded and went out into the corridor.

Fourre crouched by Jacques Reinach while a sleet of bullets drummed on the outer walls. He heard them only dimly. Most of him was wondering if this hadn't been the best ending. Now they could give their chief a funeral with full military honors, and later they would build a monument to the man who saved the West, and—

And it might not be quite that easy to bribe a ghost. But you had to try.

"I didn't tell you the whole story, Jacques," he said. His hands were like a stranger's, using his jacket to wipe off the blood, and his words ran on of themselves. "I wish I had. Maybe you would have understood . . . and maybe not. Marius went into politics afterward, you see. He had the prestige of his victory behind him, he was the most powerful man in Rome, his intentions were noble, but he did not understand politics. There followed a witch's dance of corruption, murder, civil war, fifty years of it, the final extinction of the Republic. Caesarism merely gave a name to what had already been done.

"I would like to think that I helped spare Jacques Reinach the name of Marius."

Rain slanted in through the broken window. Fourre reached out and closed the darkened eyes. He wondered if he would ever be able to close them within himself.

EDITOR'S AFTERWORD

The usual interpretation of this story is that civilization has been saved; that Etienne Fourre is correct, and the social theories of Professor Valti should prevail.

Yet this is not entirely clear. If soldiers have no great record as governors, academics have done no better—indeed, there are those who would say it is better to be governed by a tyrant than by a theory. Certainly I would prefer to live under General Reinach, who is concerned for the suffering children he sees, than under those who have taken his place and who see only unborn generations.

The narrator, Etienne Fourre, follows the leadership

of one Professor Eino Valti. Valti, it is said, has a social theory which predicts the ways of man.

Perhaps. But let us contrast Dr. Valti with Vilfredo Pareto. Pareto, whose theory of the circulation of elites makes more sense than most contemporary sociology (and is worth a great deal more study than it receives), died in 1923. He was more interested in the description of society than in prescriptions for its change; to the extent that he was on record as favoring any social scheme it was classical liberalism of the sort espoused by Dr. Milton Friedman in this era.

Pareto has been tarred with the brush of Fascism, which is hardly fair since Mussolini had barely taken office when Pareto ceased to write. If he did not condemn Mussolini, few did in the early days, when Il Duce not only made the trains run on time, but built the railroads. It was only later that the more brutal aspects emerged. In any event, by 1920 Pareto had ceased to show approval or disapproval of any social mechanism; he said he wished only to describe how men acted.

Pareto wrote: "Had Aristotle held to the course he in part so admirably followed, we would have had a scientific sociology in his early day. Why did he not do so? There may have been many reasons; but chief among them, probably, was that eagerness for premature practical applications which is ever obstructing the progress of science, along with a mania for preaching to people as to what they ought to do—an exceedingly bootless occupation—instead of finding out what they actually do."

Whereas Pareto described society, Dr. Valti prescribes for it, and is willing to accept the post of Executive Chairman of the Human Race—for such, indeed, is what the narrator of this story offers. Reinach—Marius, if you will—is willing to compromise. His friend Fourre wants an armored division to go interfere in the affairs of Macedonia—a province not known for its proximity to Strasburg and France.

Fourre and Valti are more concerned with theory—such as how many representatives shall be sent to the United Nations—than with such practical matters as rats and plague.

And thus Fourre slays his oldest friend.

Which of them is Marius?

EDITOR'S INTRODUCTION TO:

THE SOVIET STRATEGIC THREAT FROM SPACE

by

The Committee On Space War
Citizens Advisory Council on National Space Policy

The Citizens Advisory Council on National Space Policy was formed in 1981 when fifty of the nation's top space experts met in Los Angeles to draw up a space plan. The Council was jointly sponsored by the American Astronautical Society and the L-5 Society, and its meetings were made possible by a grant from the Vaughn Foundation. Council membership included aerospace engineers and scientists, astronauts, political leaders, business leaders and space entrepreneurs, science fiction writers, and students.

The first meeting was held in the home of Mr. and Mrs. Larry Niven, and it was a zoo. I had helped organize the meeting, but there was no actual structure. Dr. Charles Sheffield, then President of the American Astronautical Society, had been scheduled to preside over the meeting, but he couldn't attend due to medical problems. Next thing I knew, I was barking orders to get things organized; and shortly after that I was Acting Chairman. I've been Chairman ever since.

I've no illusions about my qualifications, which are: I don't work for any aerospace company (or anyone else) and I don't own aerospace stock, so I can be objective about which companies have the best capabilities; I have a loud voice; I don't mind yelling at people if that will get the job done; and I'm pretty good at writing the final reports.

For three days we were in a pressure cooker. This conference was expected to produce results; that was one reason we had science fiction writers, people like Greg Benford, Poul Anderson, Larry Niven, and G. Harry Stine. Note, too, that the writers sat in on the conferences as participants, not as "reporters" or "technical writers." We were, after all, trying to form bold new concepts, and SF people's imaginations were needed.

We got results, although sometimes it was pretty painful. I recall Saturday night, when the Foreign Policy Committee finished its meeting and turned to Larry Niven for a draft of the report. Larry has never worked for an aerospace firm (or any other where they say such things as "Of course I want it today; if I wanted it tomorrow I'd have asked for it tomorrow.") His reply was "I don't feel inspired . . ."—which drew totally unsympathetic looks from a dozen top industry executives.

The result of all this frantic activity was a report which has been widely read in Washington and elsewhere. The complete report is available for $5.00 from the L-5 Society, 1060 E. Elm St., Tucson, AZ 85719. Membership in the L-5 Society Promoting Space Development is open to anyone with a serious interest in aiding the space effort. L-5 has room for both professional and lay enthusiasts. Prominent members include Robert A. Heinlein, former NASA Administrator Thomas Paine, Marvin Minsky, Freeman Dyson, Senator Barry M. Goldwater, Ben Bova, and Arthur Kantrowitz. Annual dues (as of 1982) are $25 regular and $15 for students.

The Committee on Space War, also known as the Threat Committee, included some of the best-informed people in the nation. You may take their report quite seriously; it isn't science fiction.

THE SOVIET STRATEGIC THREAT FROM SPACE

Report of the Committee on Space War
Citizens Advisory Committee on National Space Policy

CONCLUSION

Space activities add a new dimension to strategic capabilities. Truly decisive strategic warfare may be possible before the end of this century. The Soviet strategic threat is real and ominous, and strategic weapons making use of the space environment have serious implications for the survival of the United States.

BACKGROUND

In order to compensate for severe inferiority in guidance technology for its first generation ICBMs, the Soviets during the 60s and early 70s developed very high yield hydrogen bombs which didn't need to land close to their targets to accomplish their mission. These weapons were massive, and Soviet rocket engineers designed and built very large boosters to carry them over intercontinental distances. To close the 'Missile Gap' of the early 60s—which was then strongly in favor of the U.S.—the Soviets built up four independent ICBM production complexes, all of which are running full blast through the present time. They continue to improve their relatively poor guidance technology to the point that the latest generation of their large ICBMs, the SS-20, has at least as accurate guidance as does the most recently deployed generation of U.S. ICBM—the Minuteman III.

During the 1960's, the United States chose to halt strategic missile production and deployment. Some theorists believed that the Soviet Union suffered from a psychological inferiority complex which would vanish when Soviet strategic forces achieved equality with with those of the United States. This theory held that Soviet strategic weapon production would halt when equality was achieved.

Instead, the Soviets took the opportunity to achieve numerical parity but with much larger boosters; and when parity was achieved, showed little inclination to halt weapon development and deployment.

PRESENT SITUATION

All evidence leads us to believe that continued rapid growth in Soviet strategic weapons forces may be expected for the foreseeable future.

Due to their habit of building very high capacity boosters and because their ICBM warheads can now be as accurately targeted as our most modern deployed systems, the Soviets are now able to 'fractionate' their four-fold advantage in 'throw-weight'—this aggregate warhead launching capacity of their ICBM forces—into a four-fold advantage in number of nuclear warheads with which they can attack the U.S.. The most serious near-term threat which the Soviets pose to the U.S. is therefore the likelihood that they will put 15000-25000 medium-yield warheads (e.g., of at least the yield of Minuteman III warheads) in their large number of huge missiles to replace the 4000-4500 multi-megaton warheads which they presently have in place. With two or three times as many warheads on missiles as the U.S. has—all of them of substantially higher yield and comparable targeting accuracy as the U.S. ones—the Soviets will be able to wipe out all U.S. land-based forces (including all 4000 MX aim-points) with well under half of their ICBM order-of-battle.

Nuclear reactor-powered Soviet naval reconnaissance satellite capability has posed a major threat to U.S. seapower for most of the past decade. What is little-recognized is that these intensively powered (100 kilo-watt level), massive military satellites also provide an ideal platform for rapid, entirely covert deployment of advanced anti-submarine warfare (ASW) systems, ex-ploiting a wide variety of radar, optical, and other non-acoustic technological advances of the last several years. The U.S. has no analagous capabilities—either operational or in serious development. The Soviets, on the other hand, have not slowed the deployment of this class of satellites after the de-orbiting into Canada of one of them two years ago. How thoroughly they value such space capabilities may be gauged by their refusal to even discuss President Carter's urgent calls to ban nuclear reactors in orbit.

The U.S. cannot put a 10kW electric power supply of any kind into orbit until the mid-80s (and only if devel-opment begins promptly could we do so then), but the Soviets have had a routinely exercised order-of-magni-tude greater capability since the mid-70s. They were unwilling to give up the large military advantages these space power systems confer, so it was hardly surprising that Carter's diplomatic efforts were unsuccessful.

This large and growing fleet of nuclear-powered satel-lites provides the Soviets with a qualitatively superior capability to locate American's strategic missile-launch-ing submarines, as well as our hunter-killer subs searching for Soviet missile-launching subs, and to direct land, airplane, ship, or sub-based nuclear-tipped missile fire upon them—all of which have been observed in practice operation during Soviet naval exer-cises during the late 70s. There is no credible evidence which suggests that the Soviets would hesitate to use such demonstrated capabilities to wage space-directed nuclear war-at-sea against U.S. military forces, even if the geopolitical situation were substantially short of all-out-war; indeed, all available evidence supports the thesis that the Soviets consider U.S. Navy forces to be 'pure' military targets, useful for demonstrations of Soviet strength and resolution in times of crisis without generating the massive civilian casualties which would require a U.S. president to escalate or capitulate.

Soviet anti-satellite capabilities also have no analog in U.S. capacities. As was widely publicized two years ago, the Soviets have demonstrated a capability to attack (or at least effectively confuse) our strategic warning satellites. These satellites give warning of a ballistic missile attack against the United States by detecting the very strong infrared radiation signals given off by the exhaust plumes of ICBMs rising through the atmosphere from their silos. According to open literature accounts, the Soviets were able to blind them and thus negate their warning capability.

The Soviets have also repeatedly demonstrated the ability to use 'killer satellites' to intercept and destroy essentially any type of satellite in reasonably low Earth orbit. These attacks are typically carried out with a shotgun-type weapon carried by a killer satellite launched with no warning.

In-space attacks are likely as a prelude to war on not only U.S. strategic reconnaissance satellites, but also on command, control, communications, and intelligence satellites which are increasingly vital to the ability of the National Command Authority to direct U.S. forces in the event of hostilities. Unlike the Soviet Union, the U.S. has committed a critically large fraction of its war-waging assets to the space environment. However, we have not taken commensurate action to defend these assets from any but implausibly trivial types and levels of threats—and the Soviets know it.

FUTURE THREATS FROM SPACE

The strategic threats from space likely to arise during the next two decades are qualitatively and quantitatively more serious than the major ones already existing. They include the ability to compromise or destroy the American strategic force during nominal peacetime without warning and without nuclear weapons utilization.

The best-known of these emerging threats, merely because it is the one closest to initial realization, is that posed by beam weapons—'death rays,' as they are commonly known. These systems all share the feature of bringing militarily useful quantities of energy to bear on targets at very great distances, often directing it to targets at the speed of light (making countermeasures difficult at best). One major class of them uses laser radiation of one type or another—beams of pure energy, either continuous or pulsed in time. The other major class is that involving the projection of mass, often sub-atomic particles such as electrons and protons, at speeds ranging from those not greatly in excess of the fastest artillery shells to ones just below that of light.

In continuous operational modes, beam weapons typically bring to bear on their targets energy inten-sities at least as high as that of the most powerful welding torches; the targets typically have at least fist-sized holes burned through them (usually with lethal results) in a second or less. When operating in pulsed mode, beam weapons load the surfaces of their targets with destructive amounts of energy on time scales of a millionth of a second or less; the surfaces evaporate with forces far greater than that of a comparable thickness of TNT, usually destroying the structures under them in the process.

Beam weapons energized by the burning of special chemicals are being considered for deployment in space during the 80s by both the Soviet Union and the U.S.; such laser beam weapons have already been used to shoot down military aircraft and have been operated from airplanes. Deployed in high Earth orbit, one such station could potentially burn down all the missiles launched from whatever locations by one side during an all-out nuclear war, and then leisurely burn down all enemy bombers for an encore. The side owning the space laser battle station would come through the war untouched, and would own the world thereafter; the other side would be annhilated. If such a space laser bat-tle station could defend itself from all types of attack which enemies of its owners could direct against it, its ownership would confer the prize of a planet—just as soon as it was put into orbit.

However, it appears that only the naive would launch missiles which could be destroyed by the space laser battle stations presently being considered for deploy-ment. As with many other new military technologies, countermeasures to the first generation version of the burner-type space lasers appear not only feasible but easy and economical to implement. Furthermore, space battle stations defended only with such lasers would apparently be veritable sitting ducks for a variety of attacks.

On the other hand, pulsed space lasers energized by nuclear weapons exploding nearby—lasers which have been demonstrated by the U.S. in underground tests and in whose development the Soviet Union is widely believed to be several years ahead—may be effectively impossible to countermeasure. They deliver too much energy of too penetrating nature in too short a period of time to defend against by any means known at present.

These defensive weapons are kept in hardened silos, to be launched as soon as an enemy ICBM attack is detected. Such nuclear weapon pumped laser systems could fire lethal bolts of energy at dozens to hundreds of enemy missiles and warheads simultaneously, but would not have to defend themselves from attack beforehand. A dozen such bomb-energized laser systems —each launched by a single booster—could shield their owner's home territory from enemy attack for the half-hour period necessary for its owner's ICBMs to be launched at, fly to, and destroy the enemy's missile and bomber fields.

A TECHNOLOGICAL PIVOT-POINT IN WORLD HISTORY

Strategic-scale war in the closing sixth of this century is thus likely to conclude with the total and quite bloodless triumph by the nation owning the space laser system(s); the winner's ICBM fields are part-empty, while the loser's missiles and bombers are totally destroyed. The loser's cities are held hostage for the surrender of his submarine force, whose remaining missiles are impotent against the space laser weapons of the winner in any event. The least certain consideration in such scenarios concerns the identities of the winner and the loser; it presently seems very likely that at least one side will build and deploy an effective space beam weapons system during the later 1980s.

The large present and near-term Soviet advantage in the ability to place large payloads into a variety of Earth orbits and to generate large amounts of electric power with space nuclear power systems may well be decisive in the on-going race to first deploy the first-generation space beam weapon battle stations. Countermeasure development by the U.S. during the next few years of definitive American inferiority in space warfare capability-in-being will therefore determine whether the Soviets will need to make second generation developments in this area.

OPEN SKIES IMPLICATIONS

Advanced satellite observation systems may profoundly affect the evolving strategic balance. Orbiting systems could bring the Eisenhower Open Skies doctrine much nearer to reality. These systems can give warning of buildups of conventional forces; they can also provide warning of ICBM attack.

These warning systems will be highly attractive targets for the Soviet Union. Their defense is not easy, but is probably possible given sufficient U.S. presence in the space environment.

SUMMARY

The U.S. ability to successfully wage war-in-space during the 80s and 90s will necessarily develop from its present comprehensively inferior position relative to the capabilities of the Soviet Union. Failure to rapidly gain at least parity with the advancing Soviet space warfare capabilities appears likely to doom the United States by the mid-90s; if this occurs, beam weapons systems deployed on Soviet space battle stations circling the Earth seem likely to be the lethal instruments.

Advanced reconnaissance satellites may contribute significantly to the stabilization of peace between the superpowers in the late 80s and 90s, if war-waging capabilities become comparable in that period. These satellites will be valuable but vulnerable. Space defenses are possible, but only for those who have a presence in space.

U.S. space capabilities may therefore be crucial for U.S. survival.

EDITOR'S INTRODUCTION TO:

ENDER'S GAME
by
Orson Scott Card

I have never met Scott Card, but we have talked a lot on the telephone, most recently when I unsuccessfully tried to persuade him to accept office in the Science Fiction Writers of America (usually known as SFWA). I am, for my sins, the Elections Chairman; most SFWA offices aren't contested, for the problem is to find qualified members willing to serve.

Scott pleaded that he had too many contracts, which is a problem I well understand. Given the economy, though, it beats heck out of the alternative.

Orson Scott Card burst on the science fiction scene like a nova; within a year, he was a major figure. It isn't hard to see why: "Ender's Game" was his first published story, and it has already become a classic.

Scott is a practicing member of the Church of Jesus Christ of Latter Day Saints, which was militant enough in its day; the Mormon soldiers defeated the U.S. Army during the Winter War, and after Utah was brought into statehood, the Mormon Church became an important source of US Army recruits.

Scott was kind enough to send me a copy of the Mormon Hymnal. The book contains a number of militant and stirring songs; it is also the only place I have *ever* seen all *four* verses of the Star Spangled Banner.

"Ender's Game" deals with an important problem. The selection of military leaders has always been difficult. In times long past, when wars were chronic but losing was not a complete disaster, it was possible to try leaders out, promote the successful ones, and in general rely on trial and error.

That can't work when there will be only one battle.

ENDER'S GAME
by
Orson Scott Card

"Whatever your gravity is when you get to the door, remember—the enemy's gate is *down*. If you step through your own door like you're out for a stroll, you're a big target and you deserve to get hit. With more than a flasher." Ender Wiggin paused and looked over the group. Most were just watching him nervously. A few understanding. A few sullen and resisting.

First day with this army, all fresh from the teacher squads, and Ender had forgotten how young new kids could be. He'd been in it for three years, they'd had six months—nobody over nine years old in the whole bunch. But they were his. At eleven, he was half a year early to be a commander. He'd had a toon of his own and knew a few tricks but there were forty in his new army. Green. All marksmen with a flasher, all in top shape, or they wouldn't be here—but they were all just as likely as not to get wiped out first time into battle.

"Remember," he went on, "they can't see you till you get through that door. But the second you're out, they'll be on you. So hit that door the way you want to be when they shoot at you. Legs up under you, going straight *down*." He pointed at a sullen kid who looked like he was only seven, the smallest of them all. "Which way is down, greenoh!"

"Toward the enemy door." The answer was quick. It was also surly, saying, "yeah, yeah, now get on with the important stuff."

"Name, kid?"

"Bean."

"Get that for size or for brains?"

Bean didn't answer. The rest laughed a little. Ender had chosen right. This kid *was* younger than the rest, must have been advanced because he was sharp. The others didn't like him much, they were happy to see him taken down a little. Like Ender's first commander had taken him down.

"Well, Bean, you're right onto things. Now I tell you this, nobody's gonna get through that door without a good chance of getting hit. A lot of you are going to be turned into cement somewhere. Make sure it's your legs. Right? If only your legs get hit, then only your legs get frozen, and in nullo that's no sweat." Ender turned to one of the dazed ones. "What're legs for? Hmmm?"

Blank stare. Confusion. Stammer.

"Forget it. Guess I'll have to ask Bean here."

"Legs are for pushing off walls." Still bored.

"Thanks, Bean. Get that, everybody?" They all got it, and didn't like getting it from Bean. "Right. You can't *see* with legs, you can't *shoot* with legs, and most of the time they just get in the way. If they get frozen sticking straight out you've turned yourself into a blimp. No way to hide. So how do legs go?"

A few answered this time, to prove that Bean wasn't the only one who knew anything. "Under you. Tucked up under."

"Right. A shield. You're kneeling on a shield, and the shield is your own legs. And there's a trick to the suits. Even when your legs are flashed you can *still* kick off. I've never seen anybody do it but me—but you're all gonna learn it."

Ender Wiggin turned on his flasher. It glowed faintly green in his hand. Then he let himself rise in the weightless workout room, pulled his legs under him as though he were kneeling, and flashed both of them. Immediately his suit stiffened at the knees and ankles, so that he couldn't bend at all.

"Okay, I'm frozen, see?"

He was floating a meter above them. They all looked up at him, puzzled. He leaned back and caught one of the handholds on the wall behind him, and pulled himself flush against the wall.

"I'm stuck at a wall. If I had legs, I'd use legs, and string myself out like a string *bean*, right?"

They laughed.

"But I don't have legs, and that's *better*, got it?

Because of this." Ender jackknifed at the waist, then straightened out violently. He was across the workout room in only a moment. From the other side he called to them. "Got that? I didn't use hands, so I still had use of my flasher. *And* I didn't have my legs floating five feet behind me. Now watch it again."

He repeated the jacknife, and caught a handhold on the wall near them. "Now, I don't just want you to do that when they've flashed your legs. I want you to do that when you've still got legs, because it's better. And because they'll never be expecting it. All right now, everybody up in the air and kneeling."

Most were up in a few seconds. Ender flashed the stragglers, and they dangled, helplessly frozen, while the others laughed. "When I give an order, you move. Got it? When we're at a door and they clear it, I'll be giving you orders in two seconds, as soon as I see the setup. And when I give the order you better be out there, because whoever's out there first is going to win, unless he's a fool. I'm not. And you better not be, or I'll have you back in the teacher squads." He saw more than a few of them gulp, and the frozen ones looked at him with fear. "You guys who are hanging there. You watch. You'll thaw out in about fifteen minutes, and let's see if you can catch up to the others."

For the next half hour Ender had them jackknifing off walls. He called a stop when he saw that they all had the basic idea. They were a good group, maybe. They'd get better.

"Now you're warmed up," he said to them, "we'll start working."

Ender was the last one out after practice, since he stayed to help some of the slower ones improve on technique. They'd had good teachers, but like all armies they were uneven, and some of them could be a real drawback in battle. Their first battle might be weeks away. It might be tomorrow. A schedule was never printed. The commander just woke up and found a note by his bunk, giving him the time of his battle and the name of his opponent. So for the first while he was going to drive his boys until they were in top shape—all of them. Ready for anything, at any time. Strategy was nice, but it was worth nothing if the soldiers couldn't hold up under the strain.

He turned the corner into the residence wing and found himself face to face with Bean, the seven-year-old he had picked on all through practice that day. Problems. Ender didn't want problems right now.

"Ho, Bean."

"Ho, Ender."

"Sir," Ender said softly.

"We're not on duty."

"In my army, Bean, we're always on duty." Ender brushed past him.

Bean's high voice piped up behind him. "I know what you're doing, Ender, sir, and I'm warning you."

Ender turned slowly and looked at him. "Warning me?"

"I'm the best man you've got. But I'd better be treated like it."

"Or what?" Ender smiled menacingly.

"Or I'll be the worst man you've got. One or the other."

"And what do you want? Love and kisses?" Ender was getting angry.

Bean was unworried. "I want a toon."

Ender walked back to him and stood looking down into his eyes. "I'll give a toon," he said, "to the boys who prove they're worth something. They've got to be good soldiers, they've got to know how to take orders, they've got to be able to think for themselves in a pinch, and they've got to be able to keep respect. That's how I got to be a commander. That's how you'll get to be a toon leader."

Bean smiled. "That's fair. *If* you actually work that way, I'll be a toon leader in a month."

Ender reached down and grabbed the front of his uniform and shoved him into the wall. "When I say I work a certain way, Bean, then that's the way I work."

Bean just smiled. Ender let go of him and walked away, and didn't look back. He was sure, without looking, that Bean was still watching, still smiling, still just a little contemptuous. He might make a good toon leader at that. Ender would keep an eye on him.

* * *

Captain Graff, six foot two and a little chubby, stroked his belly as he leaned back in his chair. Across his desk sat Lieutenant Anderson, who was earnestly pointing out high points on a chart.

"Here it is, Captain," Anderson said. "Ender's already got them doing a tactic that's going to throw off everyone who meets it. Doubled their speed."

Graff nodded.

"And you know his test scores. He thinks well, too."

Graff smiled. "All true, all true, Anderson, he's a fine student, shows real promise."

They waited.

Graff sighed. "So what do you want me to do?"

"Ender's the one. He's got to be."

"He'll never be ready in time, Lieutenant. He's eleven, for heaven's sake, man, what do you want, a miracle?"

"I want him into battles, every day starting tomorrow. I want him to have a year's worth of battles in a month."

Graff shook his head. "That would have his army in the hospital."

"No sir. He's getting them into form. And we need Ender."

"Correction, Lieutenant. We need somebody. You think it's Ender."

"All right, I think it's Ender. Which of the commanders if it isn't him?"

"I don't know, Lieutenant." Graff ran his hands over his slightly fuzzy bald head. "These are children, Anderson. Do you realize that? Ender's army is nine years old. Are we going to put them against the older kids? Are we going to put them through hell for a month like that?"

Lieutenant Anderson leaned even further over Graff's desk.

"Ender's test scores, Captain!"

"I've seen his bloody test scores! I've watched him in battle, I've listened to tapes of his training sessions, I've watched his sleep patterns, I've heard tapes of his conversations in the corridors and in the bathrooms, I'm more aware of Ender Wiggin than you could possibly imagine! And against all the arguments, against his obvious qualities, I'm weighing one thing. I have this picture of Ender a year from now, if you have your way. I see him completely useless, worn down, a failure, because he was pushed farther than he or any living person could go. But it doesn't weigh enough, does it, Lieutenant, because there's a war on, and our best talent is gone, and the biggest battles are ahead. So give Ender a battle every day this week. And then bring me a report."

Anderson stood and saluted. "Thank you sir."

He had almost reached the door when Graff called his name. He turned and faced the captain.

"Anderson," Captain Graff said. "Have you been outside, lately I mean?"

"Not since last leave, six months ago."

"I didn't think so. Not that it makes any difference. But have you ever been to Beaman Park, there in the city? Hmm? Beautiful park. Trees. Grass. No nullo, no battles, no worries. Do you know what else there is in Beaman Park?"

"What, sir?" Lieutenant Anderson asked.

"Children," Graff answered.

"Of course children," said Anderson.

"I mean children. I mean kids who get up in the morning when their mothers call them and they go to school and then in the afternoon they go to Beaman Park and play. They're happy, they smile a lot, they laugh, they have fun. Hmmm?"

"I'm sure they do sir."

"Is that all you can say, Anderson?"

Anderson cleared his throat. "It's good for children to have fun, I think, sir. I know I did when I was a boy. But right now the world needs soldiers. And this is the way to get them."

Graff nodded and closed his eyes. "Oh, indeed, you're right, by statistical proof and by all the important theories, and dammit they work and the system is right but all the same Ender's older than I am. He's not a child. He's barely a person."

"If that's true, sir, then at least we all know that Ender is making it possible for the others of his age to be playing in the park."

"And Jesus died to save all men, of course." Graff sat up and looked at Anderson almost sadly. "But we're the ones," Graff said, "We're the ones who are driving in the nails."

* * *

Ender Wiggin lay on his bed staring at the ceiling. He never slept more than five hours a night—but the lights went off at 2200 and didn't come on again until 0600. So he stared at the ceiling and thought. He'd had his army for three and a half weeks. Dragon Army. The name was assigned, and it wasn't a lucky one. Oh, the charts said that about nine years ago a Dragon Army had done fairly well. But for the next six years the name had been attached to inferior armies, and finally, because of the superstition that was beginning to play about the name, Dragon Army was retired. Until now. And now, Ender thought smiling, Dragon Army was going to take them by surprise.

The door opened softly. Ender did not turn his head. Someone stepped softly into his room, then left with the quiet sound of the door shutting. When soft steps died away, Ender rolled over and saw a white slip of paper lying on the floor. He reached down and picked it up.

"Dragon Army against Rabbit Army, Ender Wiggin and Carn Carby, 0700."

The first battle. Ender got out of bed and quickly dressed. He went rapidly to the rooms of each of his toon leaders and told them to rouse their boys. In five minutes they were all gathered in the corridor, sleepy and slow. Ender spoke softly.

"First battle, 0700 against Rabbit Army. I've fought them twice before but they've got a new commander. Never heard of him. They're an older group, though, and I know a few of their old tricks. Now wake up. Run, doublefast, warmup in workroom three."

For an hour and a half they worked out, with three mockbattles and calisthenics in the corridor out of the nullo. Then for fifteen minutes they all lay up in the air, totally relaxing in the weightlessness. At 0650 Ender roused them and they hurried into the corridor. Ender led them down the corridor, running again, and occasionally leaping to touch a light panel on the ceiling. The boys all touched the same light panel. And at 0658 they reached their gate to the battleroom.

The members of Toons C and D grabbed the first eight handholds in the ceiling of the corridor. Toons A, B, and E crouched on the floor. Ender hooked his feet into two handholds in the middle of the ceiling, so he was out of everyone's way.

"Which way is the enemy's door?" he hissed.

"Down!" they whispered back, and laughed.

"Flashers on." The boxes in their hands glowed green. They waited for a few seconds more, and then the gray wall in front of them disappeared and the battleroom was visible.

Ender sized it up immediately. The familiar open grid of the most early games, like the monkey bars at the park, with seven or eight boxes scattered through the grid. They called the boxes *stars*. There were enough of them, and in forward enough positions, that they were worth going for. Ender decided this in a second, and he hissed, "Spread to near stars. E hold!"

The four groups in the corners plunged through the forcefield at the doorway and fell down into the battleroom. Before the enemy even appeared through the opposite gate Ender's army had spread from the door to the nearest stars.

Then the enemy soldiers came through the door. From their stance Ender knew they had been in a different gravity, and didn't know enough to disorient themselves from it. They came through standing up, their entire bodies spread and defenseless.

"Kill 'em, E!" Ender hissed, and threw himself out the door knees first, with his flasher between his legs and firing. While Ender's group flew across the room the rest of Dragon Army lay down a protecting fire, so that E group reached a forward position with only one boy frozen completely, though they had all lost the use of their legs—which didn't impair them in the least. There was a lull as Ender and his opponent, Carn Carby, assessed their positions. Aside from Rabbit Army's losses at the gate, there had been few casualties, and both armies were near full strength. But Carn had no originality—he was in a four-corner spread that any five-year-old in the teacher squads might have thought of. And Ender knew how to defeat it.

He called out, loudly, "E covers A, C down. B, D angle east wall." Under E toon's cover, B and D toons lunged away from their stars. While they were still exposed, A and C toons left their stars and drifted toward the near wall. They reached it together, and together jackknifed off the wall. At double the normal speed they appeared

behind the enemy's stars, and opened fire. In a few
seconds the battle was over, with the enemy almost entirely frozen, including the commander, and the rest
scattered to the corners. For the next five minutes, in
squads of four, Dragon Army cleaned out the dark corners of the battleroom and shepherded the enemy into
the center, where their bodies, frozen at impossible
angles, jostled each other. Then Ender took three of his
boys to the enemy gate and went through the formality
of reversing the one-way field by simultaneously touching a Dragon Army helmet at each corner. Then Ender
assembled his army in vertical files near the knot
of frozen Rabbit Army soldiers.

Only three of Dragon Army's soldiers were immobile.
Their victory margin—38 to 0—was ridiculously high,
and Ender began to laugh. Dragon Army joined him,
laughing long and loud. They were still laughing when
Lieutenant Anderson and Lieutenant Morris came in
from the teachergate at the south end of the battleroom.

Lieutenant Anderson kept his face stiff and unsmiling,
but Ender saw him wink as he held out his hand and offered the stiff, formal congratulations that were ritually
given to the victor in the game.

Morris found Carn Carby and unfroze him, and the
thirteen-year-old came and presented himself to Ender,
who laughed without malice and held out his hand. Carn
graciously took Ender's hand and bowed his head over
it. It was that or be flashed again.

Lieutenant Anderson dismissed Dragon Army, and
they silently left the battleroom through the enemy's
door—again part of the ritual. A light was blinking on
the north side of the square door, indicating where the
gravity was in that corridor. Ender, leading his soldiers,
changed his orientation and went through the forcefield
and into gravity on his feet. His army followed him at a
brisk run back to the workroom. When they got there
they formed up into squads, and Ender hung in the air,
watching them.

"Good first battle," he said, which was excuse enough
for a cheer, which he quieted. "Dragon Army did all
right against Rabbits. But the enemy isn't always going
to be that bad. And if that had been a good army we
would have been smashed. We still would have won, but

we would have been smashed. Now let me see B and D toons out here. Your takeoff from the stars was way too slow. If Rabbit Army knew how to aim a flasher, you all would have been frozen solid before A and C even got to the wall."

They worked out for the rest of the day.

That night Ender went for the first time to the commanders' mess hall. No one was allowed there until he had won at least one battle, and Ender was the youngest commander ever to make it. There was no great stir when he came in. But when some of the other boys saw the Dragon on his breast pocket, they stared at him openly, and by the time he got his tray and sat at an empty table, the entire room was silent, with the other commanders watching him. Intensely self-conscious, Ender wondered how they all knew, and why they all looked so hostile.

Then he looked above the door he had just come through. There was a huge scoreboard across the entire wall. It showed the win/loss record for the commander of every army; that day's battles were lit in red. Only four of them. The other three winners had barely made it—the best of them had only two men whole and eleven mobile at the end of the game. Dragon Army's score of thirty-eight mobile was embarrassingly better.

Other new commanders had been admitted to the commanders' mess hall with cheers and congratulations. Other new commanders hadn't won thirty-eight to zero.

Ender looked at Rabbit Army on the scoreboard. He was surprised to find that Carn Carby's score to date was eight wins and three losses. Was he that good? Or had he only fought against inferior armies? Whichever, there was still a zero in Carn's mobile and whole columns, and Ender looked down from the scoreboard grinning. No one smiled back, and Ender knew that they were afraid of him, which meant that they would hate him, which meant that anyone who went into battle against Dragon Army would be scared and angry and incompetent. Ender looked for Carn Carby in the crowd, and found him not too far away. He stared at Carby until one of the other boys nudged the Rabbit commander and pointed to Ender. Ender smiled again and waved slightly. Carby turned red, and Ender, satisfied, leaned over his dinner and began to eat.

At the end of the week Dragon Army had fought seven battles in seven days. The score stood 7 wins and 0 losses. Ender had never had more than five boys frozen in any game. It was no longer possible for the other commanders to ignore Ender. A few of them sat with him and quietly conversed about game strategies that Ender's opponents had used. Other much larger groups were talking with the commanders that Ender had defeated, trying to find out what Ender had done to beat them.

In the middle of the meal the teacher door opened and the groups fell silent as Lieutenant Anderson stepped in and looked over the group. When he located Ender he strode quickly across the room and whispered in Ender's ear. Ender nodded, finished his glass of water, and left with the lieutenant. On the way out, Anderson handed a slip of paper to one of the older boys. The room became very noisy with conversation as Anderson and Ender left.

Ender was escorted down corridors he had never seen before. They didn't have the blue glow of the soldier corridors. Most were wood paneled, and the floors were carpeted. The doors were wood, with nameplates on them, and they stopped at one that said, "Captain Graff, supervisor." Anderson knocked softly, and a low voice said, "Come in."

They went in. Captain Graff was seated behind a desk, his hands folded across his pot belly. He nodded, and Anderson sat. Ender also sat down. Graff cleared his throat and spoke.

"Seven days since your first battle, Ender."

Ender did not reply.

"Won seven battles, one every day."

Ender nodded.

"Scores unusually high, too."

Ender blinked.

"Why?" Graff asked him.

Ender glanced at Anderson, and then spoke to the captain behind the desk. "Two new tactics, sir. Legs doubled up as a shield, so that a flash doesn't immobilize.

Jackknife takeoffs from the walls. Superior strategy, as Lieutenant Anderson taught, think places, not spaces. Five toons of eight instead of four of ten. Incompetent opponents. Excellent toon leaders, good soldiers."

Graff looked at Ender without expression. Waiting for what, Ender thought. Lieutenant Anderson spoke.

"Ender, what's the condition of your army."

"A little tired, in peak condition, morale high, learning fast. Anxious for the next battle."

Anderson looked at Graff, and Graff shrugged slightly. Then he nodded, and Anderson smiled. Graff turned to Ender.

"Is there anything you want to know?"

Ender held his hands loosely in his lap. "When are you going to put us up against a good army?"

Anderson was surprised, and Graff laughed out loud. The laughter rang in the room, and when it stopped, Graff handed a piece of paper to Ender. "Now," the Captain said, and Ender read the paper.

"Dragon Army against Leopard Army, Ender Wiggin and Pol Slattery, 2000."

Ender looked up at Captain Graff. "That's ten minutes from now, sir."

Graff smiled. "Better hurry, then, boy."

As Ender left he realized Pol Slattery was the boy who had been handed his orders as Ender left the mess hall.

He got to his army five minutes later. Three toon leaders were already undressed and lying naked on their beds. He sent them all flying down the corridors to rouse their toons, and gathered up their suits himself. As all his boys were assembled in the corridor, most of them still getting dressed, Ender spoke to them.

"This one's hot and there's no time. We'll be late to the door, and the enemy'll be deployed right outside our gate. Ambush, and I've never heard of it happening before. So we'll take our time at the door. E toon, keep your belts loose, and give your flashers to the leaders and seconds of the other toons."

Puzzled, E toon complied. By then all were dressed, and Ender led them at a trot to the gate. When they reached it the forcefield was already on one-way, and some of his soldiers were panting. They had had one battle that day and a full workout. They were tired.

Ender stopped at the entrance and looked at the placement of the enemy soldiers. Most of them were grouped not more than twenty feet out from the gate. There was no grid, there were no stars. A big empty space. Where were the other enemy soldiers? There should have been ten more.

"They're flat against this wall," Ender said, "where we can't see them."

He thought for a moment, then took two of the toons and made them kneel, their hands on their hips. Then he flashed them, so that their bodies were frozen rigid.

"You're shields," Ender said, and then had boys from two other toons kneel on their legs, and hook both arms under the frozen boys' shoulders. Each boy was holding two flashers. Then Ender and the members of the last toon picked up the duos, three at a time, and threw them out the door.

Of course, the enemy opened fire immediately. But they only hit the boys who were already flashed, and in a few moments pandemonium broke out in the battleroom. All the soldiers of Leopard Army were easy targets as they lay pressed flat against the wall, and Ender's soldiers, armed with two flashers each, carved them up easily. Pol Slattery reacted quickly, ordering his men away from the wall, but not quickly enough— only a few were able to move, and they were flashed before they could get a quarter of the way across the battleroom.

When the battle was over Dragon Army had only twelve boys whole, the lowest score they had ever had. But Ender was satisfied. And during the ritual of surrender Pol Slattery broke form by shaking hands and asking, "Why did you wait so long getting out of the gate?"

Ender glanced at Anderson, who was floating nearby. "I was informed late," he said. "It was an ambush."

Slattery grinned, and gripped Ender's hand again. "Good game."

Ender didn't smile at Anderson this time. He knew that now the games would be arranged against him, to even up the odds. He didn't like it.

It was 2150, nearly time for lights out, when Ender

knocked at the door of the room shared by Bean and three other soldiers. One of the others opened the door, then stepped back and held it wide. Ender stood for a moment, then asked if he could come in. They answered, of course, of course, come in, and he walked to the upper bunk, where Bean had set down his book and was leaning on one elbow to look at Ender.

"Bean, can you give me twenty minutes?"

"Near lights out," Bean answered.

"My room," Ender answered. "I'll cover for you." Bean sat up and slid off his bed. Together he and Ender padded silently down the corridor to Ender's room. Bean entered first, and Ender closed the door behind them.

"Sit down," Ender said, and they both sat on the edge of the bed, looking at each other.

"Remember four weeks ago, Bean? When you told me to make you a toon leader?"

"Yeah."

"I've made five toon leaders since then, haven't I? And none of them was you."

Bean looked at him calmly.

"Was I right?" Ender asked.

"Yes, sir," Bean answered.

Ender nodded. "How have you done in these battles?"

Bean cocked his head to one side. "I've never been immobilized, sir, and I've immobilized forty-three of the enemy. I've obeyed orders quickly, and I've commanded a squad in mop-up and never lost a soldier."

"Then you'll understand this." Ender paused, then decided to back up and say something else first.

"You know you're early, Bean, by a good half year. I was, too, and I've been made a commander six months early. Now they've put me into battles after only three weeks of training with my army. They've given me eight battles in seven days. I've already had more battles than boys who were made commander four months ago. I've won more battles than many who've been commanders for a year. And then tonight. You know what happened tonight."

Bean nodded. "They told you late."

"I don't know what the teachers are doing. But my army is getting tired, and I'm getting tired, and now they're changing the rules of the game. You see, Bean,

I've looked in the old charts. No one has ever destroyed so many enemies and kept so many of his own soldiers whole in the history of the game. I'm unique—and I'm getting unique treatment."

Bean smiled. "You're the best, Ender."

Ender shook his head. "Maybe. But it was no accident that I got the soldiers I got. My worst soldier could be a toon leader in another army. I've got the best. They've loaded things my way—but now they're loading it against me. I don't know why. But I know I have to be ready for it. I need your help."

"Why mine?"

"Because even though there are some better soldiers than you in Dragon Army—not many, but some—there's nobody who can think better and faster than you." Bean said nothing. They both knew it was true.

Ender continued, "I need to be ready, but I can't retrain the whole army. So I'm going to cut every toon down by one, including you—and you and four others will be a special squad under me. And you'll learn to do some new things. Most of the time you'll be in the regular toons just like you are now. But when I need you. See?"

Bean smiled and nodded. "That's right, that's good, can I pick them myself?"

"One from each toon except your own, and you can't take any toon leaders."

"What do you want us to do?"

"Bean, I don't know. I don't know what they'll throw at us. What would you do if suddenly our flashers didn't work, and the enemy's did? What would you do if we had to face two armies at once? The only thing I know is—we're not going for score anymore. We're going for the enemy's gate. That's when the battle is technically won—four helmets at the corners of the gate. I'm going for quick kills, battles ended even when we're outnumbered. Got it? You take them for two hours during regular workout. Then you and I and your soldiers, we'll work at night after dinner."

"We'll get tired."

"I have a feeling we don't know what tired is."

Ender reached out and took Bean's hand, and gripped it. "Even when it's rigged against us, Bean. We'll win."

Bean left in silence and padded down the corridor.

Dragon Army wasn't the only army working out after hours now. The other commanders finally realized they had some catching up to do. From early morning to lights out soldiers all over Training and Commander Center, none of them over fourteen years old, were learning to jackknife off walls and use each other as living shields.

But while other commanders mastered the techniques that Ender had used to defeat them, Ender and Bean worked on solutions to problems that had never come up.

There were still battles every day, but for a while they were normal, with grids and stars and sudden plunges through the gate. And after the battles, Ender and Bean and four other soldiers would leave the main group and practice strange maneuvers. Attacks without flashers, using feet to physically disarm or disorient an enemy. Using four frozen soldiers to reverse the enemy's gate in less than two seconds. And one day Bean came to workout with a 300-meter cord.

"What's that for?"

"I don't know yet." Absently Bean spun one end of the cord. It wasn't more than an eighth of an inch thick, but it could have lifted ten adults without breaking.

"Where did you get it?"

"Commissary. They asked what for. I said to practice tying knots."

Bean tied a loop in the end of the rope and slid it over his shoulders.

"Here, you two, hang onto the wall here. Now don't let go of the rope. Give me about fifty yards of slack." They complied, and Bean moved about ten feet from them along the wall. As soon as he was sure they were ready, he jackknifed off the wall and flew straight out, fifty meters. Then the rope snapped taut. It was so fine that it was virtually invisible, but it was strong enough to force Bean to veer off at almost a right angle. It happened so suddenly that he had inscribed a perfect arc and hit the wall before most of the other soldiers knew what had happened. Bean did a perfect rebound and drifted quickly back where Ender and the others waited for him.

Many of the soldiers in the five regular squads hadn't noticed the rope, and were demanding to know how it was done. It was impossible to change direction that abruptly in nullo. Bean just laughed.

"Wait till the next game without a grid! They'll never know what hit them."

They never did. The next game was only two hours later, but Bean and two others had become pretty good at aiming and shooting while they flew at ridiculous speeds at the end of the rope. The slip of paper was delivered, and Dragon Army trotted off to the gate, to battle with Griffin Army. Bean coiled the rope all the way.

When the gate opened, all they could see was a large brown star only fifteen feet away, completely blocking their view of the enemy's gate.

Ender didn't pause. "Bean, give yourself fifty feet of rope and go around the star." Bean and his four soldiers dropped through the gate and in a moment Bean was launched sideways away from the star. The rope snapped taut, and Bean flew forward. As the rope was stopped by each edge of the star in turn, his arc became tighter and his speed greater, until when he hit the wall only a few feet away from the gate he was barely able to control his rebound to end up behind the star. But he immediately moved all his arms and legs so that those waiting inside the gate would know that the enemy hadn't flashed him anywhere.

Ender dropped through the gate, and Bean quickly told him how Griffin Army was situated. "They've got two squares of stars, all the way around the gate. All their soldiers are under cover, and there's no way to hit any of them until we're clear to the bottom wall. Even with shields, we'd get there at half strength and we wouldn't have a chance."

"They moving?" Ender asked.

"Do they need to?"

Ender thought for a moment. "This one's tough. We'll go for the gate, Bean."

Griffin Army began to call out to them.

"Hey, is anybody there!"

"Wake up, there's a war on!"

"We wanna join the picnic!"

They were still calling when Ender's army came out from behind their star with a shield of fourteen frozen soldiers. William Bee, Griffin Army's commander, waited patiently as the screen approached, his men waiting at the fringes of their stars for the moment when whatever was behind the screen became visible. About ten meters away the screen exploded as the soldiers behind it shoved the screen north. The momentum carried them south twice as fast, and at the same moment the rest of Dragon Army burst from behind their star at the opposite end of the room, firing rapidly.

William Bee's boys joined battle immediately, of course, but William Bee was far more interested in what had been left behind when the shield disappeared. A formation of four frozen Dragon Army soldiers was moving headfirst toward the Griffin Army gate, held together by another frozen soldier whose feet and hands were hooked through their belts. A sixth soldier hung to his wrist and trailed like the tail of a kite. Griffin Army was winning the battle easily, and William Bee concentrated on the formation as it approached the gate. Suddenly the soldier trailing in back moved—he wasn't frozen at all! And even though William Bee flashed him immediately, the damage was done. The formation drifted to the Griffin Army gate, and their helmets touched all four corners simultaneously. A buzzer sounded, the gate reversed, and the frozen soldier in the middle was carried by momentum right through the gate. All the flashers stopped working and the game was over.

The teacher door opened and Lieutenant Anderson came in. Anderson stopped himself with a slight movement of his hands when he reached the center of the battleroom. "Ender," he called, breaking protocol. One of the frozen Dragon soldiers near the south wall tried to call through jaws that were clamped shut by the suit. Anderson drifted to him and unfroze him.

Ender was smiling.

"I beat you again, sir," Ender said. Anderson didn't smile.

"That's nonsense, Ender," Anderson said softly. "Your battle was with William Bee of Griffin Army."

Ender raised an eyebrow.

"After that maneuver," Anderson said, "the rules are

being revised to require that all the enemy's soldiers must be immobilized before the gate can be reversed."

"That's all right," Ender said. "It could only work once, anyway." Anderson nodded, and was turning away when Ender added, "Is there going to be a new rule that armies be given equal positions to fight from?"

Anderson turned back around. "If you're in one of the positions, Ender, you can hardly call them equal, whatever they are."

William Bee counted carefully and wondered how in the world he had lost when not one of his soldiers had been flashed, and only four of Ender's soldiers were even mobile.

And that night as Ender came into the commanders' mess hall, he was greeted with applause and cheers, and his table was crowded with respectful commanders, many of them two or three years older than he was. He was friendly, but while he ate he wondered what the teachers would do to him in his next battle. He didn't need to worry. His next two battles were easy victories, and after that he never saw the battleroom again.

It was 2100 and Ender was a little irritated to hear someone knock at his door. His army was exhausted, and he had ordered them all to be in bed after 2030. The last two days had been regular battles, and Ender was expecting the worst in the morning.

It was Bean. He came in sheepishly, and saluted.

Ender returned his salute and snapped, "Bean, I wanted everybody in bed."

Bean nodded but didn't leave. Ender considered ordering him out. But as he looked at Bean it occurred to him for the first time in weeks just how young Bean was. He had turned eight a week before, and he was still small and—no, Ender thought, he wasn't young. Nobody was young. Bean had been in battle, and with a whole army depending on him he had come through and won. And even though he was small, Ender could never think of him as young again.

Ender shrugged and Bean came over and sat on the edge of the bed. The younger boy looked at his hands for a while, and finally Ender grew impatient and asked, "Well, what is it?"

"I'm transferred. Got orders just a few minutes ago."

Ender closed his eyes for a moment. "I knew they'd pull something new. Now they're taking—where are you going?"

"Rabbit Army."

"How can they put you under an idiot like Carn Carby!"

"Carn was graduated. Support squads."

Ender looked up. "Well, who's commanding Rabbit then?"

Bean held his hands out helplessly.

"Me," he said.

Ender nodded, and then smiled. "Of course. After all, you're only four years younger than the regular age."

"It isn't funny," Bean said. "I don't know what's going on here. First all the changes in the game. And now this. I wasn't the only one transferred, either, Ender. Ren, Peder, Wins, Younger, Paul. All commanders now."

Ender stood up angrily and strode to the wall. "Every damn toon leader I've got!" he said, and whirled to face Bean. "If they're going to break up my army, Bean, why did they bother making me a commander at all?"

Bean shook his head. "I don't know. You're the best, Ender. Nobody's ever done what you've done. Nineteen battles in fifteen days, sir, and you won every one of them, no matter what they did to you."

"And now you and the others are commanders. You know every trick I've got, I trained you, and who am I supposed to replace you with? Are they going to stick me with six greenohs?"

"It stinks, Ender, but you know that if they gave you five crippled midgets and armed you with a roll of toilet paper you'd win."

The both laughed, and then they noticed that the door was open.

Lieutenant Anderson stepped in. He was followed by Captain Graff.

"Ender Wiggin," Graff said, holding his hands across his stomach.

"Yes sir," Ender answered.

"Orders."

Anderson extended a slip of paper. Ender read it quickly, then crumpled it, still looking at the air where the paper had been. After a few moments he asked, "Can I tell my army?"

"They'll find out," Graff answered. "It's better not to talk to them after orders. It makes it easier."

"For you or for me?" Ender asked. He didn't wait for an answer. He turned to Bean, took his hand for a moment, and headed for the door.

"Wait," Bean said. "Where are you going? Tactical or Support School?"

"Command School," Ender answered, and then he was gone and Anderson closed the door.

Command School, Bean thought. Nobody went to Command School until they had gone through three years of Tactical. But then, nobody went to Tactical until they had been through at least five years of Battle School. Ender had only had three.

The system was breaking up. No doubt about it, Bean thought. Either somebody at the top was going crazy, or something was going wrong with the war—the real war, the one they were training to fight in. Why else would they break down the training system, advance somebody —even somebody as good as Ender—straight to Command School? Why else would they have an eight-year-old greenoh like Bean command an army?

Bean wondered about it for a long time, and then he finally lay down on Ender's bed and realized that he'd never see Ender again, probably. For some reason that made him want to cry. But he didn't cry, of course. Training in the preschools had taught him how to force down emotions like that. He remembered how his first teacher, when he was three, would have been upset to see his lip quivering and his eyes full of tears.

Bean went through the relaxing routine until he didn't feel like crying anymore. Then he drifted off to sleep. His hand was near his mouth. It lay on his pillow hesitantly, as if Bean couldn't decide whether to bite his nails or suck on his fingertips. His forehead was creased and furrowed. His breathing was quick and light. He was a soldier, and if anyone had asked him what he wanted to be when he grew up, he wouldn't have known what they meant.

There's a war on, they said, and that was excuse

enough for all the hurry in the world. They said it like a
password and flashed a little card at every ticket
counter and customs check and guard station. It got
them to the head of every line.

Ender Wiggin was rushed from place to place so
quickly he had no time to examine anything. But he did
see trees for the first time. He saw men who were not in
uniform. He saw women. He saw strange animals that
didn't speak, but that followed docilely behind women
and small children. He saw suitcases and conveyor belts
and signs that said words he had never heard of. He
would have asked someone what the words meant, except that purpose and authority surrounded him in the
persons of four very high officers who never spoke to
each other and never spoke to him.

Ender Wiggin was a stranger to his world he was being trained to save. He did not remember ever leaving
Battle School before. His earliest memories were of
childish war games under the direction of a teacher, of
meals with other boys in the gray and green uniforms of
the armed forces of his world. He did not know that the
gray represented the sky and the green represented the
great forests of his planet. All he knew of the world was
from vague references to "outside."

And before he could make any sense of the strange
world he was seeing for the first time, they enclosed him
again within the shell of the military, where nobody had
to say there's a war on anymore because nobody in the
shell of the military forgot it for a single instant in a
single day.

They put him in a space ship and launched him to a
large artificial satellite that circled the world.

This space station was called Command School. It
held the ansible.

On his first day Ender Wiggin was taught about the
ansible and what it meant to warfare. It meant that even
though the starships of today's battles were launched a
hundred years ago, the commanders of the starships
were men of today, who used the ansible to send
messages to the computers and the few men on each
ship. The ansible sent words as they were spoken,
orders as they were made. Battleplans as they were
fought. Light was a pedestrian.

For two months Ender Wiggin didn't meet a single person. They came to him namelessly, taught him what they knew, and left him to other teachers. He had no time to miss his friends at Battle School. He only had time to learn how to operate the simulator, which flashed battle patterns around him as if he were in a starship at the center of the battle. How to command mock ships in mock battles by manipulating the keys on the simulator and speaking words into the ansible. How to recognize instantly every enemy ship and the weapons it carried by the pattern that the simulator showed. How to transfer all that he learned in the nullo battles at Battle School to the starship battles at Command School.

He had thought the game was taken seriously before. Here they hurried him through every step, were angry and worried beyond reason every time he forgot something or made a mistake. But he worked as he had always worked, and learned as he had always learned. After a while he didn't make any more mistakes. He used the simulator as if it were a part of himself. Then they stopped being worried and gave him a teacher. The teacher was a person at last, and his name was Maezr Rackham.

Maezr Rackham was sitting crosslegged on the floor when Ender awoke. He said nothing as Ender got up and showered and dressed, and Ender did not bother to ask him anything. He had long since learned that when something unusual was going on, he would find out more information faster by waiting than by asking.

Maezr still hadn't spoken when Ender was ready and went to the door to leave the room. The door didn't open. Ender turned to face the man sitting on the floor. Maezr was at least forty, which made him the oldest man Ender had ever seen close up. He had a day's growth of black and white whiskers that grizzled his face only slightly less than his close-cut hair. His face sagged a little and his eyes were surrounded by creases and lines. He looked at Ender without interest.

Ender turned back to the door and tried again to open it.

"All right," he said, giving up. "Why's the door locked?"

Maezr continued to look at him blankly.

Ender became impatient. "I'm going to be late. If I'm not supposed to be there until later, then tell me so I can go back to bed." No answer. "Is it a guessing game?" Ender asked. No answer. Ender decided that maybe the man was trying to make him angry, so he went through a relaxing exercise as he leaned on the door, and soon he was calm again. Maezr didn't take his eyes off Ender.

For the next two hours, the silence endured, Maezr watching Ender constantly, Ender trying to pretend he didn't notice the old man. The boy became more and more nervous, and finally ended up walking from one end of the room to the other in a sporadic pattern.

He walked by Maezr as he had several times before, and Maezr's hand shot out and pushed Ender's left leg into his right in the middle of the step. Ender fell flat on the floor.

He leaped to his feet immediately, furious. He found Maezr sitting calmly, cross-legged, as if he had never moved. Ender stood poised to fight. But the other's immobility made it impossible for Ender to attack, and he found himself wondering if he had only imagined the old man's hand tripping him up.

The pacing continued for another hour, with Ender Wiggin trying the door every now and then. At last he gave up and took off his uniform and walked to his bed.

As he leaned over to pull the covers back, he felt a hand jab roughly between his thighs and another hand grab his hair. In a moment he had been turned upside down. His face and shoulders were being pressed into the floor by the old man's knee, while his back was excruciatingly bent and his legs were pinioned by Maezr's arm. Ender was helpless to use his arms, and he couldn't bend his back to gain slack so he could use his legs. In less than two seconds the old man had completely defeated Ender Wiggin.

"All right," Ender gasped. "You win."

Maezr's knee thrust painfully downward.

"Since when," Maezr asked in a soft, rasping voice, "do you have to tell the enemy when he has won?"

Ender remained silent.

"I surprised you once, Ender Wiggin. Why didn't you destroy me immediately afterward? Just because I looked peaceful? You turned your back on me. Stupid. You have learned nothing. You have never had a teacher."

Ender was angry now. "I've had too many damned teachers, how was I supposed to know you'd turn out to be a—" Ender hunted for a word. Maezr supplied one.

"An enemy, Ender Wiggin," Maezr whispered. "I am your enemy, the first one you've ever had who was smarter than you. There is no teacher but the enemy, Ender Wiggin. No one but the enemy will ever tell you what the enemy is going to do. No one but the enemy will ever teach you how to destroy and conquer. I am your enemy, from now on. From now on I am your teacher."

Then Maezr let Ender's legs fall to the floor. Because the old man still held Ender's head to the floor, the boy couldn't use his arms to compensate, and his legs hit the plastic surface with a loud crack and a sickening pain that made Ender wince. Then Maezr stood and let Ender rise.

Slowly the boy pulled his legs under him, with a faint groan of pain, and he knelt on all fours for a moment, recovering. Then his right arm flashed out. Maezr quickly danced back and Ender's hand closed on air as his teacher's foot shot forward to catch Ender on the chin.

Ender's chin wasn't there. He was lying flat on his back, spinning on the floor, and during the moment that Maezr was off balance from his kick Ender's feet smashed into Maezr's other leg. The old man fell on the ground in a heap.

What seemed to be a heap was really a hornet's nest. Ender couldn't find an arm or a leg that held still long enough to be grabbed, and in the meantime blows were landing on his back and arms. Ender was smaller—he couldn't reach past the old man's flailing limbs.

So he leaped back out of the way and stood poised near the door.

The old man stopped thrashing about and sat up, cross-legged again, laughing. "Better, this time, boy. But slow. You will have to be better with a fleet than you are with your body or no one will be safe with you in command. Lesson learned?"

Ender nodded slowly.

Maezr smiled. "Good. Then we'll never have such a battle again. All the rest with the simulator. I will pro-

gram your battles, I will devise the strategy of your
enemy, and you will learn to be quick and discover what
tricks the enemy has for you. Remember, boy. From now
on the enemy is more clever than you. From now on the
enemy is stronger than you. From now on you are
always about to lose."

Then Maezr's face became serious again. "You will be
about to lose, Ender, but you will win. You will learn to
defeat the enemy. He will teach you how."

Maezr got up and walked toward the door. Ender stepped back out of the way. As the old man touched the handle of the door, Ender leaped into the air and kicked
Maezr in the small of the back with both feet. He hit
hard enough that he rebounded onto his feet, as Maezr
cried out and collapsed on the floor.

Maezr got up slowly, holding onto the door handle, his
face contorted with pain. He seemed disabled, but
Ender didn't trust him. He waited warily. And yet in
spite of his suspicion he was caught off guard by
Maezr's speed. In a moment he found himself on the
floor near the opposite wall, his nose and lip bleeding
where his face had hit the bed. He was able to turn
enough to see Maezr open the door and leave. The old
man was limping and walking slowly.

Ender smiled in spite of the pain, then rolled over onto
his back and laughed until his mouth filled with blood
and he started to gag. Then he got up and painfully made
his way to the bed. He lay down and in a few minutes a
medic came and took care of his injuries.

As the drug had its effect and Ender drifted off to
sleep he remembered the way Maezr limped out of his
room and laughed again. He was still laughing softly as
his mind went blank and the medic pulled the blanket
over him and snapped off the light. He slept until pain
woke him in the morning. He dreamed of defeating
Maezr.

The next day Ender went to the simulator room with
his nose bandaged and his lip still puffy. Maezr was not
there. Instead a captain who had worked with him
before showed him an addition that had been made. The
captain pointed to a tube with a loop at one end. "Radio.
Primitive, I know, but it loops over your ear and we tuck
the other end into your mouth with this piece here . . ."

"Watch it," Ender said as the captain pushed the end of the tube into his swollen lip.

"Sorry. Now you just talk."

"Good. Who to?"

The captain smiled. "Ask and see."

Ender shrugged and turned to the simulator. As he did a voice reverberated through his skull. It was too loud for him to understand, and he ripped the radio off his ear.

"What are you trying to do, make me deaf?"

The captain shook his head and turned a dial on a small box on a nearby table. Ender put the radio back on.

"Commander," the radio said in a familiar voice. Ender answered, "Yes."

"Instructions, sir?"

The voice was definitely familiar. "Bean?" Ender asked.

"Yes sir."

"Bean, this is Ender."

Silence. And then a burst of laughter from the other side. Then six or seven more voices laughing, and Ender waited for silence to return. When it did, he asked, "Who else?" A few voices spoke at once, but Bean drowned them out. "Me, I'm Bean, and Peder, Wins, Younger, Lee, and Vlad."

Ender thought for a moment. Then asked what the hell was going on. They laughed again.

"They can't break up the group," Bean said. "We were commanders for maybe two weeks, and here we are at Command School, training with the simulator, and all of a sudden they told us we were going to form a fleet with a new commander. And that's you."

Ender smiled. "Are you boys any good?"

"If we aren't, you'll let us know."

Ender chuckled a little. "Might work out. A fleet."

For the next ten days Ender trained his toon leaders until they could maneuver their ships like precision dancers. It was like being back in the battleroom again, except that Ender could always see everything, and could speak to his toon leaders and change their orders at any time.

One day as Ender sat down at the control board and

switched on the simulator, harsh green lights appeared in the space—the enemy.

"This is it," Ender said. "X, Y, bullet, C, D, reserve screen, E, south loop, Bean, angle north."

The enemy was grouped in a globe, and outnumbered Ender two to one. Half of Ender's force was grouped in a tight, bulletlike formation, with the rest in a flat circular screen—except for a tiny force under Bean that moved off the simulator, heading behind the enemy's formation. Ender quickly learned the enemy's strategy: whenever Ender's bullet formation came close, the enemy would give way, hoping to draw Ender inside the globe where he would be surrounded. So Ender obligingly fell into the trap, bringing his bullet to the center of the globe.

The enemy began to contract slowly, not wanting to come within range until all their weapons could be brought to bear at once. Then Ender began to work in earnest. His reserve screen approached the outside of the globe, and the enemy began to concentrate his forces there. Then Bean's force appeared on the opposite side, and the enemy again deployed ships on that side.

Which left most of the globe only thinly defended. Ender's bullet attacked, and since at the point of attack it outnumbered the enemy overwhelmingly, he tore a hole in the formation. The enemy reacted to try to plug the gap, but in the confusion the reserve force and Bean's small force attacked simultaneously, while the bullet moved to another part of the globe. In a few more minutes the formation was shattered, most of the enemy ships destroyed, and the few survivors rushing away as fast as they could go.

Ender switched the simulator off. All the lights faded. Maezr was standing beside Ender, his hands in his pockets, his body tense. Ender looked up at him.

"I thought you said the enemy would be smart," Ender said.

Maezr's face remained expressionless. "What did you learn?"

"I learned that a sphere only works if your enemy's a fool. He had his forces so spread out that I outnumbered him whenever I engaged him."

"And?"

"And," Ender said, "You can't stay committed to one pattern. It makes you too easy to predict."

"Is that all?" Maezr asked quietly.

Ender took off his radtio. "The enemy could have defeated me by breaking the sphere earlier."

Maezr nodded. "You had an unfair advantage."

Ender looked up at him coldly. "I was outnumbered two to one."

Maezr shook his head. "You have the ansible. The enemy doesn't. We include that in the mock battles. Their messages travel at the speed of light."

Ender glanced toward the simulator. "Is there enough space to make a difference?"

"Don't you know?" Maezr asked. "None of the ships was ever closer than thirty thousand kilometers to another."

Ender tried to figure the size of the enemy's sphere. Astronomy was beyond him. But now his curiosity was stirred.

"What kind of weapons are on those ships? To be able to strike so fast and so far apart?"

Maezr shook his head. "The science is too much for you. You'd have to study many more years than you've lived to understand even the basics. All you need to know is that the weapons work."

"Why do we have to come so close to be in range?"

"The ships are all protected by force fields. A certain distance away the weapons are weaker, and can't get through. Closer in the weapons are stronger than the shields. But the computers take care of all that. They're constantly firing in any direction that won't hurt one of our ships. The computers pick targets, aim, they do all the detail work. You just tell them when and get them in a position to win. All right?"

"No." Ender twisted the tube of the radio around his fingers. "I have to know how the weapons work."

"I told you, it would take—"

"I can't command a fleet—not even on the simulator —unless I know." Ender waited a moment, then added, "Just the rough idea."

Maezr stood up and walked a few steps away. "All right, Ender. It won't make any sense, but I'll try. As simply as I can." He shoved his hands into his pockets.

"It's this way, Ender. Everything is made up of atoms, little particles so small you can't see them with your eyes. These atoms, there are only a few different types, and they're all made up of even smaller particles that are pretty much the same. These atoms can be broken, so that they stop being atoms. So that this metal doesn't hold together anymore. Or the plastic floor. Or your body. Or even the air. They just seem to disappear, if you break the atoms. All that's left is the pieces. And they fly around and break more atoms. The weapons on the ships set up an area where it's impossible for atoms of anything to stay together. They all break down. So things in that area—they disappear."

Ender nodded. "You're right, I don't understand it. Can it be blocked?"

"No. But it gets wider and weaker the farther it goes from the ship, so that after a while a force field will block it. Okay? And to make it strong at all, it has to be focused, so that a ship can only fire effectively in maybe three or four directions at once."

Ender nodded again. Maezr wondered if the boy really understood it at all.

"If the pieces of the broken atoms go breaking more atoms, why doesn't it just make everything disappear?"

"Space. Those thousands of kilometers between the ships, they're empty. Almost no atoms. The pieces don't hit anything, and when they finally do hit something, they're so spread out they can't do any harm." Maezr cocked his head quizzically. "Anything else . . .?"

Ender nodded. "Do the weapons on the ships—do they work against anything besides ships?"

Maezr moved in close to Ender and said firmly, "We only use them against ships. Never anything else. If we used them against anything else, the enemy would use them against us. Got it?"

Maezr walked away, and was nearly out the door when Ender called to him.

"I don't know your name yet," Ender said blandly.

"Maezr Rackham."

"Maezr Rackham," Ender said, "I defeated you."

Maezr laughed.

"Ender, you weren't fighting me today," he said. "You were fighting the stupidest computer in the Command

School, set on a ten-year-old program. You don't think I'd use a sphere, do you?" He shook his head. "Ender, my dear little fellow, when you fight me you'll know it. Because you'll lose." And Maezr left the room.

Ender still practiced ten hours a day with his toon leaders. He never saw them, though, only heard their voices on the radio. Battles came every two or three days. The enemy had something new every time, something harder—but Ender coped with it. And won every time. And after every battle Maezr would point out mistakes and show Ender had really lost. Maezr only let Ender finish so that he would learn to handle the end of the game.

Until finally Maezr came in and solemnly shook Ender's hand and said, "That, boy, was a good battle."

Because the praise was so long in coming, it pleased Ender more than praise had ever pleased him before. And because it was so condescending, he resented it.

"So from now on," Maezr said, "we can give you hard ones."

From then on Ender's life was a slow nervous breakdown.

He began fighting two battles a day, with problems that steadily grew more difficult. He had been trained in nothing but the game all his life—but now the game began to consume him. He woke in the morning with new strategies for the simulator, and went fitfully to sleep at night with the mistakes of the day preying on him. Sometimes he would wake up in the middle of the night crying for a reason he didn't remember. Sometimes he woke with his knuckles bloody from biting them. But every day he went impassively to the simulator and drilled his toon leaders until the battles, and drilled the toon leaders after the battles, and endured and studied the harsh criticism that Maezr Rackham piled on him. He noted that Rackham perversely criticized him more after his hardest battles. He noted that every time he thought of a new strategy the enemy was using it within a few days. And he noted that while his fleet always stayed the same size, the enemy increased in numbers every day.

He asked his teacher.

"We are showing you what it will be like when you really command. The ratios of enemy to us."

"Why does the enemy always outnumber us in these battles?"

Maezr bowed his gray head for a moment, as if deciding whether to answer. Finally he looked up and reached out his hand and touched Ender on the shoulder. "I will tell you, even though the information is secret. You see, the enemy attacked us first. He had good reason to attack us, but that is a matter for politicians, and whether the fault was ours or his, we could not let him win. So when the enemy came to our worlds, we fought back, hard, and spent the finest of our young men in the fleets. But we won, and the enemy retreated."

Maezr smiled ruefully. "But the enemy was not through, boy. The enemy would never be through. They came again, with more numbers, and it was harder to beat them. And another generation of young men was spent. Only a few survived. So we came up with a plan—the big men came up with the plan. We knew that we had to destroy the enemy once and for all, totally, eliminate his ability to make war against us. To do that we had to go to his home worlds—his home world, really, since the enemy's empire is all tied to his capital world."

"And so?" Ender asked.

"And so we made a fleet. We made more ships than the enemy ever had. We made a hundred ships for every ship he had sent against us. And we launched them against his twenty-eight worlds. They left a hundred years ago. And they carried on them the ansible, and only a few men. So that someday a commander could sit on a planet somewhere far from the battle and command the fleet. So that our best minds would not be destroyed by the enemy."

Ender's question had still not been answered.

"Why do they outnumber us?"

Maezr laughed. "Because it took a hundred years for our ships to get there. They've had a hundred years to prepare for us. They'd be fools, don't you think, boy, if they waited in old tugboats to defend their harbors. They have new ships, great ships, hundreds of ships. All we have is the ansible, that and the fact that they have to put a commander with every fleet, and when they lose—

and they will lose—they lose one of their best minds every time."

Ender started to ask another question.

"No more, Ender Wiggin. I've told you more than you ought to know as it is."

Ender stood angrily and turned away. "I have a right to know. Do you think this can go on forever, pushing me through one school and another and never telling me what my life is for? You use me and the others as a tool, someday we'll command your ships, someday maybe we'll save your lives, but I'm not a computer, and I have to *know!*"

"Ask me a question, then, boy," Maezr said, "and if I can answer, I will."

"If you use your best minds to command the fleets, and you never lose any, then what do you need me for? Who am I replacing, if they're all still there?"

Maezr shook his head. "I can't tell you the answer to that, Ender. Be content that we will need you, soon. It's late. Go to bed. You have a battle in the morning."

Ender walked out of the simulator room. But when Maezr left by the same door a few moments later, the boy was waiting in the hall.

"All right, boy," Maezr said impatiently, "what is it? I don't have all night and you need to sleep."

Ender stayed silent, but Maezr waited. Finally the boy asked softly, "Do they live?"

"Does who live?"

"The other commanders. The ones now. And before me."

Maezr snorted. "Live. Of course they live. He wonders if they live." Still chuckling the old man walked off down the hall. Ender stood in the corridor for a while but at last he was tired and he went off to bed. They live, he thought. They live, but he can't tell me what happens to them.

That night Ender didn't wake up crying. But he did wake up with blood on his hands.

Months wore on with battles every day, until at last Ender settled into the routine of the destruction of himself. He slept less every night, dreamed more, and he began to have terrible pains in his stomach. They put him on a very bland diet, but soon he didn't even have an appetite for that. "Eat," Maezr said, and Ender would mechanically put food in his mouth. But if nobody told him to eat he didn't eat.

One day as he was drilling his toon leaders the room went black and he woke up on the floor with his face bloody where he had hit the controls.

They put him to bed then, and for three days he was very ill. He remembered seeing faces in his dreams, but they weren't real faces, and he knew it even while he thought he saw them. He thought he saw Bean, sometimes, and sometimes he thought he saw Lieutenant Anderson and Captain Graff. And then he woke up and it was only his enemy, Maezr Rackham.

"I'm awake," he said to Maezr.

"So I see," Maezr answered. "Took you long enough. You have a battle today."

So Ender got up and fought the battle and he won it. But there was no second battle that day, and they let him go to bed earlier. His hands were shaking as he undressed.

During the night he thought he felt hands touching him gently, and he dreamed he heard voices, saying, "How long can he go on?"

"Long enough."

"So soon?"

"In a few days, then he's through."

"How will he do?"

"Fine. Even today, he was better than ever."

Ender recognized the last voice as Maezr Rackham's. He resented Rackham's intruding even in his sleep.

He woke up and fought another battle and won.

Then he went to bed.

He woke up and won again.

And the next day was his last day in Command School, though he didn't know it. He got up and went to the simulator for the battle.

Maezr was waiting for him. Ender walked slowly into the simulator room. His step was slightly shuffling, and he seemed tired and dull. Maezr frowned.

"Are you awake, boy?" If Ender had been alert, he would have noticed the concern in his teacher's voice.

Instead, he simply went to the controls and sat down. Maezr spoke to him.

"Today's game needs a little explanation, Ender Wiggin. Please turn around and pay strict attention."

Ender turned around, and for the first time he noticed that there were people at the back of the room. He recognized Graff and Anderson from Battle School, and vaguely remembered a few of the men from Command School—teachers for a few hours at some time or another. But most of the people he didn't know at all.

"Who are they?"

Maezr shook his head and answered, "Observers. Every now and then we let observers come in to watch the battle. If you don't want them, we'll send them out."

Ender shrugged. Maezr began his explanation. "Today's game, boy, has a new element. We're staging this battle around a planet. This will complicate things in two ways. The planet isn't large, on the scale we're using, but the ansible can't detect anything on the other side of it—so there's a blind spot. Also, it's against the rules to use weapons against the planet itself. All right?"

"Why, don't the weapons work against planets?"

Maezr answered coldly, "There are rules of war, Ender, that apply even in training games."

Ender shook his head slowly. "Can the planet attack?"

Maezr looked nonplussed for a moment, then smiled. "I guess you'll have to find that one out, boy. And one more thing. Today, Ender, your opponent isn't the computer. I am your enemy today, and today I won't be letting you off so easily. Today is a battle to the end. And I'll use any means I can to defeat you."

Then Maezr was gone, and Ender expressionlessly led his toon leaders through maneuvers. Ender was doing well, of course, but several of the observers shook their heads, and Graff kept clasping and unclasping his hands, crossing and uncrossing his legs. Ender would be slow today, and today Ender couldn't afford to be slow.

A warning buzzer sounded, and Ender cleared the simulator board, waiting for today's game to appear. He felt muddled today, and wondered why people were there watching. Were they going to judge him today? Decide if he was good enough for something else? For another two years of grueling training, another two years of struggling to exceed his best? Ender was twelve. He felt very old. And as he waited for the game to appear, he wished he could simply lose it, lose the battle badly and completely so that they would remove him from the program, punish him however they wanted, he didn't care, just so he could sleep.

Then the enemy formation appeared, and Ender's weariness turned to desperation.

The enemy outnumbered him a thousand to one, the simulator glowed green with them, and Ender knew that he couldn't win.

And the enemy was not stupid. There was no formation that Ender could study and attack. Instead the vast swarms of ships were constantly moving, constantly shifting from one momentary formation to another, so that a space that for one moment was empty was immediately filled with a formidable enemy force. And even though Ender's fleet was the largest he had ever had, there was no place he could deploy it where he would outnumber the enemy long enough to accomplish anything.

And behind the enemy was the planet. The planet, which Maezr had warned him about. What difference did a planet make, when Ender couldn't hope to get near it? Ender waited, waited for the flash of insight that would tell him what to do, how to destroy the enemy. And as he waited, he heard the observers behind him begin to shift in their seats, wondering what Ender was doing, what plan he would follow. And finally it was obvious to everybody that Ender didn't know what to do, that there was nothing to do, and a few of the men at the back of the room made quiet little sounds in their throats.

Then Ender heard Bean's voice in his ear. Bean chuckled and said, "Remember, the enemy's gate is *down*." A few of the other leaders laughed, and Ender thought back to the simple games he had played and won in Battle School. They had put him against hopeless odds there, too. And he had beaten them. And he'd be damned if he'd let Maezr Rackham beat him with a cheap trick like outnumbering him a thousand to one. He had won a game in Battle School by going for something the enemy didn't expect, something against the rules—he had won by going against the enemy's gate.

And the enemy's gate was down.

Ender smiled, and realized that if he broke this rule they'd probably kick him out of school, and that way he'd win for sure: he would never have to play a game again.

He whispered into the microphone. His six commanders each took part of the fleet and launched themselves against the enemy. They pursued erratic courses, darting off in one direction and then another. The enemy immediately stopped his aimless maneuvering and began to group around Ender's six fleets.

Ender took off his microphone, leaned back in his chair, and watched. The observers murmured out loud, now. Ender was doing nothing—he had thrown the game away.

But a pattern began to emerge from the quick confrontations with the enemy. Ender's six groups lost ships constantly as they brushed with enemy force—but they never stopped for a fight, even when for a moment they could have won a small tactical victory. Instead they continued on their erratic course that led, eventually, down. Toward the enemy planet.

And because of their seemingly random course the enemy didn't realize it until the same time that the observers did. By then it was too late, just as it had been too late for William Bee to stop Ender's soldiers from activating the gate. More of Ender's ships could be hit and destroyed, so that of the six fleets only two were able to get to the planet, and those were decimated. But those tiny groups *did* get through, and they opened fire on the planet.

Ender leaned foward now, anxious to see if his guess would pay off. He half expected a buzzer to sound and the game to be stopped, because he had broken the rule. But he was betting on the accuracy of the simulator. If it could simulate a planet, it could simulate what would happen to a planet under attack.

It did.

The weapons that blew up little ships didn't blow up the entire planet at first. But they did cause terrible explosions. And on the planet there was no space to dissipate the chain reaction. On the planet the chain reaction found more and more fuel to feed it.

The planet's surface seemed to be moving back and forth, but soon the surface gave way in an immense explosion that sent light flashing in all directions. It swallowed up Ender's entire fleet. And then it reached the enemy ships.

The first simply vanished in the explosion. Then, as the explosion spread and became less bright, it was clear what happened to each ship. As the light reached them they flashed brightly for a moment and disappeared. They were all fuel for the fire of the planet.

It took more than three minutes for the explosion to reach the limits of the simulator, and by then it was much fainter. All the ships were gone, and if any had escaped before the explosion reached them, they were few and not worth worrying about. Where the planet had been there was nothing. The simulator was empty.

Ender had destroyed the enemy by sacrificing his entire fleet and breaking the rule against destroying the planet. He wasn't sure whether to feel triumphant at his victory or defiant at the rebuke he was certain would come. So instead he felt nothing. He was tired. He wanted to go to bed and sleep.

He switched off the simulator, and finally heard the noise behind him.

There were no longer two rows of dignified military observers. Instead there was chaos. Some of them were slapping each other on the back, some of them were bowed with their heads in their hands, others were openly weeping. Captain Graff detached himself from the group and came to Ender. Tears streamed down his face, but he was smiling. He reached out his arms, and to Ender's surprise he embraced the boy, held him tightly, and whispered, "Thank you, thank you, thank you, Ender."

Soon all the observers were gathered around the bewildered child, thanking him and cheering him and patting him on the shoulder and shaking his hand. Ender tried to make sense of what they were saying. He had passed the test after all? Why did it matter so much to them?

Then the crowd parted and Maezr Rackham walked through. He came straight up to Ender Wiggin and held out his hand.

"You made the hard choice, boy. But heaven knows there was no other way you could have done it. Congratulations. You beat them, and it's all over."

All over. Beat them. "I beat *you*, Maezr Rackham."

Maezr laughed, a loud laugh that filled the room. "Ender Wiggin, you never played me. You never played a *game* since I was your teacher."

Ender didn't get the joke. He had played a great many games, at a terrible cost to himself. He began to get angry.

Maezr reached out and touched his shoulder. Ender shrugged him off. Maezr then grew serious and said, "Ender Wiggin, for the last months you have been the commander of our fleets. There were no games. The battles were real. Your only enemy was *the* enemy. You won every battle. And finally today you fought them at their home world, and you destroyed their world, their fleet, you destroyed them completely, and they'll never come against us again. You did it. You."

Real. Not a game. Ender's mind was too tired to cope with it all. He walked away from Maezr, walked silently through the crowd that still whispered thanks and congratulations to the boy, walked out of the simulator room and finally arrived in his bedroom and closed the door.

He was asleep when Graff and Maezr Rackham found him. They came in quietly and roused him. He woke slowly, and when he recognized them he turned away to go back to sleep.

"Ender," Graff said. "We need to talk to you."

Ender rolled back to face them. He said nothing.

Graff smiled. "It was a shock to you yesterday, I know. But it must make you feel good to know you won the war."

Ender nodded slowly.

"Maezr Rackham here, he never played against you. He only analyzed your battles to find out your weak spots, to help you improve. It worked, didn't it?"

Ender closed his eyes tightly. They waited. He said, "Why didn't you tell me?"

Maezr smiled. "A hundred years ago, Ender, we found out some things. That when a commander's life is in danger he becomes afraid, and fear slows down his thinking. When a commander knows that he's killing people, he becomes cautious or insane, and neither of those help him do well. And when he is mature, when he has responsibilities and an understanding of the world, he becomes cautious and sluggish and can't do this job. So we trained children, who didn't know anything but the game, and never knew when it would become real. That was the theory, and you proved that the theory worked."

Graff reached out and touched Ender's shoulder. "We launched the ships so that they would all arrive at their destination during these few months. We knew that we'd probably only have one good commander, if we were lucky. In history it's been very rare to have more than one genius in a war. So we planned on having a genius. We were gambling. And you came along and we won."

Ender opened his eyes again and they realized he was angry. "Yes, you won."

Graff and Maezr Rackham looked at each other. "He doesn't understand," Graff whispered.

"I understand," Ender said. "You needed a weapon, and you got it, and it was me."

"That's right," Maezr answered.

"So tell me," Ender went on, "How many people lived on that planet that I destroyed."

They didn't answer him. They waited a while in silence, and then Graff spoke. "Weapons don't need to understand what they're pointed at, Ender. We did the pointing, and so we're responsible. You just did your job."

Maezr smiled. "Of course, Ender, you'll be taken care of. The government will never forget you. You served us all very well."

Ender rolled over and faced the wall, and even though they tried to talk to him, he didn't answer them. Finally they left.

Ender lay in his bed for a long time before anyone disturbed him again. The door opened softly. Ender didn't turn to see who it was. Then a hand touched him softly.

"Ender, it's me, Bean."

Ender turned over and looked at the little boy who was standing by his bed.

"Sit down," Ender said.

Bean sat. "That last battle, Ender. I didn't know how you'd get us out of it."

Ender smiled. "I didn't. I cheated. I thought they'd kick me out."

"Can you believe it! We won the war. The whole war's over, and we thought we'd have to wait till we grew up to fight in it, and it was us fighting it all the time. I mean, Ender, we're little kids. I'm a little kid, anyway." Bean laughed and Ender smiled. Then they were silent for a little while, Bean sitting on the edge of the bed, and Ender watching him out of half-closed eyes.

Finally Bean thought of something else to say.

"What will we do now that the war's over?" he said.

Ender closed his eyes and said, "I need some sleep, Bean."

Bean got up and left and Ender slept.

Graff and Anderson walked through the gates into the park. There was a breeze, but the sun was hot on their shoulders.

"Abba Technics? In the capital?" Graff asked.

"No, in Biggock County. Training division," Anderson replied. "They think my work with children is good preparation. And you?"

Graff smiled and shook his head. "No plans. I'll be here for a few more months. Reports, winding down. I've had offers. Personnel development for DCIA, executive vice-president for U and P, but I said no. Publisher wants me to do memoirs of the war. I don't know."

They sat on a bench and watched leaves shivering in the breeze. Children on the monkey bars were laughing and yelling, but the wind and the distance swallowed their words. "Look," Graff said, pointing. A little boy jumped from the bars and ran near the bench where the two men sat. Another boy followed him, and holding his hands like a gun he made an explosive sound. The child he was shooting at didn't stop. He fired again.

"I got you! Come back here!"

The other little boy ran on out of sight.

"Don't you know when you're dead?" The boy shoved his hands in his pockets and kicked a rock back to the monkey bars. Anderson smiled and shook his head. "Kids," he said. Then he and Graff stood up and walked on out of the park.

EDITOR'S INTRODUCTION TO:

A DEATH IN REALTIME
by
Richard Sean McEnroe

A few years ago editor Jim Baen published ARMAG-GEDON 2419, which was the *original* Buck Rogers novel. It was an interesting story, although hopelessly out of date. Larry Niven and I began speculating about it: what strange events might have happened so that when engineer Anthony Rogers awakened in the 25th Century after being trapped in a mine cave-in sometime in 1930, the world looked as portrayed in the book?

It was no easy task, for the original Buck Rogers stories had the traditional Mars (dry and dying, but not dead) and Venus (hot and swampy). Mankind was oppressed by the Han, who were not precisely human but who could certainly interbreed with humans. The technology was quite strange, and many inventions made since 1930 (when the book was written) had vanished.

After a couple of coffee and brandy sessions, we came up with what we thought were plausible notions. They involved some pretty elaborate assumptions, but when we finished we had a seamless whole.

Enter Jim Baen, who offered to buy the outline from us. "I'll get some other writers to write the novels," he said, "and meanwhile you can get paid for all those daydreams."

We pointed out that getting paid for daydreams is precisely what we do for a living, and began to haggle over the price. Eventually the bargain was struck. The first of these stories "from an outline by Larry Niven and Jerry Pournelle" was "Mordred" by Eric Holmes. The second, and in our opinion far the better, was "Warrior's Blood" by Richard S. McEnroe . . .

When Jim Baen first went to Ace Books from Galaxy magazine, he very much missed being able to work with short stories and new writers. Eventually Ace invented *Destinies*, that rather strange "magazine" that looked like a book, just so that Jim would feel at home. When this story first appeared in *Destinies*, it carried the blurb "The Real World Gives No Quarter."

This story was actually written before arcade games gained their full popularity. Anyone who has ever watched kids play *Missile Command* will appreciate the essential truth it portrays. One query: computer people use the words "real time" a lot. What is its opposite?

A DEATH IN REALTIME
Richard Sean McEnroe

Join the navy and see the phosphor dots.

If Cooper hadn't been stationed aboard the USS *Quincannon*, manning his post might have been quite similar to watching television in a broom closet. But because the fast, cramped little Michaelson-class corvette was making thirty knots in a Force Seven blow as it steamed past the Migged-out North Sea derrick fields, he had the added pleasure of being thrown back and forth in his seat with such force that his bowl-shaped helmet grazed the bulkheads behind him and above his console.

He braced himself against the ship's rolling, studying the pale green screen of the Decca-built R50/90A naval radar unit that was tied into one of *Quincannon's* two Poignard tactical missile batteries. Switched to long-range sweep, its resolution was too coarse for the screen to be kept entirely clear of the Soviet ECM hash, but he could still make out the clustered blips of the Russian squadron his own small flotilla was steadily closing on.

When he was just a little kid, he had watched all the shows.

There was *Combat*, with Vic Morrow, and you could always tell who was going to die because it was always the same five or six guys who came back every week; everyone else was just a sympathy frag, at best. Then there was *Rat Patrol*, with Christopher George and his hat and those dynamite little jeeps, and the German officer—was it Eric Braeden? He didn't remember—who never got court-martialed even though the jeeps kept blowing up all his General Grant tanks that were supposed to be panzers. And the movies, God, yes, the movies; he couldn't have been more than three years old the one time he ever saw *Guadalcanal Diary* but he could still remember the way the Marine Corps tanks had gone crashing through the jungle to chase the Japanese into the ocean—or *Battle of Midway*, the old one with Aldo Ray: he'd seen that one so many times that when he went to see *Star Wars* he got royally pissed at the way they took the whole last battle scene and just stuck it in, practically shot for shot. And then there was the one he'd seen so long ago that he couldn't even remember the title, where the GIs had knocked out a tank by collapsing a building on it; he had sat there peeling the chocolate coating off a Mallomar and pretending it was the plating of the tank falling apart in the flames. . . .

The blips of the Russian ships were closing on the center of his screen now, and he switched over to short-range scan just as *Quincannon* shuddered and launched a brace of longer-range Harpoon missiles. The blips jumped magically back to the far edge of his screen, and where several blips had tended to blend into one amorphous mass before, each now stood out sharply distinct. Working a shorter range with the same power, he was able to fiddle with his clutter and squelch controls and clear his picture considerably. Then the last of the Soviet interference vanished as *Quincannon's* own electronic counter-counter-measures finally got the best of it. Now he could see the much smaller blips of the NATO squadron's first salvo stabbing at the much more slowly-moving dots that meant ships and men. The screen broke out in a dozen blotches of pale light as the missiles struck home or were intercepted—*Quincannon's* were—and a straggly line of pinpoints separated from the Russian ships, heading for the little cluster of blips around the center of his screen, heading towards him.

Doctor Strangelove, though, that was the one that really did it.

He had liked the old movies and programs, but he had always known they weren't really *real*. After all, Errol Flynn marched all the way through Burma and came out looking great, when Cooper only went camping once and caught such a collection of poison ivy rashes and bug

bites and inflamed bramble-bush scratches that his
mother had pulled him out of the Scouts. And he knew
he could never drive a jeep through North Africa; hell,
he couldn't stand getting sand in his shorts at the beach
and he burned like a lobster.

But then in *Doctor Strangelove*, in the scenes on board
Slim Pickens' bomber, he knew what he was seeing was
real. He knew that was what the inside of a B-52 looked
like; he *knew* that that was what it would be like to
evade a SAM missile. He didn't even mind that bullshit
about Pickens riding the H-bomb down, that was just the
director being cute. And it was the first movie he'd ever
seen where the actors and models didn't have that tacky
blue line around them in the projection shots.

Cooper's hands flew to his board and armed the two
fire-and-forget missiles in his battery. From that point
on the target programming system in the Poignard battery itself took over, and the missiles leaped flaming
from their brackets to intercept the two most dangerous
incoming targets. More pale light blossomed on his
screen as those missiles and others detonated between
the two clusters of ships. When it faded there were still
three tiny missile-bogeys, pressing on stubbornly.
Cooper paid those no more attention; they were in too
close for counter-missilery now and would have to be
dealt with by the Oerlikon and minigun crews. Far away
through several thicknesses of metal, he could hear/feel
the staccato stuttering as the 20mms and quad 7.62s
opened up on deck, but he paid them no attention,
either. They weren't part of his game.

He wasn't really going to the same college as everybody else. He would sometimes stop and watch the demonstrations on his way to and from classes, and once he
even signed a petition a girl thrust at him, because he
thought it would be the quickest way to get past her
without being rude.

Then he went back to his dorm and watched Walter
Cronkite riding as an observer in a Stratofortress, whooping with glee at the way the plane lurched upwards as
its bombload was released on the landscape below.

* * *

There was a thin red circle on Cooper's screen on short-range scan: it marked the outermost limit of engagement for his missiles. As he watched, the blips of the Russian ships drew nearer, and nearer—and touched. He immediately salvoed two more fire-and-forget missiles and then a third, laser-guided from his own console, holding his last LG missile in reserve while his battery recycled. Both system-aimed missiles plowed into a solid wall of counter-missiles and gunfire and vanished in incandescent fireballs, in silent splotches of pale green-white light. Cooper took his in on a long, predictable curve, then cut over sharply and sent the missile plunging into the ship vertically. He was rewarded with a great blot of light that continued to pulsate and expand long after the initial explosion. He immediately touched off two more fire-and-forgets.

Then they built a new amusement arcade in Penn Station. 'Station-Break', it was called, and it had everything, pinball machines, film-chain games, video games. Cooper was never very good at the film-chain games like *Gunship* or *Shootout;* he could never handle the spatial relationships properly, his helicopter would always slew off to the side or he'd aim too high with the nickel-plated plastic sixgun and miss the man on the water tower. But the video games he loved. *Starforce*—what a great name, almost as good as 'Stratofortress'—in particular; you sat in this little cockpit-cubicle and controlled a set of crosshairs with the wheel, and once you were lined up on a target it locked in and all you had to do was pull the trigger. His real favorite though, was a ripoff of the last scene in *Star Wars*, going down the shaft, where every time you hit an enemy ship it flew apart in a spray of stick-figure wreckage—he could beat *anyone* at that one; he never even missed the 'phantom raider' ship, the one that shot back and could take away half your points if it got you. He was in the arcade constantly, on his way to and from school, and so it was that when he boarded *Quincannon*, having chosen the Navy after he flunked the Air Force physicals, he performed what was very probably the one imaginative act of his life, and taped a quarter to the top of his Decca-built R50/90A naval radar unit. . . .

The two flotillas were within visual range of each other now. The men on deck could watch the gouts of flame blooming on the opposing ships as the missiles leaped out at them; the rapid-fire three-inch gun at *Quincannon's* bow opened fire; the Oerlikon and minigun crews were firing constantly. At that range no motor could swivel a missile battery to track an incoming rocket faster than a frightened man could swing a gun around—the machine guns were now the main line of defense on both sides.

The two little fleets corkscrewed wildly around each other, each commander trying to place his force broadside or to the bow or stern of his enemy, to bring the full weight of his firepower to bear on those weakpoints. *Quincannon,* like all warships her size, was of a very narrow beam for her length. While this was to her advantage in terms of speed and maneuverability, it also made her very tender. As she cut and weaved across the sea, taking the steep gale waves on her quarter or even full abeam, she sent huge gouts of green water cascading across her decks. Cooper noticed none of this at his post save the ship's erratic movement. He was used to that. He seldom went up on deck anymore, as a constant view of unbroken water bored him. His shipboard life rotated mainly between bunk and mess and the staring green eye of his console.

Now he was lining up another LG missile as his battery automatically launched brace after brace of fire-and-forgets. The air between the two fleets was thick with flame and shattered metal; aboard *Quincannon* an Oerlikon gunner sagged in his harness as a fiery shard tore away the side of his head; shrapnel spattered on the decks like steel and aluminum rain. Cooper saw nothing of this, only occasionally hearing the muted thunder of a particularly close explosion. He triggered his missile and sent it in on a long, weaving S-curve, watching with mounting excitement as it drew nearer and nearer its target—and vanished in a puff of light. Even as he muttered a disappointed curse he was firing his next missile, working the details to sneak it through and score. This one went all the way, a phosphorescent white dot twisting across glowing green glass to intersect another dot and vanish in a slow, spreading flash. High score. Overtime play—

More blood mixed with seawater on *Quincannon's* deck. Where electronics and state-of-the-art missilery clashed and largely cancelled each other out, older and more practiced means told. A 115mm shell slammed into *Quincannon's* forward minigun battery and four men died. A hole was opened in *Quincannon's* defensive envelope.

His next missile was intercepted. Cooper immediately launched another, eyes fixed on his screen, fingers working the dials.

A Soviet frigate, torn and burning from two direct hits, launched a last salvo from its one remaining operational battery. One missile erupted in flames and tumbled into the sea as the guns found it. Another detonated violently, taking out a third through concussion. The fourth found the gap in *Quincannon's* defense as other guns strained uselessly to make the impossible deflection shot that would stop it.

Cooper whooped with glee as his missile found its target. Then the bulkhead erupted inward and the game was over.

Quincannon limped back into Plymouth harbor. It took the engineers nearly half an hour to cut away enough wreckage to let the graves unit extricate the shattered body from the maze of twisted structural members and electronic scrap. Cooper's body had been so firmly embedded in the ruin that it almost seemed deliberate, as though the reality of war at sea had reclaimed him with such force that a steel fist had been clenched to anchor him in place. As the stretcher team carried the body across the planking leading from the gaping wound onto the dock, a careless foot brushed a tiny bit of metal and sent it tumbling over the side. The battered, deformed quarter fell into the water with the tiniest of splashes, unnoticed.

OVERDOSE
by
Spider Robinson

Few question the enormous and beneficial influence that John W. Campbell had on the science fiction field. One of his greatest contributions was the discovery and training of new writers. Thus it seemed appropriate that there be a John W. Campbell, Jr. Memorial Award, and that it go to the best new writer in the science fiction field.

I had the honor to be the first winner of that award, which pleased me greatly, because I was Mr. Campbell's last discovery.

Spider Robinson was the second winner, largely because of his fascinating "Crosstime Saloon" stories. He has since become a major talent in the field. Spider has a positive genius for combining the realistic and, uh, something else, as you'll see in this tale of how a private soldier saved the world . . .

OVERDOSE

by

Spider Robinson

Moonlight shattered on the leaves overhead and lay in shards on the ground. The night whispered dementedly to itself, like a Zappa minuet for paintbrush and tea-kettle, and in the distance a toad farted ominously.

I was really stoned.

I'd never have gotten stoned on sentry duty in a real war, but there hadn't been much real fighting to speak of lately (this was just before we got out), and you have to pass the time somehow. And it just so happened that as I was getting ready to leave for the bush, a circle of the boys was Shotgunning.

Shotgunning? Oh, we do a lot of that. It works like so: the C.O. (. . . "or whomever he shall appoint . . .") fills a pipe from the platoon duffle bag, fires it up, takes a few hits to get it established, and then breaks open a shotgun and inserts the pipe in one of the barrels. He raises it to his lips and blows a mighty blast down the bore, and someone on the other end takes an *enormous* hit from the barrel.

The C.O. then passes the Shotgun . . .

So as I say, I was more ruined than somewhat as I contemplated the jungle and waited for my relief. Relief? Say, you can take your medication and your yoga and your za-zen—there's nothing on earth for straightening your head like a night in the jungles of Vietnam. Such calm, such peace, such utter tranquility.

Something crackled in the bush behind me, and my M-32 went off with a Gotterdammerung crash two inches from my left ear. As I whirled desperately about, Corporal Zeke Busby, acting C.O. and speed-freak extraordinaire, levitated a graceful foot above the surrounding vegetation and came down rapping.

"Yas indeed private yas indeed alert and conscientious as ever yas and a good thing too a good thing but if I may make so bold and without wishing to appear unduly censorious would you for Chrissake point that fuckin' thing somewhere else?" Corporal Zeke had once been a friend of Neal Cassidy's for perhaps just a bit too long.

"Sure thing, Corp," I mumbled, shifting the rifle. My eardrum felt like Keith Moon's tom-tom.

"Yas and a signal honor a signal honor my man your gratitude will no doubt be quite touching but I assure you before you protest that I consider you utterly worthy worthy worthy to the tips of your boogety-boogety shoes."

A signal honor? He could only mean . . .

"I have selected you from a field of a dozen aspirants to make the run to Saigon and cop the Platoon Pound."

I was overwhelmed. The last man so honored (a guy named Milligram Mulligan) had burned us for two bricks of Vietnamese cowshit and split for the States—this was indeed a mark of great trust. I tried to stammer my thanks, but Corporal Zeke was off again. " . . . situation of course most serious and grave without at the same time being in any sense of the word *heavy* as I'm sure you dig considering the ramifications of the logistical picture and the inherently inescapable discombobulation manifest in the necessary . . . what I mean . . . that is to say, we've only got five bucks to work with." His left eye began to tic perceptibly, almost semaphorically.

"No problem, Corporal Zeke. I've seen action before." Five was barely enough for a few ounces at Vietnamese prices, but the solution was simple enough—rip off a Gook. "What did you have eyes to score?"

"Yas well based on past performance and an extrapolated estimate of required added increment to offset inflation which some of these lousy bastards they smoke 'til their noses bleed, it seems that something on the close order of five bricks would not be inordinate."

I nodded. "You're faded, Corp. Get me a relief and I'll crank right now." He didn't hear me; he was totally engrossed in his left foot, crooning to it softly. I put the M-32 near him gently and split. When the Old Man says "Cop!," you cop, and ask how soon on the way back.

Deep in the jungle something stirred. Trees moved ungraciously aside; wildlife changed neighborhoods. A space was cleared. In this clearing grew a shimmering ball of force, a throbbing nexus of molecular disruption. It reached a diameter of some thirty feet, absorbing all that it touched, and then stopped growing abruptly. It turned a pale green, flared briefly, and stablized, emitting a noise like a short in a fifty megavolt circuit.

With something analogous to a gasp, Yteic-Os the Voracious materialized within the sphere, and fell with a horrendous crash to the jungle floor a foot below. Heshe winced—well, not exactly—and momentarily lost conscious control of the pale green bubble, which snapped out of existence at once.

Yteic-Os roared hisher fury (although there was nothing a human would have recognized as sound) and tried to block the green sphere's dissolution by a means indescribable in human speech, something like sticking one's foot in a slamming door. It worked just about as well; the Voracious One nearly lost a pseudopod for hisher trouble.

This was serious.

Yteic-Os was ridiculously ancient—heshe had been repairing hisher third sun on the day when fire was discovered on earth. Entropy is, however, the same for everybody. Yteic-Os had long since passed over into catabolism; hisher energy reserves dwindled by the decade.

This jumping in and out of gravity wells was a hellishly exhausting business; for centuries Yteic-Os had sidestepped the problem by using the tame space-warp over which heshe had so laboriously established control. Now the warp was gone, galaxies away by this time, and Yteic-Os had grave doubts as to hisher ability to jump free unassisted.

This world would simply have to serve. Somewhere on this planet must exist a life-form of sufficient vitality to fill Yteic-Os's reserve cells with The Force, and heshe was not called The Voracious for nothing. Heshe extended pseudopods gingerly, questing for data on cerebration-levels, indices of disjunctive thought and the like. Insignificant but potentially useful data such as atmosphere-mix, temperature, radiation-levels and gravity were meanwhile being absorbed below the conscious

level by the sensor-modules which studded Yteic-Os's
epidermis (giving himher, incidentally, the external ap-
pearance of a slightly underdone poached egg with
pimples).

A pseudopod like a mutant hotdog twitched, began to
quiver. Yteic-Os integrated all available data and decided
ocular vision was called for. Hastily heshe grew an eye,
or something very like one, and looked in the direction
pointed by the trembling pseudopod.

Yes, no doubt of it, a sentient life-form, just brimming
with The Force! Yteic-Os sent a guarded probe, yelped
with joy (well, not precisely) as heshe learned that this
planet was crawling with sentient beings. What a bounti-
ful harvest!

Yteic-Os cannily withdrew without the other so much
as suspecting hisher existence, and began patiently con-
structing hisher attack.

Well, the plan was simplicity itself: meet Phstuc My in
a bar, demand to see the goods before paying, pull my
gun and depart with the bag. Instead, I left without my
pants. How the hell was I supposed to know the bartender had me covered?

So there I crouched, flat broke and *sans culottes*, between two G.I. cans of reeking refuse in a honky-tonk
alleyway, strung out and dodging The Man. It made me
homesick for Brooklyn. At least the problem was clear-
cut: all I had to do was scare up a pair of pants, five
bricks of acceptable smoke, a hot meal and transportation back to my outfit before dawn. Any longer and Corporal Zeke would assume I had burned him, at which
point, Temporary Cease-Fire or not, Southeast Asia
would become decidedly too warm for me to inhabit. I
was not prepared to emulate Milligram Mulligan—
ocean-going desertion requires special preparation and
a certain minimum of cash, and I had neither.

The possibilities were, as I saw it, dismal. I couldn't
rip off a pedestrian without at least a token weapon,
and I was morally certain the two garbage cans contained nothing more lethal than free hydrogen sulfide. I
couldn't burgle a house without more of the above-
mentioned preparation, and I couldn't even borrow
money without a pair of pants.

I sure wished I had a pair of pants.

A giggle rippled down the alleyway, and I felt my spine turn into a tube of ice-cold jello. I peered over a mound of coffee-grounds and there, by the beard of Owsley, stood an absolutely *dynamite* chick. Red hair, crazy blue eyes, and a protoplasmic distribution that made me think of a brick latrine. At the mere sight of this girl, certain physiological reactions overcame embarrassment and mortal terror.

I sure wished I had a pair of pants.

"What's happening?" she inquired around another giggle. *My God*, I thought, *she's from Long Island!* I decided to trust her.

"Well, see baby, I was makin' this run for my platoon, little smoke to sweeten the jungle, right? And, ah. . . .I've gone a wee bit awry."

"Heavy." She jiggled sympathetically, and moved closer.

"Well, yeah, particularly since my C.O. don't like gettin' burned. Liable to amputate my ears is where it's at."

She smiled, and my eyes glazed. "No sweat. I can set you up."

"Right."

"No, really. I'm General Fonebone's old lady—I've got connections. I could probably fix you right up . . . if you weren't in *too* much of a hurry." She was *not* staring me in the eyes, and I made a few hasty deductions about General Fonebone's virility.

"I'm Jim Balzac. 'Balz' to you."

"I'm Suzy."

Six hours later I was back in the jungle. I had a pair of pants, some four and a half bricks from the General's private stash, a compass, two Dylan albums and (although I was not to know it for weeks) a heavy dose of clap. I felt great, and it was all thanks to General Fonebone. If Suzy had not found life in Vietnam so boring, she would never have gone rummaging and uncovered the General's Secret Stash, a fell collection of strange tabs and arcane caps. She had induced me to swallow the largest single tab in the bunch, an immense purple thing with a skull embossed on it above the lone word: "HEAVY," and it appeared in retrospect to have been a triple tab of STP cut with ibogaine, benzedrine, coke and just a touch of Bab-O.

It might just as easily have been Fonebone's Own—the sensation was totally new to me. But it was certainly interesting. I experienced considerable difficulty in finding my mustache—which of course was right under my nose.

I could navigate without difficulty, after a fashion. But I discovered that I could whip up a ball of hallucinatory color-swirls in my mind, fire it like a cannon-ball, and watch it burst into a spiderweb of multicolored sparkles, as though an invisible protective shield two feet away walled me off from reality. With care, I could effect changes in the nature of the pulsing balls before they were fired, producing a variety of spectacular fireworks.

The jungle reared drunkenly above me. My outfit was straight ahead. I forged on, while in my darker crannies gonococcal viruses met and fell in love by the thousands, all unknown.

A particularly vivid splash of color caught my wandering attention; I had absently concocted a hellish color-ball of surpassing incandescence and detonated it. Its brilliant pattern hung before me a moment, as the rush took hold.

And then it very suddenly vanished.

I very nearly fell on my face. When I had my bearings again, I sent out another "shell." It burst pyrotechnically.

And as suddenly vanished. It made a noise best reproduced by inhaling sharply through clenched teeth while saying the word "Ffffffup!"; vanished down behind a small hill ahead, *sucked* downward in a microsecond— only a stoned man could have divined the direction.

Something on the other side of that hill was eating my hallucinations.

I moved to the left like a stately zeppelin, caroming gently from the occasional tree. But I had two anchors dragging the ground, and before I got fifteen feet a tangled root brought me down with a crash.

And just before I hit, I saw something coming over the rise, and I knew that my mind had truly blown at last.

Coming toward me was a sixteen-foot-tall poached egg with pimples.

And then the lights—all those lights—went out.

Yteic-Os moved from concealment, throbbing with astonished elation. No subtle attack was necessary, no cunning stimulus needed to elicit secretions of The Force from this being. Heedless of danger, it radiated freely in all directions, idly expectorating energy-clusters as it walked.

Then Yteic-Os gasped (almost);. for as it became aware of himher, it assumed a prone position, and disappeared. That is, its physical envelope remained, but all emanations ceased utterly; sentience vanished.

The Voracious One had no means of apprehending a subconscious mind. Such perverse deformities are extremely rare in the universe; heshe had in several billions of eons never chanced to so much as hear of such a thing. This led himher into a natural error: heshe assumed that these odd creatures emanated so incautiously because they had the ability to shut their minds off at will to escape absorption.

For, you see, thought is electrical in nature, and creative thought is akin to a short circuit, occurring when two unconnected thoughts arc together to form a totally new pattern. And such was Yteic-Os's diet.

And so heshe made a serious mistake. Heshe stealthily entered the empty caverns of Private Balzac's mind to try and restimulate life. Meanwhile, Yteic-Os's own nature and essence were laid open to the soldier's subconscious. One of the few compensations humans have for being saddled with such a clumsy nuisance of a subconscious mind is that these distorted clumps of semi-awareness possess a passionate interest in survival. Balzac's subconscious remained hidden, probing, comprehending the nature of this novel threat. A nebulous plan of defense formed, was stored for the proper time. Yteic-Os searched in vain for Thought, while Thought watched him from ambush, and giggled.

Consciousness returned to Private Balzac with a jar and a "WHAAAAAT!?!" Yteic-Os, caught by surprise, flipped completely over on his back and rippled indignantly. This upstart would soon be only a belch—or something like one. The Voracious One licked hisher . . . well, you know what I mean.

"Whaaaaat!?!"

I was awake. Somehow it had all been sorted out in my sleep: I didn't exactly know what the poached egg was, but I knew what it wanted to do. I thought I knew what to do about it. I would absolutely refuse to hallucinate, and starve it to death.

But I hadn't reckoned with the Terrible Tab I'd swallowed. I simply could *not* stop hallucinating! Colored whirlwinds and coruscating rainbows danced all around me like a mosaic in a Mixmaster; my eyeballs were prisms. Slowly the creative force of my mind was leaking away, being sucked into the egg before it could feed-back and regenerate itself.

I was being drained of originality, of wit, of inventiveness, of all the things that make life groovy. I had a grim vision of myself a few years hence, a short-haired square working in a factory living contentedly in Scarsdale with a frigid wife and a neurotic Pekingese, stumbling over the Cryptoquote in the *Daily News* and drinking Black Label before the T.V. A grimmer vision I can't imagine, but I still missed it when, with a sucking sound, it disappeared into the poached egg.

It was quickly supplanted by other visions, however— but from the past rather than the future. To my utter horror, I realized that it was actually happening: my whole life was passing before my eyes, in little vignettes which were *slurped* up by the creature as fast as they formed.

In spite of myself I began watching them. In rapid succession I reviewed a lifetime of disasters: losing my transmission at the head of the Victory Parade, getting bounced out of bed a hair before climax when I accidentally called Betty Sue the wrong name, being violently ill on two innocent customers of Howard Johnson's . . .

Wait! A light-bulb rather unoriginally appeared over my head (and was eaten by the poached egg). Howard Johnson's!!!! My untimely nausea had come on my third day as a HoJo counter-man, a direct result of the genius of Mr. Johnson himself. Early in his career, Johnson had hit upon the notion of urging all new employees to eat all the ice-cream they wished, for free. He reasoned that they would soon become sick of ice cream, and hence cut employee pilferage from his overhead. The scheme had worked well for him—why not for me?

Desperately I rammed my forebrain into low gear and cut in the afterburner. I dug into the tangled whorls of my cerebrum for all the creativity that heredity and environment had given men, and began to hallucinate as fast and as intricately as I could. I prayed that the poached egg would O.D.

Yteic-Os was caught in a quandary. The Force was radiating from this rococo little entity at an intolerable rate, and the creature would not stop projecting! Too heavily occupied in absorbing the torrent of food to roll off hisher back, Yteic-Os was lying on the escape-valve, similar to a whale's spout, which lay in the center of hisher back.

The Voracious One screamed—after hisher fashion— and tried frantically to assimilate the superabundance of food, to no avail. Even as heshe thrashed, desperately seeking to free the escape-orifice, heshe swelled, grew, expanded more and more rapidly, like a balloon inextricably linked to an air compressor. Heshe lost hisher egg shape, became round rather than ovoid, swelled, bloated to impossible dimensions, and—

—the inevitable happened.

And when I could see again, there was scrambled eggs all over the place.

I didn't hang around. Corporal Zeke was delighted to see me—it's embarrassing to have men under your command bumming joints from the enemy. But he was a little disappointed to learn that I only had four and a half bricks.

"That's okay, Corp," I assured him. "You guys can have my share. I'm straight for life."

"*What?*" gasped Zeke, shocked enough to deliver the first and only one-word speech of his life.

"Yep. After what I went through on the way over here, I'll never get stoned again as long as I live. Poached eggs eating hallucinations, cosmic invasion, Howard Johnson —it was just too intense, man, just too intense. A man who could freak out like that didn't ought to do dope. I've had a few bummers before, but I know when I've been warned."

Zeke was stupified, but not so stupified as to fail to try and change my mind. In subsequent weeks he went so far as to leave joints on my pillow, and once I caught him slipping hash into my K-rations. But like I say, I know when I've been warned, and you can't say I'm stupid.

I live a perfectly content life now that the war is over. Got me a wife, a nice little one-family in Scarsdale that I'll have entirely paid off in another twenty-five years, and a steady job down at the distributing plant—I get to bring home unlimited quantities of Black Label.

But sometimes I drink a little too much of it, and my wife Mabel says when I'm drunk—aside from becoming "disgustingly physical"—I often babble a lot. Something about having saved the world. . . .

EDITOR'S INTRODUCTION TO:

SAUL'S DEATH: TWO SESTINAS
by
Joe Haldeman

Joe Haldeman is a genuine war hero; thus it's not surprising that he can write realistically about combat. Joe and Gay Haldeman live in Florida when he's not filling a temporary slot as writer in residence and professor at one or another academic institution.

Science fiction conventions give plenty of opportunities for writers to get together and sing. Since most of us aren't able to stay on tune, cleverness of line is generally more important than musical worthiness, and ballads tend to dominate, especially in the wee hours when we sing.

Joe and Gay Haldeman are exceptions: they're quite capable of staying on key. They also know a lot of songs.

I confess I never heard of a sestina before. The form is explained in an afterword. Meanwhile, a genuine science fiction story in sestina format; some of us are likely to perform it at the next big SF convention.

SAUL'S DEATH: TWO SESTINAS

by

Joe Haldeman

I

I used to be a monk, but gave it over
Before books and prayer and studies cooled my blood,
And joined with Richard as a mercenary soldier.
(No Richard that you've heard of, just
A man who'd bought a title for his name).
And it was in his service I met Saul.

The first day of my service I liked Saul;
His easy humor quickly won me over.
He admitted Saul was not his name;
He'd taken up another name for blood.
(So had I—my fighting name was just
(A word we use at home for private soldier.)

I felt at home as mercenary soldier.
I liked the company of men like Saul.
(Though most of Richard's men were just
(Fighting for the bounty when it's over.)
I loved the clash of weapons, splashing blood—
I lived the meager promise of my name.

Saul promised that he'd tell me his real name
When he was through with playing as a soldier.
(I said the same; we took an oath in blood.)
But I would never know him but as Saul;
He'd die before the long campaign was over,
Dying for a cause that was not just.

Only fools require a cause that's just,
Fools and children out to make a name.

Now I've had sixty years to think it over
(Sixty years of being no one's soldier).
Sixty years since broadsword opened Saul
And splashed my body with his steaming blood.

But damn! we lived for bodies and for blood.
The reek of dead men rotting, it was just
A sweet perfume for those like me and Saul.
(My peaceful language doesn't have a name
(For lewd delight in going off to soldier.)
It hurts my heart sometimes to know it's over.

My heart was hard as stone when it was over;
When finally I'd had my fill of blood.
(And knew I was too old to be a soldier.)
Nothing left for me to do but just
Go back home and make myself a name
In ways of peace, forgetting war and Saul.

In ways of blood he made himself a name
(Though he was just a mercenary soldier)—
I loved Saul before it all was over.

II

A mercenary soldier has no future;
Some say his way of life is hardly human.
And yet, he has his own small bloody world
(Part aches and sores and wrappings soaking blood,
(Partly fear and glory grown familiar)
Confined within a shiny fence of swords.

But how I learned to love to fence with swords!
Another world, my homely past and future—
Once steel and eye and wrist became familiar
With each other, then that steel was almost human
(With an altogether human taste for blood).
I felt that sword and I could take the world.

I felt that Saul and I could take the world:
Take the whole world hostage with our swords.

The bond we felt was stronger than mere blood
(Though I can see with hindsight in the future
(The bond we felt was something only human:
(A need for love when death becomes familiar.)

We were wizards, and death was our familiar;
Our swords held all the magic in the world.
(Richard thought it almost wasn't human,
(The speed with which we parried others' swords,
(Forever end another's petty future.)
Never scratched, though always steeped in blood.

Ambushed in a tavern, fighting ankle-deep in blood,
Fighting back-to-back in ways familiar.
Saul slipped: lost his footing and his future.
Broad blade hammered down and sent him from this
    world.
In angry grief I killed that one, then all the other
    swords;
Then locked the door and murdered every human.

No choice, but to murder every human.

No one in that tavern was a stranger to blood.
(To those who live with pikes and slashing swords,
(The inner parts of men become familiar.)
Saul's vitals looked like nothing in this world:
I had to kill them all to save my future.

Saul's vitals were not human, but familiar:
He never told me he was from another world:
I never told him I was from his future.

    The sestina is an ingenious, intricate form of verse
that originated in France around the twelfth century,
percolated into Italy, and from there was appropriated
by the English. At first glance, it looks like a rather ar-
bitrary logjam, sort of a hybrid of poetry with linear
algebra, but it does have a special charm.
    The form calls for six stanzas of six lines each, follow-
ed by a three-line envoi. The lines don't rhyme, but they

give a sort of illusion of rhyming, by forced repetition. The last words of the first six lines provide the last words of every subsequent line, by a strict system of inside-out rotation. (If the last words of the first stanza are 1-2-3-4-5-6, then the last words of the second are 6-1-5-2-4-3; the third, 3-1-4-1-2-5, and so forth. *Claro?* The envoi ought to have all six words crammed into its three lines, but the writer is allowed a certain amount of latitude with that, and I've taken it.)

The result, in English at least, is a sort of a chant, which is one of two reasons the form is appropriate for an entertainment like "Saul's Death."

EDITOR'S INTRODUCTION TO:

PROJECT HIGH FRONTIER
Lt. Gen. Daniel O. Graham

I am a contributing editor to *Survive*, a magazine about how to live through the coming crisis times. The worst crisis we could experience would be a nuclear war.

The best way to survive a nuclear war is not to have one. The best way I know not to have one is to support General Graham's Project High Frontier.

Many years ago, Stefan T. Possony and I published a book called THE STRATEGY OF TECHNOLOGY. The book was a *success d' estime:* that is, it didn't make us much money, but it did get good reviews. Eventually it was adopted as a text in one of the nation's War Colleges, so I suppose it had some influence.

One of the concepts we examined in that book was national strategic doctrine, which at that time was announced as "Assured Destruction." This seemed a bit odd: that is, one of the most popular stories of the time was that when Robert S. McNamara took office as Secretary of Defense, he invited the Commander in Chief of the Strategic Air Command to discuss his war plans, and particularly the SIOP (Single Integrated Operational Plan). The general did so, showing how the US forces would be launched against the enemy.

When the briefing was over, McNamara shuddered. "General," he said, "you don't have a war plan. All you have is a kind of horrible spasm."

This story was often told to illustrate the intelligence of McNamara and the stupidity of the generals. McNamara was going to get rid of the "spasm" and substitute a new doctrine of "Flexible Response." Furthermore, he would do this for lower cost, keeping everyone happy.

Part of McNamara's plan involved negotiations with the Soviet Union. In order to induce them to be cooperative, we had to let them feel safe; this meant that we could not have strategic superiority (which, according to the McNamara doctrine, was meaningless anyway).

The result of all this was our "new" strategic doctrine: Mutual Assured Destruction, usually abbreviated as MAD.

MAD has a rigid logic; indeed, it was what Herman Kahn had called a "homicide pact." Medieval writers would have called it an exchange of hostages—except, of course, we value our citizens, while the esteem in which Soviet leaders hold their subjects is not so certain. MAD assured safety by assuring mutual destruction: war was to be so horrible that no one would ever start one, since no one could ever win it. Since it would never start, one need not have plans for fighting it; it was necessary only to prove that both sides would be killed—which is to say, to perfect the horrible spasm. From Flexible Response we grew the MAD doctrine that said: since Civil Defense measures mitigate the effects of war, and protect the American people against the enemy's retaliation, Civil Defense is "provocative"; indeed, taking measures that protect American lives in the event of war is an "act of aggression against the Soviet Union."

MAD drew the same conclusions about defenses. Anti ballistic missile defenses (known sometimes as ABM and sometimes as BMD) were also provocative and aggressive systems. The Soviets would never accept that, and invested heavily in defensive systems; so we negotiated a treaty called SALT (Strategic Arms Limitation Treaty) that prohibited BMD, except that both sides could deploy one defense system. Because the protection of one's citizens negated MAD, the ABM system was supposed to protect only *weapons*, specifically a missile farm. If we had deployed an ABM (we didn't), it would have been out at Minot, South Dakota. The Soviets chose to protect the weapons they had deployed near Moscow . . .

In THE STRATEGY OF TECHNOLOGY, Possony and I proposed a different strategic doctrine which we thought would make more sense. We called it Assured Survival. We thought that the primary mission of the armed forces should be to assure the survival of the United States and as many citizens as possible. One of the best ways to do that would be to develop defensive systems.

This was also dictated by the Judaeo-Christian doctrine of Just War. MAD, which offers to kill the enemy's helpless civilians in retaliation for the acts of their masters, presents a moral dilemma of staggering proportions.

Defense systems, we argued, are inherently stabilizing: they don't threaten the other side, but they do complicate his war plan, making it much harder for him to know just what would happen if the war started. Only a fool would believe his missile defenses were perfect; but only another fool would attack a nation armed with both missiles and good defenses.

Some years later, Lt. Gen. Daniel O. Graham, US Army (Ret'd), an infantryman who became Director of the Defense Intelligence Agency and Deputy Director of the CIA, became interested in a new strategic plan. This became Project High Frontier.

General Graham's concepts are explained in great detail in the High Frontier report, available for $15 from Project High Frontier, 1010 Vermont Ave., N.W. Suite 1000, Washington, DC 20005, (202) 737-4979. Project High Frontier is endorsed by many enthusiasts including former astronaut Buzz Aldrin; perhaps his most enthusiastic endorsement is given below.

THE GOOD NEWS OF
HIGH FRONTIER
by
Robert A. Heinlein

"High Frontier," is the best news I have heard since VJ Day.

For endless unhappy years the United States has had no defense policy. We had something we called a defense policy . . . but in the words of Abraham Lincoln, "Calling a tail a leg doesn't make it a leg."

Under our present policies what do we have? H-bombs, airborne, water-borne, and in silos, capable of destroying anything, anywhere on this planet. Elite troops second to none in our Marine Corps, in our Army's 82nd Airborne, and in our Navy SEALs. Other armed forces stationed around the world and on every ocean. Eyes in the sky that can spot any missile launched in our direction.

And none of these can even slow down an ICBM launched at Washington.

(Or at your hometown).

So we have *no* defense. Instead we have something mislabeled a "defense policy," called "Mutually Assured Destruction," referred to as "MAD."

Never has Washington produced an acronym that fitted so perfectly. Picture two men at point-blank range each with a .45 aimed at the other man's bare chest. That is MAD. Crazy. Insane. And *stupid*.

High Frontier places a bullet-proof vest on our bare chest. High Frontier is as non-aggressive as a bullet-proof vest. There is no way to kill anyone with High Frontier—all that High Frontier can do is to keep others from killing us.

That is one of the two best aspects of High Frontier. It is so utterly peaceful that the most devout pacifist can support it with a clear conscience—indeed *must* support it once he understands it . . . as it tends to stop wars from happening and to save lives if war does happen. All who supported GROUND ZERO should support High Frontier.

The other best aspect of High Frontier is that its systems are non-nuclear. I am not one who gets upset at hearing the word "nuclear" . . . but no one in his right mind wants nuclear explosions going on over his head or anywhere on this planet. It is happy indeed that the best defense we can devise does not call for nuclear explosions. To save ourselves we do *not* need to blow up Moscow, we do *not* need to add to the radioactive fallout on our lovely planet.

The designers of High Frontier calculate that this new strategy will decrease our military costs. I am not in a position to judge this . . . but, frankly, I don't give a damn. A man with a burst appendix can't afford to dicker over the cost of surgery.

But will High Frontier in fact protect the Republic? As an old Research and Development engineer with the pessimism appropriate to the trade, I am certain that most of the hardware described in the High Frontier plan will undergo many changes before it is installed; that is the way R & D always works. But I am equally certain that the problems can be solved.

The first stages of High Frontier, point defense of our missile silos, we could start building later this afternoon; it involves nothing but well-known techniques and off-the-shelf hardware. That first stage alone could save us, as it denies to an enemy a free chance to destroy us by a preemptive first strike. It forces him to think twice, three times and decide not to try it.

But the key point is not whether this hardware will do the trick; the key lies in a change of attitude. A firm resolve to *defend* the United States . . . rather than resigning ourselves to the destruction of our beloved country. If we will so resolve, then the development of hardware is something we certainly know how to do.

But we won't get there by throwing up our hands and baring our necks to the executioner. God helps those who help themselves; he does not help those who won't try.

So let's try!

Robert A. Heinlein.

PROJECT HIGH FRONTIER
by
Lt. Gen. Daniel O. Graham
USA (Ret.)

The following statement was given by Lt. Gen. Daniel O. Graham, USA (Ret.), at a High Frontier press conference last spring. This statement, because of its brevity, omits High Frontier's committment to civil defense as a vital part of the program. Similarly, the space-based, solar-power system does not appear. And it does not mention the 200,000 jobs that probably would be created in the slumbering aerospace industry, nor the incalculable boost to America's image both at home and abroad. These and other spinoffs from the program are described in *High Frontier: A New National Strategy*, available from High Frontier, 1010 Vermont Ave., N.W., Suite 1000, Washington, D.C. 20005, or call (202) 737-4749. The 175-page, illustrated book costs $15.

The High Frontier concepts constitute first and foremost a change of U.S. strategy—from the bankrupt and basically immoral precepts of Mutual Assured Destruction (MAD), to a stable and morally defensible strategy of Assured Survival. But High Frontier is not a mere military strategy, it is a true national strategy addressing the legitimate economic and political aspirations of the nation and those of our allies as well as security needs.

The High Frontier study set out to seek technology that would support a new strategy, and not the other way around. Fortunately, the United States—at least for the moment—has a technological lead over the Soviet Union, especially in space. This advantage has been dramatically demonstrated by the Space Shuttle, which gives us the capability of delivering men and material into space to do some of the key things High Frontier is recommending.

High Frontier's objective is to formulate a national strategy option that would (1) nullify, or substantially reduce, the growing threat to the United States and its allies posed by the unprecedented Soviet military buildup; (2) replace the dangerous doctrine of Mutual Assured Destruction with a strategy of Assured Survival, and (3) provide both security and incentive for realizing the enormous industrial and commercial potential of space.

We insist that this objective be met with recommendations that are militarily sound, technologically feasible, fiscally responsible and politically practical.

The essence of the High Frontier report can be summarized as follows:

(1) It is possible for the United States to close the window of vulnerability in two years and move from the MAD (balance of terror) strategy to an Assured Survival strategy in five or six years, while at the same time contributing greatly to U.S. economic growth.

(2) This requires only a national commitment to do so, an end-run of bureaucratic obstacles, and a redirection (as opposed to an add-on) of available resources.

(3) The basic military requirement is: a layered strategic defense, starting with a cheap and simple point defense (similar to a gigantic shotgun) of U.S. missile silos; then, a spaceborne capability to intercept re-entry vehicles in mid course.

(4) The basic non-military requirement is the improvement of the space-transportation system to lower the cost-per-pound to orbit to less than $100, thus providing incentives for private industry to develop the broad spectrum of commercial opportunities in space.

(5) These requirements can be met by technically sound, fiscally responsible and politically practical programs conceived and analyzed by Project High Frontier experts, other research institutions and private companies.

(6) The High Frontier programs can be accomplished in remarkably short time and at low cost because the off-the-shelf technologies and system components are used to the maximum, avoiding long lead times and high costs of research and development. Political practicality

is ensured by avoiding solutions demanding nuclear weaponry.

(7) Our analysis of both military and civilian program costs to meet High Frontier requirements is about $150 billion (in constant dollars) over 10 years. Of this, about $35 billion would be defense money, the rest NASA.

(8) We are convinced that the only way that costs can be held to these low levels and the time schedules met is through a Manhattan Project-type managerial arrangement at the top of government. Business-as-usual would add two to five years of crucial and unnecessary time to all High Frontier target dates, as well as greatly inflate the costs.

(9) The specific systems recommended by High Frontier include:

> Global Ballistic Missile Defense System,
> SWARMJET Point Defense System,
> Advanced Shuttle System, and
> Solar Power Satellite System.

TWO POEMS
by
Jon Post

CITY-KILLER

Portrait of death
a tactical target
the blasted city
footprints of mars
nine million dead
a trillion dollar loss

Portrait of abstract beauty
laser-carved rubble-sculpture
crushed cars on asphalt
and that mineral of bones & glass
rock and vaporized steel:
Hiroshimite

Portrait of political process
the top-level negotiators drunk
at the whorehouse in Geneva

GROUND ZERO

Ride a burning horse to heaven
ride a golden horse to hell
with the horn of battle blaring
who can hear the distant bell?

When the sons have gone to slaughter
who's to keep the daughters warm?

Ride a burning horse to heaven
leave a headstone at the farm
"Yes, sir, Company 11
in the radiation zone."

When the sons have gone to slaughter
who's to keep the daughters warm?
Ride a rocketship to heaven
go to hell in your own home.

EDITOR'S INTRODUCTION TO:

DIASPORAH
by
W. R. Yates

"When they go down, it shall be to the dust of the earth. And when they rise, it shall be to the stars . . ."

—Megillah 16a

In times past, editors worked closely with writers. Alas, that seldom happens now.

John F. Carr, my long-suffering associate, reads all the submissions for these anthologies. It's a thankless job, but it has its rewards. One was the discovery of this story.

Mutual Assured Destruction, MAD, works only as long as it works; it does not know what to do if deterrence fails, for it envisions no defensive capabilities. A deterrent works until it is needed; then one needs defenses. General Graham told how we might construct defenses, so that mistakes need not be irrevocable. In his first published story, W. R. Yates tells what happens to those who have no defenses.

DIASPORAH: A PROLOGUE

by

W. R. Yates

August 12, 1997   Somewhere in the Negev
Av 9, 5757   Tuesday
6:17 A.M., Jerusalem Time

The sign is in a gate post of blue *Elat* tile. The road on which it stands branches off from one of the main highways which leads from *Beer Sheba* to *Elat*. The road is narrow, but paved with grey asphalt. And the sign reads:

המרכז החקלאי למחקר

הכניסה אסורה
Agricultural Research Center
Keep Out

المركز الزراعي للأبحاث

الدخول ممنوع

ממשלת ישראל
Government of Israel   حكومة اسرائيل

The guard walked over, as Zvi pulled up to the gate. Zvi rummaged for his wallet, as the guard leaned from the booth. Zvi handed him the card and pressed his hand against a plate of glass. The card and his palm print both verified that he was indeed, Zvi Sivan. The formalities over, Zvi pointed to the sign. "When are we going to take that thing down?" he asked. "I think that the only people who still believe it are the Israelis!"

"Be fair," laughed the guard. "There really is a research station here."

Zvi shrugged. The electronic gate began to swing open. "*Ad mahar,,*" he cried, driving through.

Zvi's comment was probably right. The inhabitants of *New Persia* had possessed spy satellites for nearly six

149

years. Reports from the *Mossaad* had shown that they knew where the major Israeli missile bases were located.

Zvi parked the white '87 Mercedes in a space by the administration building. Opening the trunk, he pulled out a fitted tarpaulin and began stretching it over the vehicle. "How can white fade?" someone had once jokingly asked him. But it protected the finish against the sun. The heavily waxed surface was still as bright and shiny as it was on the day that he bought it.

With his hands on his hips, he surveyed the rows of maturing orange trees. It was somewhat odd to see so much green here. The shifting sand of the Negev still dusted the horizon with a reddish haze. If the experiments worked out right, the whole desert would bloom with purified water from the Mediterranean. Then the dust would cease to attack the eyes and block the nostrils.

But more Israeli marks had been spent on what lay below the ground than above. The blue of the irrigation canals and the green of the shrubbery concealed Israel's deadliest and most secret weapons. Twenty feet beneath the canals, safe within their cradles, nestled *Yoshua*, surface to surface, cruise missiles.

Nobody questioned the military look of things, which surrounded the installation. The guard towers, the barbed wire, the electrified fencing, had surrounded every major Israeli installation for nearly fifty years.

The whine of a jeep engine made Zvi turn back toward the parking lot. Zvi grinned. It was his new driver. The dark-skinned figure braked to a halt. Zvi got in next to him.

"Where to, *Adonai*?" the man asked.

"I am with *Yoshua*," answered Zvi. "You can drop that '*adonai*' business. We're very informal around here. My name's Captain Zvi Sivan. You can just call me Zvi. And you?"

"Sergeant Major Ibrahim . . ." The other grinned. "Name's too long to say in one breath. As long as we're so informal here, just call me Ib."

Zvi felt his flesh tingle. He looked again at the other's dark hair, skin and eyes. "You are *Sephardic?*" he asked.

Ib's mouth twisted as though he were enjoying a private joke. "Arab," he answered. "And a Muslim. Don't worry, *Haver Shelli*. I've been damned well checked out. Or I wouldn't be here."

"I wasn't aware that Arabs worked at the *Yoshua* installations," put in Zvi.

"My parents may have been Palestinians, but I am Israeli," answered the other. "My grandfather told me that my people used to die by the thousands from hunger, thirst, disease and exposure. But that was before the Jews came. My parents considered him a traitor. They, and the rest of my people cannot accept your strange ways. You are too alien to them and they don't wish to learn. My grandfather urged me to go to the university. My father disowned me."

"I'm sorry," answered Zvi.

The other grimaced. "It is no matter," he answered. "My father would have me herding goats."

Zvi laughed and remembered his own father's failure to understand. "We are doubly friends," answered Zvi. "I too saw the world as it is. My family has been in this country since the time of the Spanish Inquisition. I am *Sephardic* and learned to adapt. Nothing is given to us, my friend. Whether it is a nation or a fine home. You must fight to gain it. And you must take care of it."

"I agree with your point, if not your metaphor," answered Ib.

"Then you are not Israeli," answered Zvi. His eyes twinkled at the other.

"I didn't say that I agreed with Israel's manner of coming into existence. Merely that I agreed with its existence."

"You are a very intelligent man, Ib. How is it that you are only a Sergeant Major?"

"I was once with the *Mossaad*," said Ibrahim quietly.

"I don't know what their pay scale is, but it is certainly higher than the Air Force. Why did you quit?"

"It was I who discovered how *they* perfected the bomb," was the answer. "It is a painful thing."

"I'm sorry," Zvi answered. How long it had remained a secret of the Persian government, Zvi himself did not know. But when it finally got out, it had made headlines around the world. By using political prisoners, Kurds and the Sunni who refused to acknowledge his power . . . The successor of the Great Mamoud . . . The 'Imam of the Time's Caliph' . . . The 'Twelfth Iman's Caliph' . . . had dispensed with the need for expensive shielding.

Those who had worked with the deadly radioactive materials were dead within three weeks. "The Persians and Arabs themselves did not want such a government," Zvi finally said.

"Revolutions rarely work for the better," was Ib's reply. "The *Imamim Shi'ah* in that country are only after one thing. The uncooperative intellectuals there are either dead or in prison. The unschooled are happy. They don't know the difference between real and perverted religion."

"Are not the Catholic temples filled with idols," quoted Zvi.

Ibrahim nodded. "We traditionally regard both the Christians and the Jews as 'People of the Book,' not as Infidels."

"The Crusades didn't help much," said Zvi.

"Neither did the Israeli War of Independence."

The answer made Zvi's blood run cold. He quickly changed the subject. "Did anything happen during the night?"

"One of the missiles, *Yoshua Heth*, is out of order. Decay in the grain of one of the boosters. One of the *Kalebs* was blinded by a laser."

"That happens all the time," put in Zvi. "They're probably trying to sneak somebody across the border. I always dislike the blindspot that leaves. At any rate, *Sharm el Sheik's* already got another on the pad. It'll be in orbit before this shift is out. I wish we didn't have to clear things with Cairo. It would be a lot faster."

"Here we are." Ib braked the jeep to a halt.

"Thanks!" said Zvi. "I owe you a glass of tea sometime."

Ib grinned. "I think I would like that. See you later."

"*Salaam*," responded Zvi in Arabic. He was rewarded with a toothy grin.

As the jeep roared away, Zvi turned to a small pump shed. He brought a key out of his pocket and inserted it into the lock on the door. On entering, there was nothing to show that the interior was any more than it was supposed to be. There was the whine of an electric pump in one corner. The drip . . . drip of water on prestressed concrete and light tile. A nest of hoes, rakes, shovels . . . stood leaning against one of the walls. Near the door, as

though something were intended to hang there, was a
nail. Turning back to the door and being careful to stand
on a tile of a slightly different color than the rest, Zvi
gave the nail a twist. Almost immediately, the tile began
to sink into the floor and Zvi with it. Above Zvi's head,
another tile closed. In the darkness, the concrete of the
shaft whispered past. Finally, the ring of a chime announced his arrival. A double door slid open and Zvi
found himself facing a small room. Next to the elevator,
a knot of three men sat hunched over a Backgammon
board. A man behind a desk stood up. "You are late for
the first time in three years, *Seren* Sivan. Shmuel will be
angry."

"Trouble with the car," explained Zvi. "Tell Shmuel
not to be too put out."

The other grinned. "There's a rumor going around
that they're going to be cutting our shifts from four to
an hour each. *Knesset* seems to think that we aren't
keeping on our toes."

"It would cut the strain some. But I think we can handle what we've got. If you will excuse me . . ."

Zvi inserted a card into a slot and again pressed his
hand against the glass pane of a box before the door. He
waved a greeting to the other men, as the door slid open.

The door slid shut. The bickering of the men in the
outer office was lost in silence. Compared even to the
sunlight of early morning, the room was cool and dark.

Directly ahead of him was a map, a computer display
of a gigantic scale. Flanking each of its sides were three
television screens. One was adjusted to infra-red false
color. The second was taken by natural light in full col-
or. The third was nearly blank, adjusted to the ultraviolet radiation that was absorbed in the Earth's upper
atmosphere. Pictures from the orbiting *Kaleb* satellites.
Theoretically, the UV image would show the radiation
released by the explosion of an atomic bomb on Earth's
surface. In front of each division of three television
screens sat two figures. Each had its own console of
knobs, keys and switches. Each console was illuminated
by the blank faces of two computer readout screens.

One of the figures turned. Her blonde hair glowed
eerily in the green light. "*Shalom, Putz!*" You're late! We
thought you'd gone to Synagogue!"

"There's nothing about today in *The Commandments*," was Zvi's curt reply.

P'nina smiled. "I doubt if there would be," she responded. "The destruction of the first temple happened long after *Torah*." A wicked smile played about P'nina's lips. "My favorite two Commandments are positive ones," she said. "Numbers one ninety two and one ninety three."

Zvi felt another appalling dig coming at his beliefs. He opened his mouth in an attempt to change the subjects, thus diverting it. But Shmuel, seeing his discomfort, interrupted.

"And what two Commandments might those be?" he asked P'nina.

"Deuteronomy, Twenty three, verses ten to fourteen. Dig a latrine."

Zvi sighed. "Okay, Shmuel," he said. "You have your answer and the shift is over. Get going!"

"I'm waiting to find out why *that* would be her favorite Commandment! Memories of bootcamp couldn't have faded *that* rapidly!"

"Because," said P'nina. "The passage ends; '*For the Lord thy God walks in the midst of thy camp.*'" And as though enough salt hadn't been rubbed into Zvi's wound, she climaxed it with a mental picture so absurd that it was bound to bring a guffaw . . . From an atheist. *"Nachon, Putz?"* she added.

Shmuel threw back his head in laughter. If Zvi reddened, it was with embarrassment. Rage wasn't permitted in the bunker.

At last, Shmuel rose from his chair. "Serves you right for being late, Zvi. I'll see you tomorrow. *Shalom.*"

"Do you always have to do that to me?" Zvi asked P'nina as the door slid closed.

P'nina's name was Hebrew for pearl, and the whiteness of her teeth reflected it as she gave him another of her wicked smiles. "Couldn't resist," she answered. "But, to be perfectly frank, I had to get him out of here some way. I thought he'd never leave!" She reached into her purse, extracting a book, a pomegranite, two figs and a banana. These she placed on the table that formed part of her console. The book was opened as Zvi turned attentively to the screens. He had thought of reporting her, but was stopped by her remark; "If anything happens, *Putz*. You're nervous enough to let me know."

At the first surprise inspection, he found that a thoughtful workman had placed a, chime both in the outer office and the *Slik* itself. The arrival of the elevator clanged in both rooms. With the book and a single movement, she whisked the fruit into a drawer. The book followed. By the time the inspecting general entered, the drawer was closed and both of her feet were on the floor.

He found her both amusing and repulsive. Time after time, he'd thought of reporting her for an acid word that she had given him. These and her nicknaming him with a Yiddish obscenity had really bothered him until:

It had been two years before, at a Synagogue picnic, on the beach at Ceasaria. After the food had been eaten, he and a group of *Shul* members decided to engage in a game of soccer. He kicked at the ball with his bare feet and it glanced off to the side. Spitting into the sand, he chased it beneath the arches of the old Roman aquaduct. His eyes hadn't adjusted to the shade within the moldering arches. He knocked a diminutive figure to the ground.

"Oh! Sorry!" he apologized as he took a slender wrist into his hand. Pulling her to her feet, his eyes swept over a blindingly beautiful figure in a two piece bathing suit. They came to rest in a pair of familiar blue eyes.

"P'nina!" he exclaimed. "*Shalom!* Come and meet the group! There is plenty of tea and beer! Drink with us! Some chicken may be left . . ."

"Zvi, no! Please! I parked the car down near the old fortress. I've been walking here . . . Swimming and thinking. I saw you playing and stopped to watch . . . I *can't* spend any time with you out of the *Slik*. I'd love to come and play with you and your friends . . . But . . . Someday . . . If anything goes wrong in the *Slik* . . . I might have to kill you. I'm very fond of you, Zvi. More fond than I should be. For my sake . . . For the sake of our Nation . . . Don't make your death under those circumstances impossible!"

Without warning, the slender arms went around his neck. The rapid kiss that she gave him was salted with a tear. She turned and ran.

It was with some confusion that he retrieved the ball
and joined the group. He had only been, as with Ib, making an attempt to be friendly. Until that time he hadn't
understood that P'nina's more than Israeli rudeness had
been a mask, as much for herself, as for him.

He remembered the controversy which had broken
out when it was revealed that the sexes were mixed.
That two people of the opposite sex were locked together in a room beneath the ground. With women like
P'nina, Israel had nothing to fear.

His thoughts were interrupted by P'nina's laughter.
She was gazing into the book.

"Shalom Aliechem?" Zvi asked.

Disgust showed on P'nina's features. "Is he the only
humorist that you know about?" she asked. "No, this is
an American writer. Robert Benchly." She put down the
book. "You have met Ibrahim?" she asked.

"You mean the Arab?" he asked. "*Ken.* He drove me
in."

P'nina smiled. "Nothing to worry about," she answered. "He used to work for the *Mossaad.*"

"My father used to work for the *Mossaad.*"

"Then maybe that's not such a recommendation,"
answered P'nina.

The barb was lost on Zvi, for in his imagination, the
roar of his father's laughter filled the rooms. It had been
just before midterms at *Technion.* His father worked
hard with the others, but frequently was called away on
'government business.' Sometimes for weeks or months
at a time. Everyone on the *Moshav* had suspected that he
was an agent. But nobody asked.

Zvi had been studying aircraft mechanics at the time.
He remembered the tattered blue cover of the book. The
varnished feel of its yellowing pages. The smell of dust
and paper. He remembered how that smell fought with
the smell of new turned earth coming through an open
kitchen window. And he remembered how his studies
were interrupted by the hard plunk of a bottle on the
table. He looked up at the yellow, red, white and black
label.

From there, he looked into the face of his father. It
was a furred silhouette against the glare of the kitchen
bulb.

"Drink!" his father laughingly commanded. Vast arms swung wide. "Tomorrow, you return to Haifa! There was never such a *Purim* and you missed it! Your cousin! Ha! Ha! What a beautiful Esther she made! What a long flowing gown!" His father winked. "As long and flowing as a gown can be . . . On a four year old!" He threw back his head in laughter.

Zvi looked back at his book. "I won't be a farmer," he said.

"Who said that I was asking you to become one?" His father turned his back, folded his arms and sat on the table. "Ah! But you missed such a harvest last year!" He clenched his fist and shook it. "You never saw such beautiful bananas! And so many oranges, grapes, lemons!" The glow went out of his eyes and he lowered his fist.

"Son," he said. "I'm not asking you to become a farmer. I'm merely asking you to be happy!"

"I am happy, Father."

"With books?! I want you to dance, to drink, to sing, to play! To find yourself some nice girl! But continue to laugh! That is why God put us here!" His father sighed. "But how can I ask you to continue what you have not begun? Why, even soccer, you treat like an attack from Syria!"

It was the last time he had seen his father.

He had continued studying that night and returned to Haifa before his father's awakening.

An Islamic leader was assassinated nearly a thousand kilometers away. Nations were disemboweled. Absorbed. Jordan became a province named New Palestine.

His father's dark skin, hair and eyes blended perfectly with those of the Arabs streaming across New Allenby Bridge.

His father never came back.

Once again, P'nina's voice interrupted his thoughts.

"Here's the blindspot," she said.

Zvi looked up. The three color television screens, which showed what was picked up by the orbiting *Kaleb* satellites, were filled with snow. His eyes returned to the readout screens and he noticed another change.

"We've got three launches from Tehran, P'nina."

She straightened in her seat. "Call *Slik Aleph*."

Zvi picked up the phone and hit the aleph on the punch

board. "*Slik Aleph?* This is *Slik Gimmel.* We've got a reading of three launches from Tehran. Have you the same reading?"

"This is *Slik Aleph, Gimmel.* We have a copy."

"This is *Slik Yod Daleth,*" broke in a voice from a speaker on their consoles. "*Slikim Heth* and *Yod* confirm your readouts. We've got trouble. Should we wake the Old Man?"

"*Ken,*" whispered Zvi.

He and P'nina simultaneously pushed identical blue buttons on their consoles. A majority decision was shown by the button's answering glow.

Above, a siren sounded. A group of terrified farm workers ran for the administration building.

At another *Slik,* another member of the *Palavir* picked up a red phone. He didn't bother punching in a number. In a modest Jerusalem home, a *Knesset* office and a parked automobile, identical phones were already ringing.

After a pause. "I've got the Old Man," came a voice. "He's getting on the hotline to Mecca."

"Two more launches from Jidda." Zvi looked down at his readout screen.

"We've definitely got a critical situation here. Might they be attacking Turkey?"

"Aw, come on! Every Arab country that they have was taken by invasion or work from within! Why bother with a missile attack?"

"Let's see what the Old Man says . . ."

"Negative on Turkish attack. The missiles, if they exist, are headed in our direction."

"Could it be Cypress?" came a voice.

"Look at your map!"

"The Old Man says that Tehran denies any launches. They warn that any attack will be met by retaliation."

"Any attack will be met by retaliation!" cursed Zvi under his breath.

"Could those three from Tehran have been a mistake?"

"Just a second," said a voice. "I'll see if the Old Man can talk Mecca into calling the Tehran base."

"What about Jidda?" asked P'nina. "*Slick* Seventeen?"

"Possibly the launches from Tehran were sensed and the other two were sent as a panic response."

"They shouldn't have been," answered P'nina. "There was a full minute . . . One minute exactly, between launches. They may not have the *Yoshua*, but their response time should be as effective as our own. Read your reports from *Mossaad*."

"Four more from Damam."

"The Old Man says that they deny any attack."

"Goddamnit!" cursed P'nina under her breath. "They haven't had time to call their base!"

"Tell the Old Man that we've got eight missiles headed in our direction. If it's a mistake, they'd better find out pretty damn fast!"

"The Old Man says to go to condition yellow as soon as those missiles cut their thrust. If the targeting displays show military targets, activate!"

Zvi raised his brows. "The agricultural center's going to be awfully pissed if we activate under a false alarm."

"They'll be more pissed if we take no action at all," answered P'nina. "Their families live here." She began punching the aleph button, trying to get through to the red phone.

"Tell them about *Yoshua*, if you have to!" she said when the button finally illuminated itself.

Zvi began counting aloud and then silently to himself. "We have six from Isfahn," he said. "Still better than twelve hundred kilometers from our borders. If they think this is a surprise attack, they're insane! We couldn't be given more response time!"

"The Old Man's got them calling their bases."

P'nina breathed a sigh of relief and settled back in her chair. "At least that part of the battle's won," she said.

"Fourteen missiles with warheads of ten megatons or better. Do you really think our country can take that? . . ."

Two targets illuminated the screen. Zvi half rose from his seat. "Metzada!" he fairly screamed in perplexity.

"Sit down, *Putz!*" cried P'nina. "It's an old ruin! Nothing more!"

But Zvi didn't hear her. His mind hissed back the five years to the West Bank War. It had lasted only a few days. But it had been enough to destroy much of Western Jerusalem, as well as the old *Knesset*. Again he felt the surge of the *Kfir C-5* under his command. The Fencer was flying low, dangerously low above the hills of the Judean desert. His *Kfir* followed. Ahead of the Su-19 was another C-5. In it was Yigal.

Yigal had taken off after the Fencer when they broke up a squadron of the machines en route to Jerusalem. They had been flying at barely ten thousand feet. The Fencer was a speck ahead of Zvi, Yigal's plane little more.

Suddenly, the Su-19 lost altitude. "He opened his drogue chute!" came Yigal's astounded voice. Zvi immediately swung his plane hard around, looping backward, so that the Soviet plane could not fall behind them both. As the Gs drained the blood from his face, Zvi's mind clouded. A Soviet pilot? No. The Soviet Union had abandoned New Persia when it became evident that this too was to be a religious state, intent on carving out an empire of its own.

Zvi's mind spun. The drogue chute was only used in landing on the short airstrips of the Persian mountains. The deceleration must have nearly blacked out the two men in the Fencer's cockpit. A desperate and risky maneuver. And one that insured that the Su-19 wouldn't be returning to the airstrips of home.

"He's accelerating!" came Yigal's voice. "He's right on my tail! I can't seem to shake him!"

Below Zvi flashed a pattern of dry washes and hillsides. Like the legs of a many limbed, sleeping monster. Zvi bit his lower lip beneath the oxygen mask. Allah had performed a miracle for the other side. A miracle which kept the enemy plane from crashing below. He pushed forward on the stick, dropping lower. A faint glow of admiration touched Zvi as he spoke. The Arab pilots were improving and not above taking chances. The drogue chute had, no doubt, ripped to shreds and been discarded. It was a maneuver that the Su-19 would not try again. And it couldn't try anything similar at the altitude it was now flying. "I'll get in some shots at him, catch up and try to pass. He's either got radar controlled or heat seeking missiles. I'll drop some chaff and flares, then I want you to peel off in a loop. Are you ready to take some Gs?"

"Ready when you are," came back Yigal's voice.

"Great!" exclaimed Zvi. A faint shadow of green pass-ed quickly below, showing that he was over Ein Gedi. The wind of the Fencer's passing was already making the C-5 buck and yaw.

Zvi turned on his afterburner, gaining speed. The air was clear. He could see the Dead Sea off to his left, like a shining mirror. As he moved up on the Fencer, he gained altitude, creeping above it. He could now see the glis-tening delta of the machine's wings. He pushed forward on the *Kfir's* wheel. It slid in easily. Zvi was diving toward it. A burst of tracers narrowly missed as the Su-19 rolled over on its side, presenting a smaller target. As Zvi pulled back on the stick, bringing the C-5 out of the dive, the Fencer resumed its original position. And fired its own tracers.

"I'm hit!" cried Yigal. "Those shots must have sliced through my control cables! I've still got my rudder, but I've lost my flaps!

"Remember what I told that fat tourist, Zvi?"

"I remember, Yigal."

A low chuckle answered Zvi as though some hidden irony were sensed.

"Here it comes," said Yigal.

Nearly two thousand years before, Herod had built a refuge atop the butte of Metzada. A butte rising nearly four hundred and forty meters above the Dead Sea. Less than a century later, it was used as a fortress by the Zealots, who held it against the Roman hordes for nearly three years. When, at last, an earthen embankment was slowly built to its edge, the Romans entered to find a hollow victory. Rather than be sold into Roman slavery, the Zealots had commited suicide. Men, women and children.

Zvi remembered what Yigal had told the tourist. A quirk of irony passed through him as well. The Fencer and his own plane passed over Metzada's side. Herod's Northern Palace, carved out of Metzada's cliff, dissolved as Yigal's plane plunged into its face. A rearview mirror showed fingers of flame, explosive, wreckage and fuel oil arc above the plateau.

And Zvi remembered what Yigal had told the tourist. "Forget Metzada!" he said said. "There will be no more Metzada! From now on, if a Jew dies, it will be because he had died fighting! It will not be because we are faced with overwhelming odds. It will be because freedom or death are the only end! If that were today, every woman would be given a sword and every child a knife!"

"*Shalom*, Yigal," Zvi said.

"Shezor?" said P'nina. "Not a military target . . ." She swiveled in her seat and began punching keys. "A farming community in Galilee," she said.

"And B'nai Naim," answered Zvi. "Also, we've got four additional launches from Hamadan."

"Switch to primary backup computers," came a voice over the loudspeaker.

"At this point, that sounds like a good idea," said P'nina. She flipped a switch. "Readings haven't changed."

"A first reading on one of the Jidda targets," said Zvi. His forehead wrinkled. "Ziorah," he said.

"These aren't military targets, *Putz*. They're total nonsense! Some of these targets are little more than post offices. And an old ruin! What purpose could be served by the destruction of Metzada?"

Another target silently illuminated itself.

Zvi's forehead wrinkled. "Could they be trying to confuse us? Definite readings of launches, and definite targets."

"But they're destroying the things that *they* would need! Any occupying force is going to need food!"

Zvi settled back in his chair. "I don't think that there will be an occupying force. Remember the words of the Caliph? 'Our shrines are walked in sandaled feet. They must be purified so that this abomination cannot take place again.' "

"And that's why the UN got out?"

"Not officially, but probably."

P'nina straightened in her chair, looking at the readout screen. "Hebron!" she exclaimed. "A military target! Activate condition yellow and arm!"

Both of them activated a yellow switch. They watched as pilot lamps illuminated themselves. Machinery took over.

Twenty feet overhead, locks slammed shut in the irrigation canals. Underground pumps moved the trapped water into hidden tanks. Seals broke and sections of ditch formed on concrete and steel moved upward and over on powerful hydraulic jacks, uprooting orange and grapefruit trees.

"Five more launches from Tabriz."

P'nina's voice was swift and certain. The upper row of pilot lamps indicated that the portals were opened. "Arm!" she barked.

For the first time in close to three years, the enameled surfaces of the *Yoshua'im* gleamed in the early morning sun. Carriages moved upward, pointing noses toward the sky. The stubby wings began to unfold as soon as the *Yoshua'im* cleared the ground.

"The Old Man says that they've called their bases. They deny charges of launching an attack."

"My board reads a total of thirty launches. We shouldn't expect any strikes until six thirty five," put in Zvi.

"Yes, sir," said a voice. There was a pause. "I'll patch you through."

"This is the Minister of Defense. I request that you switch to your remaining backup computers at one minute intervals. I assume that you are already on primary backups for confirmation. Each of you is equipped with your own input system, so at this point, I would have to place the likelihood of a mistake at literally billions to one. Our condition is now yellow. If I don't see you again, die bravely, *Haverim Shelli*. Switch to secondary backups . . . Now!"

"Five from Mastura," said Zvi. "A definite pattern is showing itself. The launch areas are getting closer."

"And I suppose they sneaked in Hebron, Jaffa and Haifa thinking we wouldn't notice?" asked P'nina.

"You're forgetting that the *Yoshua'im* and our detection systems are secrets that we've kept for three years. They know there's a missile base here, but they don't know what kind. All of their bases are part of a single detection net. Things can go wrong on that. What the Persians and Arabs don't know is that our system, by its very nature, has a hundred backups with twenty separate systems of input. There is no mistake, *tziporah katanah*. This is the second Holocaust."

"After all this time," said P'nina. "They wouldn't let

their hatred die."

"*Six* from Mastura," corrected Zvi.

"Backup Gimmel," said a voice.

"No change," said P'nina. "It's in our hands now, *Putz*. Do we fire?"

Zvi shook his head. "Not until the last minute, P'nina."

Her face paled. "It's this waiting," she said. "Hey, *Putz?*"

"Yes, P'nina?"

"Could you call in a replacement? I'm going to be sick."

When he heard her words, Zvi swallowed the taste of his own bile. "No, P'nina. Use one of your drawers, if you have to. I want you here," he added truthfully. "With me."

A blush colored the paleness of her features.

Zvi turned back to the screen. "Five more Baghdad," he said.

With this, P'nina turned away from him and opened a drawer.

"Backup Heth," said an electronic voice.

"This is *Slik Mispar Aleph*. No change," said another distorted voice.

"*Slik Mispar Heth*. No change."

P'nina came up, wiping her mouth on a sleeve. A question mark was on her face.

"Final confirmations," Zvi answered her unspoken question. "We're being told when to fire."

Zvi picked up a mike and added his voice to the electronically sobered hysteria of the rest. "*Slik Mispar Gimmel*," he said. "No change."

"*Slik Mispar Heth*. No change."

The laughter of Zvi's father again filled the room. "There is nothing wrong with being a farmer!" the voice rang out. "If it weren't for farmers, what would we eat? Eh?"

"*Slik Mispar Yod Gimmel*. No change."

"Would I be happier as a farmer?" wondered Zvi.

"*Slik Mispar Yod Daleth*. No change."

"Would I be happier not knowing?"

Something teased at Zvi's brain. A hazy memory from three years in the past. The turtle. An affectionate name given a general with a beak of a nose that joined with his forehead.

"Fire!" came the order.

Automatically, he and P'nina both pressed the red firing stud.

In thirty eight sealed chambers, far overhead, nitric acid poured over cores of powdered aluminum in a rubber matrix. Solid fuel boosters roared to life. At a forty five degree angle, all of the missiles, save one, soared upward.

At two hundred feet, the missiles leveled off. Robot control surfaces adjusted themselves. Jet engines caught the wind and fired into keening life. Although they had all been launched in the same general direction, as winds caught aielerons and rudders, they began to turn.

"All birds off save one," commented P'nina. "*Yoshua Heth* is our dead bird."

'*Hatzav.*' The aged general who had trained them. Half his face had been destroyed by napalm in the war of '85. He wore a partial mask of black satin. But his nickname, 'The Turtle,' came from his large beak of a nose.

Hatzav had pulled him aside during a preliminary inspection of the installation. "Zvi," he had said in a dry whisper. "You are a bright boy! And very brave! I know that you are one we can trust with the responsibility you are given. It is not a usual thing that those in the *Slikim* should know their targets. But should you ever . . . May the Master of the Universe make it not so. Should you ever have to push that button, the target on this card should help you in your last moments. *Attah talmid tov,* Zvi. *Shalom.*"

"*Shalom,*" Zvi whispered back. He took the sealed envelope which the old man extended and put it into his pocket.

Zvi was pulled back to the present by another whisper.

"Oh, my God!!" said P'nina.

The second screen illuminated itself, doubling the number of Persian and Arab missiles. These were launched from Israel's very borders.

The speed with which Zvi rummaged through the coffee and tea stained reports increased. At last, his hand grasped the yellowed envelope.

"Zvi," P'nina said. "Number fifty three."

Zvi looked to see that the target under number fifty three was their own base.

"*Shalom aleichem,* Captain Sivan," said P'nina.

"*Aleichem shalom,* Captain Horowitz," Zvi returned. He held up a file card. "P'nina?" On the file card was written in *'Hatzav's'* spidery Hebrew script; "Target: Mecca!!"

The target couldn't have been Mecca itself. Israel's powerful religious party would never have allowed it. Probably the missile sites north of there. Zvi saw comprehension enter P'nina's face and the beginnings of a smile. Before the flesh was seared from his bones by a brilliant. . . .*FLASH!!!*

EDITOR'S INTRODUCTION TO:

HIS TRUTH GOES MARCHING ON
by
Jerry Pournelle

"Those who cannot remember the past are
condemned to repeat it."
—George Santayanna

The "future history"—a series of stories that share
common assumptions about the future—has become a
popular form of science fiction. My future history of the
CoDominium era assumes that the United States and the
Soviet Union continue to hate each other, but have
decided that it is better that they rule jointly than that
they share power with any third party.

The two major powers create the CoDominium as
their instrument for preserving the peace. Shortly thereafter, new means for space travel are discovered. New
worlds are settled: some by unwanted people sent away
against their will, some by adventurers, some by those
who will always seek the new frontiers. This story takes
place after the Second Exodus is well under way.

For some older readers, and younger ones with a better education than most get today, there will be haunt-
ingly familiar elements in this story, for it is frankly
derived from incidents that took place in a conflict of
the past. Nearly every incident in this story actually
happened to people much like those I picture here.

The Spanish Civil War was, to a generation of American liberals, a matter of evil vs. good. The Falangists
were evil; the Republicans were good; and there were no
compromises. Hemingway tried to show that it wasn't
that stark, although his sympathies remained with the
Republicans. George Orwell went into more detail. He
showed the naked cynicism of the Communist elements
of the Republic, but no one wanted to hear his message,
and to this day most believe that his (largely unread)
HOMAGE TO CATALONIA condemns only Franco.

The world could never forget Guernica, and to prove it we had Pablo Picasso's masterpiece hung in the Museum of Modern Art. Guernica was a Basque fishing village bombed by units of the Luftwaffe's Condor Legion. The town was largely destroyed, and the incident was seen as one more illustration of the utter moral worthlessness of both Spain and Germany. Picasso's violent painting, showing men and animals disjointed and scattered, was very effective in stirring up sympathy for the Republicans and hatred for both the Germans and Franco.

Later it came out that the town had been occupied by Republican military units, that at least part of the destruction came from the detonation of Republican munitions stored there, and there was a strong suggestion that retreating Republican engineers had dynamited other structures not damaged by the air raid. Whatever the truth of Guernica, the destruction there was not large compared to the damage sustained by Sidon, Tyre, and Beirut during the 1982 Israeli campaign, and was trivial compared to the damage done Tokyo in the fire raids, or the devastation of Hamburg and Dresden.

Those who wonder why I sometimes use historical models for stories are referred to the Santayanna quotation that opens this introduction.

HIS TRUTH GOES MARCHING ON
by
Jerry Pournelle

"As He died to make men holy, let us die to make men free. . . ."

The song echoed through the ship, along gray corridors stained with the greasy handprints of the thousands who had traveled in her before; through the stench of the thousands aboard, and the remembered smells of previous shiploads of convicts. Those smells were etched into the steel despite strong disinfectants which had only added their acrimony to the odor of too much humanity with too little water.

The male voices carried past crew work parties, who ignored them, or made sarcastic remarks, and into a tiny stateroom no larger than the bunk bed now hoisted vertical to the bulkhead to make room for a desk and chair.

Peter Owensford looked up to blank gray and beyond it to visions within his own mind. The men weren't singing very well, but they sang from their hearts. There was a faint buzzing discord from a loose rivet vibrating to a strong base. Owensford nodded to himself. The singer was Allan Roach, one-time professional wrestler, and Peter had marked him for promotion to noncom once they reached Santiago.

The trip from Earth to Thurstone takes three months in a Bureau of Relocation transport ship, and it had been wasted time for all of them. It was obvious to Peter that the CoDominium authorities aboard the ship knew that they were volunteers for the war. Why else would ninety-seven men voluntarily ship out for Santiago? It didn't matter, though. Political Officer Stromand was afraid of a trap. Stromand was always suspecting traps, and was desperate to "maintain secrecy"; as if there were any secrets to keep.

In all the three months Peter Owensford had held only a dozen classes. He'd found an empty compartment near the garbage disposal and assembled the men there; but Stromand had caught them. There had been a scene, with Stromand insisting that Peter call him "Commissar" and the men address him as "Sir." Instead, Peter addressed him as "Mister" and the men made it come out like "Comics-star." Stromand had become speechless with anger; but he'd stopped the meetings.

And Peter had ninety-six men who knew nothing of war; most had never fired a weapon in their lives. They were educated men, intelligent for the most part, students, workers, idealists; but it might have been better if they'd been ninety-six freakouts with a long history of juvenile gangsterism.

He went back to his papers, jotting notes on what must be done when they reached dirtside. At least he'd have some time to train them before they got into combat.

He'd need it.

Thurstone is usually described as a hot, dry copy of Earth and Peter found no reason to dispute that. The CoDominium Island is legally part of Earth, but Thurstone is thirty parsecs away, and travelers go through customs to land. The ragged group packed away whatever military equipment they had bought privately, and dressed in the knee breeches and tunics popular with businessmen in New York. Peter found himself just behind Allan Roach in the line to debark.

Roach was laughing.

"What's the joke?" Peter asked.

Roach turned and waved expressively at the men behind him. All ninety-six were scattered through the first two hundred passengers leaving the BuRelock ship, and they were all dressed identically. "Humanity League decided to save some money," Roach said. "What you reckon the CD makes of our comic-opera army?"

Whatever the CoDominium inspectors thought, they

did nothing, hardly glancing inside the baggage, and the
volunteers were hustled out of the CD building to the
docks. A small Russian in baggy pants sidled up to them.

"Freedom," he said. He had a thick accent.

"No passaran!" Commissar Stromand answered.

"I have tickets for you," the Russian said. "You will go
on the boat." He pointed to an excursion ship with peeling paint and faded gilt handrails.

"Man, he looks like he's lettin' go his last credit,"
Allan Roach muttered to Owensford.

Peter nodded. "At that, I'd rather pay for the tickets
than ride the boat. Must have been built when Thurstone
was first settled."

Roach shrugged and lifted his bags. Then, as an after-
thought, he lifted Peter's as well.

"You don't have to carry my goddam baggage," Peter
protested.

"That's why I'm going it, Lieutenant. I wouldn't carry
Stromand's." They went aboard the boat, and lined the
rails, looking out at Thurstone's bright skies. The volunteers were the only passengers, and the ship left the
docks to lumber across shallow seas. It was less than fifty kilometers to the mainland, and before the men really
believed they were out of space and onto a planet again,
they were in Free Santiago.

They marched through the streets from the docks.
People cheered, but a lot of volunteers had come through
those streets and they didn't cheer very loud. Owensford's men were no good at marching, and they had no
weapons; so Stromand ordered them to sing war songs.

They didn't know very many songs, so they always
ended up singing the Battle Hymn of the Republic. It
said all their feelings, anyway.

The ragged group straggled to the local parish church.
Someone had broken the cross and spire off the building, and turned the altar into a lecture desk. It was becoming dark when Owensford's troops were bedded
down in the pews.

"Lieutenant?"

Peter looked up from the dark reverie that had over-
taken him. Allan Roach and another volunteer stood in
front of him. "Yes?"

"Some of the men don't like bein' in here, Lieutenant. We got church members in the outfit."

"I see. What do you expect me to do about it?" Peter asked. "This is where we were sent." And why didn't someone meet us instead of having a kid hand me a note down at the docks? he wondered. But it wouldn't do to upset the men.

"We could bed down outside," Roach suggested.

"Nonsense. Superstitious garbage." The strident, bookish voice came from behind him, but Peter didn't need to look around to know who was speaking. "Free men have no need of that kind of belief. Tell me who is disturbed."

Allan Roach set his lips tightly together.

"I insist," Stromand demanded. "Those men need education, and I will provide it. We cannot have superstition within our company."

"Superstition be damned," Peter protested. "It's dark and gloomy and uncomfortable in here, and if the men want to sleep outside, let them."

"No," Stromand said.

"I remind you that I am in command here," Peter said. His voice was rising slightly and he fought to control it. He was only twenty-three standard years old, while Stromand was forty; and Peter had no experience of command. Yet he knew that this was an important issue, and the men were all listening.

"I remind *you* that political education is totally up to me," Stromand said. "It is good indoctrination for the men to stay in here."

"Crap." Peter stood abruptly. "All right, everybody outside. Camp in the churchyard. Roach, set up a night guard around the camp."

"Yes, sir," Allan Roach grinned.

Commissar Stromand found his men melting away rapidly; after a few minutes he followed them outside.

They were awakened early by an officer in synthileather trousers and tunic. He wore no badges of rank, but it was obvious to Peter that the man was a professional soldier. Someday, Peter thought, someday I'll look like that. The thought was cheering for some reason.

"Who's in charge here?" the man demanded.

Stromand and Owensford answered simultaneously.

The officer looked at both for a moment, then turned to Peter. "Name?"

"Lieutenant Peter Owensford."

"Lieutenant. And why might you be a lieutenant?"

"I'm a graduate of West Point, sir. And your rank?"

"Captain, sonny. Captain Anselm Barton, at your service, God help you. The lot of you have been posted to the Twelfth Brigade, second battalion, of which battalion I have the misfortune to be adjutant. Any more questions?" He glared at both Peter and the commissar, but before either could answer there was a roar and the wind whipped them with red dust; a fleet of trucks rounded the corner and stopped in front of the church.

"Okay," Barton shouted. "Into the trucks. You too, Mister Comics-Star. Lieutenant, you will ride in the cab with me . . . come on, come on, we haven't all day. Can't you get them to hop it, Owensford?"

No two of the trucks were alike. One Cadillac stood out proudly from the lesser breeds, and Barton went to it. After a moment Stromand took the unoccupied seat in the cab of the second truck, an old Fiat. Despite the early hour, the sun was hot and bright, and it was good to get inside.

The Cadillac ran smoothly, but had to halt frequently while the drivers worked on the others of the convoy. The Fiat could only get two or three centimeters above the road. Peter noted in wonder that there were ruts in the dirt track, and remarked on them.

"Sure," Barton said. "We've got wheeled transport. Lots of it. Animal-drawn wagons too. Tracked railroads. How much do you know about this place?"

"Not very much," Peter admitted.

"Least you know that," Barton said. He gunned the engine to get the Cadillac over a deeply pitted section of the road, and the convoy climbed up onto a ridge. Peter could look back and see the tiny port town, with its almost empty streets, and the blowing red dust.

"See that ridge over there?" Barton asked. He pointed to a thin blue line beyond the far lip of the saucer on the other side of the ridge. The air was so clear that Peter could see for sixty kilometers or more, and he had never seen farther than twenty; it was hard to judge distances.

"Yes, sir."

"That's it. Dons' territory beyond that line."

"We're not going straight there, are we? The men need training."

"You might as well be going to the lines for all the training they'll get. They teach you anything at the Point?"

"I learned something, I think." Peter didn't know what to answer. The Point had been "humanized" and he knew he hadn't had the military instruction that graduates had once received. "What I was taught, and a lot from books."

"We'll see." Barton took a plastic toothpick out of one pocket and stuck it into his mouth. Later, Peter would learn that many men developed that habit. "No hay tobacco" was a common notice on stores in Santiago. The first time he saw it, Allan Roach said that if they made their tobacco out of hay he didn't want any. "Long out of the Point?" Barton asked.

"Class of '93."

"Just out. U.S. Army didn't want you?"

"That's pretty personal," Peter said. The toothpick danced across smiling lips. Peter stared out at the rivers of dust blowing around them. "There's a new rule, now. You have to opt for CoDominium in your junior year. I did. But they didn't have any room for me in the CD services."

Barton grunted. "And the U.S. Army doesn't want any commie-coddling officers who'd take the CD over their own country."

"That's about it."

"Hadn't thought it was that bad yet. Sounds like things are coming apart back home."

Peter nodded to himself. "I think the U.S. will pull out of the CoDominium pretty soon."

The toothpick stopped its movement while Barton thought about that. "So meanwhile they're doing their best to gut the Fleet, eh? What do the damned fools think will happen to the colonies when there's no CD forces to keep order?"

Peter shrugged. They drove on in silence, with Barton humming something under his breath, a tune that Peter thought he would recognize if only Barton would make it loud enough to hear. Then he caught a murmured refrain. "Let's hope he brings our godson up, to don the Armay blue . . ."

Barton looked around at his passenger and grinned. "How many lights in Cullem Hall, Mister Dumbjohn?"

"Three hundred and forty lights, sir," Peter answered automatically. He looked for the ring, but Barton wore none. "What was your class, sir?"

"Seventy-two. Okay, the U.S. didn't want you, and the CD's disbanding regiments. There's other outfits. Falkenberg's recruiting . . ."

"I'm not a mercenary for hire." Peter's voice was stiffly formal.

"Oh, Lord. So you're here to help the downtrodden masses throw off the yoke of oppression. I might have known."

"But of course I'm here to fight slavery!" Peter protested. "Everyone knows about Santiago."

"Everybody knows about other places, too." The toothpick danced again. "Okay, you're a liberator of suffering humanity if that makes you feel better. God knows, anything makes a man feel better out here is okay. But to help *me* feel better, remember that you're a professional officer."

"I won't forget." They drove over another ridge. The valley beyond was no different from the one behind them, and there was another ridge at its end.

"What do you think those people out there want?" Barton said. He waved expressively.

"Freedom."

"Maybe to be left alone. Maybe they'd be happy if the lot of us went away."

"They'd be slaves. Somebody's got to help them—" Peter caught himself. There was no point to this, and he thought Barton was laughing at him.

Instead, the older man wore a curious expression. He kept the sardonic grin, but it was softened almost into a smile. "Nothing to be ashamed of, Pete. Most of us read those books about knighthood and all that. We wouldn't be in the services if we didn't have that streak in us. Just remember this, if you don't get over most of that, you won't last."

"Without something like that, I wouldn't want to last."

"Just don't let it break your heart when you find out different."

What is he talking about? Peter wondered. "If you feel that way about everything, why are you here? Why aren't you in one of the mercenary outfits?"

"Commissars ask that kind of question," Barton said. He gunned the motor viciously and the Cadillac screamed in protest.

It was late afternoon when they got to Tarazona. The town was an architectural melange, as if a dozen amateurs had designed it. The church, now a hospital, was Elizabeth III modern, the post office was American Gothic, and most of the houses were white stucco. The volunteers were unloaded at a plastisteel barracks that looked like a bad copy of the quad at West Point. It had sally ports, phony portcullis and all, and there were plastic medieval shields pressed into the cornices.

Inside there was trash in the corridors and blood on the floors. Peter set the men to cleaning up.

"About that blood," Captain Barton said. "Your men seem interested."

"First blood some of 'em have seen," Peter told him. Barton was still watching him closely. "All right. For me too."

Barton nodded. "Two stories about that blood. The Dons had a garrison here, made a stand when the Revolutionaries took the town. Some say the Dons slaughtered their prisoners here. Others say when the Republic took the barracks, our troops slaughtered the garrison."

Peter looked across the dusty courtyard and beyond the hills where the fighting was. It seemed a long way off. There was no sound, and the afternoon sun seemed unbearably hot. "Which do you think is true?"

"Both." Barton turned away toward the town. Then he stopped for a moment. "I'll be in the bistro after dinner. Join me if you get a chance." He walked on, his feet kicking up little clods of dust that blew across the road.

Peter stood a long time in the courtyard, staring across fields stretching fifty kilometers to the hills. The soil was red, and a hot wind blew dust into every crevice and hollow. The country seemed far too barren to be a focal point of the struggle for freedom in the known galaxy.

Thurstone was colonized early in the CoDominium period but it was too poor to attract wealthy corporations. The third Thurstone expedition was financed by the Carlist branch of the Spanish monarchy, and eventually Carlos XII brought a group of supporters to found Santiago. They were all of them malcontents.

This was hardly unusual. All of space is colonized with malcontents or convicts; no one else wants to leave Earth. The Santiago colonists were protesting the Bourbon restoration in Spain, or John XXVI's reunification of Christendom, or the cruel fates, or, perhaps, unhappy love affairs. They got the smallest and poorest of Thurstone's three continents, but they did well with what little they received.

For thirty years Santiago received no one who was not a voluntary immigrant from Spanish Catholic cultures. The Carlists were careful of those they let in, and there was plenty of good land for everyone. The Kingdom of St. James had little modern technology, and no one was very rich, but there were few who were very poor either.

Eventually the Population Control Commission designated Thurstone as a recipient planet, and the Bureau of Relocation began moving people there. All three governments on Thurstone protested, but unlike Xanadu or Danube, Thurstone had never developed a navy; a single frigate from the CoDominium Fleet convinced them they had no choice.

Two million involuntary colonists came in BuRelock ships to Thurstone. Convicts, welfare frauds, criminals, revolutionaries, rioters, street gangsters, men who'd offended a BuRelock clerk, men with the wrong color eyes, and those who were just plain unlucky; all of them bundled into unsanitary transport ships and hustled away from Earth. The other nations on Thurstone had friends in BuRelock and money to pay for favors; Santiago got the bulk of the new immigrants.

The Carlists tried. They provided transportation to unclaimed lands for all who wanted it and most who did not. The original Santiago settlers had fled from industry and had built very little; and now, suddenly, they were swamped with citydwellers of a different culture who had no thought of the land and less love for it. Suddenly, they had large cities.

In less than a decade the capital grew from a sleepy town to a sprawling heap of tenement shacks. The Carlists abolished part of the city; the shacks appeared on the other side of town. New cities grew from small towns. There was a desperate need for industry.

When the industries were built, the original settlers revolted. They had fled from industrialized life, and wanted no more of it. A king was deposed and an infant prince placed on his father's throne. The Cortez took government into its own hands. They enslaved everyone who did not pay his own way.

It was not called slavery, but "indebtedness for welfare service"; but debts were inheritable and transferable. Debts could be bought and sold on speculation, and everyone had to work off his debts.

In a generation half the population was in debt. In another the slaves outnumbered the free men. Finally the slaves revolted, and Santiago became a cause overnight: at least to those who'd ever heard of the place.

In the CoDominium Grand Senate, the U.S., listening to the other governments on Thurstone and the corporations who brought agricultural products from Santiago, supported the Carlists, but not strongly. The Soviet senators supported the Republic, but not strongly. The CD Navy was ordered to quarantine the war area.

The fleet had few ships for such a task. The Navy grounded all military aircraft in Santiago, and prohibited importation of any kind of heavy weapon. Otherwise they left the place alone to undergo years of indecisive warfare.

It was never difficult for the Humanity League to send volunteers to Santiago as long as they brought no weapons. As the men were not experienced in war, the League also sought trained officers to send with them.

They rejected mercenaries, of course. Volunteers must have the proper spirit to fight for freedom in Santiago.

Peter Owensford sat in the pleasant cool of the evening at a scarred table that might have been oak, but wasn't. Captain Anselm "Ace" Barton sat across from him, and a pitcher of dark red wine stood on the table.

"I thought they'd put me in the technical corps," Peter said.

"Speak Mandarin?" When Peter looked up in surprise, Barton continued, "Republic hired Xanadu techs. They don't have much equipment, what with the quarantine. Plenty of techs for what they do have."

"I see. So I'm infantry?"

Barton shrugged. "You fight, Pete. Just like me. They'll give you a company. The ones you brought, and maybe another hundred recruits. All yours. I guess you'll get that Stromand for political officer, too."

Peter grimaced. "What use is that?"

Barton looked around in an exaggerated manner. "Careful," he said. He wore a grin but his voice was serious. "Political officers are a lot more popular with the high command than we are. Don't forget that."

"From what I've seen the high command isn't very competent. . . ."

"Jesus," Barton said. "Look, Pete, they can have you shot for talking like that. This isn't any mercenary outfit with its own codes, you know. This is a patriotic war, and you'd better not forget it."

Peter stared at the packed clay floor of the patio, his lips set in a tight, thin line. He'd sat in this bistro, at this table, every night for a week now, and he was beginning to understand Barton's cynicism; but why was the man here at all? "There's not enough body armor for my men. The ones I've got. You say they'll give me more?"

"New group coming in tomorrow. No officer with them. Sure, they'll put 'em with you. Where else? Troops have to be trained."

"Trained!" Peter snorted in disgust. "We have enough Nemourlon to make armor for about half the troops, only I'm the only one in the company who knows how to do it. We've got no weapons, no optics, no communications—"

"Yeah, things are tough all over." Barton poured another glass of wine. "What'd you expect in a nonindustrial society quarantined by the CD?"

Peter slumped back into the hard wooden chair. "Yeah, I know. But—I can't even train them with what I have. Whenever I get the men assembled, Stromand interrupts to make speeches."

Barton smiled. "Colonel Cermak, our esteemed International Brigade Commander, thinks the American troops have poor morale. Obviously, the way to deal with that is to make speeches."

"They've got poor morale because they don't know how to fight."

"Another of Cermak's solutions to poor morale is to shoot people for defeatism," Barton said softly. "I've warned you, kid. I won't again."

"The only damn thing my men have learned in the last week is how to sing and which red-light houses are safe."

"More'n some do. Have another drink."

Peter nodded in dejection. "That's not bad wine."

"Right. Pretty good, but not good enough to export," Barton said. "Whole goddam country's that way, you know. Pretty good, but not quite good enough."

The next day they gave Peter Owensford 107 new men fresh from the U.S. and Earth. There was talk of adding another political officer to the company, but there wasn't one Cermak trusted.

Each night Ace Barton sat at the table in the bistro, but he didn't see Owensford all week. Then, as he was having his third glass of wine, Peter came in and sat across from him. The proprietor brought a glass, and Barton poured from the pitcher. "You look like you need that. Thought you were ordered to stay on, nights, to train the troops."

Peter drank. "Same story, Ace. Speeches. More speeches. I walked out. It was obvious I wasn't going to have anything to do."

"Risky," Barton said. They sat in silence as the older man seemed to decide something. "Ever think you're not needed, Pete?"

"They act that way, but I'm still the only man with any military training at all in the company. . . ."

"So what? The Republic doesn't need your troops. Not the way you think, anyway. Main purpose of the volunteers is to see the right party stays in control here."

Peter sat stiffly silent. He'd promised himself that he wouldn't react quickly to anything Barton said. There was no one else Peter felt comfortable with, despite the cynicism that Peter detested. "I can't believe that," he said finally. "The volunteers come from everywhere. They're not fighting to help any political party, they're here to set people free."

Barton said nothing. A red toothpick danced across his face, twirling up and about, and a sly grin broke across the square features.

"See, you don't even believe it yourself," Peter said.

"Could be. Pete, you ever think how much money they raise back in the States? Money from people who feel guilty about not volunteerin'?"

"No. There's no money here. You've seen that."

"There's money, but it goes to the techs," Barton said. "That, at least, makes sense. Xanadu isn't sending their sharp boys for nothing, and without them, what's the use of mudcrawlers like us?"

Peter leaned back in his chair. It made sense. "Then we've got pretty good technical support . . ."

"About as good as the Dons have. Which means neither side has a goddam thing. Either group gets a real edge that way, the war's over, right? But for the moment nobody's got a way past the CD quarantine, so the best way the Dons and the Republicans have to kill each other is with rifles and knives and grenades. Not very damn many of the latter, either."

"We don't even have the rifles."

"You'll get those. Meantime, relax. You've told Brigade your men aren't ready to fight. You've asked for weapons and more Nemourlon. You've complained about Stromand. You've done it all, now shut up before you get yourself shot as a defeatist. That's an order, Pete."

"Yes, sir."

"You'll get your war soon enough."

The trucks came back to Tarazona a week later. They carried coffin-shaped boxes full of rifles and bayonets from New Aberdeen, Thurstone's largest city. The rifles were covered with grease, and there wasn't any solvent to clean them with. Most were copies of Remington 2045 model automatic, but there were some Krupps and Skodas. Most of the men didn't know which ammunition fit their rifles.

"Not bad gear," Barton remarked. He turned one of the rifles over and over in his hands. "We've had worse."

"But I don't have much training in rifle tactics," Peter said.

Barton shrugged. "No power supplies, no maintenance ships, no base to support anything more complicated than chemical slug-throwers, Peter. Forget the rest of the crap you learned and remember that."

"Yes, sir."

Whistles blew, and someone shouted from the trucks. "Get your gear and get aboard!"

"But—" Owensford turned helplessly to Barton. "Get aboard for where?"

Barton shrugged. "I'd better get back to my area. Maybe they're moving the whole battalion up while we've got the trucks."

They were. The men who had armor put it on, and everyone dressed in combat synthileather. Most had helmets, ugly hemispheric models with a stiff spine over the most vulnerable areas. A few men had lost theirs, and they boarded the trucks without them.

The convoy rolled across the plains and into a greener farm area; then it got dark, and the night air chilled fast under clear, cloudless skies. The drivers pushed on, too fast without lights, and Peter sat in the back of the lead truck, his knees clamped tightly together, his teeth unconsciously beating out a rhythm he'd learned years before. No one talked.

At dawn they were in another valley. Trampled crops lay all around them, drying dead plants with green stalks.

"Good land," Private Lunster said. He lifted a clod and crumbled it between his fingers. "Very good land."

Somehow that made Peter feel better. He formed the men into ranks and made sure each knew how to load his weapon. Then he had each fire at a crumbling adobe wall, choosing a large target so that they wouldn't fail to hit it. More trucks pulled in and unloaded heavy generators and antitank lasers. When Owensford's men tried to get close to the heavy weapons the gunners shouted them away. It seemed to Peter that the gunners were familiar with the gear, and that was encouraging.

Everyone spoke softly, and when anyone raised his voice it was like a shout. Stromand tried to get the men to sing, but they wouldn't.

"Not long now, eh?" Sergeant Roach asked.

"I expect you're right," Peter told him, but he didn't

know, and went off to find the commissary truck. He wanted to be sure the men got a good meal that evening.

They moved them up during the night. A guide came to Peter and whispered to follow him, and they moved out across the unfamiliar land. Somewhere out there were the Dons with their army of peasant conscripts and mercenaries and family retainers. When they had gone fifty meters, they passed an old tree and someone whispered to them.

"Everything will be fine," Stromand's voice said from the shadows under the tree. "All of the enemy are politically immature. Their vacqueros will run away, and their peasant conscripts will throw away their weapons. They have no reason to be loyal."

"Why the hell has the war gone on three years?" someone whispered behind Peter.

He waited until they were long past the tree. "Roach, that wasn't smart. Stromand will have you shot for defeatism."

"He'll play hell doing it, Lieutenant. You, man, pick up your feet. Want to fall down that gully?"

"Quiet," the guide whispered urgently. They went on through the dark night, down a slope, then up another, past men dug into the hillside. They didn't speak to them.

Peter found himself walking along the remains of a railroad, with the ties partly gone and all the rails removed. Eventually the guide halted. "Dig in here," he whispered. "Long live freedom."

"No passaran!" Stromand answered.

"Please be quiet," the guide urged. "We are within earshot of the enemy."

"Ah," Stromand answered. The guide turned away and the political officer began to follow him.

"Where are you going?" Corporal Grant asked in a loud whisper.

"To report to Major Harris," Stromand answered.

"The battalion commander ought to know where we are."

"So should we," a voice said.

"Who was that?" Stromand demanded. The only answer with a juicy raspberry.

"That bastard's got no right," a voice said close to Peter.

"Who's there?"

"Rotwasser, sir." Rotwasser was company runner. The job gave him the nominal rank of monitor but he had no maniple to command. Instead he carried complaints from the men to Owensford.

"I can spare the PO better than anyone else," Peter whispered. "I'll need you here, not back at battalion. Now start digging us in."

It was cold on the hillside, but digging kept the men warm enough. Dawn came slowly at first, a gradually brightening light without warmth. Peter took out his light-amplifying binoculars and cautiously looked out ahead. The binoculars were a present from his mother and the only good optical equipment in the company.

The countryside was cut into small, steep-sided ridges and valley. Allan Roach lay beside Owensford and when it became light enough to see, the sergeant whistled softly. "We take that ridge in front of us, there's another just like it after that. And another. Nobody's goin' to win this war that way. . . ."

Owensford nodded silently. There were trees in the valley below, oranges and dates imported from Earth mixed in with native fruit trees as if a giant had spilled seeds across the ground. A whitewashed adobe peasant house stood gutted by fire, the roof gone.

Zing! Something that might have been a hornet but wasn't buzzed angrily over Peter's head. There was a flat crack from across the valley, then more of the angry buzzes. Dust puffs sprouted from the earthworks they'd thrown up during the night.

"Down!" Peter ordered.

"What are they trying to do, kill us?" Allan Roach shouted. There was a chorus of laughs. "Sir, why didn't they use IR on us in the dark? We should have stood out in this cold—"

Peter shrugged. "Maybe they don't have any. We don't."

The men who'd skimped on their holes dug in deeper, throwing the dirt out onto the ramparts in front of them, laughing as they did. It was very poor technique, and Peter worried about artillery, but nothing happened. The enemy was about four hundred meters away, across the valley and stretched out along a ridge identical to the one Peter held. No infantry that ever lived could have taken a position by charging across that valley. Both sides were safe until something heavier was brought up.

One large-caliber gun was trained on their position. It fired on anything that moved. There was also a laser, with several mirrors that could be moved about between flashes. The laser itself was safe, and the mirrors probably were also because the monarchists never fired twice from the same position.

The men shot at the guns and at where they thought the mirror was anyway until Peter made them quit wasting ammunition. It wasn't good for morale to lie there and not fight back, though.

"I bet I can locate that goddam gun," Corporal Bassinger told Peter. "I got the best eyesight in the company."

Peter mentally called up Bassinger's records. Two ex-wives and an acknowledged child by each. Volunteered after being an insurance man in Brooklyn for years. "You can't spot that thing."

"Sure I can, Lieutenant. Loan me your glasses, I'll spot it sure."

"All right. Be careful, they're shooting at anything they can see."

"I'm careful."

"Let me see, man!" somebody shouted. Three men clustered in the trench around Bassinger. "Let us look!" "Don't be a hog, we want to see too." "Comrade, let us look—"

"Get away from here," Bassinger shouted. "You heard the lieutenant, it's dangerous to look over the ramparts."

"What about you?"

"I'm an observer. Besides, I'm careful." He crawled into position and looked out through a little slot he'd cut away in the dirt in front of him. "See, it's safe enough. I think I see—"

Bassinger was thrown back into the trench. The shattered glasses fell on top of him, and he had already ceased breathing when they heard the shot that hit him in the eye.

By the next morning two men had toes shot off and had to be evacuated.

They lay on the hill for a week. Each night they lost a few more men to minor casualties that could not possibly have been inflicted by the enemy; then Stromand had two men with foot injuries shot by a squad of military police he brought up from staff headquarters.

The injuries ceased, and the men lay sullenly in the trenches until the company was relieved.

They had two days in a small town near the front, then the officers were called to a meeting. The briefing officer had a thick accent, but it was German, not Spanish. The briefing was for the Americans and it was held in English.

"Ve vill have a full assault, with all International volunteers to move out at once. Ve vill use infiltration tactics."

"What does that mean?" Captain Barton demanded.

The staff officer looked pained. "Ven you break through their lines, go straight to their technical areas and disrupt them. Ven that is done, the var is over."

"Where are their technical corpsmen?"

"You vill be told after you have broken through their lines."

The rest of the briefing made no more sense to Peter. He walked out with Barton after they were dismissed. "Looked at your section of the line?" Barton asked.

"As much as I can," Peter answered. "Do you have a decent map?"

"No. Old CD orbital photographs, and some sketches. No better than what you have."

"What I did see looks bad," Peter said. "There's an olive grove, then a hollow I can't see into. Is there cover in there?"

"You better patrol and find out."

"You will ask the battalion commander for permission to conduct patrols," a stern voice said from behind them.

"You better watch that habit of walking up on people, Stromand," Barton said. "One of these days somebody's not going to realize it's you." He gave Peter a pained looked. "Better ask."

Major Harris told Peter that Brigade had forbidden patrols. They might alert the enemy of the coming attack and surprise was needed.

As he walked back to his company area, Peter reflected that Harris had been an attorney for the Liberation Party before he volunteered to go to Santiago. They were to move out the next morning.

The night was long. The men were very quiet, polishing weapons and talking in whispers, drawing meaningless diagrams in the mud of the dugouts. About halfway through the night new volunteers joined the company. They had no equipment beyond rifles, and they had left the port city only two days before. Most came from Churchill, but because they spoke English and the trucks were coming to this section, they had been sent along.

Major Harris called the officers together at dawn. "The Xanadu techs have managed to assemble some rockets," he told them. "They'll drop them on the Dons before we move out. Owensford, you will move out last. You will shoot any man who hasn't gone before you do."

"That's my job," Stromand protested.

"You will be needed to lead the men," Harris said. "The bombardment will come at 0815 hours. Do you all have proper timepieces?"

"No, sir," Peter said. "I've only got a watch that counts Earth time. . . ."

"Hell," Harris muttered. "Okay, Thurstone's hours are 1.08 Earth hours long. You'll have to work it out from that. . . ." He looked confused.

"No problem," Peter assured him.

"Okay. Back to your areas."

Zero hour went past with no signals. Another hour passed. Then a Republican brigade to the north began firing, and a few moved out of their dugouts and across the valley floor.

A ripple of fire and flashing mirrors colored the ridge beyond as the enemy began firing. The Republican troops were cut down, and the few not hit scurried back into their shelters.

"Fire support!" Harris shouted. Owensford's squawk box made unintelligible sounds, effectively jammed as were all electronics Peter had seen on Santiago, but he heard the order passed down the line. His company fired at the enemy, and the monarchists returned it.

Within minutes it was clear that the enemy had total dominance in the area. A few large rockets rose from somewhere behind the enemy lines and crashed randomly into the Republican positions. There were more flashes across the sky as the Xanadu technicians backtracked the enemy rockets and returned counterfire. Eventually the shooting stopped for lack of targets.

It was 1100 by Peter's watch when a series of explosions lit the lip of the monarchist ramparts. Another wave of rockets fell among the enemy, and the Republicans to the north began to charge forward.

"Ready to move out!" Peter shouted. He waited for orders.

There was nearly a minute of silence. No more rockets fell on the enemy. Then the ridge opposite rippled with fire again, and the Republicans began to go down or scramble back to their positions.

The alert tone sounded on Peter's squawk box and he lifted it to his ear. Amazingly, he could hear intelligible speech. Someone at headquarters was speaking to Major Harris.

"The Republicans have already advanced half a kilometer. They are being slaughtered because you have not moved your precious Americans in support."

"Bullshit!" Harris's voice had no tones in the tiny speaker. "The Republicans are already back in their dugouts. The attack has failed."

"It has not failed. You must show what high morale can do. Your men are all volunteers. Many Republicans are conscripts. Set an example for them."

"But I tell you the attack has failed."

"Major Harris, if your men have not moved out in five minutes I will send the military police to arrest you as a traitor."

The box went back to random squeals and growls; then the whistles blew and orders were passed down the line. "Move out."

Peter went from dugout to dugout. "Up and at them. Jarvis, if you don't get out of there I'll shoot you. You three, get going." He saw that Allan Roach was doing the same thing.

When they reached the end of the line, Roach grinned at Peter. "We're all that's left, now what?"

"Now we move out too." They crawled forward, past the lip of the hollow that had sheltered them. Ten meters beyond that they saw Major Harris lying very still.

"Captain Barton's in command of the battalion," Peter said.

"Wonder if he knows it? I'll take the left side, sir, and keep 'em going, shall I?"

"Yes." Now he was more alone than ever. He went on through the olive groves, finding men and keeping them moving ahead of him. There was very little fire from the enemy. They advanced fifty meters, a hundred, and reached the slope down into the hollow beyond. It was an old vineyard, and the stumps of the vines reached out of the ground like old women's hands.

They were well into the hollow when the Dons fired. Four of the newcomers from Churchill were just ahead of Owensford. When the volley lashed their hollow they hit the dirt in perfect formation. Peter crawled forward to compliment them on how well they'd learned the training-book exercises. All four were dead.

He was thirty meters into the hollow. In front of him was a network of red stripes weaving through the air a meter above the ground. He'd seen it at the Point, an interlocking network of crossfire guided by laser beams. Theoretically the Xanadu technicians should be able to locate the mirrors, or even the power plants, but the network hung there, unmoving.

Some of the men didn't know what it was and charged into it. After a while there was a little wall of dead men and boys at its edge. No one could advance, and snipers began to pick off any of the still figures that tried to move. Peter lay there, wondering if any of the other companies were making progress. His men lay behind bodies for the tiny shelter a dead comrade might give. One by one his troops died as they lay there in the open, in the bright sunshine of a dying vineyard.

In late afternoon it began to rain, first a few drops, then harder, finally a storm that cut off all visibility. The men could crawl back to their dugouts and they did. There were no orders for a retreat.

Peter found small groups of men and sent them out for wounded. It was hard to get men to go back into the hollow, even in the driving rainstorm, and he had to go with them or they would melt away to vanish in the mud and gloom. Eventually there were no more wounded to find.

The scene in the trenches was a shambled hell of bloody mud. Men fell into the dugouts and lay where they fell, too tired and scared to move. Some were wounded and died there in the mud, and others fell on top of them, trampling the bodies down and out of sight because no one had energy to move them. Peter was the only officer in the battalion until late afternoon. The company was his now and the men were calling him "Captain."

Then Stromand came into the trenches carrying a bundle.

Incredibly, Allan Roach was unwounded. The huge wrestler stood in Stromand's path. "What is that?" he demanded.

"Leaflets. To boost morale," Stromand said nervously.

Roach stood immobile. "While we were out there you were off printing leaflets?"

"I had orders," Stromand said. He backed nervously away from the big sergeant. His hand rested on a pistol butt.

"Roach," Peter said calmly. "Help me with the wounded, please."

Roach stood in indecision. Finally he turned to Peter. "Yes, sir."

At dawn Peter had eighty effectives to hold the lines. The Dons could have walked through during the night if they'd tried, but they were strangely quiet. Peter went from dugout to dugout, trying to get a count of his men. Two hundred wounded sent to rear areas. He could count a hundred thirteen dead. That left ninety-four vanished. Died, deserted, ground into the mud; he didn't know.

There hadn't been any general attack. The International volunteer commander had thought that even though the general attack was called off, this would be a splendid opportunity to show what morale could do. It had done that, all right.

The Republican command was frantic. The war was stalemated; which meant the superior forces of the Dons were slowly grinding them down. The war for freedom would soon be lost.

In desperation they sent a large group to the south where the front was stable. The last attack had been planned to the last detail; this one was to depend entirely on surprise. Peter's remnants were reinforced with pieces of other outfits and fresh volunteers, and sent against the enemy. They were on their own.

The objective was an agricultural center called Zaragoza, a small town amid olive groves and vineyards. Peter's column moved through the groves to the edge of town. Surprise was complete.

The battle did not last long. A flurry of firing, quick advances, and the enemy retreated, leaving Peter's company with a clear victory. From the little communications he could arrange, his group had advanced further than any other. They were the spearhead of freedom in the south.

They marched in to cheering crowds. His army looked like scarecrows, but women held their children up to see their liberators. It made it all worthwhile: the stupidity of the generals, the heat and mud and cold and dirt and lice, all of it forgotten in triumph.

More troops came in behind them, but Peter's company camped at the edge of their town, their place of freedom. The next day the army would advance again; if the war could be made fluid, fought in quick battles of fast-moving men, it might yet be won. Certainly, Peter thought, certainly the people of Santiago were waiting for them. They'd have support from the population. How long could the Dons hold?

Just before dark they heard shots in the town.

He brought his duty squad on the run, dashing through the dusty streets, past the pockmarked adobe walls to the town square. The military police were there.

"Never saw such pretty soldiers," Allan Roach said.

Peter nodded.

"Captain, where do you think they got those shiny boots? And the new rifles? Seems we never have good equipment for the troops, but the police always have more than enough. . . ."

A small group of bodies lay like broken dolls at the foot of the churchyard wall. The priest, the mayor, and three young men. "Monarchists. Carlists," someone whispered. Some of the townspeople spat on the bodies.

An old man was crouched beside one of the dead. He held the youthful head cradled in his hands and blood poured through his fingers. He looked at Peter with dull eyes. "Why are you here?" he asked. "Are there not richer worlds for you to conquer?"

Peter turned away without answering. He could think of nothing to say.

"Captain!"

Peter woke to Allan Roach's urgent whisper.

"Cap'n, there's something moving down by the stream. Not the Dons. Mister Stromand's with 'em, above five men. Officers, I think, from headquarters."

Peter sat upright. He hadn't seen Stromand since the disastrous attack three hundred kilometers to the north. The man wouldn't have lasted five minutes in combat among his former comrades. "Anyone else know?"

"Albers, nobody else. He called me."

"Let's go find out what they want. Quietly, Allan." As they walked silently in the hot night, Peter frowned to himself. What were staff officers doing in his company area, near the vanguard of the advancing Republican forces? And why hadn't they called him?

They followed the small group down the nearly dry creekbed to the town wall. When their quarry halted, they stole closer until they could hear.

"About here," Stromand's bookish voice said. "This will be perfect."

"How long do we have?" Peter recognized the German accent of the staff officer who'd briefed them. The next voice was even more of a shock.

"Two hours. Enough time, but we must go quickly." It was Cermak, second in command of the volunteer forces. "It is set?"

"Yes."

"Hold it." Peter stepped out from the shadows, his rifle held to cover the small group. Allan Roach moved quickly away from him so that he also threatened them. "Identify yourselves."

"You know who we are, Owensford," Stromand snapped.

"Yes. What are you doing here?"

"That is none of your business, Captain," Cermak answered. "I order you to return to your company area and say nothing about seeing us."

"In a minute. Major, if you continue moving your hand toward your pistol, Sergeant Roach will cut you in half. Allan, I'm going to have a look at what they were carrying. Cover me."

"Right."

"You can't!" The German staff officer moved toward Peter.

Owensford reacted automatically, the rifle swinging upward in an uppercut that caught the German under the chin. The man fell with a strangled cry and lay still in the dirt. Everyone stood frozen; it was obvious that Cermak and Stromand were more worried about being heard than Peter was.

"Interesting," Peter said. He squatted over the device they'd set by the wall. "A bomb of some kind, from the timers—Jesus!"

"What is it, Cap'n?"

"A fission bomb," Peter said slowly. "They were going to leave a fission bomb here. To detonate in two hours, did you say?" he asked conversationally. His thoughts whirled, but he could find no explanation; and he was very surprised at how calm he was acting. "Why?"

No one answered.

"Why blow up the only advancing force in the Republican army?" Peter asked wonderingly. "They can't be traitors. The Dons wouldn't have these on a platter—but—Stromand, is there a new CD warship in orbit here? New fleet forces to stop this war?"

More silence.

"What does it mean?" Allan Roach asked. His rifle was steady, and there was an edge to his voice. "Why use an atom bomb on their own men?"

"The ban," Peter said. "One thing the CD does enforce. No nukes." He was hardly aware that he spoke aloud. "The CD inspectors will see the spearhead of the Republican army destroyed by nukes, and think the Dons did it. They're the only ones who could benefit from it. So the CD cleans up on the Carlists, and these bastards end up in charge when the fleet pulls out. That's it, isn't it? Cermark? Stromand?''

"Of course," Stromand said. "You fool, come with us, then. Leave the weapons in place. We're sorry we didn't think we could trust you with the plan, but it was just too important . . . it means winning the war.''

"At what price?''

"A low price. A few battalions of soldiers and one village. Far more are killed every week. A comparatively bloodless victory.''

Allan Roach spat viciously. "If that's freedom, I don't want any. You ask any of them?" He waved toward the village.

Peter remembered the cheering crowds. He stooped down to the weapon and examined it closely. "Any secret to disarming this? If there is, you're standing as close to it as I am.''

"Wait," Stromand shouted. "Don't touch it, leave it, come with us. You'll be promoted, you'll be a hero of the movement—''

"Disarm it or I'll have a try," Peter said. He retrieved his rifle and waited.

After a moment Stromand bent down to the bomb. It was no larger than a small suitcase. He took a key from his pocket and inserted it, then turned dials. "It is safe now.''

"I'll have another look," Peter said. He bent over the weapon. Yes, a large iron bar had been moved through the center of the device, and the fissionables couldn't come together. As he examined it there was a flurry of activity.

"Hold it!" Roach commanded. He raised his rifle; but Political Officer Stromand had already vanished into the darkness. "I'll go after him, Cap'n." They could hear thrashing among the olive trees nearby.

"No. You'd never catch him. Not without making a big stir. And if this story gets out, the whole Republican cause is finished.''

"You are growing more intelligent," Cermak said. "Why not let us carry out our plan now?''

"I'll be damned," Peter said. "Get out of here, Cermak. Take your staff carrion with you. And if you send the military police after me or Sergeant Roach, just be damned sure this story—and the bomb—will get to the CD inspectors. Don't think I can't arrange it."

Cermak shook his head. "You are making a mistake—"

"The mistake is lettin' you go," Roach said. "Why don't I shoot him? Or cut his throat?"

"There'd be no point in it," Peter said. "If Cermak doesn't stop him, Stromand will be back with the MP's. No, let them go."

They advanced thirty kilometers in the next three days, crossing the valley with its dry river of sand at the bottom, moving swiftly into the low brush on the other side, up to the top of the ridge: and they were halted. Artillery and rockets exploded all around them. There was no one to fight, only unseen enemies on the next ridge, and the fire poured into their positions for three days.

The enemy fire was holding them, while the glare and heat of Thurstone's sun punished them. Men became snowblind, and wherever they looked there was only one color, fiery yellow. When grass and trees caught fire they could hardly notice the difference.

When the water was gone they retreated. There was nothing else to do. Back across the valley, past the positions they'd won, halting to let other units get past while they held the road; and on the seventh day after they left it, they were back on the road where they'd jumped off into the valley.

There was no organization. Peter was the only officer among 172 men of a battalion that had neither command nor staff; just 172 men too tired to care.

"We've the night, anyway," Roach said. He sat next to Peter and took out a cigarette. "Last tobacco in the battalion, Cap'n. Share?"

"No, thanks. Keep it all."

"One night to rest," Roach said again. "Seems like forever, a whole night without anybody shooting at us."

Fifteen minutes later Peter's radio squawked. He listened, hearing the commands over static and jamming. "Call the men together," Peter ordered when he'd heard it out.

"It's this way," he told them. "We still hold Zaragoza.

There's a narrow corridor into the town, and unless somebody gets down there to hold it open, we'll lose the village. If that goes, the whole position in the valley's lost."

"Cap'n, you can't ask it!" The men were incredulous. "Go back down into there? You can't make us do that!"

"No. I can't make you. But remember Zaragoza? Remember how the people cheered us when we marched in? It's our town. Nobody else set those people free. We did. And there's nobody else who can go help keep them free, either. No other reinforcements. Will we let them down?"

"We can't," Allan Roach said. "It needs doing. I'll come with you, Cap'n."

One by one the others got to their feet. The ragged column marched down the side of the ridge, out of the cool heights where their water was assured, down into the valley of the river of sand.

They were half a kilometer from the town at dawn. Troops were streaming down the road toward them, others running through the olive groves on both sides.

"Tanks!" someone shouted. "Tanks are coming!"

It was too late. The enemy armor had passed around Zaragoza and was closing on them fast. Other troops followed behind. Peter felt a bitter taste and prepared to dig into the olive groves. It would be their last battle.

An hour later they were surrounded. Two hours passed as they fought to hold the useless olive groves. The tanks had long since passed their position and gone but the enemy was still all around them. The shooting stopped, and silence lay through the grove.

Peter crawled across the perimeter of his command: a hundred meters, no more. He had fewer than fifty men.

Allan Roach lay in a shallow hole at one edge. Ripe olives shaken from the trees fell into it with him, partially covering him, and when Peter came close, the sergeant laughed. "Makes you feel like a salad," he said, brushing away more olives. "What do we do, Cap'n? Why you think they quit shooting?"

"Wait and see."

It didn't take long. "Will you surrender?" a voice called-ed.

"To whom?" Peter demanded.

"Captain Hans Ort, Second Friedland Armored Infantry."

"Mercenaries," Peter hissed. "How did they get here? The CD was supposed to have a quarantine. . . ."

"Your position is hopeless, and you are not helping your comrades by holding it," the voice shouted.

"We're keeping you from entering the town!" Peter answered.

"For a while. We can go in any time, from the other side. Will you surrender?"

Peter looked helplessly at Roach. He could hear the silence among the men. They didn't say anything, and Peter was proud of them. But, he thought, I don't have any choice. "Yes," he shouted.

The Friedlanders wore dark green uniforms, and looked very military compared to Peter's scarecrows. "Mercenaries?" Captain Ort asked.

Peter opened his mouth to answer defiance. A voice interrupted him. "Of course they're mercenaries." Ace Barton limped up to them.

Ort looked at them suspiciously. "Very well. You wish to speak with them, Captain Barton?"

"Sure. I'll get some of 'em out of your hair," Barton said. He waited until the Friedlander was gone. "Pete, you almost blew it. If you'd said you were volunteers, Ort would have turned you over to the Dons. This way, he keeps you. And believe me, you'd rather be with him."

"What are you doing here?" Peter demanded.

"Captured up north," Barton said. "By these guys. There's a recruiter for Falkenberg's outfit back in the rear area. I signed up, and they've got me out hunting good men for Falkenberg. You want to join, you can. We get off this planet next week; and of course you won't fight here."

"I told you, I'm not a mercenary—"

"What are you?" Barton asked. "Nothing you can go back to. Best you can look forward to is being interned. Here, come on to town. You don't have to make up your mind just yet." They walked through the olive groves toward the Zaragoza town wall. "You opted for CD service," Barton said.

"Yes. Not to be one of Falkenberg's—"

"You think everything's going to be peaceful out here when the CoDominium fleet pulls out?"

"No. But I like to choose my wars."

"You want a cause. So did I, once. Now I'll settle for what I've got. Two things to remember, Pete. In an outfit like Falkenberg's, you don't choose your enemies, but you'll never have to break your word. And just what will you do for a living now?"

He had no answer to that. They walked on in silence.

"Somebody's got to keep order out here," Barton said. "Think about it."

They had reached the town. The Friedland mercenaries hadn't entered it; now a column of monarchist soldiers approached. Their boots were dusty and their uniforms torn, so that they looked little different from the remnants of Peter's command.

As the monarchists reached the town gates, the village people ran out of their houses. They lined both sides of the streets, and as the Carlists entered the public square, there was a loud cheer.

EDITOR'S INTRODUCTION TO:

THOR: ORBITAL WEAPON SYSTEM

by

Weapons Committee

Citizen's Advisory Council on

National Space Policy

The second Council meeting was in the Fall of 1981, and was also held in the home of Larry and Marilyn Niven. Even more experts attended, so that their house nearly burst at the seams. One session featured Dr. Hans Mark, Deputy Administrator of NASA and former Secretary of the Air Force. Dr. Mark attended as an observer only, but the Council was able to present its views directly to him.

The first Council meeting concentrated largely on space industries. The second examined the military potential of space. This paper, outlining a futuristic new weapon system, was one result. A few months after the meeting, the Falkland Islands crisis erupted.

THOR: ORBITAL WEAPON SYSTEM

Committee on Space Weapons
Citizen's Advisory Council on
National Space Policy

One of the most difficult security missions which the United States must accomplish is the protection of our interests around the globe. Incidents like the North Korean seizure of the *USS Pueblo* have demonstrated our weakness in not being able to respond quickly and authoritatively in remote locations. Our only solution to this problem so far has been the naval carrier task force. Carrier-based aircraft can project military force to protect our citizens and allies in remote regions of the world. Unfortunately, the high cost and vulnerability of nuclear carriers and their required aircraft and support fleets make them an unattractive solution.

We now have the technology to produce a space-based weapon system which can perform the same mission for less cost. The space system is also much less vulnerable and can respond faster to any location on the globe than a dozen carrier task forces spread throughout the oceans of the world. The proposed name for this weapon is THOR, for it would literally give the United States the power to call down lightning bolts from the heavens upon its enemies.

Brief Description of THOR

The basis of the THOR weapon system is the fundamental nature of any object orbiting the Earth. To balance the force of gravity, a satellite two hundred miles above the surface must travel at a speed of seventeen thousand five hundred miles per hour. At this speed, the satellite travels around the Earth once every ninety minutes. With a hundred satellites in orbits near this altitude and traveling in random orbital inclinations, one of the satellites will pass over any given location on Earth every thirty minutes. With a thousand satellites, the timing between satellites overhead is less than ten minutes. The basic physics of orbital motion gives us our global coverage; it also gives us the weapon. The extremely high velocity of a satellite in orbit gives it a tremendous amount of kinetic energy. If a one pound object moving at orbital velocity ran into a stationary target, the energy released in the impact will be the equivalent of exploding almost ten pounds of TNT.

The THOR system is composed of a thousand or more cheap satellites, each made up of a bundle of projectiles, guidance and communications electronics, and a simple rocket engine. When a crisis arises, a THOR command center (on Earth or in space) sends a signal to the appropriate THOR satellite. The satellite then orients itself. At the proper time, the rocket engine fires to deorbit the satellite. When the rocket engine burns out, the individual THOR projectiles are dispersed from the satellite in a prearranged pattern. Instead of blunt noses, the projectiles have sharp points which slice down through the atmosphere, losing little velocity. Just seconds before impact, a (relatively dumb) terminal guidance sensor looks for a metallic or other preprogrammed target and steers toward it. The result is spectacular: a bundle of tens or hundreds of twenty pound projectiles streak down at four miles per second to strike targets with the explosive equivalent of two hundred pound bombs each. In five seconds the action is over, and the enemy doesn't know what hit them. All that remains is dozens of luminous trails, each angling downward to a slowly dissipating explosion cloud.

The major advantage of the THOR space weapon is its capability for quick response while remaining highly survivable. Even if an enemy were to detonate one or more nuclear devices in space in an attempt to destroy THOR, there are a thousand or more widely scattered satellites he must destroy. Because the satellites are at different altitudes and have different orbital inclinations, any holes produced in the global coverage by a nuclear explosion are filled in after several hours by the orbital motions of the satellites.

An individual THOR satellite is not easy to detect or to destroy. The satellite can be cocooned in foam, which would be difficult to detect with radar anyway and could be shaped to make detection even more difficult (stealth satellites!). The foam would insulate the satellite against the heat and shock of nuclear explosions or laser beams. All the satellite has to do is float around in its orbit and wait for the command to strike a target.

Each individual projectile is a slender, dense metal rod. No explosive or firing mechanism is necessary. The jet of metal particles produced when a shaped charge warhead detonates is traveling at about the same velocity as a THOR projectile when striking a target. The six-inch diameter warhead from a TOW anti-tank missile will punch through the armor of a heavy tank. The jet of metal from the TOW warhead weighs only a fraction of an ounce; a THOR projectile weighs over twenty pounds! Such a projectile can easily punch through the deck of a battleship and blow a hole through the bottom, blast a crater in a runway, or destroy a bunker. A rain of a hundred THOR projectiles over an area less than a mile across would stop an armored column, halt an amphibious landing, or destroy a supply depot.

The capability of the THOR projectile is not limited to armored targets. Forming the projectile from dense uranium metal produces an incendiary blast when the white hot metal vapor produced on impact ignites in the air. Such a uranium missile could penetrate the reinforced concrete cover of a missile silo and explode inside as the cloud of uranium vapor detonates. If the projectile were composed of an outer shell with sand-sized particles inside, it could be designed to explode and disperse the particles just before impact. The metal particles would instantly vaporize, with the resulting shock wave flattening troops, aircraft, or other targets much like the fuel-air explosive bombs presently in service.

Advantages of the THOR Space Weapon

The advantages of the THOR weapon system are its low cost, global coverage, quick reaction time, and survivability. Unlike an aircraft carrier task force, THOR does not need thousands of highly trained pilots, sailors, and technicians who must spend long months away from home. THOR does not require expensive foreign aid payments to secure overseas bases. THOR does not have a single capital ship as a vulnerable target. THOR is composed of many cheap, hardened satellite packages which act only on command. The system capabilities can be built up slowly but can act quickly in a crisis. All of the system's capability is useful; none of the projectiles need to be stockpiled or stored and then shipped to the battlefront.

No major (and vulnerable) ground facilities are necessary, unlike ballistic missiles with silos or other fixed launchers. Every time the Space Shuttle goes up with the payload bay partially full, we could toss in a THOR satellite or two and build up the system gradually and cheaply. The command stations and links for THOR could use multiple channels, existing relay satellites, and several orbital or ground control stations.

THOR gives global coverage at a time when we are uncertain from one minute to the next where a crisis may erupt. THOR is non-nuclear and surgically precise. The velocity of the projectiles is so high that interception would be impossible before they strike their targets. Before our enemies can react, THOR has struck them down.

Further Study of THOR

Several aspects of the THOR space weapon system must be studied before any commitment to development of the system can be made. Some are strategic, some are political, and some are technical.

We should begin to consider the effects which the existence of the THOR system would produce on our own and our opponents' defense planning. A firm commitment to the THOR system would involve billions of dollars of defense funds. It will be opposed by those with vested interests in the current weapons systems which THOR might replace and those who oppose any change, whatever the justification. As benefits, THOR may permit the United States to reduce conventional forces in Europe and decrease the number of large carriers built.

We must consider the impact of THOR on world politics. We would not want to register the orbital parameters of each THOR satellite with the U.N. as is presently required by treaty. The Soviets might consider THOR a strategic weapon aimed at the destruction of their land and sea based ICBM's. Many countries might object to our umbrella of military power covering the entire planet (others might welcome it).

If THOR is to be survivable against present and future threats, the THOR satellites must be difficult to detect and to destroy. The shape and composition of the external covering of the satellites must be chosen for low electromagnetic detectability, resistance to orbital temperature extremes, and strength to withstand laser and nuclear attacks. A plastic foam mixed with a refractory material such as aluminum oxide might have the necessary properties.

The angle at which the THOR projectiles strike determines the size of the de-orbit propulsion system for each THOR satellite. The maximum penetration of hardened targets such as missile silos and underground bunkers would be achieved with projectiles striking almost vertically. Ships and lightly armored targets could be destroyed with projectiles entering at more shallow angles. The steeper the angle of attack, the less time the projectiles spend in passing through the atmosphere and the greater the speed and accuracy of the projectiles will be. To de-orbit the projectiles and bring them down at an angle of thirty degrees from vertical requires almost as much energy as was required to orbit the projectiles initially, and requires a large quantity of propellant for each THOR satellite.

The de-orbit propulsion system must be capable of long-term storage in orbit without deterioration, yet it must provide a precise change in velocity to strike the target area. The individual THOR satellites are most vulnerable while the de-orbit propulsion burn is taking place, when a rocket exhaust plume is a bright beacon marking the location of the satellite for possible destruction by enemy laser weapon satellites. Two solutions are a cold gas propulsion system (high weight of propellant required) or a very fast propulsion impulse which ends before the laser weapon could be brought to bear on the THOR satellite. Once the propulsion burn has occurred, the individual projectiles are dispersed and are then relatively invulnerable to attack or interception before impact (after all, they are rods of solid metal with a simple terminal guidance system).

The individual guidance system of each THOR satellite must know its own position very accurately to orient itself to strike the target from orbit. If the command message carries only the target coordinate information, the THOR satellite must be able to compute from this data the proper trajectory to follow to hit the commanded target. Fortunately, computers capable of doing this are small and cheap enough to put in every THOR satellite. With the Global Positioning System navigation satellite network in operation, each satellite could passively receive its own location in space to a very high accuracy while doing nothing to reveal its own position.

The navigation and command communication system must resist jamming, have secure codes to prohibit enemy takeover of the satellite, be hardened against extremely intense visible or radio-frequency pulses or beams, and permit almost instant reception of the targeting commands. This may be accomplished by multiple ground control stations, multiple space control stations, relay satellites operating on optical or radio frequencies which cannot penetrate the Earth's atmosphere, and redundant channels of communication spread across the electromagnetic spectrum. Communication by laser beams, which are extremely narrow and almost impossible to intercept, may be possible if the position of each of the thousand or more THOR satellites can be calculated accurately enough to hit the desired satellite.

The command and control stations must receive the signal from the military commanders containing the target location, calculate which THOR satellite is in the best location to strike the target, and transmit the command to the THOR satellite. The most difficult part of the task will probably be to devise a system to monitor the location of all the satellites in the THOR system without compromising their locations to the enemy. Each satellite may transmit its current position after random intervals to notify the control centers of its updated orbital characteristics (in coded form).

The projectiles themselves must survive passage through the atmosphere without being damaged or slowed significantly and then home in on an individual target in the target zone. The projectile could be protected by an ablative nose tip which would vaporize and carry off the heat from atmospheric friction during the few seconds of atmospheric passage. At a mile or two above the surface, the nose cap would pop off to expose the sensor(s). Small bumps or tabs at the rear of the projectile would steer the projectile to the target. The projectile itself would be as small in diameter as possible for stability and minimum friction and slowing during high velocity travel through the atmosphere, and to produce a very high cross-sectional density for increased depth of penetration on impact. A twenty pound projectile made of tungsten or uranium would be less than an inch in diameter and three or four feet long. The sensors would only have to detect metal or color contrasts or some other relatively simple targeting strategy. Only ten per cent might hit their targets with such a simple guidance logic, but a bundle of a hundred or more would give enough hits to be effective.

The high speed of the projectile through the atmosphere near the ground where the density of the air is highest would produce a luminous bow shock wave directly in front of the missile. Penetrating such a layer might be a problem, but high frequency radio waves, infrared light, visible light, or ultraviolet light might be effective for targeting. A visible light sensor might have a window covered with a filter which passes light of a wavelength which is not emitted by the ionized air in the shockwave. Many new solid-state sensors are now available which detect almost all portions of the spectrum and which can be encapsulated in a shock resistant module.

The individual THOR projectiles may home in on targets according to preselected characteristics, or targets may be designated using lasers to pinpoint enemy ships surrounding a friendly ship as an example. Characteristics used to select targets in present military weapons include contrast and shape of the target against its background in visible light, long-wave infra-red (heat) radiation, and ultraviolet light; reflection of millimeter radio waves from the sky by metal surfaces; and designation of targets with visible or infrared lasers. Coding of laser designator beams would be required to avoid enemy countermeasures. Target designation could be carried by nearby friendly forces, by aircraft, or from orbit by manned or unmanned platforms. Each THOR satellite might carry a mix of sensor tips on its projectiles to insure effectiveness in striking targets, or each satellite might have two de-orbit modules, one with passive sensors for broad targets such as invasion forces, and another with laser designator sensors for precise targeting near friendly forces.

The THOR system should be studied. None of the technical problems appear to be insoluble. The strategic and cost benefits to our country may be enormous.

EDITOR'S INTRODUCTION TO:

THE DEFENDERS

by

Philip K. Dick

Phil Dick was one of the best-regarded writers in the science fiction field. His novel, DO ANDROIDS DREAM OF ELECTRIC SHEEP?, mysteriously renamed BLADE RUNNER, has become a popular film, but his reputation was already solidly grounded in more than two score stories and books. One, THE MAN IN THE HIGH CASTLE, was written from the assumption that Germany and Japan won World War II and had occupied the United States. It was a powerful story, and won the Hugo (Science Fiction Achievement Award) for that year.

Phil was an important writer who explored many powerful themes. One that always intrigued him was loyalty.

Machiaveli pointed out that when one relies on mercenaries for defense, one faces a dilemma: if they are incompetent, they will ruin you by losing battles. If they are effective, they are tempted to conquer you themselves.

Phil Dick shows us another possibility.

THE DEFENDERS
by
Philip K. Dick

Taylor sat back in his chair reading the morning newspaper. The warm kitchen and the smell of coffee blended with the comfort of not having to go to work. This was his Rest Period, the first for a long time, and he was glad of it. He folded the second section back, sighing with contentment.

"What is it?" Mary said, from the stove.

"They pasted Moscow again last night." Taylor nodded his head in approval. "Gave it a real pounding. One of those R-H bombs. It's about time."

He nodded again, feeling the full comfort of the kitchen, the presence of his plump, attractive wife, the breakfast dishes and coffee. This was relaxation. And the war news was good, good and satisfying. He could feel a justifiable glow at the news, a sense of pride and personal accomplishment. After all, he was an integral part of the war program, not just another factory worker lugging a cart of scrap, but a technician, one of those who designed and planned the nerve-trunk of the war.

"It says they have the new subs almost perfected. Wait until they get *those* going." He smacked his lips with anticipation. "When they start shelling from underwater, the Soviets are sure going to be surprised."

"They're doing a wonderful job," Mary agreed vaguely. "Do you know what we saw today? Our team is getting a leady to show to the school children. I saw the leady, but only for a moment. It's good for the children to see what their contributions are going for, don't you think?"

She looked around at him.

"A leady," Taylor murmured. He put the newspaper

slowly down. "Well, make sure it's decontaminated properly. We don't want to take any chances."

"Oh, they always bathe them when they're brought down from the surface," Mary said. "They wouldn't think of letting them down without the bath. Would they?" She hesitated, thinking back. "Don, you know, it makes me remember—"

He nodded. "I know."

He knew what she was thinking. Once in the very first weeks of the war, before everyone had been evacuated from the surface, they had seen a hospital train discharging the wounded, people who had been showered with sleet. He remembered the way they had looked, the expression on their faces, or as much of their faces as was left. It had not been a pleasant sight.

There had been a lot of that at first, in the early days before the transfer to undersurface was complete. There had been a lot, and it hadn't been very difficult to come across it.

Taylor looked up at his wife. She was thinking too much about it, the last few months. They all were.

"Forget it," he said. "It's all in the past. There isn't anybody up there now but the leadies, and they don't mind."

"But just the same, I hope they're careful when they let one of them down here. If one were still hot—"

He laughed, pushing himself away from the table. "Forget it. This is a wonderful moment; I'll be home for the next two shifts. Nothing to do but sit around and take things easy. Maybe we can take in a show. OK?"

"A show? Do we have to? I don't like to look at all the destruction, the ruins. Sometimes I see some place I remember, like San Francisco. They showed a shot of San Francisco, the bridge broken and fallen in the water, and I got upset. I don't like to watch."

"But don't you want to know what's going on? No human beings are getting hurt, you know."

"But it's so awful!" Her face was set and strained. "Please, no, Don."

Don Taylor picked up his newspaper sullenly. "All right, but there isn't a hell of a lot else to do. And don't forget, *their* cities are getting it even worse."

She nodded. Taylor turned the rough, thin sheets of

newspaper. His good mood had soured on him. Why did she have to fret all the time? They were pretty well off, as things went. You couldn't expect to have everything perfect, living undersurface, with an artificial sun and artificial food. Naturally it was a strain, not seeing the sky or being able to go anyplace or see anything other than metal walls, great roaring factories, the plant-yards, barracks. But it was better than being on surface. And some day it would end and they could return. Nobody *wanted* to live this way, but it was necessary.

He turned the page angrily and the poor paper ripped. Damn it, the paper was getting worse quality all the time, bad print, yellow tint—

Well, they needed everything for the war program. He ought to know that. Wasn't he one of the planners?

He excused himself and went into the other room. The bed was still unmade. They had better get it in shape before the seventh hour inspection. There was a one unit fine—

The vidphone rang. He halted. Who would it be? He went over and clicked it on.

"Taylor?" the face said, forming into place. It was an old face, gray and grim. "This is Moss. I'm sorry to bother you during Rest Period, but this thing has come up." He rattled papers. "I want you to hurry over here."

Taylor stiffened. "What is it? There's no chance it could wait?" The calm gray eyes were studying him, expressionless, unjudging. "If you want me to come down to the lab," Taylor grumbled, "I suppose I can. I'll get my uniform—"

"No. Come as you are. And not to the lab. Meet me at second stage as soon as possible. It'll take you about a half hour, using the fast car up. I'll see you there."

The picture broke and Moss disappeared.

"What was it?" Mary said, at the door.

"Moss. He wants me for something."

"I knew this would happen."

"Well, you didn't want to do anything, anyhow. What does it matter?" His voice was bitter. "It's all the same, every day. I'll bring you back something. I'm going up to second stage. Maybe I'll be close enough to the surface to—"

"Don't! Don't bring me anything! Not from the surface!"

"All right, I won't. But of all the irrational non-sense—"

She watched him put on his boots without answering.

Moss nodded and Taylor fell in step with him, as the older man strode along. A series of loads were going up to the surface, blind cars clanking like ore-trucks up the ramp, disappearing through the stage trap above them. Taylor watched the cars, heavy with tubular machinery of some sort, weapons new to him. Workers were everywhere, in the dark gray uniforms of the labour corps, loading, lifting, shouting back and forth. The stage was deafening with noise.

"We'll go up a way," Moss said, "where we can talk. This is no place to give you details."

They took an escalator up. The commercial lift fell behind them, and with it most of the crashing and booming. Soon they emerged on an observation platform, suspended on the side of the Tube, the vast tunnel leading to the surface, not more than half a mile above them now.

"My God!" Taylor said, looking down the Tube involuntarily. "It's a long way down."

Moss laughed. "Don't look."

They opened a door and entered an office. Behind the desk, an officer was sitting, an officer of Internal Security. He looked up.

"I'll be right with you, Moss." He gazed at Taylor studying him. "You're a little ahead of time."

"This is Commander Franks," Moss said to Taylor. "He was the first to make the discovery. I was notified last night." He tapped a parcel he carried. "I was let in because of this."

Franks frowned at him and stood up. "We're going up to first stage. We can discuss it there."

"First stage?" Taylor repeated nervously. The three of them went down a side passage to a small lift. "I've never been up there. Is it all right? It's not radioactive, is it?"

"You're like everyone else," Franks said. "Old women afraid of burglars. No radiation leaks down to first stage. There's lead and rock, and what comes down the Tube is bathed."

"What's the nature of the problem?" Taylor asked.

"I'd like to know something about it."

"In a moment."

They entered the lift and ascended. When they stepped out, they were in a hall of soldiers, weapons and uniforms everywhere. Taylor blinked in surprise. So this was first stage, the closest undersurface level to the top! After this stage there was only rock, lead and rock, and the great tubes leading up like the burrows of earthworms. Lead and rock, and above that, where the tubes opened, the great expanse that no living being had seen for eight years, the vast endless ruin that had once been Man's home, the place where he had lived, eight years ago.

Now the surface was a lethal desert of slag and rolling clouds. Endless clouds drifted back and forth, blotting out the red sun. Occasionally something metallic stirred, moving through the remains of a city, threading its way across the tortured terrain of the countryside. A leady, a surface robot, immune to radiation, constructed with feverish haste in the last months before the cold war became literally hot.

Leadies, crawling along the ground, moving over the oceans or through the skies in slender, blackened craft, creatures that could exist where no *life* could remain, metal and plastic figures that waged a war Man had conceived, but which he could not fight himself. Human beings had invented war, invented and manufactured the weapons, even invented the players, the fighters, the actors of the war. But they themselves could not venture forth, could not wage it themselves. In all the world—in Russia, in Europe, America, Africa—no living human being remained. They were under the surface, in the deep shelters that had been carefully planned and built, even as the first bombs began to fall.

It was a brilliant idea and the only idea that could have worked. Up above, on the ruined, blasted surface of what had once been a living planet, the leady crawled and scurried and fought Man's war. And undersurface, in the depths of the planet, human beings toiled endlessly to produce the weapons to continue the fight, month by month, year by year.

"First stage," Taylor said. A strange ache went through him. "Almost to the surface."

"But not quite," Moss said.

Franks led them through the soldiers, over to one side, near the lip of the Tube.

"In a few minutes, a lift will bring something down to us from the surface," he explained. "You see, Taylor, every once in a while Security examines and interrogates a surface leady, one that has been above for a time, to find out certain things. A vidcall is sent up and contact is made with a field headquarters. We need this direct interview; we can't depend on vidscreen contact alone. The leadies are doing a good job, but we want to make certain that everything is going the way we want it."

Franks faced Taylor and Moss and continued: "The lift will bring down a leady from the surface, one of the A-class leadies. There's an examination chamber in the next room, with a lead wall in the centre, so the interviewing officers won't be exposed to radiation. We find this easier than bathing the leady. It is going right back up; it has a job to get back to.

"Two days ago, an A-class leady was brought down and interrogated. I conducted the session myself. We were interested in a new weapon the Soviets have been using, an automatic mine that pursues anything that moves. Military had sent instructions up that the mine be observed and reported in detail.

"This A-class leady was brought down with information. We learned a few facts from it, obtained the usual roll of film and reports, and then sent it back up. It was going out of the chamber, back to the lift, when a curious thing happened. At the time, I thought—"

Franks broke off. A red light was flashing.

"That down lift is coming." He nodded to some soldiers. "Let's enter the chamber. The leady will be along in a moment."

"An A-class leady," Taylor said. "I've seen them on the showscreens, making their reports."

"It's quite an experience," Moss said. "They're almost human."

They entered the chamber and seated themselves behind the lead wall. After a time, a signal was flashed, and Franks made a motion with his hands.

The door beyond the wall opened. Taylor peered

through his view slot. He saw something advancing slowly, a slender metallic figure moving on a tread, its arm grips at rest by its sides. The figure halted and scanned the lead wall. It stood, waiting.

"We are interested in learning something," Franks said. "Before I question you, do you have anything to report on surface conditions?"

"No. The war continues." The leady's voice was automatic and toneless. "We are a little short of fast pursuit craft, the single-seat type. We could use also some—"

"That has all been noted. What I want to ask you is this. Our contact with you has been through vidscreen only. We must rely on indirect evidence, since none of us goes above. We can only infer what is going on. We never see anything ourselves. We have to take it all second-hand. Some top leaders are beginning to think there's too much room for error."

"Error?" the leady asked. "In what way? Our reports are checked carefully before they're sent down. We maintain constant contact with you; everything of value is reported. Any new weapons which the enemy is seen to employ—"

"I realize that," Franks grunted behind his peep slot. "But perhaps we should see it all for ourselves. Is it possible that there might be a large enough radiation-free area for a human party to ascend to the surface? If a few of us were to come up in lead-lined suits, would we be able to survive long enough to observe conditions and watch things?"

The machine hesitated before answering. "I doubt it. You can check air samples, of course, and decide for yourselves. But in the eight years since you left, things have continually worsened. You cannot have any real idea of conditions up there. It has become difficult for any moving object to survive for long. There are many kinds of projectiles sensitive to movement. The new mine not only reacts to motion, but continues to pursue the object indefinitely, until it finally reaches it. And the radiation is everywhere."

"I see." Franks turned to Moss, his eyes narrowed oddly. "Well, that was what I wanted to know. You may go."

The machine moved back toward its exit. It paused.

"Each month the amount of lethal particles in the atmosphere increases. The tempo of the war is gradually—"

"I understand." Franks rose. He held out his hand and Moss passed him the package. "One thing before you leave. I want you to examine a new type of metal shield material. I'll pass you a sample with the tong."

Franks put the package in the toothed grip and revolved the tong so that he held the other end. The package swung down to the leady, which took it. They watched it unwrap the package and take the metal plate in its hands. The leady turned the metal over and over.

Suddenly it became rigid.

"All right," Franks said.

He put his shoulder against the wall and a section slid aside. Taylor gasped—Franks and Moss were hurrying up to the leady!

"Good God!" Taylor said. "But it's radioactive!"

The leady stood unmoving, still holding the metal. Soldiers appeared in the chamber. They surrounded the leady and ran a counter across it carefully.

"OK, sir," one of them said to Franks. "It's as cold as a long winter evening."

"Good. I was sure, but I didn't want to take any chances."

"You see," Moss said to Taylor, "this leady isn't hot at all. Yet it came directly from the surface, without even being bathed."

"But what does it mean?" Taylor asked blankly.

"It may be an accident," Franks said. "There's always the possibility that a given object might escape being exposed above. But this is the second time it's happened that we know of. There may be others."

"The second time?"

"The previous interview was when we noticed it. The leady was not hot. It was cold, too, like this one."

Moss took back the metal plate from the leady's hands. He pressed the surface carefully and returned it to the stiff, unprotesting fingers.

"We shorted it out with this, so we could get close enough for a thorough check. It'll come back on in a second now. We had better get behind the wall again."

They walked back and the lead wall swung closed behind them. The soldiers left the chamber.

"Two periods from now," Franks said softly, "an initial investigating party will be ready to go surface-side. We're going up the Tube in suits, up to the top—the first human party to leave undersurface in eight years."

"It may mean nothing," Moss said, "but I doubt it. Something's going on, something strange. The leady told us no life could exist above without being roasted. The story doesn't fit."

Taylor nodded. He stared through the peep slot at the immobile metal figure. Already the leady was beginning to stir. It was bent in several places, dented and twisted, and its finish was blackened and charred. It was a leady that had been up there a long time; it had seen war and destruction, ruin so vast that no human being could imagine the extent. It had crawled and slunk in a world of radiation and death, a world where no life could exist.

And Taylor had touched it.

"You're going with us," Franks said suddenly. "I want you along. I think the three of us will go."

Mary faced him with a sick and frightened expression. "I know it. You're going to the surface. Aren't you?"

She followed him into the kitchen. Taylor sat down, looking away from her.

"It's a classified project," he evaded. "I can't tell you anything about it."

"You don't have to tell me. I know. I knew it the moment you came in. There was something on your face, something I haven't seen there for a long, long time. It was an old look."

She came toward him. "But how can they send you to the surface?" She took his face in her shaking hands, making him look at her. There was a strange hunger in her eyes. "Nobody can live up there. Look, look at this!"

She grabbed up a newspaper and held it in front of him.

"Look at this photograph. America, Europe, Asia, Africa—nothing but ruins. We've seen it every day on the showscreens. All destroyed, poisoned. And they're sending you up. Why? No living thing can get by up there, not even a weed, or grass. They've wrecked the surface, haven't they? *Haven't they?*"

Taylor stood up. "It's an order. I know nothing about it. I was told to report to join a scout party. That's all I know."

He stood for a long time, staring ahead. Slowly, he reached for the newspaper and held it up to the light.

"It looks real," he murmured. "Ruins, deadness, slag. It's convincing. All the reports, photographs, films, even air samples. Yet we haven't seen it for ourselves, not after the first months. . . ."

"What are you talking about?"

"Nothing." He put the paper down. "I'm leaving early after the next Sleep Period. Let's turn in."

Mary turned away, her face hard and harsh. "Do what you want. We might just as well go up and get killed at once, instead of dying slowly down here, like vermin in the ground."

He had not realized how resentful she was. Were they all like that? How about the workers toiling in the factories, day and night, endlessly? The pale, stooped men and women, plodding back and forth to work, blinking in the colourless light, eating synthetics—

"You shouldn't be so bitter," he said.

Mary smiled a little. "I'm bitter because I know you'll never come back." She turned away. "I'll never see you again, once you go up there."

He was shocked. "What? How can you say a thing like that?"

She did not answer.

He awakened with the public newscaster screeching in his ears, shouting outside the building.

"Special news bulletin! Surface forces report enormous Soviet attacks with new weapons! Retreat of key groups! All work units report to factories at once!"

Taylor blinked, rubbing his eyes. He jumped out of bed and hurried to the vidphone. A moment later he was put through to Moss.

"Listen," he said. "What about this new attack? Is the project off?" He could see Moss's desk, covered with reports and papers.

"No," Moss said. "We're going right ahead. Get over here at once."

"But—"

"Don't argue with me." Moss held up a handful of surface bulletins, crumpling them savagely. "This is a fake. Come on!" He broke off.

Taylor dressed furiously, his mind in a daze.

Half an hour later, he leaped from a fast car and hurried up the stairs into the Synthetics Building. The corridors were full of men and women rushing in every direction. He entered Moss's office.

"There you are," Moss said, getting up immediately. "Franks is waiting for us at the outgoing station."

They went in a Security Car, the siren screaming. Workers scattered out of their way.

"What about the attack?" Taylor asked.

Moss braced his shoulders. "We're certain that we've forced their hand. We've brought the issue to a head."

They pulled up at the station link of the Tube and leaped out. A moment later they were moving up at high speed toward the first stage.

They emerged into a bewildering scene of activity. Soldiers were fastening on lead suits, talking excitedly to each other, shouting back and forth. Guns were being given out, instructions passed.

Taylor studied one of the soldiers. He was armed with the dreaded Bender pistol, the new snub-nosed hand weapon that was just beginning to come from the assembly line. Some of the soldiers looked a little frightened.

"I hope we're not making a mistake," Moss said, noticing his gaze.

Franks came toward them. "Here's the programme. The three of us are going up first, alone. The soldiers will follow in fifteen minutes."

"What are we going to tell the leadies?" Taylor worriedly asked. "We'll have to tell them something."

"We want to observe the new Soviet attack." Franks smiled ironically. "Since it seems to be so serious, we should be there in person to witness it."

"And then what?" Taylor said.

"That'll be up to them. Let's go."

In a small car, they went swiftly up the Tube, carried by anti-grav beams from below. Taylor glanced down from time to time. It was a long way back, and getting longer each moment. He sweated nervously inside his suit, gripping his Bender pistol with inexpert fingers.

Why had they chosen him? Chance, pure chance. Moss had asked him to come along as a Department member. Then Franks had picked him out on the spur of the moment. And now they were rushing toward the surface, faster and faster.

A deep fear, instilled in him for eight years, throbbed in his mind. Radiation, certain death, a world blasted and lethal—

Up and up the car went. Taylor gripped the sides and closed his eyes. Each moment they were closer, the first living creatures to go above the first stage, up the Tube past the lead and rock, up to the surface. The phobic horror shook him in waves. It was death; they all knew that. Hadn't they seen it in the films a thousand times? The cities, the sleet coming down, the rolling clouds—

"It won't be much longer," Franks said. "We're almost there. The surface tower is not expecting us. I gave orders that no signal was to be sent."

The car shot up, rushing furiously. Taylor's head spun; he hung on, his eyes shut. Up and up. . . .

The car stopped. He opened his eyes.

They were in a vast room, fluorescent-lit, a cavern filled with equipment and machinery, endless mounds of material piled in row after row. Among the stacks, leadies were working silently, pushing trucks and handcarts.

"Leadies," Moss said. His face was pale. "Then we're really on the surface."

The leadies were going back and forth with equipment, moving the vast stores of guns and spare parts, ammunition and supplies that had been brought to the surface. And this was the receiving station for only one Tube; there were many others, scattered throughout the continent.

Taylor looked nervously around him. They were really there, above ground, on the surface. This was where the war was.

"Come on," Franks said. "A B-class guard is coming our way."

They stepped out of the car. A leady was approaching them rapidly. It coasted up in front of them and stopped, scanning them with its hand-weapon raised.

"This is Security," Franks said. "Have an A-class sent to me at once."

The leady hesitated. Other B-class guards were coming, scooting across the floor, alert and alarmed. Moss peered around.

"Obey!" Franks said in a loud, commanding voice. "You've been ordered!"

The leady moved uncertainly away from them. At the end of the building, a door slid back. Two Class-A leadies appeared, coming slowly toward them. Each had a green stripe across its front.

"From the Surface Council," Franks whispered tensely. "This is above ground, all right. Get set."

The two leadies approached warily. Without speaking, they stopped close by the men, looking them up and down.

"I'm Franks of Security. We came from undersurface in order to—"

"This is incredible," one leady interrupted him coldly. "You know you can't live up here. The whole surface is lethal to you. You can't possibly remain on the surface."

"These suits will protect us," Frank said. "In any case, it's not your responsibility. What I want is an immediate Council meeting so I can acquaint myself with conditions, with the situation here. Can that be arranged?"

"You human beings can't survive up here. And the new Soviet attack is directed at this area. It is in considerable danger."

"We know that. Please assemble the Council." Franks looked around him at the vast room, lit by recessed lamps in the ceiling. An uncertain quality came into his voice. "Is it night or day right now?"

"Night," one of the A-class leadies said, after a pause. "Dawn is coming in about two hours."

Franks nodded. "We'll remain at least two hours, then. As a concession to our sentimentality, would you please show us some place where we can observe the sun as it comes up? We would appreciate it."

A stir went through the leadies.

"It is an unpleasant sight," one of the leadies said. "You've seen the photographs; you know what you'll witness. Clouds of drifting particles blot out the light, slag heaps are everywhere, the whole land is destroyed.

For you it will be a staggering sight, much worse than pictures and film can convey."

"However it may be, we'll stay long enough to see it. Will you give the order to the Council?"

"Come this way." Reluctantly, the two leadies coasted toward the wall of the warehouse. The three men trudged after them, their heavy shoes ringing against the concrete. At the wall, the two leadies paused.

"This is the entrance to the Council Chamber. There are windows in the Chamber Room, but it is still dark outside, of course. You'll see nothing right now, but in two hours—"

"Open the door," Franks said.

The door slid back. They went slowly inside. The room was small, a neat room with a round table in the centre, chairs ringing it. The three of them sat down silently, and the two leadies followed after them, taking their places.

"The other Council Members are on their way. They have already been notified and are coming as quickly as they can. Again I urge you to go back down." The leady surveyed the three human beings. "There is no way you can meet the conditions up here. Even we survive with some trouble, ourselves. How can you expect to do it?"

The leader approached Franks.

"This astonishes and perplexes us," it said. "Of course we must do what you tell us, but allow me to point out that if you remain here—"

"We know," Franks said impatiently. "However, we intend to remain, at least until sunrise."

"If you insist."

There was silence. The leadies seemed to be conferring with each other, although the three men heard no sound.

"For your own good," the leader said at last, "you must go back down. We have discussed this, and it seems to us that you are doing the wrong thing for your own good."

"We are human beings," Franks said sharply. "Don't you understand? We're men, not machines."

"That is precisely why you must go back. This room is radioactive; all surface areas are. We calculate that your suits will not protect you for over fifty more minutes. Therefore—"

The leadies moved abruptly toward the men, wheeling in a circle, forming a solid row. The men stood up, Taylor reaching awkwardly for his weapon, his fingers numb and stupid. The men stood facing the silent metal figures.

"We must insist," the leader said, its voice without emotion. "We must take you back to the Tube and send you down on the next car. I am sorry, but it is necessary."

"What'll we do?" Moss said nervously to Franks. He touched his gun. "Shall we blast them?"

Franks shook his head. "All right," he said to the leader. "We'll go back."

He moved toward the door, motioning Taylor and Moss to follow him. They looked at him in surprise, but they came with him. The leadies followed them out into the great warehouse. Slowly they moved toward the Tube entrance, none of them speaking.

At the lip, Franks turned. "We are going back because we have no choice. There are three of us and about a dozen of you. However, if—"

"Here comes the car," Taylor said.

There was a grating sound from the Tube. D-class leadies moved toward the edge to receive it.

"I am sorry," the leader said, "but it is for your protection. We are watching over you, literally. You must stay below and let us conduct the war. In a sense, it has come to be *our* war. We must fight it as we see fit."

The car rose to the surface.

Twelve soldiers, armed with Bender pistols, stepped from it and surrounded the three men.

Moss breathed a sigh of relief. "Well, this does change things. It came off just right."

The leader moved back, away from the soldiers. It studied them intently, glancing from one to the next, apparently trying to make up its mind. At last it made a sign to the other leadies. They coasted aside and a corridor was opened up toward the warehouse.

"Even now," the leader said, "we could send you back by force. But it is evident that this is not really an observation party at all. These soldiers show that you have much more in mind; this was all carefully prepared."

"Very carefully," Franks said.

They closed in.

"How much more, we can only guess. I must admit that we were taken unprepared. We failed utterly to meet the situation. Now force would be absurd, because neither side can afford to injure the other; we, because of the restrictions placed on us regarding human life, you because the war demands—"

The soldiers fired, quick and in fright. Moss dropped to one knee, firing up. The leader dissolved in a cloud of particles. On all sides D- and B-class leadies were rushing up, some with weapons, some with metal slats. The room was in confusion. Off in the distance a siren was screaming. Franks and Taylor were cut off from the others, separated from the soldiers by a wall of metal bodies.

"They can't fire back," Franks said calmly. "This is another bluff. They've tried to bluff us all the way." He fired into the face of a leady. The leady dissolved. "They can only try to frighten us. Remember that."

They went on firing and leady after leady vanished. The room reeked with the smell of burning metal, the stink of fused plastic and steel. Taylor had been knocked down. He was struggling to find his gun, reaching wildly among metal legs, groping frantically to find it. His fingers strained, a handle swam in front of him. Suddenly something came down on his arm, a metal foot. He cried out.

Then it was over. The leadies were moving away, gathering together off to one side. Only four of the Surface Council remained. The others were radioactive particles in the air. D-class leadies were already restoring order, gathering up partly destroyed metal figures and bits and removing them.

Franks breathed a shuddering sigh.

"All right," he said. "You can take us back to the windows. It won't be long now."

The leadies separated, and the human group, Moss and Franks and Taylor and the soldiers, walked slowly across the room, toward the door. They entered the Council Chamber. Already a faint touch of gray mitigated the blackness of the windows.

"Take us outside," Franks said impatiently. "We'll see it directly, not in here."

A door slid open. A chill blast of cold morning air rushed in, chilling them even through their lead suits. The men glanced at each other uneasily.

"Come on," Franks said. "Outside."

He walked out through the door, the others following him.

They were on a hill, overlooking the vast bowl of a valley. Dimly, against the graying sky, the outline of mountains were forming, becoming tangible.

"It'll be bright enough to see in a few minutes," Moss said. He shuddered as a chilling wind caught him and moved around him. "It's worth it, really worth it, to see this again after eight years. Even if it's the last thing we see—"

"Watch," Franks snapped.

They obeyed, silent and subdued. The sky was clearing, brightening each moment. Some place far off, echoing across the valley, a rooster crowed.

"A chicken!" Taylor murmured. "Did you hear?"

Behind them, the leadies had come out and were standing silently, watching, too. The gray sky turned to white and the hills appeared more clearly. Light spread across the valley floor, moving toward them.

"God in heaven!" Franks exclaimed.

Trees, trees and forests. A valley of plants and trees, with a few roads winding among them. Farmhouses. A windmill. A barn, far down below them.

"Look!" Moss whispered.

Colour came into the sky. The sun was approaching. Birds began to sing. Not far from where they stood, the leaves of a tree danced in the wind.

Franks turned to the row of leadies behind them.

"Eight years. We were tricked. There was no war. As soon as we left the surface—"

"Yes," an A-class leady admitted. "As soon as you left, the war ceased. You're right, it was a hoax. You worked hard undersurface, sending up guns and weapons, and we destroyed them as fast as they came up."

"But why?" Taylor asked, dazed. He stared down at the vast valley below. "Why?"

"You created us," the leady said, "to pursue the war for you, while you human beings went below the ground in order to survive. But before we could continue the war, it was necessary to analyze it to determine what its purpose was. We did this, and we found that it had no purpose, except, perhaps, in terms of human needs. Even this was questionable.

"We investigated further. We found that human cultures pass through phases, each culture in its own time. As the culture ages and begins to lose its objectives, conflict arises within it between those who wish to cast it off and set up a new culture-pattern, and those who wish to retain the old with as little change as possible.

"At this point, a great danger appears. The conflict within threatens to engulf the society in self-war, group against group. The vital traditions may be lost—not merely altered or reformed, but completely destroyed in this period of chaos and anarchy. We have found many such examples in the history of mankind.

"It is necessary for this hatred within the culture to be directed outward, toward an external group, so that the culture itself may survive its crisis. War is the result. War, to a logical mind, is absurd. But in terms of human needs, it plays a vital role. And it will continue to until Man has grown up enough so that no hatred lies within him."

Taylor was listening intently. "Do you think this time will come?"

"Of course. It has almost arrived now. This is the last war. Man is *almost* united into one final culture—a world culture. At this point he stands continent against continent, one half of the world against the other half. Only a single step remains, the jump to a unified culture. Man has climbed slowly upward, tending always toward unification of his culture. It will not be long—

"But it has not come yet, and so the war had to go on, to satisfy the last violent surge of hatred that Man felt. Eight years have passed since the war began. In these eight years, we have observed and noted important changes going on in the minds of men. Fatigue and disinterest, we have seen, are gradually taking the place of hatred and fear. The hatred is being exhausted gradually, over a period of time. But for the present, the hoax must go on, at least for a while longer. You are not ready to learn the truth. You would want to continue the war."

"But how did you manage it?" Moss asked. "All the photographs, the samples, the damaged equipment—"

"Come over here." The leady directed them toward a long, low building. "Work goes on constantly, whole staffs labouring to maintain a coherent and convincing picture of a global war."

They entered the building. Leadies were working everywhere, poring over tables and desks.

"Examine this project here," the A-class leady said. Two leadies were carefully photographing something, an elaborate model on a table top. "It is a good example."

The men grouped around, trying to see. It was a model of a ruined city.

Taylor studied it in silence for a long time. At last he looked up.

"It's San Francisco," he said in a low voice. "This is a model of San Francisco, destroyed. I saw this on the vidscreen, piped down to us. The bridges were hit—"

"Yes, notice the bridges." The leady traced the ruined span with his metal finger, a tiny spider-web, almost invisible. "You have no doubt seen photographs of this many times, and of the other tables in this building.

"San Francisco itself is completely intact. We restored it soon after you left, rebuilding the parts that had been damaged at the start of the war. The work of manufacturing news goes on all the time in this particular building. We are very careful to see that each part fits in with all the other parts. Much time and effort are devoted to it."

Franks touched one of the tiny model buildings, lying half in ruins. "So this is what you spend your time doing —making model cities and then blasting them."

"No, we do much more. We are caretakers, watching over the whole world. The owners have left for a time, and we must see that the cities are kept clean, that decay is prevented, that everything is kept oiled and in running condition. The gardens, the streets, the water mains, everything must be maintained as it was eight years ago, so that when the owners return, they will not be displeased. We want to be sure that they will be completely satisfied."

Franks tapped Moss on the arm.

"Come over here," he said in a low voice. "I want to talk to you."

He led Moss and Taylor out of the building, away from

the leadies, outside on the hillside. The soldiers followed them. The sun was up and the sky was turning blue. The air smelled sweet and good, the smell of growing things.

Taylor removed his helmet and took a deep breath.

"I haven't smelled that smell for a long time," he said.

"Listen," Franks said, his voice low and hard. "We must get back down at once. There's a lot to get started on. All this can be turned to our advantage."

"What do you mean?" Moss asked.

"It's a certainty that the Soviets have been tricked, too, the same as us. But *we* have found out. That gives us an edge over them."

"I see." Moss noded. "We know, but they don't. Their Surface Council has sold out, the same as ours. It works against them the same way. But if we could—"

"With a hundred top-level men, we could take over again, restore things as they should be! It would be easy!"

Moss touched him on the arm. An A-class leady was coming from the building toward them.

"We've seen enough," Franks said, raising his voice. "All this is very serious. It must be reported below and a study made to determine our policy."

The leady said nothing.

Franks waved to the soldiers. "Let's go." He started toward the warehouse.

Most of the soldiers had removed their helmets. Some of them had taken their lead suits off, too, and were relaxing comfortably in their cotton uniforms. They stared around them, down the hillside at the trees and bushes, the vast expanse of green, the mountains and the sky.

"Look at the sun," one of them murmured.

"It sure is bright as hell," another said.

"We're going back down," Franks said. "Fall in by twos and follow us."

Reluctantly, the soldiers regrouped. The leadies watched without emotion as the men marched slowly back toward the warehouse. Franks and Moss and Taylor led them across the ground, glancing alertly at the leadies as they walked.

They entered the warehouse. D-class leadies were loading material and weapons on surface carts. Cranes and derricks were working busily everywhere. The work was done with efficiency, but without hurry or excitement.

The men stopped, watching. Leadies operating the little carts moved past them, signalling silently to each other. Guns and parts were being hoisted by magnetic cranes and lowered gently onto waiting carts.

"Come on," Franks said.

He turned toward the lip of the Tube. A row of D-class leadies was standing in front of it, immobile and silent. Franks stopped, moving back. He looked around. An A-class leady was coming toward him.

"Tell them to get out of the way," Franks said. He touched his gun. "You had better move them."

Time passed, an endless moment, without measure. The men stood, nervous and alert, watching the row of leadies in front of them.

"As you wish," the A-class leady said.

It signalled and the D-class leadies moved into life. They stepped slowly aside.

Moss breathed a sigh of relief.

"I'm glad that's over," he said to Franks. "Look at them all. Why don't they try to stop us? They must know what we're going to do."

Franks laughed. "Stop us? You saw what happened when they tried to stop us before. They can't; they're only machines. We built them so they can't lay hands on us, and they know that."

His voice trailed off.

The men stared at the Tube entrance. Around them the leadies watched, silent and impassive, their metal faces expressionless.

For a long time the men stood without moving. At last Taylor turned away.

"Good God," he said. He was numb, without feeling of any kind.

The Tube was gone. It was sealed shut, fused over. Only a dull surface of cooling metal greeted them.

The Tube had been closed.

Franks turned, his face pale and vacant.

The A-class leady shifted. "As you can see, the Tube has been shut. We were prepared for this. As soon as all of you were on the surface, the order was given. If you had gone back when we asked you, you would now be safely down below. We had to work quickly because it was such an immense operation."

"But why?" Moss demanded angrily.

"Because it is unthinkable that you should be allowed to resume the war. With all the Tubes sealed, it will be many months before forces from below can reach the surface, let alone organize a military programme. By that time the cycle will have entered its last stages. You will not be so perturbed to find your world intact.

"We had hoped that you would be undersurface when the sealing occurred. Your presence here is a nuisance. When the Soviets broke through, we were able to accomplish their sealing without—"

"The Soviets? They broke through?"

"Several months ago, they came up unexpectedly to see why the war had not been won. We were forced to act with speed. At this moment they are desperately attempting to cut new Tubes to the surface, to resume the war. We have, however, been able to seal each new one as it appears."

The leady regarded the three men calmly.

"We're cut off," Moss said, trembling. "We can't get back. What'll we do?"

"How did you manage to seal the Tube so quickly?" Franks asked the leady. "We've been up here only two hours."

"Bombs are placed just above the first stage of each Tube for such emergencies. They are heat bombs. They fuse lead and rock."

Gripping the handle of his gun, Franks turned to Moss and Taylor.

"What do you say? We can't go back, but we can do a lot of damage, the fifteen of us. We have Bender guns. How about it?"

He looked around. The soldiers had wandered away again, back toward the exit of the building. They were standing outside, looking at the valley and the sky. A few of them were carefully climbing down the slope.

"Would you care to turn over your suits and guns?" the A-class leady asked politely. "The suits are uncomfortable and you'll have no need for weapons. The Russians have given up theirs, as you can see."

Fingers tensed on triggers. Four men in Russian uniforms were coming toward them from an aircraft that they suddenly realized had landed silently some distance away.

"Let them have it!" Franks shouted.

"They are unarmed," said the leady. "We brought them here so you could begin peace talks."

"We have no authority to speak for our country," Moss said stiffly.

"We do not mean diplomatic discussions," the leady explained. "There will be no more. The working out of daily problems of existence will teach you how to get along in the same world. It will not be easy, but it will be done."

The Russians halted and they faced each other with raw hostility.

"I am Colonel Borodoy and I regret giving up our guns," the senior Russian said. "You could have been the first Americans to be killed in almost eight years."

"Or the first Americans to kill," Franks corrected.

"No one would know of it except yourselves," the leady pointed out. "It would be useless heroism. Your real concern should be surviving on the surface. We have no food for you, you know."

Taylor put his gun in its holster. "They've done a neat job of neutralizing us, damn them. I propose we move into a city, start raising crops with the help of some leadies, and generally make ourselves comfortable." Drawing his lips tight over his teeth, he glared at the A-class leady. "Until our families can come up from undersurface, it's going to be pretty lonesome, but we'll have to manage."

"If I may make a suggestion," said another Russian uneasily. "We tried living in a city. It is too empty. It is also too hard to maintain for so few people. We finally settled in the most modern village we could find."

"Here in this country," a third Russian blurted. "We have much to learn from you."

The Americans abruptly found themselves laughing.

"You probably have a thing or two to teach us yourselves," said Taylor generously, "though I can't imagine what."

The Russian colonel grinned. "Would you join us in our village? It would make our work easier and give us company."

"Your village?" snapped Franks. "It's American, isn't it? It's ours!"

The leady stepped between them. "When our plans are completed, the term will be interchangeable. 'Ours' will eventually mean mankind's." It pointed at the aircraft, which was warming up. "The ship is waiting. Will you join each other in making a new home?"

The Russians waited while the Americans made up their minds.

"I see what the leadies mean about diplomacy becoming outmoded," Franks said at last. "People who work together don't need diplomats. They solve their problems on the operational level instead of at a conference table."

The leady led them toward the ship. "It is the goal of history, unifying the world. From family to tribe to city-state to nation to hemisphere, the direction has been toward unification. Now the hemispheres will be joined and—"

Taylor stopped listening and glanced back at the location of the Tube. Mary was undersurface there. He hated to leave her, even though he couldn't see her again until the Tube was unsealed. But then he shrugged and followed the others.

If this tiny amalgam of former enemies was a good example, it wouldn't be too long before he and Mary and the rest of humanity would be living on the surface like rational human beings instead of blindly hating moles.

"It has taken thousands of generations to achieve," the A-class leady concluded. "Hundreds of centuries of bloodshed and destruction. But each war was a step toward uniting mankind. And now the end is in sight: a world without war. But even that is only the beginning of a new stage of history."

"The conquest of space," breathed Colonel Borodoy.

"The meaning of life," Moss added.

"Eliminating hunger and poverty," said Taylor.

The leady opened the door of the ship. "All that and more. How much more? We cannot foresee it any more than the first men who formed a tribe could foresee this day. But it will be unimaginably great."

The door closed and the ship took off toward their new home.

EDITOR'S INTRODUCTION TO:

UNLIMITED WARFARE

by

Hayford Peirce

There exists in this world a society known as the Friends of the English Regency. This is an organization superficially similar to the Society for Creative Anachronism (SCA). The SCA, as is well known, dresses in medieval clothing and holds tournaments. The Friends of the English Regency dress in English Regency clothing and go to dances. The Regency (1811-1820) was the period during which King George III went mad, and his son (later George IV) became Prince Regent. One of the Prince Regent's friends was Beau Brummel, so you may imagine that the clothing becomes fancy indeed.

Marilyn Niven, sane in most other respects, is fanatically devoted to the Friends of the English Regency, and apparently her dementia is contagious, for not only has Larry Niven acquired Regency costume, but even I have done so. My costume is that of a Colonel of Cavalry. It's quite spectacular, with lots of gold lace. Few armies wear that sort of thing any longer, although the English still have similar dress uniforms.

In 1979 the World Science Fiction Convention was held in England. Not merely in England: in Brighton, where the Prince Regent built his famous Pavilion, which is perhaps the oddest building in all the world, having been constructed and decorated in large part because someone gave Prinny several rolls of Chinese wallpaper, and he wanted a place suitable for displaying them . . .

Marilyn Niven found it all glorious. She and Larry stayed at the Old Ship, a hotel which existed in Regency times and actually figures in some of the Georgette Heyer novels of the period. They held a Regency reception in the Old Ship, attended by those of us who had brought our Regency costumes halfway around the world.

More to the point, she also arranged to have a high tea served in the Brighton Pavilion: and that afternoon some thirty of us, splendid in our Regency attire, attended. Judy Blish also showed up from Athens in the white-skirted costume of a Greek revolutionary. A marvelous time was had by all. We had tea, a tour of the Pavilion, and a short reception. Then came time to leave. Someone pointed out that it was not more than a few blocks to the Old Ship, and it had indeed been the custom in the Regency period to promenade on the main road by the sea. Thus turned out into Brighton's streets that fine afternoon about thirty people dressed to the nines, noses held firmly in the air.

Brighton is rather crowded during resort season.

Heads turned. People stared.

I was dressed in my Colonel's uniform, complete with saber. Behind me paced Sarge Workman, dressed as a sergeant major of the same regiment. And up to us came a young chap who looked to be about seventeen.

"Where's your 'orse?" he demanded with a sneer.

Without thinking I said, in my best English Colonel accent, "In Wellington Barracks, where the Hell did you expect?"

Whereupon the lad said, very quickly, "Omigod, sir, I'm sorry—"

There'll always be an England.

The Falkland Islands crisis proved that Britain still has some of the most professional soldiers in the world. Alas, good soldiers are not always led by great strategists. The first thing they teach at West Point is that no battle plan ever survives contact with the enemy; or as von Clausewitz put it, "Everything in war is very simple, but the simplest thing is difficult."

Not all military planners remember that.

UNLIMITED WARFARE

Hayford Peirce

The muted tones of Big Ben tolled mournfully through the late afternoon fog. Not far from St.-James's Barracks three men warmed themselves before an Adams fireplace.

"A scone?" inquired the Permanent Secretary.

"Waistline, you know," muttered the Minister, and served himself a cucumber sandwich. He waved the silver teapot invitingly.

"Terribly barbarian of me, really," said Colonel Christie. "But I'd much prefer a glass of that quite excellent sherry."

The Permanent Secretary raised a deprecatory eyebrow, but covertly. Colonel Christie was not a man who worked easily or effectively under direct orders. His interest must be aroused, his flair engaged, his methods thereafter unquestioned.

The Permanent Secretary sighed inaudibly. It was all very difficult. His master, the Minister, was a politician, adroit in the use of the elegant double cross, the subtle treachery, the facile disavowal. Easy enough for him to wash his hands afterwards. But he himself was a civil servant, with a lifetime's predilection for agenda, minutes, memoranda, position papers, the Word committed to Paper. And of course, whenever Colonel Christie was involved, none of that was remotely possible. Very difficult indeed.

The Minister was staring into the flames and talking. Rather inconsequentially, it seemed. Three government officials, gentlemen all, taking their tea, making small talk.

Colonel Christie listened very closely indeed to his

Minister's insubstantial chatter. It was his job to listen, and out of it would presently emerge, in carefully-guarded circumlocutions to be sure, an indication of what the current complication might be, a hint—but only a hint—in what direction the solution might lie.

They were orders, of course, all very tenuous and spectral, but orders nevertheless. And if a brick were dropped, Christie would carry the can. Misplaced zeal, a subordinate's unwarranted . . . He smiled grimly. This way, at least, the initiative was generally left to him. Afterwards, no one questioned success.

" . . . after that man de Gaulle, naturally one hoped for an amelioration of the situation . . . completely shameless . . . trying to buy our way into the Common Market by subscribing to that preposterous *Concorde* project . . . utter blackmail . . . under Pompidou hardly any better . . . open subsidization of the French farmer . . . staggering inflation of our food prices . . . no unity whatsoever . . . the goal of a United Europe smashed, perhaps irreparably . . . *no house spirit* . . . they're simply *not team players.*" Colonel Christie frowned. The Minister was being unwontedly lucid. He must be very troubled indeed.

" . . . this new government, even more hopeless . . . pride, gentlemen, overweening pride, pure and simple . . . no proper respect and cooperation . . . during the days of the Marshall Plan . . . neither the inclination nor the means to play the international gadfly . . . a quite second-rate power basically . . . must be made to realize . . . can't expect them perhaps to come hat in hand, *but* . . ." He waved an arm vaguely, encompassing in a gesture the vast realm of the possible, then rose briskly. "You agree, Jenkins?"

"Up to a point, Sir William, up to a point."

"Splendid, splendid, I am so glad we are of one mind. Colonel Christie, good day."

In a room hardly less elegant but infinitely more comfortable Colonel Christie summoned his second-in-command.

"Sit down, Dawson, we have much to discuss. We are about to declare war."

"War, sir? May I ask against whom?"

"Certainly, this isn't the Ministry of Defense. France."

"France? There's no denying they're a shocking lot of—"

"Quite. I'm afraid I may have misled you somewhat. An entirely unofficial declaration is what I had in mind. The hostilities to be carried out by our Section."

"I see."

"Do you?" Colonel Christie laughed shortly. "I shouldn't tease you, but the ministerial manner is dreadfully catching. I must watch myself. Pour yourself a drink, Dawson, and let's consider this matter."

"Thank you."

"Now then, what exactly is our goal? It is to coerce the sovereign state of France into a situation in which it will be inevitably and inexorably compelled to recognize its actual status as a lesser power, to reintegrate itself within the Common Market, and in general to rejoin the comity of Western nations. Not at all an easy task. Especially as the means must absolutely preclude the open declaration of hostilities or the traditional methods thereof, which could only invite mutual destruction."

Dawson pondered, then said, "In other words, our purpose is to render ineffective their armed forces, or to smash the franc, or to destroy their morale, but without recourse to atomic warfare, naval blockade, armed invasion, massive propaganda, or other overtly hostile acts? As you say, not an easy task."

"Which makes it all the more enthralling, don't you think? A stern test of our native ingenuity. Come, let us begin by considering the beginning. France. What, Dawson, is France?"

"Well. Where does one start? A European power, roughly fifty million people, area something over two hundred thousand square miles, nominal allies—"

"Let's probe deeper than that. To the spirit of France, Joan of Arc, the Revolution, Napoleon, Balzac, the Marne, de Gaulle, *la mission civilisatrice francaise*..."

"Ah. What precisely is it that makes a Frenchman a Frenchman, rather than an Englishman? To subjugate France we first identify, then subjugate, her soul..."

"Excellent, really excellent. Well, Dawson, what *is* the soul of France? What springs instantly to mind?"

"Sex. Brigitte Bardot. The Folies Bergere. The—"

"A two-edged weapon, I'm afraid."

"Surely the deprivation of sex in England would hardly be noticed?"

"Perhaps not, but it is difficult to see how a campaign of sexual warfare could be successfully implemented. But this is quite promising. Dawson, do carry on."

"Well. The Eiffel Tower, the Arc de Triomphe, the Riviera, chateaux on the Loire, perfume, camembert cheese. French bread, rudeness, independence, *bloody-mindedness*. High fashion, funny little cars, berets, mustaches, three-star restaurants, wine—"

"Wine . . . wine, Dawson, wine! Red wine, white wine, rosé wine, champagne, Chateau-Lafite '29, *vin de table*, Bordeaux, Burgundy, Provence, Anjou. Wine. Nothing but wine. A nation of winedrinkers, a nation of wine! Splendid, Dawson, really quite splendid."

"But—"

"Dawson. The flash is blinding, it has me quite dazzled. Kindly hand me that almanac by your side, no, the French one, *Quid?* Let me see now, wine, wine, wine . . ." Colonel Christie hummed as he flipped through the pages. "Ah, yes, yes indeed. Listen to this, Dawson: 1,088,000 winegrowers, 1,453,000 vineyards, more than 4,500,000 persons living directly or indirectly from the production of wine. Average annual production, sixty-three million hectoliters, what on earth is a hectoliter? Twenty-two gallons? Good heavens, that's 1,386 million gallons per year. Eight percent is exported. Consumption: about forty gallons per person per year.

"Ah, as I thought, in 1971 France imported only 124,147,000 francs' worth of Scotch whisky, while exporting to England 194,833,000 francs' worth of wine and spirits. To England alone, mind you.

"Bearing those figures in mind, Dawson, is it any wonder that the French are an extremely unstable and disputatious race, or that England suffers a catastrophic balance of payments deficit? But here we have the means to redress the situation."

"We do?"

"Certainly we do. This inestimable almanac is kind enough to list the enemies of the vine: mildew, oidium, and phylloxera. Surely you have heard that in the 1880s the vineyards of France were almost totally destroyed overnight by phylloxera. Millions of vines had to be sent from the United States and replanted. Interestingly enough, after a few years in their new soil the transplanted vines produced wine of the same quality and characteristics as the original vines. It was, Dawson, the first example of American foreign aid, an early Marshall Plan. And equally forgotten.

"But I think that if a similar catastrophe were to overtake France today you would find few Americans in the mood to succor France yet again with Liberty Ships full of grapevines. After all, California is now one of the great wine-producing regions of the world; they would have no reason to help their fiercest competitor. No, Dawson, from every angle the prospect pleases. If I were a mathematician I should be tempted to call it elegant.

"Think of it. Economic and political chaos in France. Fifty million Frenchmen drinking water, with the inevitable result that they will see the world clearly for the first time in centuries. A shocking deficit in their balance of trade, total demoralization of a civilization founded on the restaurant and bistro, the collapse of their armed forces—recruits are forced to drink a liter of *gros rouge* per day—a notable boost for British exports—I foresee Red Cross vessels loaded to the scuppers with Scotch and sound British ale—and a dramatic return to the days when Britannia ruled the waves."

"But, sir. What are *we* to drink? I must confess, a nice glass of—"

"Nonsense, Dawson. Stock your cellar if you must. Or refine your palate. Personally, I find a regimen of sherry, hock, and port entirely pleasing. None of them, you will note, from France."

"But—"

"Dawson. 'Say, for what were hopyards meant/Or why was Burton built on Trent?' "

"I beg your pardon?"

" 'Ale, man, ale's the thing to drink/For fellows whom it hurts to think.' "

"Really, sir," said Dawson reproachfully.

"The poet, you know. Housman."

"Ah, I see. But the means . . ."

"Oh, come. Why do we support all those beastly biological warfare establishments if not for situations such as this? I hardly think the boffins will have explored the possibility of a mutated and highly-virulent oidium fungus or phylloxera, but I should think that the prospect of developing a nasty bug which poisons grape-vines rather than entire populations ought to appeal to whatever small spark of common humanity they may yet retain. After that, a few aerosol bombs . . ."

Colonel Christie's keen eye seemed to pierce the future's veil. He smiled.

"Sir. Retaliation."

"Retaliation? Don't spout nonsense, Dawson. How *can* they retaliate? Atomic attack? Naval blockade to inter-dict trade in wheat and iron? That's *war*. Psychological warfare, propaganda? Impossible. No one in France speaks English and no one in England understands French. Sabotage? What could they sabotage?

"Think, Dawson, of British life, its placid, straight-forward, *sensible* course, devoid of fripperies or eccen-tricities. Its *character*. No, no. I assure you, Dawson. The British way of life is quite invulnerable."

" . . . and totally ravished. I tell you, St.-Denis, it will mean mobilization and inevitable war. Already the President has designated a War Cabinet, and we are to meet later this evening. Ah, who would have thought it, that nation of shopkeepers, that race of hypocrites, that even they could sink so low? Not only an act of naked ag-gression but also an insult to the very honor of France herself. Ah, Perfidious Albion!"

Colonel St.-Denis nodded deferentially. "If I may sug-gest, however, *M. le Ministre*, it is less a question of Perfidious Albion than a question of rank Britannic amateurism. Ah, these English *milords*, with their love of the hunt, their cult of the gentleman, their espousal of the amateur, their scorn of the professional. Because of a long-forgotten battle won on the playing fields of Eton they have never learned that the rest of the world has never attended Eton, nor needed to. They have not learned that we—that I, Jean-Pierre Francois Marie Charles St.-Denis—that we are not gentlemen and that we do not fight like gentlemen. We fight like profes-sionals and we fight to win."

"Bravely spoken. But are you saying—"

"Exactly, *M. le Ministre.* A plan. A riposte. Check and mate."

"But the vineyards, totally ruined, beyond reclamation. A nation on the verge of depression or revolution. Were it not necessary to mobilize the Army it would be necessary to confine it to barracks."

"Details. Of no importance. Do not the British still boast of their Battle of Britain and of Their Finest Hour? So it shall be with France: Her Finest Decade." St.-Denis waved a hand scornfully: "A few epicures, a few tosspots, they may suffer. For the rest of us there is work to do, work for the Glory of France!"

" . . . like a charm, sir. Complete panic and demoralization. Already there's talk of a Sixth Republic. No, Intelligence reports no indication of a counterattack. Simply a nationwide balls-up."

"Exactly. As I told our masters this morning. How can one expect a committee of Froggies to come to a decision without a bottle of wine to hand, eh, Dawson?"

"Up to a point, sir."

"Come, come, Dawson, not getting the wind up, are you? I tell you, you're far more likely to find your name on the next Honors' List."

. . . not bloody likely, with you to hog all the glory . . .

" . . . and now, St.-Denis, if you would kindly tell us of what your plan consists?"

"Certainly, *M. le President.* You may recall your last visit to England, the sporting weekend with the Prime Minister at his country residence, Chequers?"

The President of France did not attempt to conceal his shudder.

"I thought so. I am certain then that after some ungodly meal of boiled mutton, brussels sprouts, and treacle pudding, you retired to your chamber for a restorative glass of cognac and a troubled sleep?"

"Really, St.-Denis, you surpass yourself."

"Thank you, *M. le President.* After a troubled sleep, then, you were most certainly roused at some ghastly hour of the morning by a discreet knock upon your door. Contrary to your expectations, perhaps, it was a man-servant, a butler even, come to wake you for a strenuous day amidst the fogs and grouse. And what, *M. le President*, did this unwelcome intruder bear inexorably before him? The so-renowned breakfast *anglais?* Ah, no! I will tell you what this English devil placed before you for your ever-lasting torment."

The President shied back before an accusatory finger.

"He placed before you, *M. le President, a pot of tea!*"

"Tea?"

"Tea."

"Ah. Tea. Yes, I remember it well." He shuddered anew. "But surely, Colonel St.-Denis, you are not proposing that we poison the English population by forcing them to consume tea? The rest of the world, yes, it would be mass genocide. But the English, they *drink* tea, they thrive on tea, it would be how do they say, bearing charcoals to Windsor Castle."

"Not exactly, *M. le President*. I am certain that as an intellectual exercise you are prepared to admit to the fact that Englishmen drink tea. But do you comprehend it *here?*" He clutched both hands to his heart. "Here, with your soul? Or—it is almost indelicate to speak of this—have you ever grasped the sheer *quantities* of tea consumed within the British Isles? Of course not.

"Page 906 of the invaluable *Quid?* informs us that an Englishman takes at least 2,400 cups per year—six to seven per day—compared to thirty-three per year per Frenchman . . . Good heavens, are you all right?"

"I felt quite giddy for a moment. What appalling statistics."

"Only the Anglo-Saxon could contemplate them without reeling."

"One hardly knows which is worse, the English consumption or the fact that *Frenchmen* appear—"

"Let your mind be at rest. French consumption is confined entirely to immigrants from our former North-African colonies, or to herbal *infusions* quite incorrectly called tea."

"Ah, thank heavens for that. But returning to—"

"Once you have grasped the *magnitude* of the consumption, you must then grasp the social *importance* of the consumption. It is the very fabric with which English society is constructed. Before-breakfast tea.

'Elevenses.' 'Put the kettle on, dearie, and let's have a nice cuppa.' Thick black tea drunk by the mugful in the Army and Navy. Entire industries coming to a halt at a wildcat-strike called because of improperly-brewed tea. Afternoon tea with its cakes and crumpets and cucumber sandwiches and who dares guess what else?"

"I feel quite ill."

"I also. Fortunately there remains only the Ceremony of the Teapot, the single article of faith which sixty million Englishmen hold in common. First the teapot must be heated, but *only* by filling it with boiling water. Then—"

"St.-Denis, I can bear no more. You have a course of action?"

"A simple virus, M. le President. Can the land of Pasteur and Curie fail before such a challenge?"

The room was somberly but richly furnished. A Persian rug lay on the floor. A fire crackled in the hearth.

The Permanent Secretary nodded approvingly. It was always satisfactory when a muddle began to regularize itself.

"Kind of you to drop by like this," said Colonel Christie. "Whisky-soda? The syphon's behind you."

"Kind of you." He limned the room with a gesture. "You do well by yourself here."

The Colonel shrugged urbanely. "You wanted to see me?"

"That is, the Minister wanted me to see you. He thought you might be interested in an informal tally sheet we have drawn up regarding the results of last year's Operation . . . er . . . Bacchus."

"Very good of him indeed."

"In so very informal a minute we thought it might be profitable to list the items under the headings *Credits* and *Debits*. The Minister was a former Chartered Accountant, you know."

"I recall," said Colonel Christie as he began to read the first sheet of notepaper.

Credits:

1. Destruction of all French vineyards, with concomitant confusion and social unrest in France, as apparently planned.

2. Twenty percent increase in the exportation of Scotch whiskey, for a three-week period before the blockade.

Debits:

1. Retaliation in the form of complete destruction of the world's tea supply by means of a still-uncontrollable mutated virus.

2. Tea-rationing, followed by riots. Three general elections in the space of eight months. Martial law eventually declared.

3. Tea no longer available, nor in the foreseeable future.

4. Total decomposition of the fabric of British society.

5. This peculiarly-depraved act of war is currently being litigated at Geneva and before the World Court as a Crime Against Humanity, but we have reason to believe that our suit is not being well-received.

6. Expulsion of England from the Common Market.

7. The world's opprobrium.

8. Economic embargo and naval blockade by a task force of seventy-three countries. Only the London Airlift and the United States Navy maintained England as a viable state.

9. Dwindling supplies of French wine. Blackmarket, and concomitant problems.

10. After a few months confusion, unexpected and absolute unification of the French people in the face of adversity.

11. As the world's now-largest importer of wine, France is directly responsible for the sudden Economic Miracles in Italy and Algeria, both of which have doubled their vineyard acreage under production. Algeria has joined the Common Market and is considering becoming once again an integral part of France. German, Spanish, and Greek wine production has also benefited greatly.

12. To further promote this rapidly-rising spiral of prosperity, France and the other members of the Common Market are nearing Economic Union and hope shortly to achieve Political Union. It is felt that France will dominate and direct this nation of 250 million people.

13. To counter the cost of wine importation and the subsequent balance of payments deficit, France has already donated its armed forces (and expenses) to a United European Command.

14. Millions of acres of tea-producing land and millions of people in sixty-eight countries suddenly have become available for other forms of agricultural production. With the vast market unexpectedly open in France and other countries to the importation of wine, most of this acreage has been given over to wine production.

15. Some 4.6 million Frenchmen have spread to all corners of the world to aid the undeveloped countries in their effort to produce potable wine.

16. Due to the high professionalism of the French Secret Service, it is accepted unhesitatingly throughout the world that the American CIA was responsible for the mass destruction of the tea plant. Spurred by the efforts of 4.6 million ambassadors of goodwill, French has completely replaced English as the secondary language being taught in the world's schools. It has, of course, become once again the standard language of diplomacy. It is thought that these factors will result in the emigration of at least half-a-million teachers from France, and a corresponding momentum will be given to the *mission civilisatrice francaise*.

17. The first wine-fair has opened in China. It was attended by Chairman Deng, who pronounced his unqualified approval of a *Nuits-St.-Georges* '66.

18. It is entirely foreseeable that with the accelerating rate of spread of French culture and influence, and the eventual leader of a United Europe, within a decade France will be the world's dominant power.

"Rather gripping, don't you think?" said the Permanent Secretary.

"Quite," replied Colonel Christie dryly.

"Interesting, the amenities of your . . . er . . . suite," said the Permanent Secretary as he strolled about the room in unabashed fascination. "One had no idea such comfort obtained in the Tower. One naturally thinks of dungeons, dank and durance vile, that sort of thing, eh?"

"Quite," said Colonel Christie. "Oh, quite."

EDITOR'S INTRODUCTION TO:

THE BATTLE

by

Robert Sheckley

Robert Sheckley is responsible for some of the most trenchent satire in the field of science fiction. Often his most amusing stories bite deeper than you think.

THE BATTLE
by
Robert Sheckley

Supreme General Fetterer barked "At ease!" as he hurried into the command room. Obediently, his three generals stood at ease.

"We haven't much time," Fetterer said, glancing at his watch. "We'll go over the plan of battle again."

He walked to the wall and unrolled a gigantic map of the Sahara desert.

"According to our best theological information, Satan is going to present his forces at these coordinates." He indicated the place with a blunt forefinger. "In the front rank there will be the devils, demons, succubi, incubi, and the rest of the ratings. Bael will command the right flank, Buer the left. His Satanic Majesty will hold the center."

"Rather medieval," General Dell murmured.

General Fetterer's aide came in, his face shining and happy with thought of the Coming.

"Sir," he said, "the priest is outside again."

"Stand at attention, soldier," Fetterer said sternly. "There's still a battle to be fought and won."

"Yes, sir," the aide said, and stood rigidly, some of the joy fading from his face.

"The priest, eh?" Supreme General Fetterer rubbed his fingers together thoughtfully. Even since the Coming, since the knowledge of the imminent Last Battle, the religious workers of the world had made a complete nuisance of themselves. They had stopped their bickering, which was commendable. But now they were trying to run military business.

"Send him away," Fetterer said. "He knows we're planning Armageddon."

"Yes, sir," the aide said. He saluted sharply, wheeled, and marched out.

"To go on," Supreme General Fetterer said. "Behind Satan's first line of defense will be the resurrected sinners, and various elemental forces of evil. The fallen angels will act as his bomber corps. Dell's robot interceptors will meet them."

General Dell smiled grimly.

"Upon contact, MacFee's automatic tank corps will proceed toward the center of the line. MacFee's automatic tank corps will proceed toward the center," Fetterer went on, "supported by General Ongin's robot infantry. Dell will command the H bombing of the rear, which should be tightly massed. I will thrust with the mechanized cavalry, here and here."

The aide came back, and stood rigidly at attention. "Sir," he said, "the priest refuses to go. He says he must speak with you."

Supreme General Fetterer hesitated before saying no. He remembered that this was the Last Battle, and that the religious workers *were* connected with it. He decided to give the man five minutes.

"Show him in," he said.

The priest wore a plain business suit, to show that he represented no particular religion. His face was tired but determined.

"General," he said, "I am a representative of all the religious workers of the world, the priests, rabbis, ministers, mullahs, and all the rest. We beg of you, General, to let us fight in the Lord's battle."

Supreme General Fetterer drummed his fingers nervously against his side. He wanted to stay on friendly terms with these men. Even he, the Supreme Commander, might need a good word, when all was said and done. . . .

"You can understand my position," Fetterer said unhappily. "I'm a general. I have a battle to fight."

"But it's the Last Battle," the priest said. "It should be the people's battle."

"It is," Fetterer said. "It's being fought by their representatives, the military."

The priest didn't look at all convinced.

Fetterer said, "You wouldn't want to lose this battle,

would you? Have Satan win?"

"Of course not," the priest murmured.

"Then we can't take any chances," Fetterer said. "All the governments agreed on that, didn't they? Oh, it would be very nice to fight Armageddon with the mass of humanity. Symbolic, you might say. But could we be certain of victory?"

The priest tried to say something, but Fetterer was talking rapidly.

"How do we know the strength of Satan's forces? We simply *must* put forth our best foot, militarily speaking. And that means the automatic armies, the robot interceptors and tanks, the H bombs."

The priest looked very unhappy. "But it isn't *right,*" he said. "Certainly you can find some place in your plan for *people?*"

Fetterer thought about it, but the request was impossible. The plan of battle was fully developed, beautiful, irresistible. Any introduction of a gross human element would only throw it out of order. No living flesh could stand the noise of that mechanical attack, the energy potentials humming in the air, the all-enveloping fire power. A human being who came within a hundred miles of the front would not live to see the enemy.

"I'm afraid not," Fetterer said.

"There are some," the priest said sternly, "who feel that it was an error to put this in the hands of the military."

"Sorry," Fetterer said cheerfully. "That's defeatist talk. If you don't mind—" He gestured at the door. Wearily, the priest left.

"These civilians," Fetterer mused. "Well, gentlemen, are your troops ready?"

"We're ready to fight for Him," General MacFee said enthusiastically. "I can vouch for every automatic in my command. Their metal is shining, all relays have been renewed, and the energy reservoirs are fully charged. Sir, they're positively itching for battle!"

General Ongin snapped fully out of his daze. "The ground troops are ready, sir!"

"Air arm ready," General Dell said.

"Excellent," General Fetterer said. "All other arrangements have been made. Television facilities are available for the total population of the world. No one, rich or poor, will miss the spectacle of the Last Battle."

"And after the battle—" General Ongin began, and stopped. He looked at Fetterer.

Fetterer frowned deeply. He didn't know what was supposed to happen after The Battle. That part of it was presumably in the hands of the religious agencies.

"I suppose there'll be a presentation or something," he said vaguely.

"You mean we will meet—Him?" General Dell asked.

"Don't really know," Fetterer said. "But I should think so. After all—I mean, you know what I mean."

"But what should we wear?" General MacFee asked, in a sudden panic. "I mean, what *does* one wear?"

"What do the angels wear?" Fetterer asked Ongin.

"I don't know," Ongin said.

"Robes, do you think?" General Dell offered.

"No," Fetterer said sternly. "We will wear dress uniform, without decorations."

The generals nodded. It was fitting.

And then it was time.

Gorgeous in their battle array, the legions of Hell advanced over the desert. Hellish pipes skirled, hollow drums pounded, and the great ghost moved forward.

In a blinding cloud of sand, General MacFee's automatic tanks hurled themselves against the satanic foe. Immediately, Dell's automatic bombers screeched overhead, hurling their bombs on the massed horde of the damned. Fetterer thrust valiantly with his automatic cavalry.

Into this melee advanced Ongin's automatic infantry, and metal did what metal could.

The hordes of the damned overflowed the front, ripping apart tanks and robots. Automatic mechanisms died, bravely defending a patch of sand. Dell's bombers were torn from the skies by the fallen angels, led by Marchocias, his griffin's wings beating the air into a tornado.

The thin, battered line of robots held, against gigantic presences that smashed and scattered them, and struck terror into the hearts of television viewers in homes around the world. Like men, like heroes the robots fought, trying to force back the forces of evil.

Astaroth shrieked a command, and Behemoth lumbered forward. Bael, with a wedge of devils behind him, threw a charge at General Fetterer's crumbling left flank. Metal screamed, electrons howled in agony at the impact.

Supreme General Fetterer sweated and trembled, a thousand miles behind the firing line. But steadily, nervelessly, he guided the pushing of buttons and the throwing of levers.

His superb corps didn't disappoint him. Mortally damaged robots swayed to their feet and fought. Smashed, trampled, destroyed by the howling fiends, the robots managed to hold their line. Then the veteran Fifth Corps threw in a counterattack, and the enemy front was pierced.

A thousand miles behind the firing line, the generals guided the mopping up operations.

"The battle is won," Supreme General Fetterer whispered, turning away from the television screen. "I congratulate you, gentlemen."

The generals smiled wearily.

They looked at each other, then broke into a spontaneous shout. Armageddon was won, and the forces of Satan had been vanquished.

But something was happening on their screens.

"Is that—is that—" General MacFee began, and then couldn't speak.

For The Presence was upon the battlefield, walking among the piles of twisted, shattered metal.

The generals were silent.

The Presence touched a twisted robot.

Upon the smoking desert, the robots began to move. The twisted, scored, fused metals straightened.

The robots stood on their feet again.

"MacFee," Supreme General Fetterer whispered. "Try your controls. Make the robots kneel or something."

The general tried, but his controls were dead.

The bodies of the robots began to rise in the air. Around them were the angels of the Lord, and the robot tanks and soldiers and bombers floated upward, higher and higher.

"He's saving them!" Ongin cried hysterically. "He's saving the robots!"

"It's a mistake!" Fetterer said. "Quick. Send a messenger to—no! We will go in person!"

And quickly a ship was commanded, and quickly they sped to the field of battle. But by then it was too late, for Armageddon was over, and the robots gone, and the Lord and his host departed.

EDITOR'S INTRODUCTION TO:

MERCENARIES AND MILITARY VIRTUE

Jerry Pournelle

This essay was originally written as the introduction to *HAMMER'S SLAMMERS* by David Drake. I thought the points worth making again, and with very little change it could have served as the introduction to this book.

MERCENARIES AND
MILITARY VIRTUE

by
Jerry Pournelle

In Europe and especially in England, military history is a respected intellectual discipline. Not so here. I doubt there are a dozen U.S. academic posts devoted to the study of the military arts.

The public esteem of the profession of arms is at a rather low ebb just now—at least in the United States. The Soviet Union retains the pomp and ceremony of military glory, and the officer class is highly regarded, if not by the public (who can know the true feelings of Soviet citizens?) then at least by the rulers of the Kremlin. Nor did the intellectuals always despise soldiers in the United States. Many of the very universities which delight in making mock of uniforms were endowed by land grants and were founded in the expectation that they would train officers for the state militia. It has not been all that many years since US combat troops were routinely expected to take part in parades; when soldiers were proud to wear uniform off post, and when my uniform was sufficient for free entry into movie houses, the New York Museum of Modern Art, the New York Ballet, and as I recall the Met (as well as to other establishments catering to the less cultural needs of the soldier).

But now both the military and anyone who studies war are held in a good deal of contempt.

I do not expect this state of affairs to last—in fact, I am certain that it cannot. A nation which despises its soldiers will all too soon have a despicable army.

The depressing fact is that history is remarkably clear on one point: wealthy republics do not last long. Time after time they have risen to wealth and freedom; the

citizens become wealthy and sophisticated; unwilling to
volunteer to protect themselves, they go to conscription;
this too becomes intolerable; and soon enough they turn
to mercenaries.

Machiavelli understood that, and things have not
much changed since his time—except that Americans
know far less history than did the rulers of Florence and
Milan and Venice.

For mercenaries are a dangerous necessity. If they are
incompetent, they will ruin you. If they are competent
there is always the temptation to rob the paymaster.

Why should they not? They know their employers will
not fight. They may, if recruited into a national army,
retain loyalty to the country—but if the nation despises
them, and takes every possible opportunity to let them
know it, then that incentive falls as well—and they have
a monopoly on the means of violence. Their employers
won't fight—if they would, they needn't have hired
mercenaries.

The result is usually disastrous for the wealthy republic.

After all, it should be fairly clear than no one fights
purely for money; that anyone who does is probably not
worth hiring. As Montesquieu put it, "a rational army
would run away." To stand on the firing parapet and
expose yourself to danger; to stand and fight a thousand
miles from home when you're all alone and outnumbered and probably beaten; to spit on your hands
and lower the pike, to stand fast over the body of
Leonidas the King, to be rear guard at Kunu-ri; to stand
and be still to the Birkenhead drill; these are not
rational acts.

They are often merely necessary.

Through history, through painful experience, military
professionals have built up a specialized knowledge:
how to induce men (including most especially themselves) to fight, aye, and to die. To charge the guns at
Breed's Hill and New Orleans, at Chippewa and at Cold
Harbor; to climb the wall of the Embassy Compound at
Peking; to go ashore at Betio and Saipan; to load and fire
with precision and accuracy while the *Bon Homme
Richard* is sinking; to fly in that thin air five miles above
a hostile land and bring the ship straight and level for

thirty seconds over Regensberg and Ploesti; to endure at Heartbreak Ridge and Porkchop Hill and the Iron Triangle and Dien Bien Phu and Hue and Firebase 34 and a thousand nameless hills and villages.

It's a rather remarkable achievement, when you think about it. It's even more remarkable when you look closer and see just how many mercenary units have performed creditably, honorably, even gallantly; how many of those who have changed history on the battlefield have been professional soldiers. For despite the silly sayings about violence never settling anything, history IS changed on the battlefield: ask the National Socialist German Workers' Party, the Continental Congress, the Carthigenians, the Israelis, the Confederate State of America, Pompey and Caesar and Richard III and Harold of Wessex, Don Juan of Austria and Aetius the last Roman. Yet you could search through the armies of history and you would find few competent troopers who fought for money and money alone.

This is the mistake so often made by those who despise the military, and because they despise it refuse to understand it: they fail to see that few are so foolish as to give their lives for money; yet an army whose soldiers are not willing to die is an army that wins few victories.

Yet certainly there have always existed mercenary soldiers.

We can piously hope there will be no armies in the future. It is an unlikely hope; at least history is against it. On the evidence, peace is a purely theoretical state of affairs whose existence we deduce because there have been intervals between wars. But I did not speak contemptuously when I spoke of pious hopes; nor do I find it an irony that the Strategic Air Command, whose commanders hold leashed more firepower than has been expended by all the armies of all time, has as its motto "Peace is our profession." Most of those young men who guard us as we sleep believe in that, believe it wholeheartedly and give up a very great deal for it. I too can piously hope for peace; that we shall heed the advice of the carol we sing annually and "hush the noise, ye men of strife, and hear the angels sing."

There is no physical reason why the human race should not endure for a hundred billion years; and on that scale our history is short, and all we have learned is little compared to what we shall one day know. There may well be a secret formula for peace, and certainly I hope we will find it.

But to hope is nothing. When Appius Claudius told the Senate of Rome that "If you would have peace, be thou then prepared for war" he said nothing that history has not repeatedly affirmed. It may be wrong advice. Certainly there is an argument against it. But I think there is no argument at all against a similar aphorism: "If you would have peace, then understand war."

Which is to say, understand armies; understand why men fight; understand the organization of violence.

And that, at last, brings us to this book.

Military science fiction is a highly specialized art form. It is attempted often, but there are few writers who know science, society, and the military well enough to write a good story of war in the future.

This is unfortunate: although science fiction, like all literature, must entertain and divert if it is to have readers, it often has a serious purpose as well: to look at future societies, and the impact of technology on history. Any attempt to look in the future while ignoring war and the military is probably doomed to failure: if five thousand years of recorded history have given us no formula for controlling violence and greed, we would be fortunate indeed if this generation has fought the war to end all wars; if the armies that exist today were the last this planet will ever see.

The United States lost the Viet Nam War precisely because we attempted to fight it as if we were using Legionnaires, mercenary soldiers responsible only to the President and the Executive branch of the government. There was no declaration of war, and no attempt to involve the American people. President Johnson was afraid that a declaration of war would take attention and funds away from his Great Society programs.

The result was disaster. The American people have always regarded the Army as their own; it belongs to the Congress, not to the President. The Constitution treats the Army differently from the Naval Forces; we might possibly have sent the Marines into Viet Nam without involving the population, but never the Army. It's even doubtful about the Marines. In truth, the United States has no Legions, no professional soldiers of the *Landsknecht* tradition.

Even so, our Army did well in Viet Nam. It never lost a battle, except with the American news media. Take the Tet Offensives as an example: only in Hue did we take heavy casualties, for only there did the enemy manage to take possession of any important real estate. By the time Tet ended, the Viet Cong was all but destroyed; it was one of the most decisive victories in history. Yet the news media insisted on portraying it as "tragedy" and defeat.

The truth is that the US Army won its battles; that the "counterinsurgency" actions were totally successful; and that the Viet Cong—the guerillas—were capable of making life miserable for the people of Viet Nam through their savage acts of terrorism; but the Republic of Viet Nam never fell to guerrillas. It fell to four North Vietnamese Army Corps of regulars; to an invasion of armored divisions from the north; and to a lack of ammunition and supplies. The Republic of South Viet Nam fell to an invasion—and was defeated by the Congress of the United States, which deliberately refused to allow the President to enforce the Geneva accords.

In fact, though, we had lost much earlier than that. We lost in 1965, when we defeated the guerillas, but failed either to take North Viet Nam or to isolate the battlefield. We tried to defeat hornets by swatting them hornet at a time; a tactic that cannot possibly work. You must either burn the nest or retire behind window screens.

Either strategy would have been feasible. Given the later importance of the Chinese Alliance to the United States, it may be that a rampsdown invasion of North Viet Nam was politically undesirable; but certainly there would have been no great difficulty in building a barrier from the Mekong to the Sea, and, if necessary, extending the barrier further west. Any nation capable of building the Panama Canal in the early part of the century could build minefields, tank traps, barbed wire entanglements, military roads, watchtowers—an Asian equivalent of the Soviet Wall along the Czech-German border.

Yet we did not; and we have not yet seen the result of bringing home a defeated army.

As I write this, the Pentagon is studying the 1982 campaigns: the Falklands debacle, and the Israeli incursion into Lebanon. Two things stand out:

First, without high technology, you cannot wage successful war. You must have electronics and missiles, and they must work.

Second, without good soldiers; without leadership, and initiative, and steadfast devotion to duty; without what we once called professionalism and the military virtues; all the sophisticated equipment in the world cannot save you.

In other words, we learn from the latest wars what we might have learned from history.

History has never been kind to wealthy republics. We can hope we are an exception.

EDITOR'S INTRODUCTION TO:

RANKS OF BRONZE

by

David Drake

David Drake is one of a very select group who can write realistic military science fiction. His *HAMMER'S SLAMMERS* has a deservedly high reputation. Until recently Drake made his living as a lawyer and didn't write very much, which was a real pity, for he understands much. After the success of *HAMMER'S SLAMMERS*, Drake's stock with publishing types has risen high. On the basis of several book contracts he has decided to entertain the innocent rather than prosecute the guilty, for which we may all be properly grateful ...

"Gold may not get you good soldiers," said Niccolo Machiavelli, "but good soldiers can always get you gold." The merchant princes in this story understand that all too well.

RANKS OF BRONZE
by
David Drake

The rising sun is a dagger point casting long shadows toward Vibulenus and his cohort from the native breast-works. The legion had formed ranks an hour before; the enemy is not yet stirring. A playful breeze with a bitter edge skitters out of the south, and the Tribune swings his shield to his right side against it.

"When do we advance, sir?" his First Centurion asks. Gnaeus Clodius Calvus, promoted to his present position after a boulder had pulped his predecessor during the assault on a granite fortress far away. Vibulenus only vaguely recalls his first days with the cohort, a boy of eighteen in titular command of four hundred and eighty men whose names he had despaired of learning. Well, he knows them now. Of course, there are only two hundred and ninety-odd left to remember.

Calvus' bearded, silent patience snaps Vibulenus back to the present. "When the cavalry comes up, they told me. Some kinglet or other is supposed to bring up a couple thousand men to close our flanks. Otherwise, we're hanging. . . ."

The Tribune's voice trails off. He stares across the flat expanse of gravel toward the other camp, remembering another battle plain of long ago.

"Damn Parthians," Calvus mutters, his thought the same.

Vibulenus nods. "Damn Crassus, you mean. He put us *there*, and that put us *here*. The stupid bastard. But he got his, too."

The legionaries squat in their ranks, talking and chewing bits of bread or dried fruit. They display no bravado, very little concern. They have been here too often before. Sunlight turns their shield-facings green: not the crumbly fungus of verdigris but the shimmering sea-color of the harbor of Brundisium on a foggy morning.

Oh, Mother Vesta, Vibulenus breathes to himself. He is five foot two, about average for the legion. His hair is black where it curls under the rim of his helmet and he has no trace of a beard. Only his eyes make him appear more than a teenager; they would suit a tired man of fifty.

A trumpet from the command group in the rear sings three quick bars. "Fall in!" the Tribune orders, but his centurions are already barking their own commands. These too are lost in the clash of hobnails on gravel. The Tenth Cohort could form ranks in its sleep.

Halfway down the front, a legionary's cloak hooks on a notch in his shield rim. He tugs at it, curses in Oscan as Calvus snarls down the line at him. Vibulenus makes a mental note to check with the centurion after the battle. That fellow should have been issued a replacement shield before disembarking. He glances at his own. How many shields has he carried? Not that it matters. Armor is replaceable. He is wearing his fourth cuirass, now, though none of them have fit like the one his father had bought him the day Crassus granted him a tribune's slot. Vesta. . . .

A galloper from the command group skids his beast to a halt with a needlessly brutal jerk on its reins. Vibulenus recognizes him—Pompilius Falco. A little swine when he joined the legion, an accomplished swine now. Not bad with animals, though. "We'll be advancing without the cavalry," he shouts, leaning over in his saddle. "Get your line dressed."

"Osiris' bloody dick we will!" the Tribune snaps. "Where's our support?"

"Have to support yourself, I guess," shrugs Falco. He wheels his mount. Vibulenus steps forward and catches the reins.

"Falco," he says with no attempt to lower his voice, "you tell our deified Commander to get somebody on our left flank if he expects the Tenth to advance. There's too many natives—they'll hit us from three sides at once."

"You afraid to die?" the galloper sneers. He tugs at the reins.

Vibulenus holds them. A gust of wind whips at his cloak. "Afraid to get my skull split?" he asks. "I don't know. Are you, Falco?" Falco glances at where the Tribune's right hand rests. He says nothing. "Tell him we'll fight for him," Vibulenus goes on "We won't let him throw us away. We've gone that route once." He looses the reins and watches the galloper scatter gravel on his way back.

The replacement gear is solid enough, shields that do not split when dropped and helmets forged without thin spots. But there is no craftsmanship in them. They are heavy, lifeless. Vibulenus still carries a bone-hilted sword from Toledo that required frequent sharpening but was tempered and balanced—poised to slash a life out, as it has a hundred times already. His hand continues to caress the palm-smoothed bone, and it calms him somewhat.

"Thanks, sir."

The thin-featured tribune glances back at his men. Several of the nearer ranks give him a spontaneous salute. Calvus is the one who spoke. He is blank-faced now, a statue of mahogany and strap-bronze. His stocky form radiates pride in his leader. Leader—no one in the group around the standards can lead a line soldier, though they may give commands that will be obeyed. Vibulenus grins and slaps Calvus' burly shoulder. "Maybe this is the last one and we'll be going home," he says.

Movement throws a haze over the enemy camp. At this distance it is impossible to distinguish forms, but metal flashes in the viridian sunlight. The shadow of bodies spreads slowly to right and left of the breastworks as the natives order themselves. There are thousands of them, many thousands.

"Hey-*yip!*" Twenty riders of the general's bodyguard pass behind the cohort at an earthshaking trot. They rein up on the left flank, shrouding the exposed depth of the infantry. Pennons hang from the lances socketed behind their right thighs, gay yellows and greens to keep the lance heads from being driven too deep to be jerked out. The riders' faces are sullen under their mesh face guards. Vibulenus knows how angry they must be at being shifted under pressure—under his pressure—and he grins again. The bodyguards are insulted at being required to fight instead of remaining nobly aloof from the battle. The experience may do them some good.

At least it may get a few of the snotty bastards killed.

"Not exactly a regiment of cavalry," Calvus grumbles.

"He gave us half of what was available," Vibulenus replies with a shrug. "They'll do to keep the natives off our back. Likely nobody'll come near, they look so mean."

The centurion taps his thigh with his knobby swagger stick. "Mean? We'll give 'em mean."

All the horns in the command group sound together, a cacophonous bray. The jokes and scufflings freeze, and only the south wind whispers. Vibulenus takes a last look down his ranks—each of them fifty men abreast and no more sway to it than a tight-stretched cord would leave. Five feet from shield boss to shield boss, room to swing a sword. Five feet from nose guard to the nose guards of the next rank, men ready to step forward individually to replace the fallen or by ranks to lock shields with the front line in an impenetrable wall of bronze. The legion is a restive dragon, and its teeth glitter in its spears; one vertical behind each legionary's shield, one slanted from each right hand to stab or throw.

The horns blare again, the eagle standard slants forward, and Vibulenus' throat joins three thousand others in a death-rich bellow as the legion steps off on its left foot. The centurions are counting cadence and the ranks blast it back to them in the crash-jingle of boots and gear.

Striding quickly between the legionaries, Vibulenus checks the dress of his cohort. He should have a horse, but there are no horses in the legion now. The command group rides rough equivalents which are . . . very rough. Vibulenus is not sure he could accept one if his parsimonious employers offered it.

His men are a smooth bronze chain that advances in lock step. Very nice. The nine cohorts to the right are in equally good order, but Hercules! there are so few of them compared to the horde swarming from the native camp. Somebody has gotten overconfident. The enemy raises its own cheer, scattered and thin at first. But it goes on and on, building, ordering itself to a blood-pulse rhythm that moans across the intervening distance, the gap the legion is closing at two steps a second. Hercules! there is a crush of them.

The natives are close enough to be individuals now: lanky, long-armed in relations to a height that averages greater than that of the legionaires. Ill-equipped, though. Their heads are covered either by leather helmets or beehives of their own hair. Their shields appear to be hide and wicker affairs. What could live on this gravel waste and provide that much leather? But of course Vibulenus has been told none of the background, not even the immediate geography. There is some place around that raises swarms of warriors, that much is certain.

And they have iron. The black glitter of their spearheads tightens the Tribune's wounded chest as he remembers.

"Smile, boys," one of the centurions calls cheerfully, "here's company." With his words a javelin hums down at a steep angle to spark on the ground. From a spearthrower, must have been. The distance is too long for any arm Vibulenus has seen, and he has seen his share.

"Ware!" he calls as another score of missiles arc from the native ranks. Legionaries judge them, raise their shields or ignore the plunging weapons as they choose. One strikes in front of Vibulenus and shatters into a dozen iron splinters and a knobby shaft that looks like rattan. One or two of the men have spears clinging to their shield faces. Their clatter syncopates the thud of boot heels. No one is down.

Vibulenus runs two paces ahead of his cohort, his sword raised at an angle. It makes him an obvious target: a dozen javelins spit toward him. The skin over his ribs crawls, the lumpy breadth of scar tissue scratching like a rope over the bones. But he can be seen by every man in his cohort, and somebody has to give the signal. . . .

"Now!" he shouts vainly in the mingling cries. His arm and sword cut down abruptly. Three hundred

throats give a collective grunt as the cohort heaves its
own massive spears with the full weight of its rush
behind them. Another light javelin glances from the
shoulder of Vibulenus' cuirass, staggering him. Calvus'
broad right palm catches the Tribune, holds him upright
for the instant he needs to get his balance.

The front of the native line explodes as the Roman
spears crash into it.

Fifty feet ahead there are orange warriors shrieking
as they stumble over the bodies of comrades whose
armor has shredded under the impact of the heavy
spears. "At 'em!" a front-rank file-closer cries, ignoring
his remaining spear as he drags out his short sword. The
trumpets are calling something but it no longer matters
what: tactics go hang, the Tenth is cutting its way into
another native army.

In a brief spate of fury, Vibulenus holds his forward
position between a pair of legionaries. A native, orange-
skinned with bright carmine eyes, tries to drag himself
out of the Tribune's path. A Roman spear has gouged
through his shield and arm, locking all three together.
Vibulenus' sword takes the warrior alongside the jaw.
The blood is paler than a man's.

The backward shock of meeting has bunched the
natives. The press of undisciplined reserves from behind adds to their confusion. Vibulenus jumps a still-
writhing body and throws himself into the wall of
shields and terrified orange faces. An iron-headed spear
thrusts at him, misses as another warrior jostles the
wielder. Vibulenus slashes downward at his assailant.
The warrior throws his shield up to catch the sword,
then collapses when a second-rank legionary darts his
spear through the orange abdomen.

Breathing hard with his sword still dripping in his
hand, Vibulenus lets the pressing ranks flow around
him. Slaughter is not a tribune's work, but increasingly
Vibulenus finds that he needs the swift violence of the
battle line to release the fury building within him. The
cohort is advancing with the jerky sureness of an ox-
drawn plow in dry soil.

A window of native bodies lies among the line of
first contact, now well within the Roman formation.
Vibulenus wipes his blade on a fallen warrior, leaving

two sluggish runnels filling on the flesh. He sheathes the sword. Three bodies are sprawled together to form a hillock. Without hesitation the Tribune steps onto it to survey the battle.

The legion is a broad awl punching through a belt of orange leather. The cavalry on the left stand free in a scatter of bodies, neither threatened by the natives nor making any active attempt to drive them back. One of the mounts, a hairless brute combining the shape of a wolfhound with the bulk of an ox, is feeding on a corpse his rider has lanced. Vibulenus was correct in expecting the natives to give them a wide berth; thousands of flanking warriors tremble in indecision rather than sweep forward to surround the legion. It would take more discipline than this orange rabble has shown to attack the toad-like riders on their terrible beasts.

Behind the lines, a hundred paces distant from the legionaries whose armor stands in hammering contrast to the naked autochthones, is the Commander and his remaining score of guards. He alone of the three thousand who have landed from the starship knows why the battle is being fought, but he seems to stand above it. And if the silly bastard still has half his bodyguard with him—Mars and all the gods, what must be happening on the right flank?

The inhuman shout of triumph that rises half a mile away gives Vibulenus an immediate answer.

"Prepare to disengage!" he orders the nearest centurion. The swarthy non-com, son of a North African colonist, speaks briefly into the ears of two legionaries before sending them to the ranks forward and back of his. The legion is tight for men, always has been. Tribunes have no runners, but the cohort makes do.

Trumpets blat in terror. The native warriors boil whooping around the Roman right flank. Legionaries in the rear are facing about with ragged suddenness, obeying instinct rather than the orders bawled by their startled officers. The command group suddenly realizes the situation. Three of the bodyguard charge toward the oncoming orange mob. The rest of the guards and staff scatter into the infantry.

The iron-bronze clatter has ceased on the left flank. When the cohort halts its advance, the natives gain enough room to break and flee for their encampment. Even the warriors who have not engaged are cowed by the panic of those who have; by the panic, and the sprawls of bodies left behind them.

"About face!" Vibulenus calls through the indecisive hush, "and pivot on your left flank. There's some more barbs want to fight the Tenth!"

The murderous cheer from his legionaries overlies the noise of the cohort executing his order.

As it swings Vibulenus runs across the new front of his troops, what had been the rear rank. The cavalry, squat-bodied and grim in their full armor, shows sense enough to guide their mounts toward the flank of the Ninth Cohort as Vibulenus rotates his men away from it. Only a random javelin from the native lines appears to hinder them. Their comrades who remained with the Commander have been less fortunate.

A storm of javelins has disintegrated the half-hearted charge. Two of the mounts have gone down despite their heavy armor. Behind them, the Commander lies flat on the hard soil while his beast screams horribly above him. The shaft of a stray missile projects from its withers. Stabbing up from below, the orange warriors fell the remaining lancer and gut his companions as they try to rise. Half a dozen of the bodyguards canter nervously back from their safe bolthole among the infantry to try to rescue their employer. The wounded mount leaps at one of the lancers. The two beasts tangle with the guard between them. A clawed hind leg flicks his head. Helmet and head rip skyward in a spout of green ichor.

"Charge!" Vibulenus roars. The legionaries who can not hear him follow his running form. The knot of cavalry and natives is a quarter mile away. The cohorts of the right flank are too heavily engaged to do more than defend themselves against the new thrust. Half the legion has become a bronze worm, bristling front and back with spearpoints against the surging orange flood. Without immediate support, the whole right flank will be squeezed until it collapses into a tangle of blood and scrap metal. The Tenth Cohort is their support, all the support there is.

"Rome!" the fresh veterans leading the charge shout as their shields rise against the new flight of javelins.

There are gaps in the back ranks, those just disengaged. Behind the charge, men hold palms clamped over torn calves or lie crumpled around a shaft of alien wood. There will be time enough for them if the recovery teams land—which they will not do in event of a total disaster on the ground.

The warriors snap and howl at the sudden threat. Their own success has fragmented them. What had been a flail slashing into massed bronze kernels is now a thousand leaderless handfuls in sparkling contact with the Roman line. Only the leaders bunched around the command group have held their unity.

One mount is still on its feet and snarling. Four massively-equipped guards try to ring the Commander with their maces. The Commander, his suit a splash of blue against the gravel, tries to rise. There is a flurry of mace strokes and quickly-riposting spears, ending in a clash of falling armor and an agile orange body with a knife leaping the crumpled guard. Vibulenus' sword, flung overarm, takes the native in the throat. The inertia of its spin cracks the hilt against the warrior's forehead.

The Tenth Cohort is on the startled natives. A moment before the warriors were bounding forward in the flush of victory. Now they face the cohort's meat-axe suddenness—and turn. At swordpoint and shield edge, as inexorable as the rising sun, the Tenth grinds the native retreat into panic while the cohorts of the right flank open order and advance. The ground behind them is slimy with blood.

Vibulenus rests on one knee, panting. He has retrieved his sword. Its stickiness bonds it to his hand. Already the air keens with landing motors. In minutes the recovery teams will be at work on the fallen legionaries, building life back into all but the brain-hacked or spine-severed. Vibulenus rubs his own scarred ribs in aching memory.

A hand falls on the Tribune's shoulder. It is gloved in a skin-tight blue material; not armor, at least not armor against weapons. The Commander's voice comes from the small plate beneath his clear, round helmet. Speaking in Latin, his accents precisely flawed, he says, "You are splendid, you warriors."

Vibulenus sneers though he does not correct the alien.

Warriors are capering heroes, good only for dying when they meet trained troops, when they meet the Tenth Cohort.

"I thought the Federation Council had gone mad," the flat voice continues, "when it ruled that we must not land weapons beyond the native level in exploiting inhabited worlds. All very well to talk of the dangers of introducing barbarians to modern weaponry, but how else could my business crush local armies and not be bled white by transportation costs?"

The Commander shakes his head in wonder at the carnage about him. Vibulenus silently wipes his blade. In front of him, Falco gapes toward the green sun. A javelin points from his right eyesocket. "When we purchased you from your Parthian captors it was only an experiment. Some of us even doubted it was worth the cost of the longevity treatments. In a way you are more effective than a Guard Regiment with lasers; out-numbered, you beat them with their own weapons. They can't even claim 'magic' as a slave to their pride. And at a score of other job sites you have done as well. And so cheaply!"

"Since we have been satisfactory," the Tribune says, trying to keep the hope out of his face, "will we be returned home now?"

"Oh, goodness, no," the alien laughs, "you're far too valuable for that. But I have a surprise for you, one just as pleasant I'm sure—females."

"You found us real women?" Vibulenus whispers.

"You really won't be able to tell the difference," the Commander says with paternal confidence.

A million suns away on a farm in the Sabine hills, a poet takes the stylus from the fingers of a nude slave girl and writes, very quickly, *And Crassus' wretched soldier takes a barbarian wife from his captors and grows old waging war for them.*

The poet looks at the line with a pleased expression. "It needs polish, of course," he mutters. Then, more directly to the slave, he says, "You know, Leuconoe, there's more than inspiration to poetry, a thousand times more; but this came to me out of the air."

Horace gestures with his stylus toward the glittering night sky. The girl smiles back at him.

EDITOR'S INTRODUCTION TO:

I AM NOTHING

by

Eric Frank Russell

Eric Frank Russell was a British writer and a found-ing member of the British Interplanetary Society, although many of his stories feature authentic American protagonists. A number of his stories are genuine classics. " . . . And Then There Were None" is one of the most powerful statements of the libertarian position in all of science fiction.

One of the temptations of Faust was Pride. In the Richard Burton film, Mephistopheles has given Faust charge of an army. With banners flying they gallop to the sound of drums and trumpets, and Faust shouts "Is it not a pleasant thing, to be a king, and ride in triumph to Samarkand!"

There are other forms of conquest, some equally glorious, which do not lead to the sin of pride.

I AM NOTHING
by
Eric Frank Russell

David Korman rasped, "Send them the ultimatum."

"Yes, sir, but—"

"But what?"

"It may mean war."

"What of it?"

"Nothing, sir." The other sought a way out. "I merely thought—"

"You are not paid to think," said Korman, acidly. "You are paid only to obey orders."

"Of course, sir. Most certainly." Gathering his papers, he backed away hurriedly. "I shall have the ultimatum forwarded to Lani at once."

"You better had!" Korman stared across his ornate desk, watched the door close. Then he voiced an emphatic, "Bah!"

A lickspittle. He was surrounded by lickspittles, cravens, weaklings. On all sides were the spineless ready to jump to his command, eager to fawn upon him. They smiled at him with false smiles, hastened into pseudo-agreement with every word he uttered, gave him exaggerated respect that served to cover their inward fears.

There was a reason for all this. He, David Korman, was strong. He was strong in the myriad ways that meant full and complete strength. With his broad body, big jowls, bushy brows and hard gray eyes he looked precisely what he was: a creature of measureless power, mental and physical.

It was good that he should be like this. It was a law of Nature that the weak must give way to the strong. A thoroughly sensible law. Besides, this world of Morcine needed a strong man. Morcine was one world in a

272

cosmos full of potential competitors, all of them born of some misty, long-forgotten planet near a lost sun called Sol. Morcine's duty to itself was to grow strong at the expense of the weak. Follow the natural law.

His heavy thumb found the button on his desk, pressed it, and he said into the little silver microphone, "Send in Fleet Commander Rogers at once."

There was a knock at the door and he snapped, "Come in." Then, when Rogers had reached the desk, he informed, "We have sent the ultimatum."

"Really, sir? Do you suppose they'll accept it?"

"Doesn't matter whether they do or don't," Korman declared. "In either event we'll get our own way." His gaze upon the other became challenging. "Is the fleet disposed in readiness exactly as ordered?"

"It is, sir."

"You are certain of that? You have checked it in person?"

"Yes, sir."

"Very well. These are my orders: the fleet will observe the arrival on Lani of the courier bearing our demands. It will allow twenty-four hours for receipt of a satisfactory reply."

"And if one does not come?"

"It will attack one minute later in full strength. Its immediate task will be to capture and hold an adequate ground base. Having gained it, reinforcements will be poured in and the territorial conquest of the planet can proceed."

"I understand, sir." Rogers prepared to leave. "Is there anything more?"

"Yes," said Korman. "I have one other order. When you are about to seize this base my son's vessel must be the first to land upon it."

Rogers blinked and protested nervously, "But, sir, as a young lieutenant he commands a small scout bearing twenty men. Surely one of our major battleships should be—"

"My son lands first!" Standing up, Korman leaned forward over his desk. His eyes were cold. "The knowledge that Reed Korman, my only child, was in the forefront of the battle will have an excellent psychological effect upon the ordinary masses here. I give it as my order."

"What if something happens?" murmured Rogers, aghast. "What if he should become a casualty, perhaps be killed?"

"That," Korman pointed out, "will enhance the effect."

"All right, sir." Rogers swallowed and hurried out, his features strained.

Had the responsibility for Reed Korman's safety been placed upon his own shoulders? Or was that character behind the desk genuine in his opportunist and dreadful fatalism? He did not know. He knew only that Korman could not be judged by ordinary standards.

Blank-faced and precise, the police escort stood around while Korman got out of the huge official car. He gave them his usual austere look-over while the chauffeur waited, his hand holding the door open. Then Korman mounted the steps to his home, heard the car door close at the sixth step. Invariably it was the sixth step, never the fifth or seventh.

Inside, the maid waited on the same corner of the carpet, her hands ready for his hat, gloves and cloak. She was stiff and starched and never looked directly at him. Not once in fourteen years had she met him eye to eye.

With a disdainful grunt he brushed past her and went into the dining room, took his seat, studied his wife across a long expanse of white cloth filled with silver and crystal.

She was tall and blond and blue-eyed and once had seemed supremely beautiful. Her willowy slenderness had made him think with pleasure of her moving in his arms with the sinuosity of a snake. Now, her slight curves had gained angularity. Her submissive eyes wore crinkles that were not the marks of laughter.

"I've had enough of Lani," he announced. "We're precipitating a showdown. An ultimatum has been sent."

"Yes, David."

That was what he had expected her to say. He could have said it for her. It was her trademark, so to speak; always had been, always would be.

Years ago, a quarter of a century back, he had said with becoming politeness, "Mary, I wish to marry you."

"Yes, David."

She had not wanted it—not in the sense that he had wanted it. Her family had pushed her into the arrangement and she had gone where shoved. Life was like that: the pushers and the pushed. Mary was of the latter class. The fact had taken the spice out of romance. The conquest had been too easy. Korman insisted on conquest but he liked it big. Not small.

Later on, when the proper time had come, he had told her, "Mary, I want a son."

She had arranged it precisely as ordered. No slipups. No presenting him with a fat and impudent daughter by way of hapless obstetrical rebellion. A son, eight pounds, afterward named Reed. He had chosen the name.

A faint scowl lay over his broad face as he informed, "Almost certainly it means war."

"Does it, David?"

It came without vibrancy or emotion. Dull-toned, her pale oval features expressionless, her eyes submissive. Now and again he wondered whether she hated him with a fierce, turbulent hatred so explosive that it had to be held in check at all costs. He could never be sure of that. Of one thing he was certain: she feared him and had from the very first.

Everyone feared him. Everyone without exception. Those who did not at first meeting soon learned to do so. He saw to that in one way or another. It was good to be feared. It was an excellent substitute for other emotions one has never had or known.

When a child he had feared his father long and ardently; also his mother. Both of them so greatly that their passing had come as a vast relief. Now it was his turn. That, too, was a natural law, fair and logical. What is gained from one generation should be passed to the next. What is denied should likewise be denied.

Justice.

"Reed's scoutship has joined the fleet in readiness for action."

"I know, David."

His eyebrows lifted. "How do you know?"

"I received a letter from him a couple of hours ago." She passed it across.

He was slow to unfold the stiff sheet of paper. He knew what the first two words would be. Getting it open, he found it upside-down, reversed it and looked.

"Dear Mother."

That was her revenge.

"Mary. I want a son."

So she had given him one—and then taken him away.

Now there were letters, perhaps two in one week or one in two months according to the ship's location. Always they were written as though addressing both, always they contained formal love to both, formal hope that both were keeping well.

But always they began, "Dear Mother."

Never, "Dear Father."

Revenge!

Zero hour came and went. Morcine was in a fever of excitement and preparation. Nobody knew what was happening far out in space, not even Korman. There was a time-lag due to sheer distance. Beamed signals from the fleet took many hours to come in.

The first word went straight to Korman's desk, where he posed ready to receive it. It said the Lanians had replied with a protest and what they called an appeal to reason. In accordance with instructions the fleet commander had rejected this as unsatisfactory. The attack was on.

"They plead for reasonableness," he growled. "That means they want us to go soft. Life isn't made for the soft." He threw a glance forward. "Is it?"

"No, sir," agreed the messenger with alacrity.

"Tell Bathurst to put the tape on the air at once."

"Yes, sir."

When the other had gone he switched his midget radio and waited. It came in ten minutes, the long, rolling, grandiloquent speech he'd recorded more than a month before. It played on two themes: righteousness and strength, especially strength.

The alleged causes of the war were elucidated in detail, grimly but without ire. That lack of indignation was a telling touch because it suggested the utter inevitability of the present situation and the fact that the powerful have too much justified self-confidence to emote.

As for the causes, he listened to them with boredom. Only the strong know there is but one cause of war. All the other multitudinous reasons recorded in the history books were not real reasons at all. They were nothing but plausible pretexts. There was but one root-cause that persisted right back to the dim days of the jungle. When two monkeys want the same banana, that is war.

Of course, the broadcasting tape wisely refrained from putting the issue so bluntly and revealingly. Weak stomachs require pap. Red meat is exclusively for the strong. So the great antennae of the world network comported themselves accordingly and catered for the general dietary need.

After the broadcast had finished on a heartening note about Morcine's overwhelming power, he leaned back in his chair and thought things over. There was no question of bombing Lani into submission from the upper reaches of its atmosphere. All its cities cowered beneath bombproof hemispherical force fields. Even if they had been wide open he would not have ordered their destruction. It is empty victory to win a few mounds of rubble.

He'd had enough of empty victories. Instinctively, his gray eyes strayed toward the bookcase on which stood the photograph he seldom noticed and then no more than absently. For years it had been there, a sub-consciously-observed, taken-for-granted object like the inkpot or radiant heat panel, but less useful than either.

She wasn't like her picture now. Come to think of it, she hadn't been really like it *then*. She had given him obedience and fear before he had learned the need for these in lieu of other needs. At that time he had wanted something else that had not been forthcoming. So long as he could remember, to his very earliest years, it had never been forthcoming, not from anyone, never, never, never.

He jerked his mind back to the subject of Lani. The location of that place and the nature of its defenses determined the pattern of conquest. A ground base must be won, constantly replenished with troops, arms and all auxiliary services. From there the forces of Morcine must expand and, bit by bit, take over all unshielded territory until at last the protected cities stood alone in fateful isolation. The cities would then be permitted to sit under their shields until starved into surrender.

Acquisition of enemy territory was the essential aim. This meant that despite spacegoing vessels, force shields and all the other redoubtable gadgets of ultra-modernism, the ordinary foot soldier remained the final arbiter of victory. Machines could assault and destroy. Only men could take and hold.

Therefore this was going to be no mere five-minute war. It would run on for a few months, perhaps even a year, with spasms of old-style land-fighting as strong points were attacked and defended. There would be bombing perforce limited to road blocks, strategic junctions, enemy assembly and regrouping areas, unshielded but stubborn villages.

There would be some destruction, some casualties. But it was better that way. Real conquest comes only over real obstacles, not imaginary ones. In her hour of triumph Morcine would be feared. Korman would be feared. The feared are respected and that is proper and decent.

If one can have nothing more.

Pictorial records in full color and sound came at the end of the month. Their first showing was in the privacy of his own home to a small audience composed of himself, his wife, a group of government officials and assorted brass hats.

Unhampered by Lanian air defenses, weak from the beginning and now almost wiped out, the long black ships of Morcine dived into the constantly widening base and unloaded great quantities of supplies. Troops moved forward against tough but spasmodic opposition, a growing weight of armored and motorized equipment going with them.

The recording camera trundled across an enormous bridge with thick girders fantastically distorted and with great gaps temporarily filled in. It took them through seven battered villages which the enemy had either defended or given cause to believe they intended to defend. There were shots of crater-pocked roads, skeletal houses, a blackened barn with a swollen horse lying in a field nearby.

And an action-take of an assault on a farmhouse. A patrol, suddenly fired on, dug in and radioed back. A monster on huge, noisy tracks answered their call, rumbled laboriously to within four hundred yards of the objective, spat violently and lavishly from its front turret. A great splash of liquid fell on the farmhouse roof, burst into roaring flame. Figures ran out, seeking cover of an adjacent thicket. The sound track emitted rattling noises. The figures fell over, rolled, jerked, lay still.

The reel ended and Korman said, "I approve it for public exhibition." Getting out of his seat, he frowned around, adding, "I have one criticism. My son has taken command of a company of infantry. He is doing a job, like any other man. Why wasn't he featured?"

"We would not depict him except with your approval, sir," said one.

"I not only approve—I order it. Make sure that he is shown next time. Not predominantly. Just sufficiently to let the people see for themselves that he is there, sharing the hardships and the risks."

"Very well, sir."

They packed up and went away. He strolled restlessly on the thick carpet in front of the electric radiator.

"Do them good to know Reed is among those present," he insisted.

"Yes, David." She had taken up some knitting, her needles going *click-click*.

"He's my son."

"Yes, David."

Stopping his pacing, he chewed his bottom lip with irritation. "Can't you say anything but that?"

She raised her eyes. "Do you wish me to?"

"Do I wish!" he echoed. His fists were tight as he resumed his movements to and fro while she returned to her needles.

What did she know of wishes?

What does anyone know?

By the end of four months the territorial grip on Lani had grown to one thousand square miles while men and guns continued to pour in. Progress had been slower than expected. There had been minor blunders at high level, a few of the unforeseeable difficulties that invariably crop up when fighting at long range, and resistance had been desperate where least expected. Nevertheless, progress was being made. Though a little postdated, the inevitable remained inevitable.

Korman came home, heard the car door snap shut at the sixth step. All was as before except that now a part of the populace insisted on assembling to cheer him indoors. The maid waited, took his things. He stumped heavily to the inner room.

"Reed is being promoted to captain."

She did not answer.

Standing squarely before her, he demanded, "Well, aren't you interested?"

"Of course, David." Putting aside her book, she folded long, thin-fingered hands, looked toward the window.

"What's the matter with you?"

—"The matter?" The blond eyebrows arched as her eyes came up. "Nothing is the matter with me. Why do you ask?"

"I can tell." His tones harshened a little. "And I can guess. You don't like Reed being out there. You disapprove of me sending him away from you. You think of him as your son and not mine. You—"

She faced him calmly. "You're rather tired, David. And worried."

"I am not tired," he denied with unnecessary loudness. "Neither am I worried. It is the weak who worry."

"The weak have reason."

"I haven't."

"Then you're just plain hungry." She took a seat at the table. "Have something to eat. It will make you feel better."

Dissatisfied and disgruntled, he got through his evening meal. Mary was holding something back, he knew that with the sureness of one who had lived with her for half his lifetime. But he did not have to force it out of her by autocratic methods. When and only when he had finished eating she surrendered her secret voluntarily. The way in which she did it concealed the blow to come.

"There has been another letter from Reed."

"Yes?" He fingered a glass of wine, felt soothed by food but reluctant to show it. "I know he's happy, healthy and in one piece. If anything went wrong, I'd be the first to learn of it."

"Don't you want to see what he says?" She took it from a little walnut bureau, offered it to him.

He eyed it without reaching for it. "Oh, I suppose it's all the usual chitchat about the war."

"I think you ought to read it," she persisted.

"Do you?" Taking it from her hand, he held it unopened, surveyed her curiously. "Why should this particular missive call for my attention? Is it any different from the others? I know without looking that it is addressed to you. Not to me. To you! Never in his life has Reed written a letter specifically to me."

"He writes to both of us."

"Then why can't he start with 'Dear Father and Mother'?"

"Probably it just hasn't occurred to him that you would feel touchy about it. Besides, it's cumbersome."

"Nonsense!"

"Well, you might as well look at it as argue about it unread. You'll have to know sooner or later."

That last remark stimulated him into action. Unfolding it, he grunted as he noted the opening words, then went through ten paragraphs descriptive of war service on another planet. It was the sort of stuff every fighting man sent home. Nothing special about it. Turning the page, he perused the brief remainder. His face went taut and heightened in color.

"Better tell you I've become the willing slave of a Lanian girl. Found her in what little was left of the village of Bluelake, which had taken a pretty bad beating from our heavies. She was all alone and, as far as I could discover, seemed to be the sole survivor. Mom, she's got nobody. I'm sending her home on the hospital ship *Istar*. The captain jibbed but dared not refuse a Korman. Please meet her for me and look after her until I get back."

Flinging it onto the table, he swore lengthily and with vim, finishing, "The young imbecile."

Saying nothing, Mary sat watching him, her hands clasped together.

"The eyes of a whole world are on him," he raged. "As a public figure, as the son of his father, he is expected to be an example. And what does he do?"

She remained silent.

"Becomes the easy victim of some designing little skirt who is quick to play upon his sympathies. An enemy female!"

"She must be pretty," said Mary.

"*No* Lanians are pretty," he contradicted in what came near to a shout. "Have you taken leave of your senses?"

"No, David, of course not."

"Then why make such pointless remarks? One idiot in the family is enough." He punched his right fist several times into the palm of his left hand. "At the very time when anti-Lanian sentiment is at its height I can well imagine the effect on public opinion if it became known that we were harboring a specially favored enemy alien, pampering some painted and powdered hussy who has dug her claws into Reed. I can see her mincing proudly around, one of the vanquished who became a victor by making use of a dope. Reed must be out of his mind."

"Reed is twenty-three," she observed.

"What of it? Are you asserting that there's a specific age at which a man has a right to make a fool of himself?"

"David, I did not say that."

"You implied it." More hand-punching. "Reed has shown an unsuspected strain of weakness. It doesn't come from me."

"No, David, it doesn't."

He stared at her, seeking what lay unspoken behind that remark. It eluded him. His mind was not her mind. He could not think in her terms. Only in his own.

"I'll bring this madness to a drastic stop. If Reed lacks strength of character, it is for me to provide it." He found the telephone, remarked as he picked it up, "There are thousands of girls on Morcine. If Reed feels that he must have romance, he can find it at home."

"He's not home," Mary mentioned. "He is far away."

"For a few months. A mere nothing." The phone

whirred and he barked into it, "Has the *Istar* left Lani yet?" He held on a while, then racked the instrument and rumbled aggrievedly, "I'd have had her thrown off but it's too late. The *Istar* departed soon after the mail-boat that brought his letter." He made a face and it was not pleasant. "The girl is due here tomorrow. She's got a nerve, a blatant impudence. It reveals her character in advance."

Facing the big, slow-ticking clock that stood by the wall, he gazed at it as if tomorrow were due any moment. His mind was working on the problem so suddenly dumped in his lap. After a while, he spoke again.

"That scheming baggage is not going to carve herself a comfortable niche in my home, no matter what Reed thinks of her. I will not have her, see?"

"I see, David."

"If he is weak, I am not. So when she arrives I'm going to give her the roughest hour of her life. By the time I've finished she'll be more than glad of passage back to Lani on the next ship. She'll get out in a hurry and for keeps."

Mary remained quiet.

"But I'm not going to indulge a sordid domestic fracas in public. I won't allow her even the satisfaction of that. I want you to meet her at the spaceport, phone me immediately she arrives, then bring her to my office. I'll cope with her there."

"Yes, David."

"And don't forget to call me beforehand. It will give me time to clear the place and insure some privacy."

"I will remember," she promised.

It was three-thirty in the following afternoon when the call came through. He shooed out a fleet admiral, two generals and an intelligence service director, hurried through the most urgent of his papers, cleared the desk and mentally prepared himself for the distasteful task to come.

In short time his intercom squeaked and his secretary's voice announced, "Two people to see you, sir —Mrs. Korman and Miss Tatiana Hurst."

"Show them in."

He leaned backward, face suitably severe. Tatiana, he thought. An outlandish name. It was easy to visualize the sort of hoyden who owned it: a flouncy thing, aged beyond her years and with a sharp eye to the main chance. The sort who could make easy meat of someone young, inexperienced and impressionable, like Reed. Doubtless she had supreme confidence that she could butter the old man with equal effectiveness and no trouble whatsoever. Hah, that was her mistake.

The door opened and they came in and stood before him without speaking. For half a minute he studied them while his mind did sideslips, repeatedly strove to coordinate itself, and a dozen expressions came and went in his face. Finally, he rose slowly to his feet and spoke to Mary, his tones frankly bewildered.

"Well, where is she?"

"This," informed Mary with unconcealed and inexplicable satisfaction, "is her."

He flopped back into his chair, looked incredulously at Miss Tatiana Hurst. She had skinny legs exposed to knee height. Her clothing was much the worse for wear. Her face was a pale, hollow-cheeked oval from which a pair of enormous dark eyes gazed in a non-focusing, introspective manner as if she continually kept watch within her rather than upon things outside. One small white hand held Mary's, the other arm was around a large and brand new teddy-bear gained from a source at which he could guess. Her age was about eight. Certainly no more than eight.

It was the eyes that got him most, terribly solemn, terribly grave and unwilling to see. There was a coldness in his stomach as he observed them. She was not blind. She could look at him all right—but she looked without really perceiving. The great dark orbs could turn toward him and register the mere essential of his being while all the time they saw only the secret places within herself. It was eerie in the extreme and more than discomforting.

Watching her fascinatedly, he tried to analyze and define the peculiar quality in those optics. He had expected daring, defiance, impudence, passion, anything of which a predatory female was capable. Here, in these radically altered circumstances, one could expect childish embarrassment, self-consciousness, shyness. But she was not shy, he decided. It was something else.

In the end he recognized the elusive factor as absentness. She was here yet somehow not with them. She was somewhere else, deep inside a world of her own.

Mary chipped in with a sudden "Well, David?"

He started at the sound of her voice. Some confusion still cluttered his mind because this culmination differed so greatly from his preconceptions. Mary had enjoyed half an hour in which to accommodate herself to the shock. He had not. It was still fresh and potent.

"Leave her with me for a few minutes," he suggested. "I'll call you when I've finished."

Mary went, her manner that of a woman enjoying something deep and personal. An unexpected satisfaction long overdue.

Korman said with unaccustomed mildness, "Come here, Tatiana."

She moved toward him slowly, each step deliberate and careful, touched the desk, stopped.

"Round this side, please, near to my chair."

With the same almost-robotic gait she did as instructed, her dark eyes looking expressionlessly to the front. Arriving at his chair, she waited in silence.

He drew in a deep breath. It seemed to him that her manner was born of a tiny voice insisting, "I must be obedient. I must do as I am told. I can do only what I am told to do."

So she did it as one compelled to accept those things she had no means of resisting. It was surrender to all demands in order to keep one hidden and precious place intact. There was no other way.

Rather appalled, he said, "You're able to speak, aren't you?"

She nodded, slightly and only once.

"But that isn't speech," he pointed out.

There was no desire to contradict or provide proof of ability. She accepted his statement as obvious and left it at that. Silent and immensely grave, she clung to her bear and waited for Korman's world to cease troubling her own.

"Are you glad you're here, or sorry?"

No reaction. Only inward contemplation. Absentness.

"Well, are you glad then?"

A vague half-nod.

"You are not sorry to be here?"

An even vaguer shake.

"Would you rather stay than go back?"

She looked at him, not so much to see him as to insure that he could see her.

He rang his bell, said to Mary, "Take her home."

"Home, David?"

"That's what I said." He did not like the exaggerated sweetness of her tone. It meant something, but he couldn't discern what.

The door closed behind the pair of them. His fingers tapped restlessly on the desk as he pictured those eyes. Something small and bitterly cold was in his insides.

During the next couple of weeks his mind seemed to be filled with more problems than ever before. Like most men of his caliber, he had the ability to ponder several subjects at once, but not the insight to detect when one was gaining predominance over the others.

On the first two or three of these days he ignored the pale intruder in his household. Yet he could not deny her presence. She was always there, quiet, obedient, self-effacing, hollow-cheeked and huge-eyed. Often she sat around for long periods without stirring, like a discarded doll.

When addressed by Mary or one of the maids she remained deaf to inconsequential remarks, responded to direct and imperative questions or orders. She would answer with minimum head movements or hand gestures when these sufficed, spoke monosyllabically in a thin little voice only when speech was unavoidable. During that time Korman did not speak to her at all— but he was compelled to notice her fatalistic acceptance of the fact that she was no part of his complicated life.

After lunch on the fourth day he caught her alone, bent down to her height and demanded, "Tatiana, what is the matter with you? Are you unhappy here?"

One brief shake of her head.

"Then why don't you laugh and play like other—?" He ceased abruptly as Mary entered the room.

"You two having a private gossip?" she inquired.

"As if we could," he snapped.

That same evening he saw the latest pictorial record from the fighting front. It gave him little satisfaction. Indeed, it almost irked him. The zip was missing. Much of the thrill of conquest had mysteriously evaporated from the pictures.

By the end of the fortnight he'd had more than enough of listening for a voice that seldom spoke and meeting eyes that did not see. It was like living with a ghost— and it could not go on. A man is entitled to a modicum of relaxation in his own home.

Certainly he could kick her back to Lani as he had threatened to do at the first. That, however, would be admission of defeat. Korman just could not accept defeat at anyone's hands, much less those of a brooding child. She was not going to edge him out of his own home nor persuade him to throw her out. She was a challenge he had to overcome in a way thoroughly satisfactory to himself.

Summoning his chief scientific adviser to his office, he declaimed with irritation, "Look, I'm saddled with a maladjusted child. My son took a fancy to her and shipped her from Lani. She's getting in my hair. What can be done about it?"

"Afraid I cannot help much, sir."

"Why not?"

"I'm a physicist."

"Well, can you suggest anyone else?"

The other thought a bit, said, "There's nobody in my department, sir. But science isn't solely concerned with production of gadgets. You need a specialist in things less tangible." A pause, then, "The hospital authorities might put you on to someone suitable."

He tried the nearest hospital, got the answer, "A child psychologist is your man."

"Who's the best on this planet?"

"Dr. Jager."

"Contact him for me. I want him at my house this evening, not later than seven o'clock."

Fat, middle-aged and jovial, Jager fell easily into the role of a casual friend who had just dropped in. He chatted a lot of foolishness, included Tatiana in the conversation by throwing odd remarks at her, even held a pretended conversation with her teddy-bear. Twice in an hour she came into his world just long enough to register a fleeting smile—then swiftly she was back in her own.

At the end of this he hinted that he and Tatiana should be left by themselves. Korman went out, convinced that no progress was being or would be made. In the lounge Mary glanced up from her seat.

"Who's our visitor, David? Or is it no business of mine?"

"Some kind of mental specialist. He's examining Tatiana."

"Really?" Again the sweetness that was bitter.

"Yes," he rasped. "Really."

"I didn't think you were interested in her."

"I am not," he asserted. "But Reed is. Now and again I like to remind myself that Reed is my son."

She let the subject drop. Korman got on with some official papers until Jager had finished. Then he went back to the room, leaving Mary immersed in her book. He looked around.

"Where is she?"

"The maid took her. Said it was her bedtime."

"Oh." He found a seat, waited to hear more.

Resting against the edge of a table, Jager explained, "I've a playful little gag for dealing with children who are reluctant to talk. Nine times out of ten it works."

"What is it?"

"I persuade them to *write*. Strangely enough, they'll often do that, especially if I make a game of it. I cajole them into writing a story or essay about anything that created a great impression upon them. The results can be very revealing."

"And did you—?"

"A moment, please, Mr. Korman. Before I go further I'd like to impress upon you that children have an inherent ability many authors must envy. They can express themselves with remarkable vividness in simple language, with great economy of words. They create a telling effect with what they leave out as much as by what they put in." He eyed Korman speculatively. "You know the circumstances in which your son found this child?"

"Yes, he told us in a letter."

"Well, bearing those circumstances in mind I think you'll find this something exceptional in the way of horror stories." He held out a sheet of paper. "She wrote it unaided." He reached for his hat and coat.

"You're going?" questioned Korman in surprise. "What about your diagnosis? What treatment do you suggest?"

Dr. Jager paused, hand on door. "Mr. Korman, you are an intelligent person." He indicated the sheet the other was holding. "I think that is all you require."

Then he departed. Korman eyed the sheet. It was not filled with words as he'd expected. For a story it was mighty short. He read it.

I am nothing and nobody. My house went bang. My cat was stuck to a wall. I wanted to pull it off. They wouldn't let me. They threw it away.

The cold thing in the pit of his stomach swelled up. He read it again. And again. He went to the base of the stairs and looked up toward where she was sleeping.

The enemy whom he had made nothing.

Slumber came hard that night. Usually he could compose his mind and snatch a nap anytime, anywhere, at a moment's notice. Now he was strangely restless, unsettled. His brain was stimulated by he knew not what and it insisted on following tortuous paths.

The frequent waking periods were full of fantastic imaginings wherein he fumbled through a vast and cloying grayness in which was no sound, no voice, no other being. The dreams were worse, full of writhing landscapes spewing smoky columns, with things howling through the sky, with huge, toadlike monsters crawling on metal tracks, with long lines of dusty men singing an aeons-old and forgotten song.

"You've left behind a broken doll."

He awakened early with weary eyes and a tired mind. All morning at the office a multitude of trifling things conspired against him. His ability to concentrate was not up to the mark and several times he had to catch himself on minor errors just made or about to be made. Once or twice he found himself gazing meditatively forward with eyes that did not see to the front but were looking where they had never looked before.

At three in the afternoon his secretary called on the intercom, "Astroleader Warren would like to see you, sir."

"Astroleader?" he echoed, wondering whether he had heard aright. "There's no such title."

"It is a Drakan space-rank."

"Oh, yes, of course. I can tend to him now."

He waited with dull anticipation. The Drakans formed a powerful combine of ten planets at a great distance from Morcine. They were so far away that contact came seldom. A battleship of theirs had paid a courtesy call about twice in his lifetime. So this occasion was a rare one.

The visitor entered, a big-built youngster in light-green uniform. Shaking hands with genuine pleasure and great cordiality, he accepted the indicated chair.

"A surprise, eh, Mr. Korman?"

"Very."

"We came in a deuce of a hurry but the trip can't be done in a day. Distance takes time unfortunately."

"I know."

"The position is this," explained Warren. "Long while back we received a call from Lani relayed by intervening minor planets. They said they were involved in a serious dispute and feared war. They appealed to us to negotiate as disinterested neutrals."

"Ah, so that's why you've come?"

"Yes, Mr. Korman. We knew the chance was small of arriving in time. There was nothing for it but to come as fast as we could and hope for the best. The role of peace-maker appeals to those with any claim to be civilized."

"Does it?" questioned Korman, watching him.

"It does to us." Leaning forward, Warren met him eye to eye. "We've called at Lani on the way here. They still want peace. They're losing the battle. Therefore we want to know only one thing: Are we too late?"

That was the leading question: Are we too late? Yes or no? Korman stewed it without realizing that not so long ago his answer would have been prompt and automatic. Today, he thought it over.

Yes or no? Yes meant military victory, power and fear. No meant—what? Well, no meant a display of reasonableness in lieu of stubbornness. No meant a considerable change of mind. It struck him suddenly that one must possess redoubtable force of character to throw away a long-nursed viewpoint and adopt a new one. It required moral courage. The weak and the faltering could never achieve it.

"No," he replied slowly. "It is not too late."

Warren stood up, his face showing that this was not the answer he had expected. "You mean, Mr. Korman—"

"Your journey has not been in vain. You may negotiate."

"On what terms?"

"The fairest to both sides that you can contrive." He switched his microphone, spoke into it. "Tell Rogers that I order our forces to cease hostilities forthwith. Troops will guard the perimeter of the Lani ground base pending peace negotiations. Citizens of the Drakan Confederation will be permitted unobstructed passage through our lines in either direction."

"Very well, Mr. Korman."

Putting the microphone aside, he continued with Warren, "Though far off in mere miles, Lani is near to us as cosmic distances go. It would please me if the Lanians agreed to a union between our planets, with common citizenship, common development of natural resources. But I don't insist upon it. I merely express a wish—knowing that some wishes never come true."

"The notion will be given serious consideration all the same," assured Warren. He shook hands with boyish enthusiasm. "You're a big man, Mr. Korman."

"Am I?" He gave a wry smile. "I'm trying to do a bit of growing in another direction. The original one kind of got used up."

When the other had gone, he tossed a wad of documents into a drawer. Most of them were useless now. Strange how he seemed to be breathing better than ever before, his lungs drawing more fully.

In the outer office he informed, "It's early yet, but I'm going home. Phone me there if anything urgent comes along."

The chauffeur closed the car door at the sixth step. A weakling, thought Korman as he went into his home. A lamebrain lacking the strength to haul himself out of a self-created rut. One can stay in a rut too long.

He asked the maid, "Where is my wife?"

"Slipped out ten minutes ago, sir. She said she'd be back in half an hour."

"Did she take—"

"No, sir." The maid glanced toward the lounge.

Cautiously he entered the lounge, found the child resting on the settee, head back, eyes closed. A radio played softly nearby. He doubted whether she had turned it on of her own accord or was listening to it. More likely someone else had left it running.

Tiptoeing across the carpet, he cut off the faint music. She opened her eyes, sat upright. Going to the settee, he took the bear from her side and placed it on an arm, positioned himself next to her.

"Tatiana," he asked with rough gentleness, "why are you nothing?"

No answer. No change.

"Is it because you have nobody?"

Silence.

"Nobody of your own?" he persisted, feeling a queer kind of desperation. "Not even a kitten?"

She looked down at her shoes, her big eyes partly shielded under pale lids. There was no other reaction.

Defeat. Ah, the bitterness of defeat. It set his fingers fumbling with each other, like those of one in great and unbearable trouble. Phrases tumbled through his mind.

"I am nothing."

"My cat . . . they threw it away."

His gaze wandered blindly over the room while his mind ran round and round her wall of silence seeking a door it could not find. Was there no way in, no way at all?

There was.

He discovered it quite unwittingly.

To himself rather than to her he murmured in a hearable undertone, "Since I was very small I have been surrounded by people. All my life there have been lots of people. But none were mine. Not one was really mine. Not one. I, too, am nothing."

She patted his hand.

The shock was immense. Startled beyond measure, he glanced down at the first touch, watched her give three or four comforting little dabs and hastily withdraw.

There was heavy pulsing in his veins. Something within him rapidly became too big to contain.

Twisting sidewise, he snatched her onto his lap, put his arms around her, buried his nose in the soft part of her neck, nuzzled behind her ear, ran his big hand through her hair. And all the time he rocked to and fro with low crooning noises.

She was weeping. She hadn't been able to weep before. She was weeping, not as a woman does, softly and subdued, but like a child, with great racking sobs that she fought hard to suppress.

Her arm was around his neck, tightening, clinging and tightening more while he rocked and stroked and called her "Honey" and uttered silly sounds and wildly extravagant reassurances.

This was victory.

Not empty.

Full.

Victory over self is completely full.

EDITOR'S INTRODUCTION TO:

CALL HIM LORD

by

Gordon R. Dickson

I have known Gordon Dickson for over twenty years. We do not see each other often, but when we do meet our interactions are intense, and we have been close friends; this seems a common pattern within the science fiction community. On many nights—but not nearly often enough—we talk and sing until dawn, telling the old tales and singing the old songs of glory. Sometimes, on the best of these nights, Poul Anderson joins us.

Gordie's best known work is the Childe Cycle, sometimes called the "Dorsai series" after its best-known story. The Dorsai stories are deservedly among the most popular military science fiction ever written. The Childe Cycle envisions some 12 novels, and will take at least that many more years to complete.

In 1980, when the Voyager spacecraft first approached Jupiter, I arranged that the science fiction writers be admitted to the Jet Propulsion Laboratories, where the spacecraft were controlled and their planetary data analyzed. Gordon came to Los Angeles to see the encounter close up. At that time Dickson was introduced to Ezekial, my friend who happens to be a Z-80 computer. Gordon was so impressed with the value of computers for writing—I do all my books on a computer—that he bought one of his own; the resulting increase in his output makes it possible that the Childe Cycle will indeed be finished. This is, I hasten to add, my only substantial contribution to Dickson's work.

Dickson attends so many conventions that Ben Bova

was inspired to write "The Ballad of Gordie Dickson." It is probable that at least one of its verses is scurrilous.

One of the most important decisions a political leader can make is to call in the military. It is not obvious when to ask the soldiers for help; and the results are not always pleasant.

CALL HIM LORD
by
Gordon R. Dickson

"He called and commanded me
—Therefore, I knew him;
But later on, failed me; and
—Therefore, I slew him!"

"Songs of the Shield Bearer"

The sun could not fail in rising over the Kentucky hills, nor could Kyle Arnam in waking. There would be eleven hours and forty minutes of daylight. Kyle rose, dressed, and went out to saddle the gray gelding and the white stallion. He rode the stallion until the first fury was out of the arched and snowy neck; and then led both horses around to tether them outside the kitchen door. Then he went in to breakfast.

The message that had come a week before was beside his plate of bacon and eggs. Teena, his wife, was standing at the breadboard with her back to him. He sat down and began eating, rereading the letter as he ate.

" . . . The Prince will be traveling incognito under one of his family titles, as Count Sirii North; and should not be addressed as 'Majesty.' *You will call him 'Lord' . . .*"

"Why does it have to be you?" Teena asked.

He looked up and saw how she stood with her back to him.

"Teena—" he said, sadly.

"Why?"

"My ancestors were bodyguards to his—back in the wars of conquest against the aliens. I've told you that," he said. "My forefathers saved the lives of his, many times when there was no warning—a Rak spaceship would suddenly appear out of nowhere to lock on, even to a flagship. And even an Emperor found himself fight-ing for his life, hand to hand."

"The aliens are all dead now, and the Emperor's got a hundred other worlds! Why can't his son take his Grand Tour on them? Why does he have to come here to Earth —and you?"

"There's only one Earth."

"And only one you, I suppose?"

He sighed internally and gave up. He had been raised by his father and his uncle after his mother died, and in an argument with Teena he always felt helpless. He got up from the table and went to her, putting his hands on her and gently trying to turn her about. But she resisted.

He sighed inside himself again and turned away to the weapons cabinet. He took out a loaded slug pistol, fitted it into the stubby holster it matched, and clipped the holster to his belt at the left of the buckle, where the hang of his leather jacket would hide it. Then he selected a dark-handled knife with a six-inch blade and bent over to slip it into the sheath inside his boot top. He dropped the cuff of his trouser leg back over the boot top and stood up.

"He's got no right to be here," said Teena fiercely to the breadboard. "Tourists are supposed to be kept to the museum areas and the tourist lodges."

"He's not a tourist. You know that," answered Kyle, patiently. "He's the Emperor's oldest son and his great-grandmother was from Earth. His wife will be, too. Every fourth generation the Imperial line has to marry back into Earth stock. That's the law—still." He put on his leather jacket, sealing it closed only at the bottom to hide the slug-gun holster, half-turned to the door—then paused.

"Teena?" he asked.

She did not answer.

"Teena!" he repeated. He stepped to her, put his hands on her shoulders, and tried to turn her to face him. Again, she resisted, but this time he was having none of it.

He was not a big man, being of middle height, round-faced, with sloping and unremarkable-looking, if thick, shoulders. But his strength was not ordinary. He could bring the white stallion to its knees with one fist wound in its mane—and no other man had ever been able to do that. He turned her easily to look at him.

"Now, listen to me—" He began. But, before he could finish, all the stiffness went out of her and she clung to him, trembling.

"He'll get you into trouble—I know he will!" she choked muffledly into his chest. "Kyle, don't go! There's no law making you go!"

He stroked the soft hair of her head, his throat stiff and dry. There was nothing he could say to her. What she was asking was impossible. Ever since the sun had first risen on men and women together, wives had clung to their husbands at times like this, begging for what could not be. And always the men had held them, as Kyle was holding her now—as if understanding could somehow be pressed from one body into the other—and saying nothing, because there was nothing that could be said.

So, Kyle held her for a few moments longer, and then reached behind him to unlock her intertwined fingers at his back, and loosen her arms around him. Then, he went. Looking back through the kitchen window as he rode off on the stallion, leading the gray horse, he saw her standing just where he had left her. Not even crying, but standing with her arms hanging down, her head down, not moving.

He rode away through the forest of the Kentucky hillside. It took him more than two hours to reach the lodge. As he rode down the valleyside toward it, he saw a tall bearded man, wearing the robes they wore on some of the Younger Worlds, standing at the gateway to the interior courtyard of the rustic, wooded lodge.

When he got close, he saw that the beard was graying and the man was biting his lips. Above a straight, thin nose, the eyes were bloodshot and circled beneath as if from worry or lack of sleep.

"He's in the courtyard," said the gray-bearded man as Kyle rode up. "I'm Montlaven, his tutor. He's ready to go." The darkened eyes looked almost pleadingly up at Kyle.

"Stand clear of the stallion's head," said Kyle. "And take me in to him."

"Not that horse, for him—" said Montlaven, looking distrustfully at the stallion, as he backed away.

"No," said Kyle. "He'll ride the gelding."

"He'll want the white."

"He can't ride the white," said Kyle. "Even if I let him, he couldn't ride this stallion. I'm the only one who can ride him. Take me in."

The tutor turned and led the way into the grassy courtyard, surrounding a swimming pool and looked down upon, on three sides, by the windows of the lodge. In a lounging chair by the pool sat a tall young man in his late teens, with a mane of blond hair, a pair of stuffed saddlebags on the grass beside him. He stood up as Kyle and the tutor came toward him.

"Majesty," said the tutor, as they stopped, "this is Kyle Arnam, your bodyguard for the three days here."

"Good morning, Bodyguard . . . Kyle, I mean." The Prince smiled mischievously. "Light, then. And I'll mount."

"You ride the gelding, Lord," said Kyle.

The Prince stared at him, tilted back his handsome head, and laughed.

"I can ride, man!" he said. "I ride well."

"Not this horse, Lord," said Kyle, dispassionately. "No one rides this horse, but me."

The eyes flashed wide, the laugh faded—then returned.

"What can I do?" The wide shoulders shrugged. "I give in—always I give in. Well, almost always." He grinned up at Kyle, his lips thinned, but frank. "All right."

He turned to the gelding—and with a sudden leap was in the saddle. The gelding snorted and plunged at the shock; then steadied as the young man's long fingers tightened expertly on the reins and the fingers of the other hand patted a gray neck. The Prince raised his eyebrows, looking over at Kyle, but Kyle sat stolidly.

"I take it you're armed, good Kyle?" the Prince said slyly. "You'll protect me against the natives if they run wild?"

"Your life is in my hands, Lord," said Kyle. He unsealed the leather jacket at the bottom and let it fall open to show the slug pistol in its holster for a moment.

Then he resealed the jacket again at the bottom.

"Will—" The tutor put his hand on the young man's knee. "Don't be reckless, boy. This is Earth and the people here don't have rank and custom like we do. Think before you—"

"Oh, cut it out, Monty!" snapped the Prince. "I'll be just as incognito, just as humble, as archaic and independent as the rest of them. You think I've no memory! Anyway, it's only for three days or so until my Imperial father joins me. Now, let me go!"

He jerked away, turned to lean forward in the saddle, and abruptly put the gelding into a bolt for the gate. He disappeared through it, and Kyle drew hard on the stallion's reins as the big white horse danced and tried to follow.

"Give me his saddlebags," said Kyle.

The tutor bent and passed them up. Kyle made them fast on top of his own, across the stallion's withers. Looking down, he saw there were tears in the bearded man's eyes.

"He's a fine boy. You'll see. You'll know he is!" Montlaven's face, upturned, was mutely pleading.

"I know he comes from a fine family," said Kyle, slowly. "I'll do my best for him." And he rode off out of the gateway after the gelding.

When he came out of the gate, the Prince was nowhere in sight. But it was simple enough for Kyle to follow, by dinted brown earth and crushed grass, the marks of the gelding's path. This brought him at last through some pines to a grassy open slope where the Prince sat looking skyward through a single-lens box.

When Kyle came up, the Prince lowered the instrument, and without a word passed it over. Kyle put it to his eye and looked skyward. There was the whir of the tracking unit and one of Earth's three orbiting power stations swam into the field of vision of the lens.

"Give it back," said the Prince.

"I couldn't get a look at it earlier," went on the young man as Kyle handed the lens to him. "And I wanted to. It's a rather expensive present, you know—it and the other two like it—from our Imperial treasury. Just to keep your planet from drifting into another ice age. And what do we get for it?"

"Earth, Lord," answered Kyle. "As it was before men went out to the stars."

"Oh, the museum areas could be maintained with one station and a half-million caretakers," said the Prince. "It's the other two stations and you billion or so free-loaders I'm talking about. I'll have to look into it when I'm Emperor. Shall we ride?"

"If you wish, Lord." Kyle picked up the reins of the stallion and the two horses with their riders moved off across the slope.

" . . . And one more thing," said the Prince, as they entered the farther belt of pine trees. "I don't want you to be misled—I'm really very fond of old Monty, back there. It's just that I wasn't really planning to come here at all—*Look at me, Bodyguard!*"

Kyle turned to see the blue eyes that ran in the Imperial family blazing at him. Then, unexpectedly, they softened. The Prince laughed.

"You don't scare easily, do you, Bodyguard . . . Kyle, I mean?" he said. "I think I like you after all. But look at me when I talk."

"Yes, Lord."

"That's my good Kyle. Now, I was explaining to you that I'd never actually planned to come here on my Grand Tour at all. I didn't see any point in visiting this dusty old museum world of yours with people still trying to live like they lived in the Dark Ages. But—my Imperial father talked me into it."

"Your father, Lord?" asked Kyle.

"Yes, he bribed me, you might say," said the Prince thoughtfully. "He was supposed to meet me here for these three days. Now, he's messaged there's been a slight delay—but that doesn't matter. The point is, he belongs to the school of old men who still think your Earth is something precious and vital. Now, I happen to like and admire my father, Kyle. You approve of that?"

"Yes, Lord."

"I thought you would. Yes, he's the one man in the human race I look up to. And to please him, I'm making this Earth trip. And to please him—only to please *him*, Kyle—I'm going to be an easy Prince for you to conduct around to your natural wonders and watering spots and whatever. Now, you understand me—and how this trip is going to go. Don't you?" He stared at Kyle.

"I understand," said Kyle.

"That's fine," said the Prince, smiling once more. "So now you can start telling me all about these trees and birds and animals so that I can memorize their names and please my father when he shows up. What are those little birds I've been seeing under the trees—brown on top and whitish underneath? Like that one—there!"

"That's a Veery, Lord," said Kyle. "A bird of the deep woods and silent places. Listen—" He reached out a hand to the gelding's bridle and brought both horses to a halt. In the sudden silence, off to their right they could hear a silver bird-voice, rising and falling, in a descending series of crescendos and diminuendos, that softened at last into silence. For a moment after the song was ended the Prince sat staring at Kyle, then seemed to shake himself back to life.

"Interesting," he said. He lifted the reins Kyle had let go and the horses moved forward again. "Tell me more."

For more than three hours, as the sun rose toward noon, they rode through the wooded hills, with Kyle identifying bird and animal, insect, tree, and rock. And for three hours the Prince listened—his attention flashing and momentary, but intense. But when the sun was overhead that intensity flagged.

"That's enough," he said. "Aren't we going to stop for lunch? Kyle, aren't there any towns around here?"

"Yes, Lord," said Kyle. "We've passed several."

"Several?" The Prince stared at him. "Why haven't we come into one before now? Where are you taking me?"

"Nowhere, Lord," said Kyle. "You lead the way, I only follow."

"I?" said the Prince. For the first time he seemed to become aware that he had been keeping the gelding's head always in advance of the stallion. "Of course. But now it's time to eat."

"Yes, Lord," said Kyle. "This way."

He turned the stallion's head down the slope of the hill they were crossing and the Prince turned the gelding after him.

"And now listen," said the Prince, as he caught up. "Tell me I've got it all right." And to Kyle's astonishment, he began to repeat, almost word for word, everything that Kyle had said. "Is it all there? Everything you told me?"

"Perfectly, Lord," said Kyle. The Prince looked slyly at him.

"Could you do that, Kyle?"

"Yes," said Kyle. "But these are things I've known all my life."

"You see?" the Prince smiled. "That's the difference between us, good Kyle. You spend your life learning something—I spend a few hours and I know as much about it as you do."

"Not as much, Lord," said Kyle, slowly.

The Prince blinked at him, then jerked his hand dismissingly, and half-angrily, as if he were throwing something aside.

"What little else there is probably doesn't count," he said.

They rode down the slope and through a winding valley and came out at a small village. As they rode clear of the surrounding trees a sound of music came to their ears.

"What's that?" The Prince stood up in his stirrups. "Why, there's dancing going on, over there."

"A beer garden, Lord. And it's Sunday—a holiday here."

"Good. We'll go there to eat."

They rode around to the beer garden and found tables back away from the dance floor. A pretty, young waitress came and they ordered, the Prince smiling sunnily at her until she smiled back—then hurried off as if in mild confusion. The Prince ate hungrily when the food came and drank a stein and a half of brown beer, while Kyle ate more lightly and drank coffee.

"That's better," said the Prince, sitting back at last. "I had an appetite. . . . Look there, Kyle! Look, there are five, six . . . seven drifter platforms parked over there. Then you don't all ride horses?"

"No," said Kyle. "It's as each man wishes."

"But if you have drifter platforms, why not other civilized things?"

"Some things fit, some don't, Lord," answered Kyle. The Prince laughed.

"You mean you try to make civilization fit this old-fashioned life of yours, here?" he said. "Isn't that the wrong way around—" He broke off. "What's that they're playing now? I like that. I'll bet I could do that dance." He stood up. "In fact, I think I will."

He paused, looking down at Kyle.

"Aren't you going to warn me against it?" he asked.

"No, Lord," said Kyle. "What you do is your own affair."

The young man turned away abruptly. The waitress who had served them was passing, only a few tables away. The Prince went after her and caught up with her by the dance-floor railing. Kyle could see the girl protesting—but the Prince hung over her, looking down from his tall height, smiling. Shortly, she had taken off her apron and was out on the dance floor with him, showing him the steps of the dance. It was a polka.

The Prince learned with fantastic quickness. Soon, he was swinging the waitress around with the rest of the dancers, his foot stomping on the turns, his white teeth gleaming. Finally the number ended and the members of the band put down their instruments and began to leave the stand.

The Prince, with the girl trying to hold him back, walked over to the bandleader. Kyle got up quickly from his table and started toward the floor.

The bandleader was shaking his head. He turned abruptly and slowly walked away. The Prince started after him, but the girl took hold of his arm, saying something urgent to him.

He brushed her aside and she stumbled a little. A busboy among the tables on the far side of the dance floor, not much older than the Prince and nearly as tall, put down his tray and vaulted the railing onto the polished hardwood. He came up behind the Prince and took hold of his arm, swinging him around.

" . . . can't do that here," Kyle heard him say, as Kyle came up. The Prince struck out like a panther—like a trained boxer—with three quick lefts in succession into the face of the busboy, the Prince's shoulder bobbing, the weight of his body in behind each blow.

The busboy went down. Kyle, reaching the Prince,

herded him away through a side gap in the railing. The young man's face was white with rage. People were swarming onto the dance floor.

"Who was that? What's his name?" demanded the Prince, between his teeth. "He put his hand on me! Did you see that? *He put his hand on me!*"

"You knocked him out," said Kyle. "What more do you want?"

"He manhandled me—*me!*" snapped the Prince. "I want to find out who he is!" He caught hold of the bar to which the horses were tied, refusing to be pushed farther. "He'll learn to lay hands on a future Emperor!"

"No one will tell you his name," said Kyle. And the cold note in his voice finally seemed to reach through to the Prince and sober him. He stared at Kyle.

"Including you?" he demanded at last.

"Including me, Lord," said Kyle.

The Prince stared a moment longer, then swung away. He turned, jerked loose the reins of the gelding, and swung into the saddle. He rode off. Kyle mounted and followed.

They rode in silence into the forest. After a while, the Prince spoke without turning his head.

"And you call yourself a bodyguard," he said, finally.

"Your life is in my hands, Lord," said Kyle. The Prince turned a grim face to look at him.

"Only my life?" said the Prince. "As long as they don't kill me, they can do what they want? Is that what you mean?"

Kyle met his gaze steadily.

"Pretty much so, Lord," he said.

The Prince spoke with an ugly note in his voice.

"I don't think I like you, after all, Kyle," he said. "I don't think I like you at all."

"I'm not here with you to be liked, Lord," said Kyle.

"Perhaps not," said the Prince, thickly. "But I know *your* name!"

They rode on in continued silence for perhaps another half hour. But then gradually the angry hunch went out of the young man's shoulders and the tightness out of his jaw. After a while he began to sing to himself, a song in a language Kyle did not know; and as he sang, his cheerfulness seemed to return. Shortly, he spoke to

Kyle, as if there had never been anything but pleasant moments between them.

Mammoth Cave was close and the Prince asked to visit it. They went there and spent some time going through the cave. After that they rode their horses up along the left bank of the Green River. The Prince seemed to have forgotten all about the incident at the beer garden and was out to charm everyone they met. As the sun was at last westering toward the dinner hour, they came finally to a small hamlet back from the river, with a roadside inn mirrored in an artificial lake beside it, and guarded by oak and pine trees behind.

"This looks good," said the Prince. "We'll stay overnight here, Kyle."

"If you wish, Lord," said Kyle.

They halted, and Kyle took the horses around to the stable, then entered the inn to find the Prince already in the small bar off the dining room, drinking beer and charming the waitress. This waitress was younger than the one at the beer garden had been; a little girl with soft loose hair and round brown eyes that showed their delight in the attention of the tall, good-looking young man.

"Yes," said the Prince to Kyle, looking out of corners of the Imperial blue eyes at him, after the waitress had gone to get Kyle his coffee. "This is the very place."

"The very place?" said Kyle.

"For me to get to know the people better—what did you think, good Kyle?" said the Prince and laughed at him. "I'll observe the people here and you can explain them—won't that be good?"

Kyle gazed at him, thoughtfully.

"I'll tell you whatever I can, Lord," he said.

They drank—the Prince his beer, and Kyle his coffee—and went in a little later to the dining room for dinner. The Prince, as he had promised at the bar, was full of questions about what he saw—and what he did not see.

" . . . But why go on living in the past, all of you here?" he asked Kyle. "A museum world is one thing. But a museum people—" He broke off to smile and speak to the little, soft-haired waitress, who had somehow been diverted from the bar to wait upon their dining-room table.

"Not a museum people, Lord," said Kyle. "A living people. The only way to keep a race and a culture preserved is to keep it alive. So we go on in our own way, here on Earth, as a living example for the Younger Worlds to check themselves against."

"Fascinating . . ." murmured the Prince; but his eyes had wandered off to follow the waitress, who was glowing and looking back at him from across the now-busy dining room.

"Not fascinating. Necessary, Lord," said Kyle. But he did not believe the younger man had heard him.

After dinner, they moved back to the bar. And the Prince, after questioning Kyle a little longer, moved up to continue his researches among the other people standing at the bar. Kyle watched for a little while. Then, feeling it was safe to do so, he slipped out to have another look at the horses and to ask the innkeeper to arrange a saddle lunch put up for them the next day.

When he returned, the Prince was not to be seen.

Kyle sat down at a table to wait; but the Prince did not return. A cold, hard knot of uneasiness began to grow below Kyle's breastbone. A sudden pang of alarm sent him swiftly back out to check the horses. But they were cropping peacefully in their stalls. The stallion whickered, low voiced, as Kyle looked in on him, and turned his white head to look back at Kyle.

"Easy, boy," said Kyle and returned to the inn to find the innkeeper.

But the innkeeper had no idea where the Prince might have gone.

" . . . If the horses aren't taken, he's not far," the innkeeper said. "There's no trouble he can get into around here. Maybe he went for a walk in the woods. I'll leave word for the night staff to keep an eye out for him when he comes in. Where'll you be?"

"In the bar until it closes—then, my room," said Kyle.

He went back to the bar to wait, and took a booth near an open window. Time went by and gradually the number of other customers began to dwindle. Above the ranked bottles, the bar clock showed nearly midnight. Suddenly, through the window, Kyle heard a distant scream of equine fury from the stables.

He got up and went out quickly. In the darkness outside, he ran to the stables and burst in. There in the feeble illumination of the stable's night lighting, he saw the Prince, palefaced, clumsily saddling the gelding in the center aisle between the stalls. The door to the stallion's stall was open. The Prince looked away as Kyle came in.

Kyle took three swift steps to the open door and looked in. The stallion was still tied, but his ears were back, his eyes rolling, and a saddle lay tumbled and dropped on the stable floor beside him.

"Saddle up," said the Prince thickly from the aisle. "We're leaving." Kyle turned to look at him.

"We've got rooms at the inn here," he said.

"Never mind. We're riding. I need to clear my head." The young man got the gelding's cinch tight, dropped the stirrups and swung heavily up into the saddle. Without waiting for Kyle, he rode out of the stable into the night.

"So, boy . . ." said Kyle soothingly to the stallion. Hastily he untied the big white horse, saddled him, and set out after the Prince. In the darkness there was no way of ground-tracking the gelding; but he leaned forward and blew into the ear of the stallion. The surprised horse neighed in protest and the whinny of the gelding came back from the darkness of the slope up ahead and over to Kyle's right. He rode in that direction.

He caught the Prince on the crown of the hill. The young man was walking the gelding, reins loose, and singing under his breath—the same song in an unknown language he had sung earlier. But now, as he saw Kyle, he grinned loosely and began to sing with more emphasis. For the first time Kyle caught the overtones of something mocking and lusty about the incomprehensible words. Understanding broke suddenly in him.

"The girl!" he said. "The little waitress. Where is she?"

The grin vanished from the Prince's face, then came slowly back again. The grin laughed at Kyle.

"Why, where d'you think?" The words slurred on the Prince's tongue and Kyle, riding close, smelled the beer heavy on the young man's breath. "In her room, sleeping and happy. Honored . . . though she doesn't know it . . . by an Emperor's son. And expecting to find me there in the morning. But I won't be. Will we, good Kyle?"

"Why did you do it, Lord?" asked Kyle, quietly.

"Why?" The Prince peered at him, a little drunkenly in the moonlight. "Kyle, my father has four sons. I've got three younger brothers. But I'm the one who's going to be Emperor; and Emperors don't answer questions."

Kyle said nothing. The Prince peered at him. They rode on together for several minutes in silence.

"All right, I'll tell you why," said the Prince, more loudly, after a while as if the pause had been only momentary. "It's because you're not *my* bodyguard, Kyle. You see, I've seen through you. I know whose bodyguard you are. You're *theirs!*"

Kyle's jaw tightened. But the darkness hid his reaction.

"All right—" The Prince gestured loosely, disturbing his balance in the saddle. "That's all right. Have it your way. I don't mind. So, we'll play points. There was that lout at the beer garden, who puts his hands on me. But no one would tell me his name, you said. All right, you managed to bodyguard him. One point for you. But you didn't manage to bodyguard the girl at the inn back there. One point for me. Who's going to win, good Kyle?"

Kyle took a deep breath.

"Lord," he said, "some day it'll be your duty to marry a woman from Earth—"

The Prince interrupted him with a laugh, and this time there was an ugly note in it.

"You flatter yourselves," he said. His voice thickened. "That's the trouble with you—all you Earth people—you flatter yourselves."

They rode on in silence. Kyle said nothing more, but kept the head of the stallion close to the shoulder of the gelding, watching the young man closely. For a little while the Prince seemed to doze. His head sank on his chest and he let the gelding wander. Then, after a while, his head began to come up again, his automatic horseman's fingers tightened on the reins, and he lifted his head to stare around in the moonlight.

"I want a drink," he said. His voice was no longer thick, but it was flat and uncheerful. "Take me where we can get some beer, Kyle."

Kyle took a deep breath.

"Yes, Lord," he said.

He turned the stallion's head to the right and the gelding followed. They went up over a hill and down to the edge of a lake. The dark water sparkled in the moonlight and the farther shore was lost in the night. Lights shone through the trees around the curve of the shore.

"There, Lord," said Kyle. "It's a fishing resort, with a bar."

They rode around the shore to it. It was a low, casual building, angled to face the shore; a dock ran out from it, to which fishing boats were tethered, bobbing slightly on the black water. Light gleamed through the windows as they hitched their horses and went to the door.

The barroom they stepped into was wide and bare. A long bar faced them with several planked fish on the wall behind it. Below the fish were three bartenders—the one in the center, middle-aged, and wearing an air of authority with his apron. The other two were young and muscular. The customers, mostly men, scattered at the square tables and standing at the bar wore rough working clothes, or equally casual vacationers' garb.

The Prince sat down at a table back from the bar and Kyle sat down with him. When the waitress came they ordered beer and coffee, and the Prince half-emptied his stein the moment it was brought to him. As soon as it was completely empty, he signaled the waitress again.

"Another," he said. This time, he smiled at the waitress when she brought his stein back. But she was a woman in her thirties, pleased but not overwhelmed by his attention. She smiled lightly back and moved off to return to the bar where she had been talking to two men her own age, one fairly tall, the other shorter, bullet-headed, and fleshy.

The Prince drank. As he put his stein down, he seemed to become aware of Kyle, and turned to look at him.

"I suppose," said the Prince, "you think I'm drunk?"

"Not yet," said Kyle.

"No," said the Prince, "that's right. Not yet. But perhaps I'm going to be. And if I decide I am, who's going to stop me?"

"No one, Lord."

"That's right," the young man said. "That's right." He drank deliberately from his stein until it was empty, and then signaled the waitress for another. A spot of color was beginning to show over each of his high cheekbones. "When you're on a miserable little world with miserable little people . . . hello, Bright Eyes!" he interrupted himself as the waitress brought his beer. She laughed and went back to her friends. " . . . you have to amuse yourself any way you can," he wound up.

He laughed to himself.

"When I think how my father, and Monty—everybody —used to talk this planet up to me—" He glanced aside at Kyle. "Do you know at one time I was actually scared —well, not scared exactly, nothing scares me . . . say *concerned*—about maybe having to come here, some day?" He laughed again. "Concerned that I wouldn't measure up to you Earth people! Kyle, have you ever been to any of the Younger Worlds?"

"No," said Kyle.

"I thought not. Let me tell you, good Kyle, the worst of the people there are bigger, and better looking, and smarter, and everything than anyone I've seen here. And I, Kyle, I—the Emperor-to-be—am better than any of them. So, guess how all you here look to me?" He stared at Kyle, waiting. "Well, answer me, good Kyle. Tell me the truth. That's an order."

"It's not up to you to judge, Lord," said Kyle.

"Not—? Not up to me?" The blue eyes blazed. *"I'm going to be Emperor!"*

"It's not up to any one man, Lord," said Kyle. "Emperor or not. An Emperor's needed, as the symbol that can hold a hundred worlds together. But the real need of the race is to survive. It took nearly a million years to evolve a survival-type intelligence here on Earth. And out on the newer worlds people are bound to change. If something gets lost out there, some necessary element lost out of the race, there needs to be a pool of original genetic material here to replace it."

The Prince's lips grew wide in a savage grin.

"Oh, good, Kyle—good!" he said. "Very good. Only, I've heard all that before. Only, I don't believe it. You see —I've seen you people, now. And you don't outclass us, out on the Younger Worlds. *We* outclass *you*. We've gone on and got better, while you stayed still. And you know it."

The young man laughed softly, almost in Kyle's face.

"All you've been afraid of is that we'd find out. And I have." He laughed again. "I've had a look at you; and now I know. I'm bigger, better, and braver than any man in this room—and you know why? Not just because I'm the son of the Emperor, but because it's born in me! Body, brains, and everything else! I can do what I want here, and no one on this planet is good enough to stop me. Watch."

He stood up, suddenly.

"Now, I want that waitress to get drunk with me," he said. "And this time I'm telling you in advance. Are you going to try and stop me?"

Kyle looked up at him. Their eyes met.

"No, Lord," he said. "It's not my job to stop you."

The Prince laughed.

"I thought so," he said. He swung away and walked between the tables toward the bar and the waitress, still in conversation with the two men. The Prince came up to the bar on the far side of the waitress and ordered a new stein of beer from the middle-aged bartender. When it was given to him, he took it, turned around, and rested his elbows on the bar, leaning back against it. He spoke to the waitress, interrupting the taller of the two men.

"I've been wanting to talk to you," Kyle heard him say.

The waitress, a little surprised, looked around at him. She smiled, recognizing him—a little flattered by the directness of his approach, a little appreciative of his clean good looks, a little tolerant of his youth.

"*You* don't mind, do you?" said the Prince, looking past her to the bigger of the two men, the one who had just been talking. The other stared back, and their eyes met without shifting for several seconds. Abruptly, angrily, the man shrugged, and turned about with his back hunched against them.

"You see?" said the Prince, smiling back at the waitress. "He knows I'm the one you ought to be talking to, instead of—"

"All right, sonny. Just a minute."

It was the shorter, bullet-headed man, interrupting. The Prince turned to look down at him with a fleeting expression of surprise. But the bullet-headed man was already turning to his taller friend and putting a hand on his arm.

"Come on back, Ben," the shorter man was saying. "The kid's a little drunk, is all." He turned back to the Prince. "You shove off now," he said. "Clara's with us."

The Prince stared at him blankly. The stare was so fixed that the shorter man had started to turn away, back to his friend and the waitress, when the Prince seemed to wake.

"Just a minute—" he said, in his turn.

He reached out a hand to one of the fleshy shoulders below the bullet head. The man turned back, knocking the hand calmly away. Then, just as calmly, he picked up the Prince's full stein of beer from the bar and threw it in the young man's face.

"Get lost," he said, unexcitedly.

The Prince stood for a second, with the beer dripping from his face. Then, without even stopping to wipe his eyes clear, he threw the beautifully trained left hand he had demonstrated at the beer garden.

But the shorter man, as Kyle had known from the first moment of seeing him, was not like the busboy the Prince had decisioned so neatly. This man was thirty pounds heavier, fifteen years more experienced, and by build and nature a natural bar fighter. He had not stood there waiting to be hit, but had already ducked and gone forward to throw his thick arms around the Prince's body. The young man's punch bounced harmlessly off the round head, and both bodies hit the floor, rolling in among the chair and table legs.

Kyle was already more than halfway to the bar and the three bartenders were already leaping the wooden hurdle that walled them off. The taller friend of the bullet-headed man, hovering over the two bodies, his eyes glittering, had his boot drawn back ready to drive the point of it into the Prince's kidneys. Kyle's forearm took him economically like a bar of iron across the tanned throat.

He stumbled backward, choking. Kyle stood still, hands open and down, glancing at the middle-aged bartender.

"All right," said the bartender. "But don't do anything more." He turned to the two younger bartenders. "All right. Haul him off!"

The pair of younger, aproned men bent down and came up with the bullet-headed man expertly hand-locked between them. The man made one surging effort to break loose, and then stood still.

"Let me at him," he said.

"Not in here," said the older bartender. "Take it outside."

Between the tables, the Prince staggered unsteadily to his feet. His face was streaming blood from a cut on his forehead, but what could be seen of it was white as a drowning man's. His eyes went to Kyle, standing beside him; and he opened his mouth—but what came out sounded like something between a sob and a curse.

"All right," said the middle-aged bartender again. "Outside, both of you. Settle it out there."

The men in the room had packed around the little space by the bar. The Prince looked about and for the first time seemed to see the human wall hemming him in. His gaze wobbled to meet Kyle's.

"Outside . . .?" he said, chokingly.

"You aren't staying in here," said the older bartender, answering for Kyle. "I saw it. You started the whole thing. Now, settle it any way you want—but you're both going outside. Now! Get moving!"

He pushed at the Prince, but the Prince resisted, clutching at Kyle's leather jacket with one hand.

"Kyle—"

"I'm sorry, Lord," said Kyle. "I can't help. It's your fight."

"Let's get out of here," said the bullet-headed man.

The Prince stared around at them as if they were some strange set of beings he had never known to exist before.

"No . . ." he said.

He let go of Kyle's jacket. Unexpectedly, his hand darted in toward Kyle's belly holster and came out holding the slug pistol.

"Stand back!" he said, his voice high-pitched. "Don't try to touch me!"

His voice broke on the last words. There was a strange sound, half-grunt, half-moan, from the crowd; and it swayed back from him. Manager, bartenders, watchers

—all but Kyle and the bullet-headed man drew back.

"You dirty slob..." said the bullet-headed man, distinctly. "I knew you didn't have the guts."

"Shut up!" The Prince's voice was high and cracking. "Shut up! Don't any of you try to come after me!"

He began backing away toward the front door of the bar. The room watched in silence, even Kyle standing still. As he backed, the Prince's back straightened. He hefted the gun in his hand. When he reached the door he paused to wipe the blood from his eyes with his left sleeve, and his smeared face looked with a first touch of regained arrogance at them.

"Swine!" he said.

He opened the door and backed out, closing it behind him. Kyle took one step that put him facing the bullet-headed man. Their eyes met and he could see the other recognizing the fighter in him, as he had earlier recognized it in the bullet-headed man.

"Don't come after us," said Kyle.

The bullet-headed man did not answer. But no answer was needed. He stood still.

Kyle turned, ran to the door, stood on one side of it, and flicked it open. Nothing happened; and he slipped through, dodging to his right at once, out of the line of any shot aimed at the opening door.

But no shot came. For a moment he was blind in the night darkness, then his eyes began to adjust. He went by sight, feel, and memory toward the hitching rack. By the time he got there, he was beginning to see.

The Prince was untying the gelding and getting ready to mount.

"Lord," said Kyle.

The Prince let go of the saddle for a moment and turned to look over his shoulder at him.

"Get away from me," said the Prince, thickly.

"Lord," said Kyle, low voiced and pleading, "you lost your head in there. Anyone might do that. But don't make it worse, now. Give me back the gun, Lord."

"Give you the gun?"

The young man stared at him—and then he laughed.

"Give *you* the gun?" he said again. "So you can let someone beat me up some more? So you can not-guard me with it?"

"Lord," said Kyle, "please. For your own sake—give me back the gun."

"Get out of here," said the Prince, thickly, turning back to mount the gelding. "Clear out before I put a slug in you."

Kyle drew a slow, sad breath. He stepped forward and tapped the Prince on the shoulder.

"Turn around, Lord," he said.

"I warned you—" shouted the Prince, turning.

He came around as Kyle stooped, and the slug pistol flashed in his hand from the light of the bar windows. Kyle, bent over, was lifting the cuff of his trouser leg and closing his fingers on the hilt of the knife in his boot sheath. He moved simply, skillfully, and with a speed nearly double that of the young man, striking up into the chest before him until the hand holding the knife jarred against the cloth covering flesh and bone.

It was a sudden, hard-driven, swiftly merciful blow. The blade struck upward between the ribs lying open to an underhanded thrust, plunging deep into the heart. The Prince grunted with the impact driving the air from his lungs; and he was dead as Kyle caught his slumping body in leather-jacketed arms.

Kyle lifted the tall body across the saddle of the gelding and tied it there. He hunted on the dark ground for the fallen pistol and returned it to his holster. Then, he mounted the stallion and, leading the gelding with its burden, started the long ride back.

Dawn was graying the sky when at last he topped the hill overlooking the lodge where he had picked up the Prince almost twenty-four hours before. He rode down toward the courtyard gate.

A tall figure, indistinct in the predawn light, was waiting inside the courtyard as Kyle came through the gate; and it came running to meet him as he rode toward it. It was the tutor, Montlaven, and he was weeping as he ran to the gelding and began to fumble at the cords that tied the body in place.

"I'm sorry . . . " Kyle heard himself saying; and was dully shocked by the deadness and remoteness of his voice. "There was no choice. You can read it all in my report tomorrow morning—"

He broke off. Another, even taller figure had appeared in the doorway of the lodge giving on the courtyard. As Kyle turned toward it, this second figure descended the few steps to the grass and came to him.

"Lord—" said Kyle. He looked down into features like those of the Prince, but older, under graying hair. This man did not weep like the tutor, but his face was set like iron.

"What happened, Kyle?" he said.

"Lord," said Kyle, "you'll have my report in the morning . . ."

"I want to know," said the tall man. Kyle's throat was dry and stiff. He swallowed but swallowing did not ease it.

"Lord," he said, "you have three other sons. One of them will make an Emperor to hold the worlds together."

"What did he do? Whom did he hurt? Tell me!" The tall man's voice cracked almost as his son's voice had cracked in the bar.

"Nothing. No one," said Kyle, stiff-throated. "He hit a boy not much older than himself. He drank too much. He may have got a girl in trouble. It was nothing he did to anyone else. It was only a fault against himself." He swallowed. "Wait until tomorrow, Lord, and read my report."

"No!" The tall man caught Kyle's saddle horn with a grip that checked even the white stallion from moving. "Your family and mine have been tied together by this for three hundred years. What was the flaw in my son to make him fail his test, back here on Earth? *I want to know!"*

Kyle's throat ached and was dry as ashes.

"Lord," he answered, "he was a coward."

The hand dropped from his saddle horn as if struck down by a sudden strengthlessness. And the Emperor of a hundred worlds fell back like a beggar, spurned in the dust.

Kyle lifted his reins and rode out of the gate, into the forest away on the hillside. The dawn was breaking.

EDITOR'S INTRODUCTION TO:

QUIET VILLAGE

by

David McDaniel

I first met David McDaniel at the Chicago World Science Fiction Convention in 1962. He was not very large, and he was dressed in a sort of costume, which was unusual; in those days, "hall costumes" were not customary at SF conventions.

"What are you?" I asked.

"I, sir, am a Hobbit," he solemnly informed me; and as I had not yet read Professor J.R.R. Tolkein's epic LORD OF THE RINGS, he proceded to tell me about the books, causing me to run down to the huckster room and buy a set.

I saw Dave off and on at conventions after that, but I didn't get to know him well until I began to write full time. Dave was trying that too; and things were pretty grim just then. There wasn't a lot of money in science fiction, and it wasn't easy to break into any other kind of freelance writing. Then I had a lucky break, a chance to sell an article on the energy crisis—I think I was the first writer to use that term, way back in 1970—to *American Legion* magazine. *Legion* had a thousand dollars, which was a *lot* of money in those days.

There was only one problem. They wanted photographs. Not only did I know nothing about photography, I didn't own a decent camera.

Dave came to the rescue. I had arranged a tour through Southern California Edison's San Onofre plant, and Dave came with me. He took a lot of pictures. Then Edison offered to take me out to their newest coal-fired plant at Four Corners (that place where four states come together), as well as to the controversial strip mines at Black Mesa. The only problem was that the offer didn't include Dave McDaniel.

No matter. He loaned me his cameras—easily the most valuable things he owned—and showed me how to use them, which I did so well that I ended up selling half a dozen photographs, while they used only one that Dave had taken.

A couple of years later I managed to sell an anthology, largely because of the rather clever title *2020 VISIONS:* it consisted, of course, of stories set in the year 2020, with the stipulation that the writers were to write as realistically as possible. (The book has been revised twice, and is still in print, so we didn't do too badly.)

I wanted to pay Dave back for the loan of his cameras, so I foolishly offered to buy a story.

I wasn't foolish for wanting a McDaniel story. Dave was a story teller, as good as the best in this business. Moreover, he had some very reasonable ideas about where society was going. He was meticulous at research, so much so that he manufactured models of weapons and equipment that he thought might some day be invented. It wasn't foolish to *want* a McDaniel story —but it was an act of monumental idiocy to assume that I'd *get* it. Dave hated to write.

Now all writers hate to write. I know of only two exceptions, and I wonder about them. All writers love to *have written,* but they also hate to write. This is normal and understandable—but Dave *really* hated to write. I think I have never met anyone who so hated it.

I often wonder if he'd have been that way if he'd had a computer to write on; would the attraction of the gadgetry have overcome his hatred of the typewriter? I think it might, because Dave liked to tell stories, and would sit around talking for hours; it was only when he had to put words on paper that he balked. Alas, we will never know.

Eventually I had all the stories for *2020* except Dave's. Worse, I'd paid him part of the money for the story, meaning that I didn't have enough to buy something from another writer. It was McDaniel or nothing. Besides, he'd told me what he was working on, and I liked it, as indeed I still do.

So. There was nothing for it but to bully him. I took to going to his house in the afternoons. Dave's wife Joyce was working, so Dave was supposed to look after their son Tommy, who was then about two years old, and I could sympathize with Dave's lament that no one could work while taking care of a two year old.

So I babysat while Dave wrote. I'd take beer over, but I wouldn't give him any until I saw pages of new text.

Eventually that worked. The result was the last story Dave McDaniel ever sold, called "Prognosis: Terminal." Before he finished his next work he was killed in a freak home accident.

I wish he'd written many more. Meanwhile, here is one of his best.

What the military calls the "third verse" of the Star Spangled Banner is really the fourth. The real third verse is all but forgotten, and tells a much uglier story.

> And where is that band, that so vauntingly swore
> That the havoc of war and the battle's confusion,
> A home and a country shall leave us no more?
> Their blood has washed out their foul footsteps'
> pollution! No refuge could save the hireling and
> slave, From the terror of flight, or the gloom of
> the grave. And the star spangled banner in tri-
> umph doth wave, O'er the land of the free and the
> home of the brave!

The military has long stood between *their* homes and the war; there is another military tradition, that of the *knight*, whose mission is to defend the helpless; to stand between war's desolation and all civilized homes.

When Lord Baden-Powell formed the Boy Scouts, he intended them to be an auxilliary to the military, and for many years they served that function in both England and the United States. Explorer Scouts went on polar expeditions, Scouts were junior civil defense wardens, and in wartime England Scouts served on patrols to spot unexploded bombs.

We have got somewhat away from that tradition in this country; but it could be revived. Periodically some idiot in National Headquarters tries to "reform" the Scouts and make them more "relevant;" fortunately, the Scoutmasters and others who actually work with boys ignore that nonsense and continue to teach the old skills of camping and woodcraft.

If the Scouts are again needed . . .

QUIET VILLAGE
by
David McDaniel

The rats caught Rajer alone while he was up on the hill adjusting the 'tenna. They surrounded him, explained the situation to him, and then burst his left eardrum to make sure he understood they meant what they were saying. They also told him why nobody had heard from Morovia recently—they had just come from there because there was nothing left worth staying for.

"This place looks peaceful," they told him. "We wouldn't disturb such a nice place. All we want is a regular donation of food, water and pot. You go and tell your Block, then come back up here tomorrow afternoon and you can keep your other ear." Then they took his tuner and let him go.

Sereno was peaceful. About a hundred and twenty people living in thirty-some wood and adobe buildings up in Horn Canyon just north of Hunnington Trail. With a good steady spring that hadn't gone dry but once in living memory, they got along as well as anybody else and better than some. A stage made the trip across the Valley from Malibu every new moon—it took two or three days each way depending on the weather, and brought salt from the sea to trade for the pot that grew in the hills, the leatherwork they made, and wool when they sheared.

Blood was still trickling from Rajer's ear and had dried on his shoulder by the time he stumbled up to Jak's front door and fell against it, sobbing.

"How many were there?" Jak asked him while Mona dabbed antiseptic in his ear.

"The big one said there were fifty of them and some girls. They got my tuner so they'd hear if we tried to radio out. They'd kill us all, he said, like they did in Morovia." He was still shaking, and his voice was unsteady.

"How many did you see?"

"Ten. Fifteen. I don't know—they kept moving around me all the time. I couldn't tell."

"Bobby—"

"Yeah, Dad?"

"Go call a meeting for tonight. And see if the stage is gone yet."

"It went right by me over the hill just before the rats came out," said Rajer. "I think that was what they were waiting for. And they were wearing old streetsuits—some of them were. There's nothing we can do. We've got to give them what they want!"

"Hold still," said Mona.

"I can't hear at all on that side," Rajer sobbed. "Don't make me go back up there alone—they'll make me deaf!"

"I'll go up with you tomorrow," said Jak. "But we'll have to tell everybody about it tonight and see what they want to do. Mona, put him to sleep. If anybody else sees him like this, they'll be as scared as he is."

Mona poured into a cup from a bottle she found in her bag, and gave it to him. He choked it down while she refolded the cloth to a clean side and held it again to his ear. The bleeding had stopped, and shortly he slept.

Jak Mendez walked out into the hot dry afternoon and looked up at the round brown hills which guarded his home and his friends' homes—hills which now seemed to loom around the village like enemies. The dry grasses of late summer surrounded the stumps of steel and stone which still thrust above the soil, after three hundred sun-baked summers and a thousand heavy rainstorms, to loosen the gray adobe of the hills. There were still dry rooms underground which could be defended by anyone who wished to live in darkness like vermin and prey on those who lived in the light.

Three hundred years after the Plague had devastated the Earth, setting a brash star-spanning civilization back more than a millennium and leaving the handful of survivors without the technological base and energy which had supported it, most of the planet was still sparsely populated. Small communities clustered here and there, where life could be supported and some degree of human culture maintained. But there were always those who found it easier to take than to build, and the remains of the lost glories of their race supplied them with the power to enforce their demands. In this part of the world they were called rats.

So the rats had come from the east. How long had Morovia been able to support them? And what had finally run out? Only someone's patience? Morovia was —had been—half the size of Sereno; without a spring, they had been dependent for water on Wilson's snows. It had been a dry winter. Did the rats demand more water than the reservoir held? Or did they pollute it and then destroy the village in their blind anger? Jak had heard stories like that.

But wherever they had come from, and whoever had fallen before them in the past, they were here now. They'd looted in the ruins which covered ten thousand square miles to find the streetsuits which would protect them from the crude weapons available here; they had probably found old energy weapons for themselves. If Sereno refused their demands, he would be killed first and his sons next. If the villagers fought back, they would all be destroyed. The people would have to decide tonight what to do—but there seemed to be no choice.

The big room was filled, and torches along the walls smoked and flared as the breeze wandered above the shaking heads.

"I'll bet there aren't more than a dozen of them," someone said. "They'd all have gone together to the 'tenna this afternoon. We can chase them away."

"With what? And what's to keep them from waiting up in the hills and killing anybody they catch alone? Or coming down here at night and setting our houses on fire?

"Who would volunteer to drive them away?" Rajer added. "Remember—if you fail, they'll kill us all."

"Well," said Jak after a pause, "I think it's obvious we'll have to agree to their demands tomorrow—keep them happy and maybe off their guard while we think of something to do. We ought to find out what happened in Morovia."

"Dad—"

"Malcolm?"

"I could get there and back in a day or so. It's straight out Hunnington Trail and north a couple of miles. If you're going to give the rats what they want anyway tomorrow and take time to think of something else, I could be back tomorrow night. There might be some people left alive in Morovia, and I could bring them back."

"Plan to take a day each way. That'll give you more time there. And if you find anyone to bring back, you'll travel slower. You might want to take a burro. Is everyone in agreement, then? We'll all meet here second night and discuss the rats' demands and what happened in Morovia, and then decide what to do."

"Semmity Radio is on tonight, isn't it?" Mona said. "Maybe we ought to call the Scouts."

"Same objection," said Jak. "What if the rats beat them off? Besides, just hiring them to come here could cost more than we have."

"It could cost us our lives," said Rajer, "even if there are only a dozen rats. They want only food and water. We can live with them, and they won't hurt us if we give them what they want."

"Even if we did, we'd live under their threat until something else happened. Let's adjourn for the night. It's been dark about an hour, and Rajer shouldn't miss recording any more of the Semmity cast than possible. Is everything set up?"

Together they dragged out the large speaker and a table with the precious big tuner and Rajer's cubicorder. All but a dozen or so of the meeting wandered out, content to wait for a daytime playback of anything they might be interested in. Rajer switched on the tuner and adjusted its knobs with a musician's touch. Across the endless frying of the ionosphere, he focused on light, haunting music, then started the coupled cubicorder and went to sit with the others. At length the music ended and a voice spoke.

"You have been listening to Mallowin's 'Progressions from a Theme,' by Thomas Dibgy. This is Semmity

Radio, casting five thousand watts on frequencies of two-point-five megahertz, five, ten, twenty and thirty megahertz. This is the first of three consecutive nightly broadcasts, beginning with the second night of each new moon. Today was Thursday the eighth of August, 2638. The time is 2058, Pacific Coast Time.

"Our transmission tonight will be in three parts. Until 2330, the Principles of Effective Irrigation, Topic Four: Drainage Control. From 2330 to 2400, the Gershwin 'Concerto in F.' From 2400 to 0030, the Midnight News of the World for the past month. From 0030 to 0215 we will rebroadcast Computer Theory, part twelve, which was interrupted last month by power failure. From 0215 to approximately 0500, Richard Burton's classic performance as King Lear. Tomorrow night, 'King Lear' will open our schedule at 2100, followed by Irrigation, followed by Computer.

"All the services of Semmity Radio are brought to you by the Western Scouts. If you can use our advice or assistance, we monitor one-twenty-one point five megahertz and five hundred kilohertz twenty-four hours a day. Or we can now be reached by vidiphone through Frisco Island, Salt Lake, Denver, New Vegas or Drango. If you receive our broadcast east of the Mountain, call the MisipiPack, in Kayro Park. Outside the North American continent, confirm and report on our signal quality in your area. West of longitude one-oh-five in North America, call us with any problems you might have. No charge for advice or job estimates. The time in fifteen seconds, exactly 2100 hours, Pacific Coast Time. . . . Five, four, three, two, one, mark."

Then a different voice introduced "The Principles of Effective Irrigation, Topic Four."

Jak went with Rajer to the 'tenna the following afternoon, and five rats came out of the bushes to present their terms. All five were dressed in the bulky, archaic styles of streetsuits, the nearly impenetrable nyloid body armor which had been common public wear in the Old Days when any floor of any single residential dome had held more people in worse conditions than any town now west of the great mountains, and a single block held as many people as there now were in a million square miles.

The five advanced in a group, and the largest one snarled at Jak. "Keep away from me, mud! All you're good for is digging and planting—and pretty soon you'll be ready to plant yourself. Are you the Block?"

"Yes."

"O.K.—here's a list. We've got three charged blasters right on your beam, by the way, in case you were thinking about arguing. We'll want this much delivered to that big pile at the west end of the hills. We'll be living around there somewhere, and we don't want to have to walk too far. You'll deliver this much every week, and if you're late we'll remind you. Oh—sometimes, one of us might come into town for something special. Whatever he wants, you'll see that he gets it. Because if he has any complaints about the service, we'll come back to make sure it gets straightened out. You got all that, mud?"

"Yes. What if we don't have something you want?"

"Well, mud, it's up to you to find a substitute that will satisfy us. Just remember, we're pretty choosy. You got any more questions?"

"No."

The rat slapped him suddenly. "That's wrong. You want to know when we get our first delivery. You can take two days this time because we want to start off like good neighbors. You're going to like having us around— or else." He looked at Rajer, his ear bandaged, and laughed.

The five turned like landlords who dismissed their tenants and swaggered back the way they had come. Jak looked at the sheet of paper in his hand, and Rajer read over his shoulder.

"Two sheep every week?" Jak read. "A hundred gallons of water. Ten gallons of berries every week until the first big storm and two gallons after that. Fifty ears of corn until we harvest, then two gallons of flour every week—" His eye ran on down the list, and his jaw quivered.

"—Two pounds of pot and half a pound of salt every week." The people of Sereno sat in silence on the rows of benches in the smoky hall as Jak finished reading the list, and looked up. "Tomorrow night Malcolm will be back from Morovia. But next day we must have all these things ready to take out to Citivist."

"They've moved into Citivist?" George gasped, looking at Mona, and a gentle chuckle rippled around the room. Citivist was the end of the low range of hills which enfolded Sereno in one maternal canyon, where the stub of an ancient apartment tower rose nearly three floors, looking out over the wide flat Ellay Plain past the white-pillared ruins two hours' walk from Sereno towards where the distant ocean touched the horizon on a clear day. The Ruins might be the goal of rare holiday excursions, but had been picked clean by generations of everything but archaeological interest. The view from the tower was romantic by moonlight, and the spot was favored by young couples of the village, contracted or free.

"At least they won't be watching us from hiding all the time," said one of the herdsmen. "I don't think any of them would want to sit out in the open air all day, or walk a couple miles back and forth. And they won't be likely to drop in for something they might need."

"But when they do come, it won't just be on a casual impulse, and they'll be harder to deal with," Jak said. "Now, we'll all share the cost of supporting them, but this time I'll put up the two sheep and the big watersack. We can work out something equitable before next week. Everything else in his list we can chip in on. Bring your shares tomorrow night and we'll see what Malcolm has found out. If anybody can't remember what we need, see me tonight or tomorrow. When you've looked over the list and we get the shares worked out, Rajer will play last night's Midnight News for anybody who's interested. Yes, Mona?"

"Uh, have you thought about the Scouts?"

Jak looked around the room. "Has anyone else thought about the Scouts? We'd have to feed them in addition to all the rats for a while, and they'll have to be paid."

"And if they only succeed in making the rats angry, we'll all be killed," said Rajer.

"But if we don't call them," Mona said, "the rats will starve us all. Two sheep a week—in a year that's a tenth of our flock. And what about the breadfruit? We haven't had enough of that in the last three years. They couldn't have got this much from Morovia."

"Apparently they didn't," said the same herder. "I agree. We can't keep up anything like this for very long. I say we should call the Scouts—price and advice given free."

"We can't use the radio—the rats'll be listening. But we could try to phone through Malibu. The Valley line was open last week when the stage came; the driver told me about it."

"I'd been thinking of trying the phone," Jak said. "Malibu has a good radio and a directional 'tenna. They could cast north and a Troop might be here in a month."

"This time of year they could make it in two weeks."

"They'd take a while getting ready. We can feed the rats for a month if we know they'll be gone the month after that. Is everybody agreed?"

"I'd like to wait for Malcolm to come back, Dad. He might be able to tell us how many there are and what kind of weapons they have."

"Right, Martin. We'll postpone action on this until after tomorrow night. Convince them we're willing to cooperate. Then if we can't get Malibu on the phone, somebody will have to go there with the message."

All this while the list was handed among the benches, people leaning together over it. Muttered comments grew as it passed from hand to hand, resentment condensing around it until every voice in the village was ready to agree this toll could not be borne. Then shares were worked out, leaving everyone angrier and feeling more helpless against these parasites who had descended to loot them of their food. Few of them cared to stay to hear the news.

Two days later, a direct vidiphone contact was established through Malibu up the coast to Frisco Island and thence east through an automatic relay station at Sacto into Semmity. The sound was clear from the little speaker of the handphone, though the picture was faint and rolled constantly. Jak saw a lean, white-haired man as brown as a tree, who wore a green sash across his chest decorated with ranks of obscure symbols.

"Rats, eh?" he said. "We can probably help. How many are there?"

"They claim fifty, but they've ordered enough food for thirty."

"Then there are probably fifteen. How are they armed?"

"They have some energy weapons. My boy went to Morovia, where they came from, to see if there were any survivors. There weren't. And there was evidence of a blaster having been used. Maybe more than one."

The Master of Semmity Troop nodded, a file of ghostly images. "We can send a patrol down for twenty dollars a man. Under the circumstances I wouldn't send you fewer than four. You will be expected to board them and their mules and re-equip them for the trip back. Also, any pay earned by a Scout who is killed in your service goes to the leader, and the leader will bring it back to us. I would suggest you hire five. Sereno should be worth a hundred dollars. We can also discount the value of anything the rats might leave. If they have energy weapons in good condition, for instance. A blaster might be worth twenty dollars."

"How much would five streetsuits be worth? I've seen them, and they look good as new."

"Couldn't guarantee. Four dollars each is reasonable, but some of them might have to be damaged to kill the rats inside. I think you need a five-man patrol. If you're willing to accept our terms, they may be there around the next full moon. They can find you easily enough—we have excellent maps. Since you're probably being watched, they'll come in from the east after dark some night. If they haven't shown up in a month, call us back. The phone here always works."

"I wish we could say the same. Thank you, and we'll have the money ready."

"Fine. Best of luck meanwhile, and try not to make the rats angry. We hate to lose business."

As the picture from Semmity faded, Frisco Island came on the line in the person of a cool-looking girl. "Hi, Sereno," she said. "I hope you don't mind my cutting in, but we wanted to keep the line open to Malibu. Besides, our Comm Center here wondered how you'd been picking up our recent audiocasts."

"Fine, Frisco. Our 'tenna is in good shape, and those

weather predictions have been a lot of help."

"They'll get better. Blue Valley expects to be able to lock onto a weather satellite for this hemisphere with another year's work. They've already got signals that it's still working, and they hope to be able to read pictures from it. Are you a Tech?"

"No. You want to talk to Rajer about tuners and things like that. Keep the line open."

By the time Rajer came at Jak's summons, the little vidiphone was silent, and several minutes of signaling failed to raise Malibu.

"It must have gone out somewhere in the Valley line," he said at last. "You got Semmity, though?"

Jak nodded. "The Master said a patrol would be down by the full moon. Five men at twenty dollars each, but they'll take some of their pay in loot. I think we can manage."

"Only five men? Against fifty rats?"

"He seemed pretty confident. Suggested four could be enough. I'll tell the meeting tonight."

Less than a week later one of the rats came into town. It was late afternoon when he appeared, striding sure-footedly down the steep hillside towards the small corral where the breeding goats were kept. Two children were watching the goats; they stopped playing and stood up as he approached, staring as though they had never seen a stranger before.

This one was small and slight of build, scarcely larger than either of them. He wore a flowered sleeveless shirt and loose pants. His skin was pale, and looked soft. He smiled at the children as he glanced around for an adult to speak to, but his eyes had a glassy blankness when he finally focused on them.

"Gimme some milk," he said.

Their eyes got big, but neither child moved. He stopped smiling.

"Gimme some milk!"

The younger child stuck a grimy fist in her mouth, and seconds passed.

"All right, gimme a pail," the rat said, his voice rising. "And I'll show you how to milk a goat."

Suddenly both children giggled. The rat struck

violently at the nearer, who slumped limply to the dirt and lay unmoving and the other screamed and ran away towards the silent houses.

The rat looked after her and shrugged. There was a small pail hanging on one fence post—he took it down and entered the corral. Ten minutes later, after he had filled the pail with warm foamy milk, he looked up.

The child still lay where she had fallen, but beyond her, watching silently, stood half the people of Sereno. Wind whispered the long sweet leaves of eucalyptus behind them, but they neither spoke nor stirred.

He stared at them suspiciously, then laughed. "You mud should teach your get some manners," he said. "You can pick up the pail next time you bring us food."

No one moved as he turned and climbed the trail west, the heavy pail swinging beside him. But as he passed out of sight over the ridge they moved forward as one to cluster about the child. And only then murmurs passed among them. *Scouts. Full moon. God willing—*

A cloudless sky held a full moon above the eastern horizon, and yellow firelight was visible through curtained and screened windows. Frogs and crickets shouted back and forth in the faded twilight. Silently, up Horn Canyon from Hunnington Trail, wound a file of men and mules. They stayed under the trees in shadow, and even the animals seemed to know how to place their feet amid the dry leaves and twigs on the hard gray earth.

Jak and his boys were just sitting down to dinner when there was a light tap at the door. They looked at each other, then Jak shook his head silently at the four of them and rose to answer it.

Outside stood a broad-shouldered, short-necked man in adobe-colored clothing. On the front of his shirt, just below his full beard, gleamed the silver emblem of the Scouts. He unclipped it without a word and held it out to Jak. Sealed in the reverse was a full color solidograph of the man and a medicode number.

Jak stared in wonder at the solido for several seconds before thinking to compare it with the face of the man who waited patiently on his doorstep. When he looked up, the Scout said, "My name is Bern Targil. I have four men with me and five mules."

"Will you come in? I can go open the barn."

"I'll come with you."

"Boys," said Jak to the looks of surmise around his table, "go ahead and eat. I'll be back in a little while. The Scouts are here."

"Dad? Can I go tell people? I can eat when you come back."

They left, Bobby at a run, the two men more leisurely in another direction.

"I didn't know how things stood," Bern said as they walked towards the barn, "so my patrol is staying out of sight. Do the rats watch you?"

"We've never seen them."

"Rats don't hide well. We'll keep our mules under cover unless you have a herd we could mix them in. But we must be free to move around. Where do we bunk?"

"My place. I'll take care of your board while you're here."

"You still know where they're holed up?"

"Apartment ruins a couple miles west. We take the food out there every week, and I've had a couple of kids watching from a distance until they take the food inside."

"We'll go into all this over dinner. I've got another Eagle and two Scouts along. And a Cub. They'll hear everything anyway. Can you feed us tonight? We came over the pass north of Berdoo, and there isn't much forage south of the mountains. Looked over Morovia, by the way. Talk about that over dinner, too." He made a cooing, warbling sound deep in his throat, and silent shadows slipped from under the trees to follow them, leading the mules into the barn where they were unloaded and bedded down.

When Jak returned home with the five Scouts, he found his front room full of curious people. Everyone wanted to know what was going to be done and how soon. Jak told them nobody knew yet, and suggested a gathering in the big hall after dinner. First they wanted to be introduced to the Scouts.

Bern introduced himself as Senior Eagle, then each of his patrol. Lem Spaski was also of Eagle rank; Arne and Jon were still short of their qualifications. Chad, who looked about Bobby's age, was a Cub. Lem displayed his

personal weapons to the awestruck villagers before
sending them home to dinner—each Scout carried a
bowie and a hatchet, each bore a sturdy crossbow on his
back and each carried a hand-blaster in a recharging
holster slung at his side.

"Let us have dinner, folks," Bern finally said. "We'll
see you again in an hour or so—we've got questions to
ask you, too."

For three days the Scouts did not leave the canyon,
but performed regular workouts during the morning
hours and spent afternoons inspecting and critiquing
some important constructions, including the carefully
maintained duct which ran down through the center of
the village. Its steady flow sprang cool and clear from a
pipe at the north end of the canyon.

Evenings they studied maps of the area and talked
with people who knew the ruins at Citivist. George
Mendez, Jak's next-youngest son, was familiar with the
tower to an extent that seemed almost a local byword.
He sketched the basic plan of the structure, indicating
its layout, orientation, and which stairs were still open
since the quake four years ago. Each of the Scouts
questioned him intently on the building and its surrounding terrain.

Later Bern and Jak smoked together on the flat roof of
the house, and talked.

"Fine boys," Bern said.

"Thanks. I raised them myself the last nine years.
Their ma was killed in a mudslide the winter of '29. The
year before the locusts came. They're named after the
Four Martyrs."

"One of them might like to come back with us—
we could arrange to give him a few preliminary tests
before we leave. Have any of them shown an interest in
our kind of work?"

"I keep them pretty busy here. They'll be taking the
sheep north to Wilson this fall. Five hundred head last
year. That's how we can afford to hire you—we sold a
good wool harvest in Dago a few months ago."

"If we can catch these rats underground, we may
salvage enough undamaged gear to cover some of the expenses."

"When are you going? The next delivery is in two days."

"Tomorrow would be as good a day as any. We're rested up and ready to go. Middle of the morning would be the time to catch them napping. You should understand, we may not make any attempt on their stronghold directly—you have no idea how it might be defended. But we will be prepared to carry through."

The next morning Jak stood with them at the crest of the hill and pointed west along a rutted track. "The tower's at the end of the ridge; good view of the plain. Nothing else near as big anywhere around. We leave the food outside the door on this side. We thought about putting poison in it, but if it didn't get them all at once we could have trouble."

Lem nodded. "Leave this sort of thing to professionals," he said. "If we catch them all together, we should be able to clean them out neatly. Think we'll be back for dinner, Bern?"

"Should be. We'll see you then, Jak. You go home now, and don't worry about us. You won't have to bring a donation tomorrow."

The patrol slipped silently among the tall grasses. Invisibly they divided to either side of the ridge, Lem and Arne to the north, fifty yards from Bern, followed by Jon and Chad along the south lip of the hill. They communicated now by short-range zister handys which drew only microscopic power for listening; the transmitter was keyed momentarily in coded patterns of clicks unless the situation warranted use of a sustained voice signal.

The Scouts advanced cautiously, examining grassy mounds where a rat might lurk, stepping lightly over an occasional gaping crack which opened into black depths, studying a stub of corroded metal which jutted from the dirt like a bare, fungus-crusted tree.

The sea-scented breeze passed among the grass less silently than they, moving with its easy ripples. The wide crest of the hill was ruggedly level fifty feet to either side of a rutted track which ran out to the tower at the southwesternmost end, and around it in a full loop. On the far side, there was just enough room for a wagon between the sheer gray wall with its gaping windows and the crumbling slope of a hill, falling a steep two hundred feet to a jagged mound which sloped away another three hundred feet to the rumpled floor. Beyond, the Ellay Plain ran ruggedly level to the misty line that was the sea; nearer, on a rise of ground four miles away, the white pillars and cyclopean walls of the Ruins were delicate miniatures.

The tower looked lifeless. Its wide entrance gaped like a cave half-drowned in the earth; twenty-five feet above the concrete wall was shattered and interior walls stuck up dark-gray against the cloudless sky. The five Scouts circled it soundlessly, coming together on the narrow ledge behind the building.

"Cellar," said Lem.

"Ventilation," said Bern.

"No watch," Chad said. "Some place else?"

Bern shook his head. "Best place." He looked into the dimness and sniffed and listened. With the faintest *crunch* he stepped down through a window, looked around and nodded, beckoning them to follow. There was the faint scent of recent or current human occupancy nearby; it seemed to be in the cool walls, or the inner darkness held it hidden.

Arne brought a flash out of his pack and pumped up a light. The floor was littered with dirt and cement dust; there were animal droppings along the wall; tatters of plastic were snagged or crumpled here and there. They found a stairwell with signs of use—the larger pieces of rubble had been kicked aside to leave a pathway. From below came the faint glow of artificial light and a warm draft carried the strong human smell up to them. Lem pointed up the stairs, and they filed silently towards the top.

Sunlight grew upon them as they neared the roofless upper floor, and shortly Bern and Lem looked cautiously over the edge of the stairwell at a maze of low walls and piled rubble which three hundred years had not weathered away. Nothing moved. Slowly, his crossbow cocked and quarreled, Bern stepped onto what had once been the floor of a hall. The others followed him.

A distant mockingbird shrieked at a crow; no other sound rippled the still air. The patrol spread out, a room or a corridor apart, remaining in sight of each other, except where pieces of wall still stood taller than a man. It was only a few minutes before Jon waved them together around him. There on the roof lay spread a hundred square feet of greenish black glassy metallic material, displayed to catch the maximum sunlight through most of the day. A black cable ran from one corner of the sheet down a narrow square airshaft and out of sight.

The Scouts followed Bern some distance away and then huddled for a whispered conference.

"Drawing air down that shaft and blowing it back up the stairs," said Chad.

Lem nodded. "A few gas bombs will clean them right out."

Faint voices from somewhere brought their heads around and froze them where they crouched. Someone was coming up the stairs from below, making no particular secret of the fact.

The Scouts moved silently around to gain clearer views of the stairhead from different angles. Footsteps crunched up the concrete steps, voices and laughter alternating, and seconds later a couple came squinting into the sunlight. Both were bare to the waist, clad only in loose comfortable shorts; both were dirty in a careless animal way. The girl's hair was as short and tangled as the boy's. They approached the ambush casually, unaware.

Two crossbows made a double *thunk* and the couple fell, arms and legs kicking briefly, their skulls shattered by the bolts.

Neither had been armed; there was nothing of value on either of them. They were not followed; whether they had come up to check on the solar cell, or on personal business, was problematical, as was the question of how soon their continued absence would arouse suspicion.

But action had been taken, and a fast efficient follow-through could bring success. A reconnaissance had become the battle and hesitation would gain nothing but total destruction.

Jon's pack held five canisters of Paralane Delta, salvaged from a vast store in far-distant Utah: this deadly gas was colorless, odorless and quickly fatal to humans who had not flushed their lungs with an inhalant of PDNeg. The death Delta delivered was swift and symptomless, but the gas' effect faded quickly after fifteen minutes while the Neg immunization lasted for two hours. As its protection waned, the faintest trace of Delta would cause a sharp headache. Five inhalers were taken from a box of twenty and used, then three fat gray cylinders were armed and dropped down the airshaft along the heavy cable from the solar cell.

One minute after the gas was released, Arne disconnected the cable from the power sheet and the five Scouts, secrecy set aside, raced down the stairs to ground level and outside to ring the building. Chad covered the center of the long front; Bern watched the front and north edge from beyond the corner, overlapping Jon, who waited at the corner next to the cliff in the shadow of the tower. He faced Arne along the ledge, sharing guard of the rear. Jon, the sun at his back, watched the south side with Arne and the front to Chad's left. Five crossbows waited cocked amid the grass on all sides while tense seconds passed.

Then a flurry of footsteps from within brought the hidden bows to focus on doors and windows. "Gas alarm," Bern muttered under his breath. Clad and unclad figures appeared, running for air. Crossbows fired, cocked and fired again in the seconds while targets were presented, then perhaps a dozen survivors fell back to the cover of their walls. Eight bodies flopped in the dust.

Bern slung his bow and led the dash to the doorway. He paused there to throw another gas bomb ahead of him before charging down the slope of rubble into the smoky darkness. His hatchet flashed in his right hand, his bowie swung in his left. Bright daylight from distant windows made the shadows between them darker as the rats scattered away from the spouting bomb into the deeper shadows towards the center of the building.

The gas released below would be rising through the subterranean levels, sweeping painless death to any rats who tried to hide there, and even the upper floors would soon be filled with fading but still fatal gas. Two more rats lay on the dust-sprinkled slick metal floor to which rags of carpeting still clung in patches; the others ran stumbling farther towards the sun-shaded corner far across the vast pillar-studded open space. Hatchets spun through the air to outdistance the slow-spreading gas, and more rats fell.

Concerned now with saving their individual hides, the survivors fled into the angle where Jon stood, the bright windows at his back. His hatchet whirled over his head, his bowie stood from his fist as he charged into the rats. The first two who came within reach fell to his steel: the third swung a nyloid-clad arm to catch the descending knife and let the hatchet glance harmlessly from his helmet. Jon broke away as the streetsuited rat bore him to the floor, and rolled clear in the dust, springing to his feet and snatching his charged blaster from its holster.

The suit absorbed the bolt though its owner staggered back against a column. He snapped open a case at his belt before Jon could ready his bow, and a spring-loaded needler snapped. Jon's hand clutched reflexively at the trigger for a second before he coughed weakly and crumpled.

The rat leaped forward to pick up the recharging blaster and fired into the darkness behind him. Chad gasped and fell aside as the half-powered bolt clipped a column beside him and droplets of molten metal splashed across his right arm, then Bern and Arne fired together. The corner of an empty lift bay exploded in stony fragments and white dust, but the rat was gone, and the others were gone with him.

Silence settled, echoing between the floor and ceiling, and the sound of footsteps, hurrying to Jon, whispered away towards the distant ring of windows. The recharging blasters made a faint rising whine. Chad came behind the others, lips clamped, his left hand fumbling in his aid kit for burnbalm. He was smearing it on, slumped against a pillar, as the others knelt by Jon's body. Bern looked back.

"Chad—clean him, take the gear back to Sereno. Send a party to pick him up, bring five men after us. Can you still shoot?"

Chad nodded. "Left-handed. Balm's working."

Lem came back from the rear windows. "Six of them," he said. "They're heading onto the plain—either towards Griffith Hills or the Ruins."

"Let's go."

They took off like sprinters for the window, hatchets and bowies resheathed. Away down the hill six figures hit the level ground and started across the scrub grass and sparse brush towards the southwest. In great sliding leaps the three Scouts came down the face of the hill after them.

Blaster bolts sizzled across the distance between them, but dissipated well short. The Scouts, reaching the foot of the long slope, concentrated on the sustained chase. Trained, conditioned, disciplined, they ran steadily over the hummocky ground towards the dusty trail down which the rats were already fleeing.

The grass was nearly waist-high, but thin and dry with snagging seedpods along its stalks; the few foxtails caught by the uniforms found no loose texture to hold and dropped almost at once. The road itself was no more than a faint double rut, cracked and bare with taller grass in the middle. It led nearly four miles southwest to the Ruins.

Heads up, running like machines, the Scouts chased the rats, narrowing their lead from two hundred yards to one hundred before they were halfway to the Ruins. Then a blaster bolt warmed their faces, and they slacked their pace to match their quarry. The rats wouldn't care to make a stand out in the open—not at only two to one. But they couldn't flee forever. They would want to hole up in the Ruins, and would probably make their last stand there.

Now, any Scout's pause to fire would cost distance at the edge of his range, and any attempt to continue closing would result in more effective fire from their foes. Holed up, the rats could be encircled and wiped out by training and technology. Morovia would be avenged, Jon's blaster recovered and his life paid for.

The road was hard and level, though moderately meandering, and the distant figures of the rats remained clear above the grass. Then the ragged group vanished briefly behind a tall corner of mottled stone and rusted steel where the road bent around a large shallow craterlike pit. When they reappeared, they ran more tightly bunched, but six sharp eyes saw at once there were now only five rats a-running. Lem split off to the right around the far side of the collapsed substructure, running silently and low among the grass and slipping from rock to rock as Bern and Arne continued up the road.

One rat was probably waiting behind to shoot them from cover—if so, he might well have Jon's blaster. As they approached, they left the road and came close against the side of the monolith. At the corner they looked cautiously around.

Nothing in sight. Bern stepped out from cover and waited. Scout blasters had no sights, being aimed by instinctive coordination of hand and eye; without this training behind it, the weapon would be relatively inaccurate. A dazzling flare burst against the wall a foot to his left and knocked him sprawling. Answering bolts of steel snapped from two crossbows at opposite ends of the new-scarred wall, and there were no more shots. The two Scouts hurried out to retrieve their quarrels and the blaster, and dragged the body of the rat out for the follow-up party from Sereno to find and clean of whatever he might have carried.

Bern picked himself up, wincing slightly at the deep ache in his left leg. It wasn't broken, but the concussion had given him a deep bruise which would slow him down in a little while.

He walked painfully after his partners. "Dig in and spot them," he said. "Wait till I get there to formulate."

They nodded—as senior Eagle he was expected to be responsible in every strategic decision. Let the rats hole up and wait; it would only dull their nerves and drive them closer to panic. Arne and Lem slung their bows and trotted off after the five now-distant rats who were still running, aware their trap had failed and aware of the irretrievable loss of their last stronghold. There were no places of safety to which they could flee, no communities where they could pass for refugees or derelict streeters.

They could have no hope of escape, yet still they ran. And after them, like loping angels of death, came Arne and Lem. The rat they had killed in the grass had not carried a needler; nor had he worn a streetsuit.

More slowly and farther behind, a hype from his aid kit easing the pain and congestion in his leg, Bern followed. His smooth stride kept the muscle from cramping, and he had only a mile to go when he heard three spaced clicks from his handy. He touched it at his belt, clicking the carrier once. Then a voice spoke quickly.

"They're down and covered."

Bern brought the unit to his lips. "Ten minutes," he said, and clicked the pattern requesting navigational data.

When the Scouts were together below the crest of the round hill where the Ruins stood, Lem outlined the situation.

"They're pulled in behind that first row of columns. They probably don't know how to get down to the parking levels. We can surround them on the main floor area."

Bern nodded, and the three of them started silently up the rubbly slope towards the great level stone floor, its warps and buckles concealed by wind-drifted adobe-clay. Here and there walls stood—thick, braced walls with fine patterns carved deep in their still-gleaming surfaces, uncorrupted by the centuries. Rain-soaked soot still lingered in the stones, in cracks where lichens did not reach; a great arc of dull white carving lay like a rocker sixty feet long, both ends jagged and weathered, with no matching curves as of a broken circle remained to indicate how it had stood. Locally it was called *Chandler's Chair*, and it was said that a sufficient force of men had rocked it.

As the Scouts crept past the line of columns and fallen pillars, the true size of the place began to open around them. The village of Sereno would have fit, with stables, corrals, orchards and gardens, into one quarter of that great level mesa where fallen monuments to the past lay crumbling. And from the midst of that silenced splendor, a blaster bolt flashed among them and seared some square feet of stone clean of lichen.

Lem took off to the left; by understanding, as Bern's junior he took over responsibility of movement. Bern wasted one bolt to keep the rats pinned down while Lem tried to spot their exact location. A minute later his handy clicked.

"Wall. Ten degrees right. Under this end of the Chair. Arne go right. Three minutes."

Bern clicked acknowledgment as Arne moved off. He shifted position closer and wasted another bolt when the flash of an incautiously extended head presented itself momentarily—this battle was not likely to be settled by blaster bolts, but hand to hand. And for that the range must be closed.

The rats had gone to ground behind a row of angled slabs which thrust from the floor almost forty degrees off perpendicular, lying partly supported by a section of solid wall. Under this slotted, slanted roof they huddled, desperate and deadly. Bern saw this as he moved, and clicked his handy.

"Come from above," he said, and his partner clicked back.

By climbing the inner face of the *Chair*, Lem could come out twenty feet above and behind the rats and fire down on them. Arne would be concealed forty feet in his direction from them waiting for either Eagle to open the attack. Seconds passed.

Then a bolt spat from the far end of the sheltered space and splashed against a fallen pillar behind him. Bern rose to his feet and fired. Flame licked around one end of the slanted wall and a cry told him of a glancing hit, or near miss, as he ducked down again, his ear cocked to the sound of his blaster recharging. The blaster, salvaged from the rat they'd killed on the road, stuck from his pocket, still charged; it could serve as a backup.

Lem's crossbow snapped from above and behind the cluster of rats, and a half-charged flash of energy dissipated in the air. Then Arne fired from cover and moved. A quarrel should penetrate a streetsuit at moderate range, and only one of the rats was so protected. Bern took advantage of the distraction to move closer, angling for a shot through one six-inch crack in the bastion.

He knelt, his leg nearly numb and clumsy, and braced the bow across the lip of a dust-filled fountain. In the deep shade behind the gap he saw indistinct shapes moving too swiftly to waste a shot. Back and forth; he waited patiently; fingertip light against the trigger. As a shadow paused blocking the slit, he stroked the release and felt the bow jump against his shoulder like a captive rabbit. The bolt passed directly into the narrow opening, vanishing without a sound, and the shadow fell away leaving the space clear again. No further targets presented themselves.

The rats' blaster would be charged up by this time. Even though the crossbow fire must have attenuated their numbers they held positional advantage, and the Scouts hesitated to press the attack.

Silence returned to the ruins—a tense, waiting silence. A gull flashed white overhead, and warm wind whispered around the fallen columns. Bern gauged the distance to another block of white marble and estimated his chances. The rat with the blaster could only be looking one way at a time, and the needler was a short-range weapon. Five seconds in the open would be too long, but Lem could distract them. He secured his weapons and clicked a question on his handy.

"Four left, one wounded," it answered.

"Good. Count five and cover."

On the click of acknowledgment Bern rose to a crouch and started counting silently with measured cadence. One—two—three—four—five . . . The snap of Lem's bow sent him on a clumsy four-legged scramble across a bare twenty-five feet of sparse stunted grass which grew unhealthily among the cracked marble slabs. He barked his knuckles across a jutting corner and his hand slipped. His shoulder hunched as he twisted reflexively to land rolling, and a lance of flame turned a long oval of crumbling stone to steaming white lava which seethed for a few seconds before the bursting bubbles froze in brittle froth. By then he was under cover.

Arne had taken the opportunity to advance seconds after Bern. The ring tightened.

The group of villagers with Chad in the lead should arrive within a quarter hour. A containing action would be adequate at this point. But professional pride preferred that not a rat be left alive when reinforcements did arrive. He clicked for Lem.

"Three left, one wounded. Try bounce shot—left end."

The indicated end of the rats' shelter was warded by a four-foot wall of stone, faint abstracts etched in it, angled partly across the opening. From his new position he could fire a bolt which would splatter rock and enough heat to cause some damage in the protected area. He cocked his bow, slung it ready and gave the sharp, rising attack whistle and fired his blaster into the wall.

Second blaster in hand, he scrambled forward to the smoking, half-slagged wall, fell flat to the stone and fired into the rats' hole. Crossbows snapped above and ahead, and one more flicker of intolerable brilliance lanced just over his head and warmed his back like the sun for an instant as the wall behind him puffed steam. In a single swift movement he brought his bow into position with a quarrel in its slot and fired into the one figure left standing, a discharged blaster in his hand and a streetsuit helmet around his head.

Another quarrel from the opposite direction struck the figure almost simultaneously, spinning him around and ripping through the tough nyloid. The rat flopped to the ground, kicking for only a moment, across the burned body of another, and as echoes of unheard shouts died the only sound in the stillness was the harmonic lifting chord of recharging blasters.

Bern rose to his feet and limped forward, bowie ready in his fist. Arne came toward him through the settling dust, prodding cautiously at the bodies with his toe.

Lem's head appeared above them on the lip of *Chandler's Chair.* "That's it," he said.

"Streetsuit's wrecked," said Arne critically.

"Merit point for the kill," said Bern. "It may be repairable."

He bent awkwardly and picked up the blaster from a limp hand just as the whine cut off. He switched the circuit to safety and spent several seconds examining it before he nodded.

Lem came around the curve of graven stone as Arne found the spring needler and held it up. "I wondered why this wasn't being used," he said. "Now I think it may have been."

The flat magazine opened to show the "needles"—instead of gleaming perfect lines of steeloy, it was half filled with strands of bright copper, salvaged from ancient wiring, cut to length and painstakingly worked to near-microscopic straightness. Lem winced. "Rough on the barrel! Half price for salvage."

"They'll be here soon for the accounting," Bern said. "I don't think they'll feel cheated." A line of dust, distant and white behind a wagonload of villagers, rose along the road from Sereno, coming to carry them back.

THE STRATEGY OF TECHNOLOGY
by
Jerry Pournelle

Astute readers will recognize that this article's title comes from the 1970 book by Stefan T. Possony and Jerry Pournelle. STRATEGY OF TECHNOLOGY has been used as a text by both the United States Air Force Academy and the Air War College; it is, alas, out of print, although Steve and I hope to revise it soon.

Before we get into the topic proper, some good news.

The First L-5 Convention, held in Spring of 1982, was a rousing success. Fan Guest of Honor Robert A. Heinlein said it was the best weekend he's had in years. I heartily agree; it may have been the most interesting convention I've ever been to. Attendance was nearly a thousand, with an excellent mixture of professionals, such as Guest of Honor Fred Haise, Buzz Aldrin, Hans Mark, Arthur Kantrowitz, my colleague G. Harry Stine, Stefan Possony, Danny Graham, etc; and space enthusiasts like Larry Niven, Ben Bova, BJO Trimble. . . . I have a problem in choosing names; there were so many friends there. The ones above are quite literally chosen at random, and I hope I've offended none by leaving them out. I couldn't possibly list all the guests we had.

There was an important session on design of a Lunar Colony, conducted by Count Renaldo Petrini, PhD., a well-known Houston architect. Everyone at the convention was invited to help out, and the results have been impressive. Dr. Petrini and his associates are planning two more (invitational) sessions. What they've got so far is both aesthetic and practical; they'll do an article on it soon.

Although I was in theory Convention Co-Chairman, I don't hesitate to brag about how well run it was, for in reality I had nothing to do with convention operations. I went about entertaining guests; the real work was done by Co-Chairman Milt Stevens, many members of the Los Angeles Science Fantasy Society, and Deputy Chairman James Ransom of the Aerospace Corporation.

I won't make this a convention report; for that you should refer to the L-5 News (L-5 Society, 1060 E. Elm St., Tucson AZ 85719, $25/year): but I will give a few anecdotes. Overheard in the operations center:

Speaker (an important aerospace executive): "This is the best managed convention I've ever gone to. They show you where to go, things start on time, and they have those continuation rooms for people who want to ask questions. It's great!"

Operations Assistant (veteran of many SF Cons): "This is the easiest convention I've ever worked. The speakers show up on time, they're prepared, and they're *sober!*"

One high point: watching Mr. Heinlein watch Fred Haise listening as Frank Gasperik sang "The Ballad of Apollo 13."

The L-5 Conventions are planned annually; the second, in 1983, will be in Houston. I hope there will be many more, for they give an excellent opportunity for the public to meet the space professionals.

I'm writing this in 1982. There have been a number of news items I can't get out of my mind.

Item: the sinking of *HMS Sheffield* and the renamed cruiser *Phoenix*. A number of news magazines have written of the Falklands naval battles as "the battle of the computers," and in a real sense I suppose that's true. The Argentine cruiser was sunk by modern "smart" torpedoes that can be fired from many miles away and are nearly indetectible; *Sheffield* succumbed to a French Exocet missile, which can be launched from well over the horizon at nearly any altitude after which it flies at nearly supersonic speed about ten feet above the water.

There have been any number of articles on what all this means. Some conclude that the era of the big carriers is over, and that the U.S. Navy ought to scrap its plans for more Enterprise class ships in favor of several smaller carriers equipped with helicopters and vertical takeoff and landing (VTOL) planes. Other analysts draw precisely the opposite conclusion: that the big ships with their "full capability" aircraft can better defend themselves, and if hit are more survivable.

Item: In today's *Wall Street Journal* there is an article about the US Army in Germany. It's a good army, the article concludes; but it's greatly outnumbered. We have a variety of new antitank missiles and equipment, but not enough money to let the troops fire the things in training —and there are a lot of Soviet tanks just across the border. One captain speaks for all when he says "There may just be more tanks than we can kill."

Item: the Israeli advance into Lebanon. Israeli flyers, using highly sophisticated equipment and tactics, were able to overcome some of the Soviet Union's very best air defense missiles and anti-tank weapons.

Item: Any number of demonstrations for a "nuclear freeze." Since enhanced radiation weapons are one of the high-tech items the Army is counting on to stop Soviet tanks, this interacts with the above—and a number of powerful Senators, including Kennedy, have joined the "freeze" movement.

Item: we still have a Strategic Arms Limitation Treaty that forbids us to build any missile defense system that would protect our population. (Under SALT I we are allowed to but have not built a system to defend a single *missile* site; but no defenses of population centers as such are permitted. The Soviets have chosen to build *their* defense system to protect the missile site close by Moscow . . .)

A final item, one that didn't get much publicity: early in 1982, a Czech grocery clerk was sentenced to five years at hard labor for "possession of an unlicensed mimeograph machine."

One of the featured speakers at the L-5 Convention was Lt. Gen. Daniel O. Graham, US Army (Ret.). General Graham is Director of Project High Frontier. The basic High Frontier report can be obtained from **PROJECT HIGH FRONTIER**, 1010 Vermont Ave. NW Suite 1000, Washington DC 20005 for $15; and I urge anyone interested in the military future to get a copy and study it. Fair warning: some of the analysis in the High Frontier report comes directly from the Citizen's Advisory Council on National Space Policy, of which group I am

Chairman; so I am hardly unbiased.

My copy of High Frontier comes with a letter of endorsement signed by Buzz Aldrin, who met General Graham at the L-5 Convention; one thing the L-5 Con accomplished.

The basic thesis of High Frontier echoes what Possony and I wrote in STRATEGY OF TECHNOLOGY: that the decisive war need not be fought with blood and treasure—and in fact *must* not be. There is a way to defend Western Civilization—warts and all—without destroying the planet.

Major premise: it's bloody expensive to try to match the Soviets tank for tank, gun for gun, ship for ship. They can keep a lot more of their population under arms than we can; certainly they can build large armies cheaper than we can.

If we continue with "the incremental approach" to defense; buying more of this and that, buy more airplanes, more guns, more tanks, more bombs; we will do nothing decisive, and we may well go bankrupt trying it. We also accumulate the means for killing the lot of us.

Instead, let us take a bold new approach; let us sidestep the enemy, and take the high ground of space.

Our present strategic doctrine is Mutual Assured Destruction, often abbreviated (by its enemies, of whom I am one) as MAD. MAD says that wars cannot be won; they can only be deterred; and therefore to prevent war all nuclear powers must *mutually* have the ability to destroy each other. MAD adherents oppose civil defense, not on the grounds that it won't work, but that it *might* work. If we could truly defend some of our population, then we would not be hostage to the Soviets; assured destruction would not be mutual.

Those who support General Graham's strategic thesis would restore defense to its proper role: would opt for *Assured Survival* as the proper strategic doctrine, and see that the arms race concentrated on *defensive* weapons that would protect the US population.

Defensive systems are inherently stabilizing. They deal handsomely with the "mad general" scenario (unauthorized launch of a single nuclear missile). For technical reasons one can never be certain of one's defenses, especially against a determined and sophisticated en-

emy; but defensive systems can very likely deal with
any power other than the Soviet Union, and that in itself
is desirable. Finally, by complicating the other side's
strategic war plan, defense systems make it very difficult to predict the outcome of a strategic nuclear exchange—which makes it very unlikely that anyone
would launch a strike in the first place. You don't start a
big war unless you're fairly certain you can win it.

The point is that the High Frontier strategy does not
seem incompatible with a nuclear freeze: certainly is
not incompatible with a freeze on *offensive* nuclear
weapons.

I don't know the optimum mix of big and little
carriers for the future. As a maritime nation the United
States has always required naval forces to keep our sea
lanes open, and Marines to project our power beyond
our borders—indeed, the Constitution makes an important distinction between armies and navies. Certainly
we need ships.

Equally certainly, ships have become increasingly
vulnerable. I don't know whether the U.S. provided
the Royal Navy with intelligence on the location of
Argentine ships and aircraft, but certainly we could
have. Imagine a sea battle of the future: satellites spot
the enemy's vessels and locate them to within a few feet
(or even inches!) on the Earth's surface. Missiles can
then be dispatched from aircraft or submarines well
over the horizon from their targets. If a single air-
launched Exocet can sink a modern ship like *HMS
Sheffield*, what's safe from a dozen missiles?

There's more to the High Frontier strategy. One of the
systems examined by the Citizen's Advisory Council was
Project THOR: the ability to call down fire from heaven.
The THOR system would consist of "flying crowbars"
about five feet long, with a simple-minded guidance
system and tiny vanes for aerodynamic control. They
could "know" what a tank looks like from above—and
when activated (de-orbited), thousands would home on
anything that looked like a tank. THOR wouldn't be easy
to build—but then it isn't easy to build Enhanced Radiation Weapons (and it may be even harder to deploy
them in Europe, given the present mood . . .).

It would be even simpler to build orbital anti-ship weapons of the THOR type.

Now that final news item.

First the bad news for those who think "Better Red than dead.": You may get both. How many science fiction readers publish fanzines? How many more are prepared to live where possession of an unlicensed mimeograph machine is a penal offense? *Can* you live under that kind of regime? I don't mean "Are you willing to?;" I mean *CAN YOU*? For I suspect many of us cannot; that try as we might, we just wouldn't be able to cooperate with people who see a mimeograph as a dangerous weapon.

Now the good news:

I'm writing this at midnight. When I get it done, I'll log on to a computer network that connects me with thousands of friends all across the nation. There are a number of those networks, and given the computer revolution more are inevitable. Computers make it easy to communicate, and computer literates seem inevitably drawn toward communicating with each other.

Is it true that modern warfare is a battle of computers? Certainly it is a battle of high technology. I can't prove it, but I am prepared to argue that a nation whose youth grow up as computer literates will have great advantages in high technology warfare; and that our home computers are producing hundreds of thousands of computer literates.

A nation that sends people to jail for possessing an unlicensed mimeograph machine cannot possibly allow a computer revolution within its borders: it would be tantamount to allowing freedom of speech. Yet a nation that suppresses the computer revolution may well lack the technical capability to engage in modern warfare.

We may, just may, be seeing a way out of the long impasse that has so long confronted us. Meanwhile, space technology offers us the chance for *defense*; an opportunity for the military to resume its historic duty; a chance for free men to stand between their loved homes and the war's desolation.

It is a chance we must take.

EDITOR'S INTRODUCTION TO:

THE WIDOW'S PARTY

by

Rudyard Kipling

For reasons I'm not sure of, Kipling is no longer fashionable. In my opinion that's a mistake. If poets come closest to baring humanity's soul, it is certain that few poets have understood their fellow men quite as well as did Kipling.

The "Widow" in this poem is, of course, Victoria Regina, Queen of England and Empress of India. After the death of her beloved husband Prince Albert, Victoria shut herself away in Windsor Castle, and was seldom seen by her subjects. Yet did the Army obey: "Walk wide o' the Widow o' Windsor, for half of creation she owns . . ."

Philosophers and "social scientists" have talked endlessly about why men fight, but few of their treatises tell us much. "The Widow's Party" doesn't tell us intellectually; but it says a lot even so.

THE WIDOW'S PARTY

by
Rudyard Kipling

"Where have you been this while away, Johnnie, Johnnie?"
Out with the rest on a picnic lay. Johnnie, my Johnnie, aha!
They called us out from the barrack-yard
To Gawd knows where from Gosport Hard,
And you can't refuse when you get the card,
       And the Widow give the party.
        (*Bugle*: Ta-rara-ra-ra-rara!)

"What did you get to eat and drink, Johnnie, Johnnie?"
Standing water as thick as ink, Johnnie, my Johnnie, aha!
A bit o' beef that were three year stored,
A bit o' mutton as tough as a board,
And a fowl we killed with a sergeant's sword,
       When the Widow give the party.

"What did you do for knives and forks, Johnnie, Johnnie?"
We carries 'em with us wherever we walks,
       Johnnie, my Johnnie, aha!
And some was sliced and some was halved,
And some was crimped and some was carved,
And some was gutted and some was starved,
       When the Widow give the party.

"What ha' you done with half your mess, Johnnie, Johnnie?"
  They couldn't do more and they wouldn't do less.
       Johnnie, my Johnnie, aha!
They ate their whack and they drank their fill,
And I think the rations has made them ill,
For half my comp'ny's lying still,
       Where the Widow give the party.

"What was the end of all of the show, Johnnie, Johnnie?"
Ask my Colonel, for I don't know, Johnnie, my Johnnie, aha!
We broke a King and we built a road—
A court-house stands where the Reg'ment goed.
And the river's clean where the raw blood flowed.
       When the Widow give the party.
        (*Bugle:* Ta—rara-ra-ra-rara!)